DREAMLA

DUTY ROST

LT. COLONEL TECUMSEH 'DOG' BASTIAN
Once one of the country's elite fighter jocks, now Dog is whipping Dreamland into shape the only way he knows how—with blood, sweat, and tears—and proving that his bite is just as bad as his bark....

CAPTAIN BREANNA BASTIAN STOCKARD
Like father, like daughter. Breanna is brash, quick-witted, and one of the best test pilots at Dreamland. But she wasn't prepared for the biggest test of her life: a crash that grounded her husband in more ways than one....

MAJOR JEFFREY 'ZEN' STOCKARD
A top fighter pilot until a runway crash at Dreamland left him paraplegic. Now, Zen is at the helm of the ambitious Flighthawk program, piloting the hypersonic remote-controlled aircraft from the seat of his wheelchair—and watching what's left of his marriage crash and burn....

MAJOR MACK 'KNIFE' SMITH
A top gun with an attitude to match. Knife had two MiG kills in the Gulf War—and won't let anyone forget it. Though resentful that his campaign to head Dreamland stalled, Knife's the guy you want on your wing when the bogies start biting....

MAJOR NANCY CHESHIRE
A woman in a man's world, Cheshire has more than proven herself as the Megafortress's senior project officer. But when Dog comes to town, Cheshire must stake out her territory once again—or watch the Megafortress project go down in flames....

CAPTAIN DANNY FREAH
Freah made a name for himself by heading a daring rescue of a man in Bosnia. Now, at the ripe old age of twenty-three, Freah's constantly under fire as commander of the top-secret 'Whiplash' rescue and support team—and Dog's right-hand man....

DALE BROWN'S DREAMLAND

Dale Brown's Dreamland is the first in a brand-new series of novels written by Dale Brown and Jim DeFelice, centred on 'Dreamland', a high-tech aerospace-weapons testing facility in Nevada. Dale Brown, a former US Air Force captain, is the author of thirteen acclaimed *New York Times*-bestselling thrillers, all of which are available from HarperCollins.

'When a former pilot with years of experience in America's Strategic Air Command turns his hand to writing thrillers you can take their authenticity for granted. His writing is exceptional and the dialogue, plots and characters are first-class . . . far too good to be missed.'

Sunday Mirror

'You have to hug the seat when reading Dale Brown. The one-time US Air Force captain navigates his way at such a fearsome pace it is impossible to take your eyes off the page.'

Oxford Times

'Dale Brown is a master at mixing technology and action. He puts readers right into the middle of the inferno.'   LARRY BOND

'Like the thrillers of Tom Clancy, Stephen Coonts and Larry Bond, the novels of Dale Brown brim with action, sophisticated weaponry and political intrigue . . . first-rate.'

San Francisco Chronicle

'Dale Brown is a superb storyteller.'

Washington Post

DALE BROWN'S
DREAMLAND

**WRITTEN BY DALE BROWN
AND JIM DEFELICE**

HarperCollins*Publishers*

HarperCollins*Publishers*
77–85 Fulham Palace Road,
Hammersmith, London W6 8JB

www.**fire**and**water**.com

A Paperback Original 2001
Special overseas edition 2001
1 3 5 7 9 8 6 4 2

First published in the USA by
Berkley Books 2001

A catalogue record for this book
is available from the British Library

ISBN 0 00 710966 0

Set in Times

Printed and bound in Great Britain by
Omnia Books Limited, Glasgow

I
Down for doubles

Air Force High Technology Aerospace Weapons Center (Dreamland), Nevada
10 October 1995, 0530 PDT

GRAVITY SMASHED AGAINST HIS HEAD SO HARD HE nearly eased off on the stick. That would have been fatal—the butt of Major Jeff "Zen" Stockard's Strike Eagle was dancing across the boresight of a pursuing fighter at optimum cannon range. Stockard's only hope was to yank and bank away, zigging and zagging in a wild twist across the desert sky, pulling between six and seven g's as he tried to escape. He tightened his fingers around the control stick and hung on.

Zen had done this a million times—in fact, he'd fought this very same dogfight on a simulator the day before. But that was then, this was now. The simulator could only approximate what the slashing maneuvers did to his body. His neck and shoulders especially—the helmet he had to wear to control his remote escorts weighed more than forty pounds. The helmet used holographic imaging to provide enhanced optical and sensor views from both his plane and the escorts; its oval master view could be divided in half or quarters by voice command or the push of a button on his specially designed control stick. The skull bucket, with its onboard microprocessors, thick layers of LEDs, and retina-scan circuits, was critical to his mission, but that was no comfort when the sudden slash of his maneuvers increased its weight exponentially. The F-15E's ACES II ejector seat had been modified to help support it, but Zen still worried that his head was going to snap right off his body as he pushed through the seven-g turn.

Even with normal gear, seven g's would have hurt. The cells in his pressurized suit worked against his body like a masseuse's hands, fighting to keep his blood in place. But he was out at the edge of his endurance. Zen's heart pounded violently in his chest as he rammed his F-15E Eagle back to the right, picking his nose up and then flailing back over in a barely controlled reverse dive.

Bitchin' Betty—the plane's English-language audio warning system—whined that he was about to become toast. Too many g's, too fat a target, too little airspeed.

It might also have complained about his housekeeping, for all the attention he paid to it.

Stockard pushed the nose around, gaining just enough momentum to miss his pursuer's snap shot as he recovered. He had to hold on for at least another ten seconds before his escorts caught up. If he lasted that long, the fighter hunting him would become the hunted.

If he didn't: toast.

Major Mack "Knife" Smith cursed as Stockard's Strike Eagle once more slid out of his targeting pipper without cuing the signal that meant he'd splashed the SOB. If there had been real slugs in his F-15C's M61A1 cannon, he was sure he'd have nailed Stockard by now. But even though the laser designator had danced back and forth across the Strike Eagle's left wing and fuselage, the computer-controlled SiCS, or Simulated Cannonfire Scoring system, refused to record a fatal hit.

Only reason for that, he decided, was that he was supposed to be profiling an Su-27, with its notoriously inaccurate fire-control system. Had to be. That or someone had rigged the gear against him.

Knife tucked his Eagle down to follow Stockard into a rolling dive. Stockard was clever—he was trying to get Knife to either speed up and fly right by him, or slow down enough to let the two Flighthawks catch up. The Flighthawk U/MF-3's were the purpose of this exercise. Flying as escorts controlled by Zen, the two robot aircraft were supposed to keep Knife from shooting down the Strike Eagle. The exercise was designed to push the mini-planes and their human commander to the limit.

Which was fine with Knife. As long as he nailed the SOB.

Stockard's left wing slid downward, and the plane seemed to literally drop from the sky. Knife pushed his nose down before realizing what was going on. Zen was twirling through an invert as he dove, aiming to swoop off at close to ninety degrees. Knife had no choice now but to follow—anything else would let the escorts catch up.

He matched the spin, catching a glimpse of one of the Flighthawks trailing him. He ignored it—if he could see it, it wasn't in position to nail him, he decided—and concentrated on Stockard, whose rear tail fins were still disappearing below his HUD. Stockard was below ten thousand feet.

So much for the rules of engagement. Not that Knife would have let them stop him from winning either. But it was a relief that the other guy had ignored them first.

Stockard's fantail sailed into Mack's targeting pipper, and he pressed the trigger.

No good. Stockard pulled left just in time to duck the shot, recovering at eight thousand feet.

The g forces kicked up by the maneuvers tore Knife in all different directions; he felt like he was being pinched and pulled at the same time. A dark cloud began edging toward the corners of his eyes as he saw Zen flicking to the right. He pulled at the Eagle's stick to follow, worrying in the back of his mind that the extreme maneuvers would flame the Eagle's nearly unflammable engines.

And then he realized he'd blown it.

ZEN PUSHED HIS STICK TO LEVEL HIS WINGS, FEELING for the plane with his arms and legs. He'd faked Smith out, but the rush of gravity was nearly too much; he felt his head starting to implode. If he were flying only the Strike Eagle he'd be fine, but he had to guide the Flighthawks as well. Even with the computer guidance system carrying most of the load, it was too much work; his brain started caving under the physical and mental stress.

That was the point of all this, right? To find the limits?

Okay, he told himself, I'm here, I'm doing this. The bar at the top of his visor screen flashed green. It meant one of his escorts was now within firing range.

Okay, he repeated to himself. I'm home. All I have to do is flick my thumb down and enable the Flighthawk forward cams.

If Zen could do that, the heavy visor in his helmet would project two three-dimensional holograms in front of his eyes, each view projected from the nose of one of the U/MF-3's. He'd say "Hawk One" or "Hawk Two," look directly at his target, select cannon, fire. End of exercise.

But before he could do that, the center of his screen flashed red, indicating that the F-15C behind him was firing its simulated cannon. He jinked left, his consciousness narrowing to a pinprick of pure white light in a round black night.

Smith had all the stops out. He wasn't flying the F-15C as if it were a Sukhoi, with its limited avionics and conservative flight regimes. He'd tossed aside the flight protocol and briefed plan and was flying like an American—balls-out, over the line.

Fair enough, thought Zen, pulling back left, swirling in a scissors. The green firing bar disappeared—the Flighthawks had lost the shot. The little planes were extremely agile, but the computers that helped control them were not yet as creative as human pilots in close-in furballs.

Zen yanked his nose down hard, barely escaping one more time.

His head started to float. He'd pushed too far.

Zen forced air into his lungs, forced his muscles to relax, forced the blackness away. The green bar appeared and this time he mashed his thumb downward right away, saw Smith's butt hanging fat in Hawk One's boresight.

"Hawk One," he told the control computer. "Cannon."

"Ready," replied the computer.

"Fire."

KNIFE CURSED AS THE SICS BUZZER ANNOUNCED THAT he had been fried. He eased off on his stick and checked his power, leveling off as he reoriented himself. The dog-fight had taken them to the edge of the restricted airspace Dreamland had set aside for the Flighthawk test; he began a bank south.

"Dreamland Playboy One, this is Hawk Mother," Zen radioed. "You're dirt."

"Yeah, no shit," Smith snapped. The transmissions were monitored as well as recorded, but at the moment Knife didn't care if anyone thought he was a sore loser. It was the first time he'd lost to Zen in three weeks' worth of mock battles. The point of the exercises was to test and improve the Flighthawk U/MF-3's, and it could be argued that his previous victories had greatly enhanced the un-manned escort program, helping to improve the combat computer programming so the miniature planes would be useful twenty-first-century weapons.

It could also be argued that three against one wasn't a fair fight. Nor were the exercise's rules of engagement, which called for him to approach the Strike Eagle as if he were an Su-27, slower and higher than optimum.

Somehow, none of those things made him feel any better.

"Let's go again," suggested Stockard. "Down for doubles."

"Oh, you got it," said Knife. He glanced at his fuel gauge to make sure he had gas, then ran his eyes over the rest of the Eagle's instruments. He knew from feel that the plane was at dash-one spec—but he also knew that relying on feel could be a quick ticket to the boneyard.

"Point Zero in zero one," added Stockard, meaning that he and his escorts would be back at his starting position in sixty seconds.

Knife gave a terse acknowledgment and headed toward the end of the range. What he wouldn't give to be flying the Cheetah, the advanced-airframe F-15. Its forward canards and maneuverable thrust nozzles enabled the plane to cut nearly straight lines in the sky. He would have nailed Stockard on his first pass.

He would have nailed him if he hadn't had to worry about the Flighthawks. Three against one.

All right, he told himself. Stop making excuses and get to work.

Knife pushed himself forward against his restraints as he reached his starting point at the edge of the restricted airspace. He was ready. He'd nail that SOB, Flighthawks or no Flighthawks. This time he wasn't holding back.

ZEN REPLAYED THE FINAL THIRTY SECONDS OF THE dogfight in the lower left quadrant of his high-tech visor while he waited for Smith. The herky-jerky images made it clear the Flighthawk project had a long way to go. The U/MF-3 flight computers simply hadn't been able to keep up with the two manned planes; luck as well as skill had saved Zen's butt from being fried.

Admittedly, carrying a dedicated Flighthawk remote pilot in the Eagle's backseat would have helped. But the point of this particular experiment, and indeed the entire program, was to see if the remote planes could operate with minimal human guidance—if, in fact, a single pilot on a combat mission could control them while trying to evade an enemy aircraft. Besides, the com equipment and communications gear were so large there was no way to get anyone else into the plane.

Even though Zen had just nailed Smith, he felt that he had failed. He knew he was being incredibly hard on himself. But he'd had to go all out to do it. If he had been flying a strike mission, he would not have been able to complete the bombing run. Zen was the sort of pilot, the sort of man, who accepted nothing less than perfection. Settling for what was possible simply wasn't good enough.

The U/MF-3's were in a shadow orbit, slightly offset and trailing his wings at a half mile as he circled over the Nevada desert. It was a standard Flighthawk maneuver, one that he could tell the computer to execute and forget about, though he had the Flighthawks' God's-eye view selected on his helmet monitor just in case.

The U/MF's were about the size of Miata sports cars, with delta-shaped knife wings and small canard wings. Their tail sections looked like miniature versions of the F-23's, canted off in a squashed V. Powered by specially designed and downsized versions of the Pratt & Whitney F-119-PW-100 without an afterburner section, the planes were theoretically more maneuverable than the F-15 or even the F-22, but without the top-end speed of either plane. On the other hand, their size and wing configurations made them essentially invisible to radar beyond three miles. The Flighthawks were intended as multi-role escort craft for high-performance attack planes on difficult deep-strike missions. They could be configured for reconnaissance as well as close combat, and the engineers who had drawn up the plans foresaw the day when a high-megawatt oxygen-iodine laser would fill the robots' weapons bays.

That day seemed far, far in the future. The smallest oxygen-iodine laser in the world—not coincidentally under development at the top-secret base below—wouldn't fit inside a 747 without some serious alterations.

The Flighthawks themselves had a way to go. Routine flight patterns were preprogrammed, and the small planes had enough "native" intelligence to follow simple commands, like prepare a nose-intercept with an approaching bandit. But complex commands and maneuvers had to be broken down and explained to the planes. That took time and computing power. The scientists responsible for the project had promised faster and smaller computers based on near-room-temperature superconducting chips (NRTSC) similar to those in the XF-34A DreamStar, the next-generation interceptor seen as a potential successor to the F-22 Raptor. DreamStar's computer advances were numerous and so complicated that Zen had only a vague idea what they involved; still, he knew it was just a matter of time before they found their way from the XF-34A to the Flighthawks.

Even when they did, communications bandwidth might still be a problem. Since any communications could be jammed or compromised in a combat situation, the Flighthawks used an elaborate mix of laser and radio bands. Once they were in combat mode, everything went through three layers of 128-byte encryption. There was a brief but noticeable delay between command and execution in some flight regimes.

Zen checked his fuel and reviewed his flight data. He was back at twenty thousand feet, meandering at the edge of the restricted test range at 420 knots. Smith should have reached the end of the range by now. Zen stared out the canopy toward the southeast. Nellis Air Force Base, one of the busiest in the world, lay fifteen miles to the south, but with the heavy air restrictions in force, you'd never know it was so close.

Zen flicked the Eagle's radar into air-to-air medium-range mode, scanning out ten miles to where his opponent ought to be turning around.

No contact.

No contact?

Zen started to key his mike when he realized what Knife was up to. His left hand pulled the throttle to goose the afterburners and get away.

IT WAS ALMOST TOO EASY. KNIFE GUNNED THE ENGINES and jerked the nose of his Eagle off the deck, rising from fifty feet AGL as he swung up behind the Flighthawks. Stockard lit his afterburners, but that didn't matter—the Flighthawks were caught flat-footed. Hawk One tried to follow its mother ship, but its small engine was over-matched: The silvery hull slid precisely into the middle of the square target indicator of Knife's HUD. The Flight-hawk started to jink left, but it was too late—the M61A1 Vulcan chewed it up.

Or rather, the SiCS bleeped to say it did.

Knife's P&Ws were burning at 115 percent, and within seconds his F-15's APG-63 radar tapped the second Flighthawk, just out of cannon range. Knife nudged his stick to the left as he closed, squaring in for a bull's-eye.

Except the Flighthawk ducked off to the right, dropping down so fast he couldn't react. But that was fine—his goal was to splash Zen, not the high-tech UAVs. And now that the Flighthawk had run away, Zen's unprotected butt loomed at the top of his windscreen. Knife took a breath, adrenaline careening through his veins as he closed for the kill.

DAMN GOOD THING THEY WERE PLAYING BY CANNON rules or he'd be dead, Zen thought as he jerked Hawk

Two away. Sidewinder would have walloped him.

Then again, according to the rules, Knife was supposed to be about ten thousand feet higher, not flying low enough to stop for traffic lights.

Not that fighter pilots were expected to follow the rules, let alone fight fair.

Smith was probably pissed that he'd beaten him in the first round, and wanted revenge. That would make beating him again all the sweeter, wouldn't it?

Zen waited until he was sure Mack was coming for him before ordering the remaining Flighthawk to try to acquire his opponent's tail. Then he brought his full attention back to his own plight. The two planes were fairly well matched; Zen's slightly more powerful power plants made up for the fact that Smith's plane was a tad lighter. As long as they both had the pedal to the metal, Smith couldn't catch him.

Then again, Zen wouldn't be able to get away either. Nor would he be able to splash Smith, which was what he really wanted.

Duck and roll?

Smith wouldn't be fooled by it twice.

Feint left, plunge right, swing back in a high-speed scissors, twisting around to let the Flighthawk nail Smith in a front-quarter attack.

Not easy, but also probably the last thing Smith would be expecting, since the U/MF-3's were not adept at head-on attacks. As the Flighthawk took its shot, Zen could buck into a tight loop and come up behind him. He'd have him for dinner.

Maybe. Very hard to execute, especially with half of his attention on the Flighthawk.

Go for it.

Zen backed his power off, sucking Smith toward him. As his warner buzzed, telling him that he was about to be nailed, Zen pushed left. He counted off two seconds, then came back hard right, rolling the plane downward with a burst of speed that got him out to Mach 1.2. Knife hesitated for a second, then began to follow.

Perfect. Zen slashed through the air like a ribbon unwinding from a spool, Smith barely hanging on. Stockard opened the Flighthawk visual screen in the lower right quadrant of his viewer, and asked for a sit map—a synthetic overhead or God's-eye view—in the lower left.

Hawk Two was too far off the pace to complete the deal.

Cursing, Zen threw the Eagle over his shoulder, sliding and spinning downward to try to buy more time. Smith managed a snap shot, but couldn't keep him in his target aperture long enough for the SiCS system to register a hit.

"Yo, scumbag, I would have put a half-dozen slugs in your wing on that shot," snarled Knife. "Damn SiCs."

Zen didn't give him the satisfaction of an answer. He had to go hard on the stick as Smith dashed downward, cutting between him and the approaching Flighthawk.

Nice. Though the maneuver left Smith without a shot and potentially vulnerable himself, Zen was cut off and without enough forward energy to do anything but put his nose back down and try to pick up steam. Smith was on him again, accelerating across his path just when he thought he might try to recover. Zen threw the Eagle back down, slicing down to his left and then over into another invert as Smith somehow managed to twist his F-15C onto his tail.

The two planes twirled an elaborate ribbon in the sky, at times only ten feet apart. Zen played slapstick, ducking and bobbing just enough to keep from getting waxed. Finally he managed to get into a turn too tight for Smith to stay with; his pursuer had to back off or run the risk of overshooting him and becoming the target.

At that point, Zen should have transmitted the command "Knock it off" and ended the exercise. He'd fallen below three thousand feet and was low on fuel. He had only nominal control of Hawk One. He was far outside the stated parameters of the test. Both he and Knife had been rockin' and rollin' for more than an hour. Both had gotten out of bed shortly after midnight to begin the rigorous preflight procedures that were considered an important part of the experiment. He had also, by the standards of the experiment if not those he personally lived by, won the engagement.

The inquiry would note all of this, in a pointed aside.

But neither Zen, nor Smith for that matter, was about to give up.

Zen cut south on a direct intercept for Hawk Two, determined to get his robot escort back into the furball. He'd used his air brake to make his last slash, which had cost him considerable flight energy, and as he jinked onto the new vector he got a stall warning. He dropped lower, quickly picking up speed, pouring on the gas as he streaked toward the desert floor. The Flighthawk, apparently confused by the twists of its target, was flying toward him at roughly ten o'clock, its own speed down to four hundred knots. Zen told the Flighthawk computer to plot a fresh nose-on-nose intercept with Smith, who by now had turned back around and had the stops out in pursuit. The plan was simple, a slight variation of the one he'd originally intended—the Flighthawk would force Knife to break; Zen would come back around and nail him from the rear.

Then he'd go home. He was bingo fuel.

"I'm coming for you, Zen," gloated Smith.

"Hawk One, cannon," Zen commanded.

"Not locked," replied the computer, voice mode duplicating the visual indicator. "Outside range."

They were at six hundred feet indicated, descending at a very slight angle. Smith was right on his tail, almost in range.

"Extreme range. Cannon," commanded Zen.

"Not locked," answered the computer. "Outside range."

"Time to range," said Zen.

"Five seconds," said the computer.

Three too many. Zen twinged the rudder, hoping Smith would think he was planning a sharp cut. Then he held steady.

Knife bought it, but only for a second. Zen could practically feel his bad breath on his neck.

"I'm coming," hissed Knife.

The Flighthawk bar went green.

"Fire!" screamed Zen.

As the Flighthawk fired, Knife broke downward. The move—dangerous as well as brilliant, since they were now only five hundred feet over the desert floor—caught Zen by surprise. Zen started to pull up, then realized Knife had simply yo-yoed beneath him and was about to nail his belly. Stockard shoved the F-15 into a hard right turn. As he did, he gave the Flighthawk a command to break off its attack.

In the next second, a shudder ran through Zen's body, something he'd never felt before. It was like a tickle from inside, starting in the middle of his spine and flashing like lightning into every muscle. His hands and feet went cold, his toes froze. The steady roar of the big Pratt & Whitneys behind Zen stopped.

The sensation lasted a bare millionth of a second. It was followed by a hard slam and an unbearably loud screech, then silence.

The Flighthawk had sheared through the wing of Zen's plane.

BY THE TIME THE SICS BLEEPED WITH THE HIT, KNIFE had pulled the plane onto its back, rolled level, and was trying desperately to regain altitude and forward airspeed. For a moment, he lost track of everything—his target, the Flighthawk, even the ground and the sky. Blood rushed furiously around his brain, its flow distorted by the centrifugal forces of his hard-stick maneuvers. For a second or two,

Knife flew on instinct alone, his arms and legs sorting what his mind could not. They got the plane stable, kept it in the air, even pushed his eyes where they belonged.

Okay, he heard himself say. Okay. I nailed him.

The fuzz cleared and he was back in control, banking and climbing. Something big was tumbling across the sky above him. Gray foam seemed to shoot from its sides.

It took Knife nearly three full seconds to realize it was Stockard's plane. Somehow he'd lost control and was cartwheeling across the sky.

THERE WAS NO WAY TO HOLD THE PLANE. IT DEFIED gravity and every known law of Newtonian physics, moving in four directions at once, backward and forward, up and down.

Then everything stopped, time as well as the plane. It seemed to Zen that he could pop the canopy, undo his restraints, and step out. It seemed to Zen that he could stand on the seat and walk over the fuselage and look down at the sheared wing. He'd crouch and shake his head. Straightening with a grunt, he'd walk to the other wing and step off. It seemed to Zen he would trot down into the desert, running at an easy pace across the test range, back to his bunk at Dreamland.

Just when he decided he would do that, things began moving again, spinning with the force of a tornado. Zen's eyes fell to the yellow eject handles next to the seat. He realized he was too low and moving too fast to eject; the plane was tumbling and there was no way he was getting out alive. At best, he'd go out sideways and the chute wouldn't open and with his luck he'd fly through Smith's wing, though that would serve the SOB right.

His arms were paralyzed and he couldn't move anyway, and Zen took a breath and closed his eyes, ready to die.

Then there was a fierce wind around him and he realized he'd already yanked the handles.

II
The hottest stick on the patch

One year later . . .

Dreamland
7 October 1996, 1930

IN THE PINK LIGHT OF THE LATE FALL SUNSET, THE DESert complex looked abandoned. Four large shedlike hangars stood off to the right, beyond the long, wide concrete runway that Lieutenant Colonel Tecumseh "Dog" Bastian and his F-16 were heading for. A lone Humvee sat near the access ramp; another vehicle, a station wagon or SUV, was parked next to one of the hangars. There was no tower building, and in fact the only structures that seemed inhabitable were one-story dormlike buildings made of yellow bricks near the double fence. A few scratch roads, barely visible from the sky, wound across the flat terrain toward an old boneyard, or plane cemetery, at the extreme western end of the fence. Two, perhaps three ramshackle shacks guarded the old metal hulks, whose skeletons glittered red with the reflected light, as if they were still burning with the desire to fly.

If there were more desolate posts on earth, few seemed so ordinary or bland. Dry lake beds spread out before the mountains in the distance, crisscrossed by strange shadows and shapes, marks on the earth that could have been left by a race of desert giants, long since vanquished by the coming of man.

These immense hieroglyphics were actually a clue that the restricted desert and airspace north of Nellis Air Force base in Nevada was special indeed. For the shadows were manmade concoctions designed to confuse optical satellites orbiting above. Despite appearances, the base at the corner of Groom Lake was one of the most secure on the planet. Colonel Bastian's presence was being monitored not only by three different ground radars, but by two AWACS planes flying circuits around the restricted air corridors. And while nothing much might be happening on the surface of the desert, the bunkers and laboratories below were teeming with enough activity to shame a dozen ant colonies. There was indeed an air traffic control facility; it was equipped with state-of-the-art equipment, including a brand-new three-dimensional rendering system that projected Bastian's F-16 in a holographic display for the controller. The high-tech "tower" was located underground—beneath enough cement to withstand a ten-megaton nuclear blast. And so was the facility it connected to, with suites of some of the most sophisticated aeronautical and electronics research labs in the country. For Lieutenant Colonel Tecumseh Bastian was approaching the Air Force High Technology Aerospace Weapons Center, otherwise known as HAWC or, more colloquially, "Dreamland." The four cavernous hangars—and the facilities connected by special elevators beneath them—contained some of the most advanced aircraft and weapons imaginable.

And a few that were unimaginable.

"Dream Tower, this is DCAF Flight One," said Bastian after keying Dreamland's frequency on his F-16's radio.

"DCAF Flight One, squawk 2351 and ident," responded the tower, asking the colonel to prod the electronic identifying equipment aboard his plane. Even though the controller's sophisticated equipment had already independently ID'd the plane, Bastian moved quickly to comply; failing to do so could result in a no-questions-asked shoot-down by one of the MIM-23 I-HAWK batteries covered by desert camo netting just to the west of the base.

The controller did not verbally acknowledge the ID. Instead, he asked Bastian to give his security clearance.

"Diamond-diamond-black," replied the colonel.

There was a pause.

"Yes, sir," replied the controller finally. "Welcome to Dreamland, Colonel Bastian. We, uh, weren't expecting you today or in an F-16, sir."

"I assume you're not asking me to change planes," Bastian snapped. He had already begun to line up for his final approach, although technically he had not yet received clearance.

"Sir, no, sir," said the flustered controller, who immediately cleared Dreamland's new commander for a landing on the main runway. He added in a final aside that the weather was "desert fine."

The Block 1 F-16A Viper or Fighting Falcon Bastian flew was an old soldier. Dating from the very first production run of the versatile "light" fighter series, the plane had been scheduled to be "surplused" under the latest round of Pentagon budget slashings. Dog had managed to wangle it as a pilot-proficiency craft for his new command. It was his first victory over the bean counters; he hoped to hell it wouldn't be his last.

The fighter chirped its wheels appreciatively as Dog touched down. A row of lights sprang to life from the tarmac in front of him as the plane trundled toward the access ramp; the lights blinked yellow, helping to guide him toward Hangar Four, which housed transport and auxiliary craft assigned to the base. As he approached, the hangar door began to open. All of these functions were being performed by a brand-new Automated Airport Assistance computer being tested by the HAWC wizards. When perfected, the system would be able to do much more than turn on a few lights and open some doors. With minimal human assistance, AAA and its Series S IBM mainframes would be able to run routine maintenance inspections after every flight, scanning physical flight surfaces as well as avionics equipment. The system would automate maintenance procedures and, probably in the not-too-distant future, accomplish some of the work itself. The engineers envisioned a day when combat-ready versions of AAA would do the work of a hundred or more maintenance pukes, keeping a squadron in the air around the clock.

Dog wasn't necessarily sure he'd want to see that day. Not that he didn't want the Air Force to get maximum use of its planes and people—"bang for the buck" was the order of the day. But in his opinion, machines could only do so much. Taking away human error and inefficiency also meant taking away human judgment and creativity. To his way of thinking judgment and creativity were what made the Air Force—any organization really—work.

As he approached the hangar, a regular welcome-wagon parade came out to join the half-dozen ground crewmen waiting for him: A trio of black security Hummers zipped out from behind Hangar One. Combat-dressed Air Force Special Operations troops poured out of the modern-day jeeps, M-16A3 laser-dot-targeted rifles in their paws.

A good sign, Dog thought to himself—it meant Captain Danny Freah had gotten to the base ahead of schedule.

Freah's sourpuss face was the first to greet him when he climbed down the ladder.

"Colonel, welcome to Dreamland." The captain snapped off an impressive salute. Dog had known him for a little more than a year; in all that time, he'd never seen the twenty-three-year-old African American smile.

He liked that.

"Captain." Dog gave the detail a quick once-over, nodding appreciatively. "We'll be having a meeting for all officers and senior NCOs as soon as I'm squared away here. Set that up for me, will you, Danny? Let's say thirty minutes. My office."

"Excuse me, Colonel," said a civilian, walking slowly from the hangar. His blue shirt was open at the collar, and while his blond hair was cropped military-style, he wore a tiny gold-post earring in his left ear. "You'll never fit that many people in your office."

"And you're who?"

"I am Dr. Rubeo, senior scientist." Rubeo heaved his shoulders back like a skinny cock preening before a fight. His oversized nose dominated his bony face; though at least six-two, he looked to weigh maybe 150 pounds.

"And what do you suggest, Doctor?"

"Frankly, I would suggest you postpone your meeting until tomorrow," said Rubeo. "Assuming it's necessary."

Dog pitched his arms onto his hips. "Unacceptable."

"Colonel, let me suggest Conference Room Two," said Freah.

Dog locked eyes with Rubeo, then slowly turned to Freah and nodded.

"You'll be looking for Major Thomas, sir," Danny added. "I can take you over to him myself."

"Very good," said Dog.

"Life support this way, sir," said a young staff sergeant, indicating where he could leave his flight gear. The sergeant pointed toward the F-16's large travel pod, lashed to the side of the fuselage. "We'll get your bags."

"Thank you, Sergeant," said Bastian, starting toward the hangar.

"Excuse me, Colonel." Rubeo said the word "colonel" as if it belonged to a foreign language.

"Yes?"

"You want staff at the meeting as well?"

"I want all senior scientists there, yes," said Dog, snapping each word from his mouth. "I believe that would include staff."

"I don't know about that. Most aren't even on the base at this hour. They could be—"

"Thirty minutes," said Dog, setting off to get out of his speed suit.

DANNY FREAH HAD FIRST MET LIEUTENANT COLONEL Bastian during the planning session for a classified mission in Bosnia. Freah, then a lieutenant, had been tapped to help rescue a high-ranking Serbian defector, one of the Yugoslavian generals responsible for military planning during the Bosnian ethnic war. As originally drawn up, Freah's job was minor; he was heading a security team on the second helo in the backup flight. But the primary helicopters had to be scrapped, and by the time the backups arrived at the pickup zone the insertion team was taking heavy fire. Freah and his men saved the day. Danny hoisted the wounded general on his shoulders, and ran through a minefield with him to the MH-60K Pave Hawk just as the craft lifted off. The exploit had earned Danny a promotion and the right to wear a fancy medal on his dress uniform. It also got him assigned to the Pentagon, where he'd stayed just long enough to know he never wanted to go back there again.

Bastian helped get him transferred into Special Operations—and then pulled some strings to get him out here just a few days ago.

A lot of guys pointed out that "Bastian" sounded like "bastard." A lot of other guys pointed out that the colonel's nickname—"Dog"—was "God" spelled backward. But in Freah's opinion, the colonel was just a no-nonsense ballbuster who wanted things done right and fast. More importantly, the colonel had treated him fairly and respectfully from day one.

Though he'd only been at Dreamland for a few days, Freah already knew the base as well as anyone. Showing the colonel into Main Building One—they mockingly called the bland rectangle "The Taj"—he stepped quickly to the retina-scan device that stood in front of the elevator. Two of his men watched silently from a few feet away as the computer beeped clearances.

"Elevator won't descend unless each passenger has gone through the device," Freah told Bastian. "It's brand-new. Installed after, uh, their problems."

Bastian nodded. Like many pilots, Dog was barely average height, though his broad shoulders and squat legs betrayed the fact that he could probably out-bench Freah, who was no slouch himself. The forty-something colonel also ran five miles every morning, usually in just under thirty minutes.

The elevator arrived with a slow, pained hiss. It had never been exactly fast, but the addition of the security equipment made it excruciatingly slow. Having used the retina scan to identify them, the security system now reconfirmed its initial decision with an elaborate sensor array that measured fifteen physical attributes, from height to heartbeat. Any parameter that was out of line with recorded norms would cause an alert; the equipment was so sensitive that personnel were regularly briefed not to drink more than their usual allotment of coffee in the morning, for fear of pushing their heartbeat too high. In theory, the gear was supposed to make it impossible for an impostor to infiltrate the base. Freah was skeptical, to say the least.

"This thing taking us down, or what?" asked Bastian as they waited for the doors to close.

"Sorry, Colonel. The procedure takes a while."

Bastian frowned as Freah explained how the device worked.

"We'll have to find something better," said Bastian as the doors finally closed. "With the amount of time this takes, people will be looking for shortcuts."

"Yes, sir," said Freah. He smiled—he had come to the same conclusion.

They had barely started downward when Bastian reached over to the panel and pulled out the stop button. The car halted immediately.

"How's morale here, Danny?" asked the colonel.

"Colonel, I've only been here three days," said Freah.

He could tell from the way Bastian pursed his lips that wasn't going to do.

"To be honest, I'd say they're waiting to be nuked or closed down. They'd probably prefer to be nuked."

Bastian nodded. He might have wanted more, but Freah had nothing more to add. He honestly couldn't blame the men and women assigned here for feeling so dejected. While the scientists were a bit flaky, by and large everyone at Dreamland ranked in the top percentiles of intelligence and ability. They were the elite, charged with an elite mission—take cutting-edge ideas and turn them into usable hardware. But in the last few months, they'd seen their ability, work, and even loyalties questioned. A spy had been discovered in one of Dreamland's top projects.

The spy hadn't been just anyone. He'd been the top pilot on the top project at Dreamland: the XF-34A DreamStar next-generation interceptor and flight-control system. He'd stolen the plane, doing irreparable damage to the program and the careers of maybe a hundred people, including the three-star general who had run the place. As if the scandal and investigations weren't enough, the budget cutters' ax had arbitrarily slashed Dreamland's funds so severely even toilet paper was in short supply. And things were bound to get worse. Rumor had it that Bastian had been tasked with slicing Dreamland's budget even further—and ultimately closing it down.

But it wasn't Freah's job to complain, nor was it his

way. And while he'd actually majored in math for a while as a college undergraduate, he'd just as soon let someone else put the numbers in a row. So he merely stood at attention, waiting for his boss to reset the elevator.

"Hal Briggs says hello," Bastian told him when he finally pushed the button. "I saw him in Washington last week."

Freah nodded. Briggs had headed security at Dreamland until the spy scandal. It was an ironic twist. Briggs had mentored his career, and Freah felt more than a little awkward succeeding him.

Typical Briggs: He'd found out about the offer somehow and immediately called Freah to urge him to grab it. "Even if they close the base," Briggs had told him, "it's a plum assignment. Go for it."

Briggs had somehow landed on his feet after the DreamStar debacle, getting an assignment so classified he couldn't even hint about it. They kept in fairly constant touch—especially during football season, when they traded weekly and sometimes daily predictions about games. Briggs had sent him a secure e-mail message about Bastian just yesterday, detailing an account he'd heard from someone in Washington about how many arms Bastian had had to break to get his personal "pilot check" F-16. It was thanks to that message that Freah was ready for the colonel's early arrival.

"The major's office will be this way," Freah told them as the elevator stopped on Underground Level One, which was devoted to administration and support. "I'll take you there, and then alert people about the meeting. Major's a nice guy, but as you probably know, strictly a caretaker. He was about the only one left standing after the scandal and political BS, outside of the pilots and scientists."

"Yes," said Dog, stepping out.

*   *   *

"I EXPECT THAT A FEW OF YOU HAVE HEARD OF ME. I'M a pilot by avocation. A zipper suit. That means I don't accept no for an answer. I have an engineering background, but I don't pretend to be as scientifically adept as any of you. Frankly, that's not my job."

Dog took a step away from the podium, pausing for a moment to let his words sink in. Nearly two hundred men and women had crammed into the bowl-shaped lecture hall. Most had been either just going off duty or already at home, which in some cases meant Las Vegas, some miles to the southwest. A few looked like they had been sleeping. There were sharp divisions in the crowd, and not just between civilians and military. Air Force officers who had strictly administrative functions at the base were front-row-center. Two knots of senior noncoms filled the flanks, wearing respectful though perhaps slightly skeptical expressions. The scientists filled most of the middle and the back rows; their eyes betrayed a "now-what" attitude. That sentiment was common too among the senior officers standing along the back row. Unlike the civilians near them, they stood ramrod-straight—though Dog suspected this was more because they didn't want to touch their neighbors than out of any respect toward him.

And then there were the pilots, sitting in the two rows nearest the door, barely concealing smirks, each undoubtedly teeming with wisecracks.

Dog gave them his most severe frown before continuing.

"You've taken a lot of shit here in the past six or seven months," he said. "I know all about Maraklov—or Captain James, as he was calling himself." Dog made sure to spit out the name of the traitor, who had wreaked so much havoc during his so-called Day of the Cheetah. "I'm not going to belabor the point. You've all had to put up with enough BS on that account. Dreamland is in trouble. You know it. I know it. People are talking about closing it down. Important people, including Congress. And including the President."

The requisite jeers followed. Dog let them get them out of their system for a moment before putting his hand up.

"I can tell you right now, that's not going to happen."

The jeers turned to silence, and then something deeper, as if his words had created a black hole in the room, as if they had sucked every sound and every potential for sound away.

"I'm here to kick some ass," Bastian said quickly. "And I'm going to put Dreamland back at the top of the agenda. Anyone who doesn't want to be a part of that, leave now." He waited a beat, then continued. "Good. At 0600 hours tomorrow, we'll start mission-orientation flights. That means everybody—engineers, scientists, security, secretaries—hell, everybody, even the cleaning people—every last person on this base is going aboard an aircraft to see just exactly what the hell it is we do."

Dog ignored the murmurs of approval from the staff people and turned to Major Thomas, who had been acting as base director of operations until his arrival. "Major Thomas will work with whoever needs to be worked with to make it go off smoothly."

Thomas looked at him as if he'd just declared war on Canada. But Dog wasn't about to get into a discussion.

"Dismissed," he said, waving his hand. "I'll see you on the tarmac in the morning."

Dog hadn't actually expected applause, but he took it in stride. The surprising thing was that it seemed to have started with the NCOs. He buttoned his mouth tight against a grin, gesturing to Thomas so he could explain what he had in mind while people started to file out of the room.

"No offense, Colonel," said Thomas, whose forehead was dotted by beads of sweat, "but I would have appreciated, uh, maybe a heads-up?"

"You just got it," Dog told him. Assuming Dreamland survived, Dog intended on picking his own staff and Thomas wasn't going to make the cut. Still, he meant him no ill will. "There's no problem with arranging flights, is there?" he said, trying to modulate his voice into something almost friendly.

"Well, we have to work around the spy satellites. And the pilots aren't going to like it," sputtered Thomas.

"I'll take care of the pilots," said Dog. He smiled. "I speak their language."

"Yes, sir. But, uh, is it worth it? If we get the order to, uh, to, uh—"

"Abandon ship?" suggested Dog.

"Well, uh, no, I think they'll keep us open. I mean, there's so much invested here that it would be foolish, but, uh—"

"I didn't come here to mothball Dreamland, Major. Yes, I'm aware that I'm replacing a three-star general. The political implications are not entirely lost on me," added Dog in his most severe voice. The matter was more than merely one of prestige, since in effect it demoted Dreamland far down the command chain. "However, we will carry on. Maybe they'll even promote me," he added wryly.

"I'm sure, uh, yes, sir," said Thomas, taking a step backward.

"Colonel, can I have a word?"

Dog couldn't immediately place the voice, or the face that went with it.

"Mack Smith." A tallish major grabbed his hand and began pumping. "You might remember me from the Gulf, Colonel. I was just a captain back then, flying CAP while you were at Black Hole. A lot of guys call me Knife."

"Mack, of course. How the hell are you?" Dog mimicked the pilot's aw-shucks routine, trying to put the name and face together.

"First Tactical Wing," said Smith.

"Smith. Knife. You bagged a MiG," said Dog, suddenly putting the name—and deed—to the face.

"Actually two," said Smith. "Glad to have you with us. I heard you were coming in tomorrow."

"I was restless."

Smith gave him a puckish grin. "About those, what are we calling them, morale-booster flights?"

"Mission-orientation flights." Dog grinned wider than Smith had. "Don't make anybody throw up when you put them in the backseat."

Smith lost his grin, but only for a second. "I'm lead pilot on the F-119 project, Colonel, the Joint Strike Fighter. I've had that assignment since DreamStar was canceled."

"And?" Dog let just the hint of impatience creep into his voice. He remembered Smith pretty well now. He was a great pilot. And he *had* bagged two planes—except that the second was initially listed as unconfirmed, due to some problem on the AWACS covering the area. Smith had raised a fuss about getting credit, bypassing his squadron commander and complaining to Centcom about it as soon as he heard the kill was in doubt.

"The, uh, we have the prototype," Smith continued, growing less sure of himself. "The F-119. I don't know if you're up to speed on it yet, Dog."

If Dog was up to speed on anything, it was the F-119. And while ordinarily he didn't mind another pilot using his handle, something about the way Smith said it bothered him.

"I realize it's a one-seater," said Bastian. "So unless you're planning on strapping someone on the wing, Knife, I think we can leave it in the barn for these missions." He paused just long enough to let Smith think he had wormed his way out of the morale flights. "But your combat record shows you're the best Eagle pilot—by far—on the base.

So obviously you ought to be the first one off the flight line. Hell, I insist on it. You're top man; you get the most seat time. I believe there are two F-15Es here. You have one all day. Move up the starting time to 0500."

Bastian started to step away from Smith when a bony hand grabbed his arm. He turned to see Rubeo, the scientist he'd met outside earlier.

"Colonel, do you really feel these airplane rides are necessary?" asked Rubeo.

Before Dog could reply, a squeaky voice piped up behind the scientist.

"Hell, I think it's blastoff idea. About time the enlisteds got into the game."

Dog peered around Rubeo—it wasn't exactly difficult—and smiled at Chief Master Sergeant Terence "Ax" Gibbs.

"Hey, Graybeard," he said to the burly, gray-haired sergeant, who had adopted the falsetto to mock the scientist.

Not that Dog officially approved of that sort of thing.

"Colonel, what took you?" said the sergeant. "I've been here since lunchtime."

"Then why weren't you on the runway waiting?" Dog asked.

"Priorities, sir. Priorities." If regulations allowed beards, Ax would look like Santa Claus after a year's worth of Nautilus sessions. He'd served in various capacities with Dog over the past decade in a dozen commands. The colonel had asked him to come to Dreamland as his senior staff NCO; there was no one better at slicing red tape and tending to things that needed tending.

"Great speech, sir," said Ax, elbowing Rubeo out of the way. "One of your best. Morale-boosting, us against the world, we're all in it together. Nine on a ten scale."

"Only nine?"

"You haven't had supper, I'd bet." Ax winked at him. "Sandwich waiting for you in your office."

"You're going to make somebody a fine wife someday,

Ax." Dog raised his eyes to scan the rest of the room. Smith and Rubeo had decided to retreat. There were only a few people left in the small auditorium. Two lieutenants and a captain, holdovers from the previous commander's staff, were waiting respectfully a few feet away. Everyone else seemed to have someplace else to go.

Just as well.

"Every base needs a good wife," said Ax. "Of course, we may be put out of business any minute. And if we're not, there are half a dozen people with shiny stars on their shoulders who want your job. I've had three offers already."

"That's all?" Dog took a step toward the waiting officers, but Ax stopped him with a subtle raise of his hand.

"She's over there by the door," said the sergeant, gesturing behind him.

Dog turned and saw her, sandy brown hair that managed to look alluringly feminine despite the military cut, sleeves rolled up to reveal well-sculpted forearms, hands on trim hips, fierce green eyes.

Her mother's eyes.

The rest—such as the captain's bars and the hard gaze of a pilot old before her time—might be traced to her father.

Him.

Dog took a deep breath, then began walking toward her. She took a breath as well, obviously tense.

"Breanna," he said.

"Daddy."

They winced simultaneously. Dog started to lean toward her, intending to give her a peck on the cheek. He stopped. She leaned up, then stopped. For a moment, neither one spoke. Then they both spoke together.

"I didn't—"

"I wanted—"

"Tell you what, Captain," said Dog, "let me go first."

"Yes, sir," she said.

Her eyes met his, and for a moment he almost asked how her mother was. But he'd already decided that was out of bounds.

"You'll be treated like any other officer on the base," he told her.

"I would expect nothing less, sir."

Dog nodded.

"I was hoping to introduce you to Jeff," she said. He noticed that she lowered her gaze as well as her voice.

Dog didn't know what to say. He hadn't approved of the marriage.

He hadn't disapproved either. He simply hadn't been consulted.

"But Jeff's not here yet," said Breanna. "He wasn't due until next week. But he's coming tomorrow."

"I see."

Dog frowned, wondering if he shouldn't have his daughter removed from his command. But that would undoubtedly hurt her career—she was among the Air Force's top-rated test pilots. And if Dog took pride in the fact that he had never done anything to help her career, he also was loath to hurt it.

Everyone knew she was here when they offered him the assignment. Maybe they didn't think it would be a problem.

More likely, they didn't think Dreamland would last.

"Orientation flights first thing in the morning?" she said.

"I expect you to be among the first pilots off the tarmac," he said.

"I intend on it. Wait until you see the Megafortress. Even you'll be impressed." Her frown turned into an impish grin, something the typical young flier might betray at the thought of a good joke. Then it morphed into something else, something barely familiar—the grin of a three-year-old playing hide-and-seek the day after her birthday. "At some point, I expect to have some personal face time," she told him. "Have you found an apartment yet?"

"I'll be on base," he snapped.

Breanna's face changed back to stone, eyes focused on a blank spot in the distance.

"I understand, Colonel," she said. "No favors, please."

He didn't want to be mad at her—hell, if she were anyone else, he'd be joking, taking her under his wing. She was one of the future's bright stars, the kind of officer he wanted working for him. "We'll have dinner, okay?" he said softly. "Once I'm oriented."

Either his words were too low or she simply ignored him.

"It was a hell of a speech. We're pulling for you," she said, turning away.

"And I'm pulling for you, Bree," he said.

Dreamland
8 October, 0530

THERE WAS NO PRISON LIKE THE HUMAN BODY. IT clamped bars stronger than titanium steel around your chest, your legs, your head. It held you every waking moment; it mocked you when you slept. It infected time itself, poisoning both past and future.

There was no future for Captain Jeff "Zen" Stockard; there was only now. He sat in his wheelchair, long fingers wrapped stiffly around the spokes of the wheels, hard rubber against his palms. He stared directly ahead, eyes fixed on the closed door of the HH-53 as the big helicopter skirted the fringes of Nellis Air Force Base, rumbling toward Dreamland. The helo's crew chief sat on a narrow bench seat a few feet away, having given up his attempts at starting a conversation.

Zen hated conversations, especially with strangers.

There was always pity in their voices. The only thing worse was conversations with friends. He preferred not to talk at all. He preferred to be left to himself. He wanted . . .

What he wanted was to be able to walk. He couldn't have that, so he didn't want anything else.

He'd worked tremendously hard the past eleven months—nine actually, since most of the first two were spent mostly under sedation, in and out of operations. He'd built up his arms and upper body. He'd been in reasonably good condition before the accident, but the workout routines were a revelation. Zen welcomed the pain; he drove himself into the stinging bite of exhaustion, as if weariness were a physical place. He pushed weights around. He learned to swim with his arms and chest and head. He discovered the different balance of a body that couldn't use its legs.

The humiliation was the hard part. Needing someone to open a door for him. Needing someone to lift him into the cramped backseat of a van. Needing someone to help him with a thousand things he used to take for granted in the course of a day.

Getting past the humiliation had been his first goal. He hadn't totally accepted it, but he had at least gotten used to it.

Getting back to Dreamland was his next goal. And here he was, seconds from touching down.

It hadn't been easy. Zen had had to call in every favor, and lean heavily on his family connections besides. He'd had to find a service lawyer who knew the Disability Act and could wangle and bluff its language into places where it didn't belong.

Worse—much worse—he'd had to play the pity angle.

His lawyer, an Army captain wounded in Panama, was also in a wheelchair. Louis Whitson wasn't so much an inspiration as a slap in the face. "The bottom line," Whitson had said one morning when things looked particularly crappy, "is this: We use whatever we can use. Pity, fear, ignorance, stupidity. If it's to our advantage, we use it. Bottom line."

Like almost everything Whitson said, it was useful advice. They found a sympathetic Senator and an important Congressman. And an Air Force general whose brother had been confined to a wheelchair since he was six. They built a case for remaining on active duty. Reed-thin—hell, thinner than air. But with favors and pity, they got him a chance.

Better than that. Brad Elliott, the former commander of Dreamland, was under a cloud. But he still had a lot of influence—and he also had an artificial leg. The general helped twist arms and bend ears for Jeff, who had been one of his "boys" before the accident. Elliott managed to find a way to use his dismissal and the resulting confusion at Dreamland to Jeff's advantage. Technically, the general pointed out, Zen was still on the active-duty roster as a test pilot assigned to the Flighthawk program, which was one of the few Dreamland projects besides the F-119 not suspended in the wake of DreamStar. So technically, that's where he had to report.

Air-thin.

But now, as the helo pushed through the thin desert air en route to its landing, Zen felt something he hadn't had the luxury of feeling since his accident: fear. He realized he might not be ready to come back—certainly not here.

He slipped the chair backward against the restraining straps as the Super Jolly Green Giant began banking into its final approach. Earlier HH-53 types had been used as rescue choppers during the Vietnam War. More than likely somebody else with a broken spine had been sitting where he was sitting, staring at a door, wondering what he was going to do for the next fifty or sixty years, wondering if he was ready.

Wondering was a sucker's strategy. Zen fixed his eyes on a bolt in the door handle, then bit his teeth together. The helicopter settled downward, the T64-GE-413 Turboshafts throttling back as the craft touched onto the long, smooth run of concrete. Zen kept his eyes pasted ahead as the crew chief kicked open the door; he waited without moving a muscle until the restraints on his wheelchair were removed. As the last belt slipped off, he pushed forward, rolling to the open portal.

There wasn't a ramp. His choices were to banzai it, or wait for the crew chief and copilot to lift him down.

He waited.

"Here you go, Major," said the copilot, a paunchy six-footer who strained as he took hold of the side of the chair.

Zen grunted. The sun threw its yellow arms from over the nearby mountains, greeting him. It would soon get warmer, but at the moment it was barely fifty. Zen felt cold despite his thick jacket as they released him onto the tarmac.

Two members of the security detail—specially assigned Air Force Spec Ops troops with rifles ready—stood a few yards away, near the entrance to Hangar One. There had been a few changes in his absence; he thought two of the hangars had been painted. Otherwise, it seemed very familiar.

Different, but familiar.

Zen waited as the crew chief retrieved his briefcase and bag from the helo.

"Sergeant. Put the bags on my lap, please."

The sergeant looked down at him.

Pity. The worst thing.

"The guards won't let you past them," Zen said. "Let's go."

"Sir—" The sergeant seemed to lose his voice for a moment. "Yes, sir," he said finally. He placed the bag and briefcase on Zen's legs, then stood back and snapped off a respectful and well-intentioned salute.

Zen was only vaguely aware of it. He'd turned his attention back to the guards, who had been joined by a third person just emerging from the hangar.

It was his wife.

SHE KNEW HE'D COME EARLY, TRY TO SNEAK IN WITH-out any fanfare. He'd been vague on the telephone, and that was a dead giveaway.

Breanna watched Jeff take the bags and wheel his way toward the security men. For a moment she twinged with anger that the crewman hadn't carried the bags for her husband; then she realized Jeff had probably told him not to.

The Air Force security sergeants snapped to attention before challenging him. She'd stopped to talk to them earlier, warning them that Jeff would be arriving soon. She'd brought them coffee, then asked for a favor—treat him no differently than anyone. In fact, if they could be a little surly, that would be better.

He hated people treating him like a cripple. He'd told her that the very first night, when he regained conscious-ness—used that ugly word, "cripple," before he even knew he was one.

It hurt to watch him wheel across the open cement. It made her want to cry, but that was the last, the very last thing she could do. It would be like kicking him in the face.

Breanna forced her arms to hang down at her sides. She could do this. She had to do this.

"Sir, your orders, sir," snapped one of the two ser-geants, his voice cold enough to chill the heart of a Rus-sian paratrooper.

Zen scowled. The look was so familiar Breanna felt her

heart snap. He placed the bag with his clothes and other personal items on the ground next to him. He undid the clasp on his leather attaché—an old gift from his mother before she died—and slipped out a small sheaf of paperwork. The routine was, of course, not necessary, since the captain was well known and in any event would soon have his identity checked at a retina scanner at their station inside the hangar. His status and orders, like those of everyone at Dreamland, were recorded on the security computer. But it was a good touch.

The first sergeant inspected the documents while the other sergeant remained watchful. "Sir, I have to ask you if you are armed," said the man finally, holding the papers in his hand.

Before, Jeff would have smiled wryly and said something like, "The girls all think so."

Now he stared straight ahead, his words snapping taut in the chilly morning breeze. "My personal weapon is in storage. I am presently unarmed."

The guard handed him back his orders.

"Your bags, sir. I have to ask that you present them for inspection."

Zen handed them over.

"If you'll follow us, Major, we can complete the protocol inside. We require a retina scan. It's a new procedure."

The men turned smartly and began striding toward the hangar. One of them gave Breanna the faintest wink.

"Jeff." The word slipped out faintly as he drew parallel to her. He didn't answer; she put her hand gently on his upper arm, stopping him.

"I'm okay, Bree."

"I know that," she said.

She stepped back and watched him wheel into the hangar. An F-15C Eagle—coincidentally the one Mack Smith had been flying when the accident happened—sat at the far end. Jeff kept his head pointed straight ahead, following the two sergeants to the computerized security device.

Breanna held her breath as Greasy Hands—Chief Master Sergeant Clyde Parsons, the senior NCO in charge of the maintenance crews—ambled up with a cup of coffee in his fist.

"Yo, Zen. Good to have you back, Major. About goddamn time."

Jeff snorted.

"Been a slew of changes around here during your R&R. Flighthawks only got back in the air two months ago. Civilian pilot—nice guy, but not for nothin' his nickname's 'Rock.' " Greasy Hands offered Jeff the coffee. "Dab a milk. Alzheimer's hasn't caught up with me yet."

She couldn't see Jeff's face. He didn't say anything, but did take the coffee. Jeff and Greasy Hands had gotten along particularly well before the accident, the sergeant looking after the pilot like a doting parent.

Parsons caught her gaze. "Megafortress'll be ready for you in ten shakes, Captain. Just checked with the crew chief."

"Thank you, Sergeant."

The old geezer smirked. "Better watch out for Major Cheshire. Hear she's on the rag today."

Breanna wasn't exactly sure how to take that; she was rarely sure exactly how to take anything Parsons said. Though Dreamland's excellent work teams were a testimony to the first sergeant's abilities as an organizer and mother hen, Parsons was old school and very uncomfortable with women being in the military. She thought that he was trying to treat her like one of the guys, which probably in his mind was a big honor. His approach to Cheshire—the senior project officer on the EB-52 Megafortress and Breanna's immediate superior—was very different, stiff to the point of being overly correct.

"Your dad's sure gonna stir things up," added Parsons. "He's a bee-whacker."

"A bee-whacker?"

"Really likes to whack the old bees' nest," explained the sergeant. "Shake things up. Got all the officers jumpin', even the pilots."

"I wouldn't know," said Bree.

"He's a butt-kicker," Parsons told Jeff. His admiration seemed genuine. "You best watch your fanny, Major. Place isn't going to be the same with him in charge. Now I admired the general—a damn fine man. An excellent officer. But Colonel Bastian, hell, he's a bee-whacker. Just what we need," Greasy Hands added, shaking his head and grinning. "I've heard stories."

"So have I," said Breanna sharply. "Jeff, I have to go get ready for a mission."

He ignored her. It was pretty much what she expected; pretty much what he'd done in the hospital and all during rehab, after the doctors had told him he'd never walk again.

Not sure what else to do, she turned quickly and started for the Megafortress's underground bunker.

COLONEL BASTIAN LOOKED UP AS AX MADE HIS WAY across the office.

"Cup number two, not quite as strong," said the sergeant, placing down the coffee mug. "As per request."

Dog grunted and rubbed his eyes. He'd gotten less than two hours of sleep last night, spending the rest of the time reviewing project notes and trying to correlate some of the reports with the Pentagon data he'd come west with. His desk was littered with folders, printouts, white pads, photocopies, notes, index cards, Post-its, and even a few old-fashioned carbons.

"Sunday *Times* crossword puzzle in that mess some-where?"

"Very funny, Ax."

"You want to run through the day's agenda yet, Colonel? I figure we wait any longer the day'll be over and then we'll be behind."

"Yeah, okay." Dog took the coffee and leaned back in the well-padded leather chair. One thing about Ax's coffee: Even the weak cups were gut-burning strong. And hot—Dog backed his lips off without taking a full sip.

"It'll cool down," said the sergeant.

"Thanks for the advice. Well?"

"Okay, let's see. Number-one priority—hire a secretary. Preferably one who can make coffee."

"Agreed."

"Number-two priority, we need some typists, clerks, etc., etc. I can't be expected to do real work forever, you know."

Ax folded his arms in front of his chest. He was joking. Dreamland had a full complement of military and civilian clerks, probably more than the ever-efficient Ax needed. But instead of giving himself away with a laugh as he usually did, his expression turned serious.

"You okay, Colonel? Usually, you're rolling on the floor by now."

"This is a worse mess than I thought, Sergeant."

"Yes, sir." Ax ran his left hand up behind his neck, scratching an imaginary itch. Gibbs's actual age was a closely guarded military secret, but he gave every impression of being old enough to be Bastian's father. There were many times, like now, when he reminded Dog of the old man—kinder, without the temper. Maybe smarter, though Bastian's father had been sharp enough to make admiral and get himself elected to Congress.

"Colonel, you've been in worse messes," said the sergeant. "It's just the paper-shuffling's got you down."

"Five of these programs have to go," said Bastian, pointing to the papers. "Ms. O'Day is calling this morning for my recommendation."

Deborah O'Day was the National Security Advisor and the reason Bastian was here.

"Eenie, meeney, minee, moe."

Dog laughed.

"Finally," said the sergeant. "I was beginning to worry you left your sense of humor back in Washington somewhere."

Dog smiled and took a sip of the coffee. The problem wasn't deciding which programs *should* be cut. The problem was that the programs that *should* be cut were exactly the ones the brass, the White House, and the Congress *wouldn't* cut. Worse, by recommending they be cut, all he would succeed in doing was anger people and administer the final coup de grace to Dreamland.

An argument could be made to close the base. The spy scandal aside, in many ways HAWC belonged to an earlier era. Bastian realized that the dissolution of the Soviet Union and the end of the Cold War meant that big-ticket development projects with almost unlimited budgets were a thing of the past. Without the constant threat of a high-tech arms race, Congress would be loath to approve the immense "black" budget lines that had funded Dreamland.

But on the other hand, the end of the Cold War didn't remove the threats to national security; it just changed what they were. In Bastian's opinion—and in the opinion of the Secretary of Defense, the National Security Advisor, and the President, as far as he could tell—cutting-edge technology would be even more important in fighting the sort of brushfire wars and terrorist actions America would face in the twenty-first century. With the future so unpredictably fluid and budget constraints the order of the day, high-tech weapons were going to be a critical force-multiplier. Delta Force was the model of the

twenty-first-century Army—a highly trained, extremely
mobile group ready to strike at a moment's notice. The
Air Force needed an equivalent. And it needed to multiply
its limited resources with the country's top asset—brain-
power. That would be Dreamland's role, providing
cutting-edge technology to deal with a myriad of
next-generation crises.

Bastian had written a briefing paper to that effect while
working for the NSC under President Bush after the Gulf
War. While it had gone largely unnoticed in the Administration at the time, it had attracted the attention of Deborah O'Day, a policy wonk and university professor doing
consulting work for the NSC back then. O'Day had struck
up a friendship with Bastian, even having him in to talk
to her classes at George Washington University. Her appointment as National Security Advisor by President
Lloyd Taylor had surprised a lot of people outside the
government, but not Bastian, who realized she was as
sharp as anyone in D.C.

Technically, Bastian was a long way down the chain
of command from O'Day. But he'd worked for her in
D.C. and she had personally pulled the strings to get him
here.

"Assuming your phone call with Ms. O'Day is only its
normal marathon length," said Ax, "we can do this today
like you wanted. You start seeing your section commanders, one by one, at 0800. Fifteen minutes a pop, that gets
you to 1145, with a thirty-minute time-out for Ms. O'Day.
Lunch at your desk. Senior scientists, two minutes apiece,
you'll be done by one."

Dog looked up from his papers. "Two minutes?"

"Just checking to see if you were awake," said the sergeant. "Fifteen minutes for the eggheads, like everybody
else. Brings you to 1545, or maybe 1630. I can't quite
figure out their damn organization chart."

"That will be fixed by tomorrow," said Dog. "Each

project gets a specific commander, with staff attached. Line officers in charge. This is a working squadron."

Bastian hadn't worked out all of the details yet, but his idea was relatively simple and followed the plan he had outlined years before. You got the technology onto the front lines by using it right away. The best way to do that was to slim down your organization. The people who had to use the weapons would be the people running the show.

"I'll have the paperwork in two batches for you this morning," said Ax. "Usual routine. And seriously, there are two guys I'd like to bring in to fill out the staff."

"There's a personnel freeze," Dog reminded him.

"Oh, that's no problem." Ax grinned. He glanced down at the desk. "You want a piece of unsolicited advice, Colonel?"

"No."

"I'd eighty-six this fancy desk and the bookshelves and the paintings, the whole bit. I mean, if you were a three-star like the last commander, it would be austere. Hell, simple even. But some Congressman comes wandering in here, he's going to wonder why your office is fancier than his."

"No Congressman's wandering around Dreamland," said Dog. "But thanks for the advice."

"Anytime, Colonel. It's free."

"And worth every cent."

SMITH PUNCHED THE TWO-PLACE F-15E NEARLY straight up, letting the big warbird feel her oats. The Pratt & Whitneys unleashed nearly sixty thousand pounds of thrust, easily overpowering gravity.

"Eeeeyow!!!!" shouted the major's backseat rider, a young staff sergeant selected from the engine maintenance shop. His yell of enthusiasm was so loud Smith had to knock the volume down on the plane's interphone circuit.

At five thousand feet, Knife sliced the plane's right wing in a sharp semicircle, leveling off in an invert that had the sergeant squealing with delight.

"Hot shit! Hot shit!" said the man as Smith brought the Strike Eagle right-side-up. His next comments were lost as Knife pulled a six-g bank and roll, literally spinning the plane on her back before heading off in the other direction.

"I love it! I love it!" said the sergeant when he got his breath back.

Knife grinned in spite of himself. He loved it too. The F-15E was designated as a strike aircraft, a bomber. But she had been developed from the basic F-15 Eagle design, and was still an Eagle at heart—a balls-out hard rocker that could load g's on her wings like feathers and accelerate as easily as a bird hummed a tune.

Rolling through a fresh invert at near-supersonic speed, Knife realized he'd been on the damn F-119 project so long he'd almost forgotten that flying was supposed to be fun. *This* was why he'd joined the Air Force.

Two weeks before, Major Smith had been offered a slot in a provisional unit known only as Wing A. The details about its mission were sketchy—according to a friend who was helping put it together, it was going to be a blood-and-guts quick-response unit, a kind of Air Force equivalent of Delta Force. Smith would be Director of Operations for a four-plane F-16 sub-squadron connected with a black operation called Madcap Magician. It had been a while since he'd flown F-16's, but all in all it sounded promising. When he checked it out through the back channels, however, he got mixed responses. One general whom he trusted a great deal thought it would be an A-1 career ticket to the upper ranks. Another said it was Hot Dog Heaven, a sure way to be shunted off the fast track into a career culvert.

But damn—it was a real live flying gig, and if it *was*

like Delta Force, he'd at least be where the action was. Besides, it seemed obvious that Dreamland was about to be flushed. The previous commander was a three-star general; no way they were going to put a lieutenant colonel in charge if they were intending on keeping HAWC up and running.

And what a colonel. If last night's self-important rant was any indication, Colonel Bastian—aka "God," as everyone in the Gulf had called the one-time hotshot pilot turned Centcom strategic planner—had succumbed to serious delusions of grandeur. Knife was willing to concede that Bastian was an okay pilot and a reasonably good thinker; he knew that Dog had helped set up some good mission schemes while working with Black Hole, the central planning unit that ran the Gulf Air War out of a bunker in Riyadh. Bastian had also briefly served as a wing commander in action after the war, again supposedly doing a good job. But Dog's ego had obviously gotten the better of him since.

Knife had been ninety percent sure he would take the new gig when he slipped into the Eagle this morning. Now he was committed. Good riddance, Dreamland. Good riddance, F-119, chariot of slugs.

Knife yanked the Eagle into another hard turn, leveled off, then reached for the throttle to see if the afterburners would work this early in the morning.

They did. His backseater let out a yelp as the plane threw off her shackles and started to *move*. The plane bucked for a moment, then seemed to tuck her wings back, sailing through the sky as if she were a schooner gliding across a glass-smooth lake.

"You ever break the sound barrier, Sergeant?" Knife asked as the engines swirled.

"Sir—no!" yelled his passenger.

"Well, now you have," said Smith. He backed off the engines as they passed the boundary into Test Range K, which he'd been cleared to use as long as he stayed above five thousand feet. The airspace below was reserved because of static tests of an Army electronic-pulse system, due to begin within the half hour.

"See the tank down on the ground, Sergeant?" Knife asked.

"Affirmative, sir. That's the EMF target. Think it'll get nuked?"

"Couldn't tell you. We're talking Army here."

"Yes, sir," said the sergeant with a laugh. "We're shielded against those pulses, aren't we?"

"Well, allegedly their weapon defeats standard shielding," answered Knife, who knew that the test had been conducted about twenty times over the past month—obviously because the device didn't work. "But, like I say, we're talking Army."

"Yes, sir," said the sergeant, snickering again.

"We'll give it plenty of room," said Smith, starting to bank.

They'd been using Range K the day Stockard got nailed.

Poor bastard.

Stockard was a good pilot, but he hadn't been quite good enough. A blink too slow, and it cost him.

Knife curled his hand around his stick and took another turn, a truly hard one this time, briefly touching eight g's.

"What'd you think of that one?" Knife asked, easing back on the stick. "Sergeant?"

There was no answer.

"Sergeant?"

There was a low moan. Apparently the force of the turn had knocked his passenger unconscious.

Laughing out loud, Knife gunned the plane back toward the runway.

*   *   *

"CAN'T DISAGREE, MS. O'DAY. CAN'T." COLONEL BAStian picked up his pen and began tracing a series of triangles on his white notepad. He leaned his left elbow against the chair's armrest, the phone pressed against his ear. The National Security Advisor had just reminded him how important it was to keep Dreamland going.

"Well, then," said O'Day, "what can we give them to cut?"

Bastian sighed. "I've been here a little more than twelve hours."

"The Joint Chiefs' recommendation is full closure and shutdown," said O'Day. "I'm meeting with them in less than an hour. What bones do I throw them?"

"Well, I'd say preliminarily Megafortress, the Achilles laser array, definitely the Nightfighter A-10 upgrade. The Flighthawk U/MFVs, all the crap we're doing for the Army—"

"Crap?"

"Excuse me. All of the joint-service projects can go."

"No," said O'Day firmly. "Those contracts are going to help keep you alive. I'm fairly certain we can keep the Army Secretary on board. They're gaga over the EM pulse weapon and their smart bullets. And that carbon-boron vest thing, the body-armor project."

Bastian rolled his eyes. "If we let politics guide weapons development—"

"Oh, cut the crap, Colonel," snapped O'Day. "Since when hasn't it? Look, the first battle we wage is for survival. We keep Dreamland running, then we move it into the twenty-first century. I'll take care of the politics," she added, her tone softening. "Just give me a bottom-line number. We'll work the details out later."

"If we could take the money from the F-119 project—"

"Why don't you just suggest you'd like to sleep with the Speaker's wife?" snarled O'Day. "That would go over better."

Dog laughed despite himself. One thing he'd say for O'Day—she could be as irreverent as anyone he knew in the military. She was just very choosy about it.

"It wasn't meant as a joke," added O'Day.

"I'm sorry, ma'am," said Bastian contritely.

"All right, listen, Dog, I have a subcommittee meeting on Somalia and Iran in thirty seconds, so I'm going to have to sign off. Solid numbers by Tuesday."

The scrambled line snapped clear.

Bastian gave himself a moment to recover, then called to Ax to let his next appointment in.

The sergeant appeared in the doorway. "Bit of a complication, Colonel."

"What happened, he got tired of waiting?"

"No, sir," said Ax. "Problem is, he might not get through the door. It's, uh, Major Stockard, Colonel," added the sergeant. "He's in a wheelchair."

"Stockard's next?"

"Yes, sir. Projects in alpha order. He's the senior officer on the Flighthawks."

Dog stood up. He wasn't particularly looking forward to this. Even before Stockard's accident their relationship was at best chilly, at worst nonexistent.

"I suggested Room 103B," added Ax. "That would be the conference room two doors down the hallway. It has double doors. He's waiting. You're backed up three appointments already," added the sergeant as Bastian got up. Ax pointed to a side door, which opened into a vacant office. "Shortcut, sir."

As he reached the door, Bastian realized the frame was actually fairly wide, more than enough for a wheelchair. His sergeant had arranged the meeting place to give both men more privacy. Typical Ax. "Thanks, Sergeant."

"Lunch'll be waiting."

* * *

ZEN ROLLED BACK AND FORTH, TRYING TO WORK OFF some of his energy, some of his nervousness. He felt like a nugget pilot, moving an F-15 up to the flight line for his first takeoff, jiggling the rudder pedals up and down. You could always tell who was new or at least nervous— the twin rudders whacked back and forth like loose shingles in the wind.

He willed himself to stop. You didn't want to tip off the enemy to your vulnerabilities.

Everyone was the enemy, including his father-in-law. The fact that Zen greatly respected Bastian—whom he'd met during the Gulf War while liaisoning as an intel officer for his squadron—was an argument only for greater vigilance.

The creak of the side door took him by surprise. Zen sat up stiffly in his chair as Colonel Bastian brushed into the room.

"Major, good morning." Bastian's tone gave nothing away; he could have been greeting a Chinese military attaché. He closed the door with a slap and then folded his arms in front of his chest. "It's been a while."

"Yes, sir."

"You're still assigned on the Flighthawk project." Bastian's tone was somewhere between a question and a statement.

"Yes, sir." Stockard resisted the impulse to add something—anything—to the statement. He and his lawyer had gone over and over this point. Don't argue, don't justify, don't explain. Just state your assignment and presence as a fact. Anything else will inevitably weaken our position.

Zen's position. As supportive as his lawyer was, Jeff was in this alone.

"I think we have an unusual situation," said the colonel.

"The Flighthawks are an unusual project," said Zen.

"Major, I'm going to spare you the rah-rah bullshit," said Bastian. He pulled out a chair and sat down. "Dreamland's on the chopping block. Even if HAWC survives, at least a dozen projects are going to be killed. Everything's in play. The Flighthawks especially. Playing with robots is a luxury we can't afford right now."

"Flying with a pair of Flighthawks is like having two wing mates at your beck and call," said Zen. He was surprised to be talking about the project instead of himself. "We're just scratching the surface."

"Nonetheless—"

"Look at what UAVs did on the first day of the Air War in the Gulf," said Zen. "They were the ones responsible for helping knock out the Iraqi air defenses."

"You don't have to tell me what happened on the first day of the Air War," snapped Bastian.

"Excuse me, Colonel. I know you helped plan the attacks. But I can tell you, as someone who was there too— if we had Flighthawks, the F/A-18 that was splashed in air-to-air on Day One would not have gone down."

Bastian said nothing. The Navy plane had been knocked down by an Iraqi air-to-air missile, the only air-to-air casualty of the war. Had the Iraqi Air Force been more capable, there would undoubtedly have been many more.

"Colonel, simply using these planes as scouts will double strike effectiveness and survivability," continued Zen. "They can provide close escort to AWACS and transport types, freeing F-15's and eventually F-22's for more important work. Fit them with iron bombs and they can do the job of A-10A Warthogs, close-in ground support on the front lines without anywhere near the human risk. The Flighthawks are the future. I wouldn't have come back here if I didn't believe it."

"That's not the issue," said Bastian dryly.

"If you want to cut something, cut the damn JSF. It's a flying camel. Hell, the Warthogs go faster. You could build two hundred of them for the price of one F-119."

The comparison to the A-10 was an exaggeration—but only just. Bastian scowled, but said nothing.

"The Flighthawks need work. I'm proof of that," said Zen. "But in five years, maybe three, they'll own the skies. I guarantee."

"Robots will never outfly men," said Bastian.

They glared at each other.

"We're reorganizing our command structure," said the colonel finally, still holding Zen's eyes with his stare. "Each project will be its own flight. Pilots are going to be much more active and important in the command structure. It'll be a lot like a combat squadron."

"You mean I'm going to be in charge of the Flighthawks?"

"It means the senior pilot or officer will be responsible, yes. Everyone is going to be involved. Everybody responsible. No glamour-boy hotshots. No complicated chain of command where everyone can point a finger at everyone else. Each person will have one flight—one project, one assignment."

Zen nodded. "And if the Flighthawks get canceled?"

"We'll deal with that when the time comes. I know where you stand." Bastian winced, but plunged on. "And you know where I stand. That's the way I run things."

"That's a good way to run things," said Zen.

"As for your relationship—marriage—to my daughter," added the colonel, his voice regaining its formal tone, "that's not my concern. And it should never be. You're no different than any other officer on this base."

"Fair enough."

Zen began wheeling himself backward, swinging around to pull open the door.

The colonel beat him to it. Zen felt his face flush red as Bastian reached past him and opened it for him. He bit his teeth together and rolled on.

* * *

"FORT TWO, MOVE TO LINE ONE, AWAIT FURTHER INstructions."

Breanna acknowledged the controller's transmission. She leaned against the left window of the big Megafortress, peering down past the plane's drooping SST-style nose to give her crew chief the thumbs-up. Then she eased back in her seat, adjusted the headset's microphone, and eased the big jet forward from its parking spot in front of the hangar entrance. One of three Megafortress test beds currently active at Dreamland, Fort Two had started life as a B-52H, the last production model of the Stratofortress. The enhanced B-52, also known as the EB-52, was a pet project of General Brad Elliott, the past commander of Dreamland, who envisioned it as a relatively low-cost, high-capability twenty-first-century flying battleship. The first Megafortress had become famous as "Old Dog," aka Dog Zero-One Fox; it had at least arguably prevented World War III with a still highly classified preemptive strike on a Soviet laser system some years before. While various EB-52 scenarios had been proposed as production models, the Megafortress concept had never quite made it to permanent funding, losing out to "sexier"—and much more expensive—projects like the B-2.

Each of the three Megafortresses currently flying at Dreamland was configured differently, with different power plants, avionics, and weapons systems. Three more B-52's, including one older G model, were being converted. All made use of the same basic skeleton: a carbontitanium hull and remodeled bismaleimide (BMI) resin wings. All were considerably more capable than the admittedly versatile and robust design Boeing engineers had drawn up nearly fifty years before.

Breanna nudged her rudder pedal, gently pushing the plane to the right. Fort Two's controls were "fly-by-wire";

instead of hydraulics, the control surfaces were moved by small motors directed by electronic impulses in the pedals and yoke. The system was still being perfected, and a hydraulic backup system could be selected by throwing a manual override switch near the throttle panel. Many of Fort Two's recent experiments involved the control system's interface with an advanced flight computer capable of flying the plane on its own through a complicated mission set. The engineers were also debating whether traditional controls—such as the yoke that looked like a sawed-off steering wheel—or more contemporary ones like fighter-jet sidesticks were better. Fort Two's control set aimed to meld some of the originals with new technology; when Breanna pulled back on the yoke, it would at least theoretically feel as if she were pulling back on the wheel of a stock model H.

Besides the control systems, Fort Two was testing uprated P&W JT9D-7Rxx2 engines. The power plants allowed for greater speed and less fuel consumption; their increased thrust allowed the designers to replace the B-52's stock eight power plants with four. That took a bit of getting used to; the new engine set was not only more powerful but considerably quieter. If the Xs—as the engines were called—were adopted as standard, the EB-52 would probably rate as the quietest warplane ever.

"Electric panel one, green," said the copilot, Captain Chris Ferris. Ferris proceeded through the preflight checklist projected on one of his three multi-use displays. "Two, green. Three, green. Four, green. Crosswind crab."

"Zeroed," said Breanna, reading her own tube. The computer was doing the work she would have done in testing and adjusting the equipment in a stock B-52.

"We have pitot heat. We have instruments in the green. We have computers making pilot and copilot completely redundant," joked Chris.

"As it should be," groused Dr. Ray Rubeo, one of their

two flight deck "tourists." In rebuilding Fort Two, the forward deck had been stretched and revamped, allowing two large stations to be added immediately aft of the pilot and copilot seats. The walls on either side of the cockpit near the stations featured double banks of video monitors tied to test and monitoring equipment. Rubeo was sitting at station one; Steven McCormick, a somewhat reserved computer scientist, sat at the other.

Chris laughed, continuing through the list of systems that were ready to go. Breanna told the two passengers on the radar-navigation deck below—Greasy Hands and a staff sergeant from the motor pool—that they were proceeding to the runway.

"We'll take off, do a low-slow circuit of the range, then we'll have some fun," she told them over the interphone system, which could be piped to everyone on the plane.

Once manpower-intensive functions, radar and navigation were now handled completely by Fort Two's prototype flight computer; even the weapons operators, whose "office" was located behind the flight deck just forward of the wing area, were redundant. On Fort Two their panels had been replaced by banks of computers and test circuitry. Had the Megafortress been an active warplane, it would have required only pilot and copilot to complete its mission, though a defensive weapons specialist and a navigator would be preferred additions until all the flight computer systems were at production status. In some ways, Breanna liked the old B-52's better, with their six-member overworked crews. But this was no time for nostalgia; the tower gave her final clearance as she slipped up to the end of the runway.

"Takeoff power," she told the flight computer. She glanced at the four-pronged throttle bar, which replaced the multi-fingered mechanical control. Responding to her voice command, the throttle slid into position, thrust precisely and automatically calculated to match not only the plane's present weight, but the runway and weather conditions. The Xs rumbled on the wings, ready to boogie.

"Noisy things," groused Rubeo.

"Flaps. Optimum takeoff configuration. Go," Breanna told the computer as she manually released the brakes. They started down the runway, quickly picking up speed.

"Seventy knots, eighty," read the copilot.

The wings strained at the top of the plane, anxious to lift her into the sky. Breanna nudged her left rudder pedal ever so slightly, keeping the plane centered on the runway as she pulled back on the stick. Depending on its weight and configuration, a standard B-52 might get off the ground in three thousand meters or so; Fort Two lifted off cleanly at just over a thousand, not even breaking a sweat.

"Gear up," Bree told the computer.

"Gear up and safe," reported the computer as the giant wheel assemblies folded into the undercarriage.

Breanna checked her altitude, speed, and bearing in the HUD screen. The control system responded instantly to the optical-servers in the yoke housing as she entered a right bank. Whether flying at shoelace level or over fifty thousand feet, dodging enemy fighters or out for a pleasure cruise, the flight computer automatically trimmed the plane's control surfaces for the most efficient flight regime, essentially reading the pilot's mind—or rather, her hands and feet.

Breanna glanced back at Rubeo as the plane climbed easily upward. "Okay, Doc, change places with Chris."

"Why?"

"Come on. You can't see anything from there."

"You're not afraid of flying, are you, Ray?" asked the copilot.

Rubeo narrowed his eyes into a glare; he hated to be called Ray.

"Any monkey can fly," he said as Chris eased out from behind the copilot's station. Still, Rubeo hesitated, and Breanna realized that Chris was right. Rubeo was the senior scientist at the base, personally responsible for nearly fifty breakthroughs so secret they couldn't be openly patented. His work on logic chips was critical not only for their flight computers, but for the actuators used by the Megafortress's control surfaces. But it turned out he was petrified of flying.

Not that he would admit it. He frowned deeply as he sat down next to her.

"You might want to hitch up the restraints," she suggested.

"I intend on it," said Rubeo.

She noticed a definite green tint around his gills. Breanna hit the mike button, switching on the intercom circuit.

"Good morning, and thank you for choosing Dreamland Airlines," she said. "I'm Captain Breanna 'Rap for Rapture' Stockard and I'll be your tour guide this morning. I have to ask you to remain in your restraints at all times, and please, keep your hands inside the cars. We will be moving at close to the speed of sound, and I'd hate for anyone to lose their jewelry."

"Yuk, yuk," mouthed Rubeo.

"On a serious note," Bree continued, "I would remind you that we are an experimental aircraft. Our systems are held together by bubble gum and duct tape. I do expect that you will remain strapped to your parachutes and snug your skull buckets. You too, Sergeant Parsons."

"Don't worry about me, Captain," answered Greasy Hands.

"If you look out the port windows, you'll see the Z27 test range, where our friends in the Army are testing their new pulse antimissile system." Breanna tweaked the control stick, ducking the plane to its left. "Whoa," she joked.

"Don't everybody look out the windows at once."

"Very funny," said Rubeo. His voice was an octave higher than before.

Breanna smirked, launching into a tour-guide dissertation on the history of the venerable B-52. Though she tried to make it sound spontaneous, it was a well-practiced speech; she had given it four times over the past few weeks to Air Force VIPs as part of the effort to keep the Megafortress program alive.

"The B-52 is sometimes called the BUFF—for big, ugly, fat uh, fella, shall we say?" Breanna chortled, knowing everyone would laugh at the obligatory joke. "As a matter of record, the base plane for Fort Two is older than—hell, it's older than our copilot, Dr. Ray."

Rubeo ignored her, staring straight out the front windscreen.

"In June 1946," continued Breanna, "the U.S. government awarded the Boeing company a study contract for a long-range bomber. That seemingly innocuous event led to the design of a turboprop-powered behemoth superficially similar to the B-50, which had evolved from the B-29. You don't have to have one of Dr. Ray's four Ph.D.s to realize that a lumbering turboprop would have been no match for the interceptors under development at the time, let alone surface-to-air missiles. The problem was primarily the engines; even optimally engineered turboprops can only turn so fast, as our Communist friends found out with their Tu-95 Bear. But at the time, pure jet engines were equally unacceptable; they were thirsty things in the mid-1940's, not very powerful and, as Greasy Hands might put it, 'tarnation and hell' to work on."

"Damn straight," said Greasy Hands.

Breanna thought he might be speaking from experience.

"It was just about that time when the wizards at Pratt & Whitney came up with the J57 jet engine. It was a V-8 for airplanes, capable of delivering 7,500 pounds of thrust

without popping a gasket. An Air Force officer looked at
the Boeing turboprop proposal one cold Thursday in October 1948 and declared it obsolete. Then he showed the
team the specs for the P&Ws and sent them away. They
called the next morning from their hotel and promised
he'd have a design on his desk Monday. The engineers
worked like demons, even building a balsa-wood model.
When Monday rolled around, they had invented history's
longest flying bomber, arguably the most versatile and
successful military aircraft ever conceived. Through 774
iterations, encompassing eight major families and an almost unfathomable number of alterations and updates, the
B-52 has served for nearly fifty years as America's primary manned strategic bomber."

"Jeez, it *is* older than Dr. Ray," said the staff sergeant
sitting with Parsons below.

"Hardy, har, har," answered Rubeo.

His response got a better laugh than the original line.

Breanna checked her flight position on the global po-
sitioning system—accurate to within half a centimeter—
then did a quick scan of the vital information on the flight
monitor on the right side of her dash before continuing
with her historical narrative.

"Now where was I?" she said. "Oh, yes. I should probably note that our new power plants are derived from the
engines used by the Boeing 767. They feature considerably more thrust, so much so that Fort Two is currently
fitted with one at each engine root instead of the original
pair. If my math is correct, that's four instead of eight.
Even so, Fort Two has broken the sound barrier in level
flight at 55,000 feet."

That was an incredibly impressive statistic, since it was
impossible for even a "clean" B-52 with minimal load and
stock power plants.

"We are, as you may know, testing several engine configurations for the Megafortress," she continued. "Fort

Two is presently the only one with the Xs. And one of our planes—Raven, which we've used for ECM tests and Flighthawk drops—still has the original P&Ws. Needless to say, these power plants are better, increasing the plane's already prodigious range to slightly over ten thousand miles—though most of that's downhill."

No one laughed. Tough crowd.

"The B-52 was at least theoretically obsolete by the 1960's," said Breanna. "The sheer size of the plane, once dictated by the thirst of the engines, had become as much a liability as an asset. On the other hand, its large size meant we could keep piling equipment on, increasing its life as well as capability. The add-ons and alterations made a not particularly pretty plane one ugly MF, as the saying goes. But the BUFF was—is, I should say—one versatile airframe. You can't hot-stick her—or at least, we're not *supposed* to hot-stick her. But let me tell you something: If you're beneath the bomb bay when it opens—well, fresh underwear is the least of your problems."

"Hear, hear," snarled Rubeo.

"She takes a lickin' and keeps on tickin'," said Chris, obviously annoyed by the scientist's disdain. "I have a picture somewhere of a B-52H model landing without her stabilizer. Try that in a Bone."

"Bone"—from B-One—was the nickname for the B-1B, also known as the Excalibur and Lancer. Ferris had served with a B-1 squadron before coming to Dreamland.

"Don't get me wrong," Chris added. "I love the B-1B. There's no better low-level penetrator in the world. Mach 9 at five hundred feet wakes you up, let me tell you."

"Humph," said Rubeo.

"Much of the technology we're testing," continued Breanna sharply, "represents the next wave of development beyond the B-1B and the B-2. Our resin wings, for example, are lighter than those of the B-2. The avionics and control suite that we are currently working on, when perfected, may be used in upgrades to the B-2 or perhaps whatever its successor will be."

"We know all that," hissed Rubeo.

Annoyed by the scientist, Breanna punched the plane into a roll.

"And as you can see, the physical improvements to the control surfaces, as well as the reinforcements to the skeleton, make Fort Two as maneuverable as a late-teen fighter."

"Whoa!" yelled McCormick as Breanna put the plane back on its keel. "Better than a roller coaster."

"Now I'm not saying a B-52 couldn't have done that," Breanna told the passengers as they settled down. "But there's really no comparison between the two airplanes' flight profiles. I could demonstrate spin recovery, for example," she added pointedly, glancing over at her erstwhile copilot.

Rubeo had his hands wrapped around his neck, obviously trying to choke the bile back down.

"But maybe I'll wait for another time," Breanna said.

The words were barely out of her mouth when the plane fell out from under her in an uncontrolled, full-power dive.

DOG OPENED THE SIDE DOOR INTO HIS OFFICE AND stepped back fifteen years. Instead of lunch, Patrick McLanahan was sitting on the edge of his desk, wearing civilian clothes and a smile nearly as wide as his shoulders.

"Dog, how the hell are you?" said McLanahan with a laugh. "You're damn lucky you're not sitting in a pilot's seat right now, or your fanny would be waxed solid."

"I'd just hand the controls over to you and expect to have my butt saved," replied Dog with a laugh, grabbing his long-ago radar operator in a bear hug. "How the hell are you, Patrick?"

"Still kicking," said McLanahan. "Despite rumors to the contrary."

"I'll bet," said Dog. McLanahan had been the senior Air Force officer on the DreamStar project, and one of the heads that had rolled after the debacle.

Supposedly. He was looking awful cheerful for someone who'd recently been forced into retirement. And downright natty, with a leather jacket, sharp chinos, and expensive-looking cowboy boots.

Not to mention the fact that his shirt was tucked in.

Obviously something was up. McLanahan may have been the best bombardier in the Air Force, but he had also arguably been the worst dressed, a walking catalog of Reg. 35-10 dress and appearance violations.

"Civilian life agrees with you, I guess," said Bastian.

"In a way."

"You want some lunch?" Dog asked.

"Sounds good," said McLanahan.

"You here on business?"

"In a way."

Dog stuck his head out the door. "I'm going over to find some lunch," he told Ax.

"They're waiting for you in the base commander's lounge at the end of Level B. I've rearranged your afternoon. You're free until 1400."

"Thanks."

"I expect it will show up in the next fitness review," said the sergeant.

"I thought you told me there was a new directive requiring self-evaluation only," retorted the colonel. "How do we get to Level B?"

"I know the way," McLanahan told him.

Bastian matched his pace as they headed down a long corridor to a set of steel doors. Inside they descended two

levels and emerged in a hallway lined with framed photographs of old Air Force fighters. A thick carpet lay on
the floor. A wooden door at the end of the hall gave way
to a small, well-appointed room with hunter-green walls
and heavy drapes. A sergeant and an airman stood at the
side of a row of four tables, each outfitted with fresh lin-
ens. The place looked like an exclusive D.C. restaurant.

"I'm going to fix this," Dog said as they sat down.

"How's that?" asked McLanahan.

Before Bastian could say anything else, the airman
swept in and filled their water glasses. The sergeant
slipped a stiff piece of cardboard in front of Dog and
stepped back.

It was a wine list.

"I hear the Duck Walk by the glass is a good buy,"
quipped McLanahan.

"We won't be having wine, thank you," said Bastian,
handing the card back. "Damn. I can't believe Brad Elliott
stood for this."

"Well, first of all, General Elliott was a three-star general," noted McLanahan. He seemed rather amused. "This
sort of thing comes with the territory. And second of all,
the lounge was used only for VIPs. Congressmen, the Secretary of Defense, important contractors the general had
to impress. Otherwise, Brad ate mostly at his desk."

"Humph."

"Being a general means being a politician," said
McLanahan.

"Thank God I'm not a general," said Dog.

"Listen, I'd appreciate it if you didn't close the place
until after lunch. I didn't get a chance to have breakfast."

Dog settled back in the chair. He'd known when he
accepted the assignment that he was entering a different
world than he'd inhabited before—a world of privilege
and power. What McLanahan said about the lounge's use
was undoubtedly true. Hell, from what he'd seen back

East, this was austere. It was also likely that the facility—
and its wine list—had been donated by defense contractors.

But that didn't mean it was going to survive. Bastian
was a lieutenant colonel and would live like one. And so
would everyone else. As of tomorrow morning, he decided as he surveyed the room, all "cafeterias"—strike
that, all facilities, all mess halls, all lounges, hell, all dor-
mitories and soda machines—would be "all-ranks."
Everyone was equal, military and civilian, officer and enlisted man.

"Dog?"

"What exactly is it that you want, Patrick?"

McLanahan glanced up as the sergeant returned with
menus. Dog took the card silently, scanning it quickly.

Roast leg of lamb in a raspberry mustard sauce. Pureed
lentils in a sake-cream soup. Pheasant saltimbocca with
squid-ink linguine.

Dog looked up at the sergeant. The man's arms were
straight down at his sides, his thumbs circling rapidly
around his fingers. His cheeks were purple, but his forehead was white.

"Look," Dog told him, trying to smile, "can you get
me a medium-rare burger with fries?"

"Gladly, sir," said the sergeant.

"Me too," said McLanahan, handing the menu back to
the sergeant. "Although I have to say that pheasant was
tempting."

"You didn't set this up with Ax, did you?" Dog asked
McLanahan.

McLanahan laughed and shook his head. "I wish I did.
Just to see your face."

"Are you here to lobby for Megafortress or Cheetah?"

"Neither actually," said McLanahan, his tone instantly
serious. "And not DreamStar or ANTARES either. If you
want, I'll tell you anything you want to know about any

of the projects I was involved in. But they're not why I'm here."

"Megafortress isn't going to make the cut, Patrick," said Dog. "As much as I liked what the Old Dog did, and whatever I think of the flying-battleship idea, there's no support."

"I'm not here about that," said McLanahan. "This is all your headache, not mine. I have new ones to deal with."

"Such as?"

"ISA," said McLanahan. ISA stood for Intelligence Support Agency, a high-level covert project funded by the CIA and DOD to support "special" actions. Dog knew it well—he had helped develop the briefing papers and the draft intelligence finding that established the organizational framework. ISA operated outside of the normal military command structure, to put it mildly.

"What's up?" Dog asked.

"ISA is putting together a special strike package. One of the pilots and two of the support personnel on Dreamland's roster are going to be asked to join. It's strictly voluntary, but, uh, there have been some back-channel discussions, as I'm sure you would expect."

"They need my permission?"

"No, but some of the people back East thought you'd want to be in the loop," said McLanahan carefully. "I was at Nellis and since we know each other, they asked me to give you a heads-up."

"You're running ISA?"

"No. I'm more like a consultant. A freelancer," said McLanahan. "The pilot is Mack Smith."

"You want the F-119 too?"

Dog hadn't meant it as a joke, but McLanahan laughed. "Just Smith," he said. "The 119 can stay in the shed forever as far as I'm concerned. The technical people are listed as specialists in avionics and engines respectively, but their records show they could build planes from scratch."

While Smith was an arrogant SOB, Colonel Bastian didn't particularly want to lose him; the fighter jock was the hottest stick on the patch. And he was the senior officer on the JSF.

"It's about Somalia," added McLanahan, obviously sensing his reluctance to part with the pilot.

"Oh," said Dog. He hadn't seen the intelligence briefings since a few days before leaving Washington, but McLanahan's tone made it clear that things there had continued to worsen. The Iranian mullahs had been equipping one of the warlords in the eastern African country, apparently with the intention of helping him take over the government. That would allow them to control access to the Red Sea and Suez Canal, as well as the Gulf of Aden—and thereby manipulate the price and flow of oil. Which itself was supposed to be a prelude to their "Greater Islamic League," a coalition of Middle Eastern countries dedicated to the prospect of giving America a headache.

"ISA is involved with Somalia?" Dog asked.

"ISA is part of a contingency plan." McLanahan took a sip of his water. "Iran's warlord will be in charge inside two weeks."

"Then what happens?"

"Well, maybe nothing. The analysts are all over the place."

"I wouldn't count on nothing," said Dog. "If the mullahs are feeling strong enough, they'll base the Silkworms they bought from China there. And after that, they'll move in the new aircraft they're buying from Russia. Two dozen Su-35's and the same number of Su-27's equipped for surface attack could bottle up half the world's oil fleet within three hours."

"Oil prices will go to one hundred dollars a barrel,"

said McLanahan. "I read your white paper on it. Hard to believe you wrote it a year ago."

"The Sukhois are good warplanes."

"CIA says they haven't been sold." McLanahan frowned, but it was impossible to tell whether he believed that or not. "They have the Silkworms ready to go. And rumor has it that they're working with the Chinese on an aircraft carrier, which should be ready within a few months, if not weeks. The NSC is recommending that this thing be cut off quickly. Which is why I—ISA, that is, wants Smith."

The sergeant emerged from the kitchen pushing a large cart. On top of it were two deluxe burger plates, with oversized hamburgers on grilled potato-bread rolls. Large saucers of ketchup, mustard, and relish flanked a massive heap of steak fries at the side of the plates.

"Now this is what I call first class," said Dog, thanking the sergeant.

"I would have thought you'd be used to fancy food, having come from Washington," said McLanahan. "I hear they love you at the White House."

"I met the President exactly once," said Dog. "And that was in a room with fifty people."

The burger was excellent, perfectly charred on the outside and pink on the inside. Maybe not the healthiest lunch, but tasty enough to justify the risk.

"Like I say, the analysts are all over the place on this. We're not exactly knee-deep in intelligence on what Iran is up to," McLanahan said, picking up the napkin from his lap and dabbing at the side of his mouth. "Good burger."

"Very good," said Dog. "The Iranians have studied the Oil Shock of the seventies. They know what the impact on the Western economies would be of doubling or quadrupling the price of oil. And don't forget, they'll benefit from the extra money. They'll go straight to Russia and lure another fifty or sixty scientists for their nuclear program. As well as plutonium."

"You sound like you're still working for Ms. O'Day." McLanahan picked up one of the large steak fries with his fork. "CIA says they're at least six years away from a bomb."

"They're crazy. More like six months. You should talk to Jack O'Connell."

"I have," said McLanahan. O'Connell was a CIA ground officer who'd been in Africa and the Middle East as well as Russia, tracking Russian nuclear technology.

"Is ISA hooked up with Madcap Magician?" asked Bastian.

McLanahan didn't answer. From what Dog had been told at the NSC, Madcap Magician was an interservice Spec Ops "program" consisting of volunteers from different branches trained to operate as a covert intervention or first-strike force in the Middle East. Different Spec Ops groups—including a small unit at Dreamland under Danny Freah known as Whiplash—were attached as call-up units; they were supposed to be available on twenty-four-hour notice. Madcap Magician itself was so secret that Bastian didn't know much about it—but he realized from McLanahan's silence that he had just nailed the connection.

"Obviously, you can have Smith," said Dog. He held his half-eaten burger and roll in his hand. It was too good; it tempted him to reconsider his "all ranks" decision.

He put the burger down and pushed the plate away. McLanahan looked at him with an expression close to shock.

"What else do you need?" Dog asked.

"Food's fine."

"I mean planes. Hell, I've got the hottest weapons on the planet here. Cheetah? The Scorpion AMRAAM-Plus? Tell me what you need and it's yours."

"Sounds tempting."

"We're an important part of the Air Force," continued Dog. "With the top talent the military and private enterprise can offer. I have a base full of cutting-edge weapons just begging to be used."

"I used to work here, remember? You sound like you're making a funding pitch."

"No. I'm stating a fact. And maybe a pitch. A little pitch," conceded Dog. "Because if we put some of these high-tech doodads we're working on here to work, no one will close us down."

"Those high-tech doodads you're working on still have bugs in them," said McLanahan. "Believe me, I know."

"Nothing's without risk. If Dreamland's going to survive—now there's a white paper you should read," he added, referring to the report that had led him to this post.

"What makes you think I haven't?"

Dog stood up. "I have to get back to work, Patrick. Whoever you need, he's yours. And I'm serious about the planes and weapons. You know more about what Dreamland can offer than I do."

McLanahan nodded thoughtfully. "Say hi to Rap for me when you see her."

Dog nodded, then turned and started back for his office.

THE FIRST THING BREANNA THOUGHT AS THE MEGA-fortress slammed downward was: Damn, this is going to screw up the project big-time.

The next thing she was: Damn, we have a serious problem here.

The plane didn't respond to her yoke. Rap commanded the computer to restore full pilot control. As she did, the legends on the heads-up displays, or HUDs, glowed bright and then flashed out.

"Computer, restore pilot control," Breanna calmly told

the computer, but even as the words left her mouth she realized the computer had been taken off-line. Fort Two's nose was aimed toward the earth. The g's were piling up; they were pulling four, then five, the pressure increasing exponentially.

"Okay, we're going to backup hydraulic control," she said calmly, reaching for the heavy lever to the right of her seat that would kill the fly-by-wire system and bring the backup hydraulics on line. "Chris, change places with Dr. Ray."

Her thoughts and actions blurred in chaotic soup smeared by the effects of adrenaline and gravity. She had both hands on the control wheel as the hydraulics kicked in, pulling back for all she was worth and trying to prevent the plane from going into a spin at the same time. She had no engine indicators, but guessed the power plants must be close to flaming out, if they hadn't already.

No, she had power; she could tell by the light hum somewhere in the back of her brain.

Chris slid in beside her. Rubeo was hanging on to her seat, shouting something about the electronic systems.

"They're off-line. There's been a massive computer failure," he yelled.

"Well, no shit, Doc," Breanna said. "Relax and enjoy the ride, please."

There were any number of possible causes, from a loose wire—highly unlikely—to an anomaly caused by the Army's weapon tests on the range below. There'd be time to sort it all out later.

Assuming, of course, she regained control.

"Still accelerating and dropping," said Chris tersely. "Passing five thousand on the way to four thousand, three thousand."

He could easily have said zero. The aircraft began to shudder; they were through the sound barrier and still accelerating. The windshield filled with a brown blur.

Somewhere around here, she thought, the wing aerodynamics are going to help us. Eventually, the shape of the wing and the speed of the air flowing over it are going to give us enough lift to pull up. Then the trouble will be controlling it.

Breanna felt their momentum shifting and checked her trim tabs quickly, making sure the plane's control surfaces weren't working against the rest of the airfoil. The nose lifted steadily as the plane's inherent flying capabilities finally took over.

"Good, okay, good. Chris?"

"Yeah, yeah, yeah," he said as they roller-coasted upward. Blue flew into the windshield.

"This is easy," she lied. The plane pulled sharply to the left, as if it were trying to turn itself into a Frisbee.

"We just lost an engine," guessed Chris. "No instruments. Sorry. I can't get power into the panel no way, no how."

"Restart. Just go for it," she told him. Without the instruments they could only guess by feel which engine it was—probably number one, the furthest out on the left wing. "It's got to be number one."

"Yeah. No restart. Retrying. Nothing." He was flying through the procedures, hitting the manual backup switches instead of using the recalcitrant computer.

"Kill four," she told her copilot. "Balance us out before I lose it."

"Throttling back," he said, reaching for the control.

It worked. The loss of power was also in their favor, in effect helping to slow the plane and bring it back under control. Breanna was back on top, flying the plane instead of being flown. She felt it starting to stall, and nosed down gently, had it in her hands. Fort Two was a colt that had bolted in fright; all she had to do was pat its sides gently, reassure it, then ease it back to the barn.

If she could get the landing gear down and fly the mammoth airplane with no instruments or gauges except for a backup altimeter and compass.

Actually, the compass seemed to have quit too.

"Radio circuit completely dead, even on backups," reported Chris. He was hyperventilating.

"You may be able to get power into the circuits by using the remote-start battery array," said Dr. Rubeo.

Bree turned and saw him leaning over her. His face was whiter than a piece of marble, but the words were flat and calm.

"Won't the circuit breakers prevent that?" Breanna asked.

"I'll get around it," he said.

Before she could say anything else, Rubeo slipped out of the cabin, passing back into the defensive weapons station where the revamped Fort Two's flight-control computers were now located.

The plane began sheering sideways again. Breanna punched her rudder pedals, holding the yoke against the sharp turbulence. She brought her spoilers up to compensate.

"We're losing another engine," she told Chris.

"Yeah."

"Okay." It was theoretically possible to fly the plane on one power plant—but only just. Breanna had never done it outside the simulator. "I think it's time to land," she told Chris.

"We can eject," he suggested.

"Crew will never make it," she said, dismissing the idea.

"I agree."

She had miles of dry lake bed in front of her. All she had to do was get the wheels down. "Beginning descent," she said, trimming and preparing her flaps. "Gear?"

"I don't know," said Chris, pulling on the manual control without noticeable effect. "We may have jammed the backup release or something in that descent."

THE INSTANT FORT TWO DIPPED INTO ITS DIVE, SER-geant Parsons felt déjà vu hit him in the chest.

It was either that or the extra helping of bacon he'd had for breakfast.

No, definitely déjà vu. He'd been aboard a stinking B-36 in what? 1962 maybe? '63? Done the same damn thing.

Engines out, tearing up to shit.

B-36, now there was an airplane. Had to be before 1963, though. Damn things were retired in the late fifties.

Parsons hooked his thumbs against his restraints and waited for the pilot to regain control. He didn't put a lot of stock in females in the military, let alone as pilots. But Rap was different. He knew she'd get the upper hand, sooner or later.

Greasy Hands thought back to the B-36 that had taken its nosedive. If he remembered correctly, the plane had been hit by a massive bolt of lightning and a serious wind shear.

So that wasn't much help here, because they were fly-ing in a clear sky. Still, the lights were out on the displays in front of him, so maybe it was a working model for what was happening here. Always good to have a working model when you were chewing into a problem.

The Convair had hydraulic controls—real controls, in his opinion. But something like this had happened in one of their E-3 testers, oh, five or six years before. Freak accident—pilot lost his flight computer. He'd been on au-topilot and the damn thing went psycho, taking out the fly-by-wire system somehow. Had to go to manual rever-sion.

No, he was thinking of the two-seat A-10. It lost its

hydraulic pumps and the pilot had to muscle it in.

The E-3 did lose its fire-by-wire system. Went to the backup. Not really a big deal. Landing gear was the only problem. Had to land on foam because the gear just wouldn't unstick. Turned out one of the idiot computers had locked the doors. Damnedest thing. Sounded like all hell was breaking loose.

Nasty sound, metal on concrete. No way he wanted to hear that again, especially up close.

They figured out later that the only real problem was the damn fuses—if they'd simply bypassed the blown circuit breakers, the plane would have been fine. Instead, half of his people had spent nearly a month fixing the damn thing. Hell of a waste.

The Megafortress roller-coasted upward and pushed Greasy Hands back in the seat. Wouldn't be long now before Cap'n Rap got her even. Then he'd go play with the breakers, just in case.

Parsons waited patiently for the plane to level off. As soon as the forces pushing against his ancient frame eased, the sergeant squeezed out of his seat restraints.

"Well, now, I'd appreciate you skippin' forward an' telling the captain that I'll give her electricity as soon as I can," Greasy Hands told the staff sergeant next to him as he started up to the defensive-weapons station.

ZEN HAD JUST ROLLED OUT INTO THE HANGAR AREA when he heard the alert. He looked up and saw the black hull of a Megafortress flashing out of the sun, obliterating the huge yellow disk. He pushed his chair back half a foot, then shielded his eyes; he knew even before he saw the engines it was Breanna's plane.

She was obviously in trouble. The large black plane stuttered in the sky, its wings jittery as it took a wide bank above the base. The wings began to shake and it pulled off to the left, hanging in the air.

He could taste metal in his mouth. Zen pushed his wheelchair backward, tilting his head to watch as the big plane flew toward the mountains in the distance. A Phantom crossed from the south. For a second it looked as if it was going to plow right into the Megafortress. Then Zen realized it was flying about five hundred feet above the big bomber.

His accident a year ago had changed everything between them. He knew she tried. But he also knew it would only be a matter of time before she realized she couldn't be with him, couldn't really love half a man.

Still, he didn't want to see her hurt.

The Megafortress continued toward the far end of the range. Zen realized there were a dozen people around him now, all staring up at the plane. Somebody said that it had lost its radio. Somebody else mentioned the Army tests and rumors about problems with Fort Two's flight-control computer and the new power plants, and then everybody was talking. And then everyone stopped talking.

Zen cringed as an F-15 appeared from the east, angling toward the Megafortress. Perspiration ran down his back as the plane veered off just short of a collision.

How damn helpless I am, he thought to himself.

GREASY HANDS FOUND RUBEO SPRAWLED ON THE floor, his head half inside one of the computer units. Obviously the scientist had had the same idea he had.

"Excuse me, Doc," said the senior NCO, squatting down. "What's up?"

Rubeo backed out from under the access panel. "I'm trying to bypass the circuit breakers and feed the flight computer off the battery," said the scientist.

Parsons nodded. It seemed to him the scientist sounded a tad less arrogant than normal, a pleasant development.

"If you let me take a look, I believe I can bypass enough circuit breakers to get the landing gear down and some of the instruments back," Greasy Hands told him.

"Be my guest."

The sergeant slipped in under the panel. The solid-state regulator arrays snapped into the bus. Spares were lined up in a separate section at the right. Bing-bang-boing.

"The flight-computer panel is on the far left," said Rubeo behind him.

"Aw, we don't want the computer, Doc," said Greasy Hands, pulling out one of the long, thin plastic-encased assemblies. "That's given us enough problems as it is."

KNIFE HAD JUST TAKEN OFF ON HIS SECOND ORIENTA-tion flight when he saw the Megafortress jerking into a wild, uncontrolled dive. He immediately called a range emergency, trying to clear traffic as he climbed up and out of the way. Banking back as he reached five thousand feet, Knife saw the black bomber level off, in obvious distress. Neither he nor the tower controller could raise it on the base or emergency frequencies.

Following toward the end of the range from the south as another plane cleared out of the way, Knife realized Fort Two was flying on two engines, just barely hanging in the sky. Its gear was still stowed, but it gave every impression of preparing for a crash landing on the dry lake bed.

That would be a mistake. It was rapidly running out of clear ground. Even with gear, brakes, and massive amounts of reverse thrust, it would run into the massive boulders that marked the craggy start of the mountain range.

He was too far off to do anything but watch.

*   *   *

THE CONTROLS NEARLY PULLED OUT OF BREANNA'S hands as the plane's forward airspeed plummeted. The landing-gear door had snapped open and the gear assemblies were trundling downward.

"Jesus," she said. The control panels flickered back to life with instrument readings.

"Doc gave us back some electric power," said Chris, quickly going over the flight data. "Gear have extended. Primary controls took over for the backups on the circuit."

"I'm still on manual," she told him. "And I'm staying there."

"Roger that," snapped Chris. "Our speed—"

"Sergeant Parsons says he's going to try to get you electric," yelped the staff sergeant, rolling onto the command deck as the Megafortress lurched almost straight down.

"I'd say he succeeded," grunted Chris.

"All right, I've got it." Breanna fought the big plane level. They were nearing the end of their restricted airspace. More importantly, she had run out of safe lake bed to land on, the ground below turning back into desert. The mountains loomed ahead.

"We're going to have to turn ourselves around," she told Chris.

"We're on one engine," he said.

She was so busy trying to hold the plane in the sky, she didn't have time to snap back with something sarcastic.

KNIFE ROCKED THE EAGLE GENTLY ON HER RIGHT WING as Fort Two banked away from the mountain range, one of her wing tips so close it was a miracle it didn't scrape. Her wheels were down and he doubted she was flying more than a half knot over the stall speed. But she was still in the air.

He pushed his plane through a sharp turn to get behind the lumbering bomber, now slowing and then starting to descend. He put his own gear out to help himself slow down as he pulled parallel to Fort Two. He had a clear view into the Megafortress's cockpit. Rap's hands were working overtime; her head bobbed up and down in the cockpit, as if she were talking to the crew.

There were, at most, twenty meters—sixty feet—between the two planes. He kept one eye on her and the other on her plane, his hands ready to jerk the Eagle out of the way.

"She's giving us a thumbs-up," said his passenger, Dr. Jennifer Gleason, one of the computer scientists.

"Okay, give it to her back," said Smith, nudging forward to give her a better view.

"She's pointing down."

"Okay. Ask if she has full control," he said. "Make like you're driving a truck—"

"I'm way ahead of you," Gleason said sharply.

Dr. Gleason was in her mid-twenties and extremely good looking, with long strawberry-colored hair and a body that would melt a polar bear. But Smith found her, like most of the scientific and engineering personnel, stuck-up.

"On a scale of one to five, she has about a three," Gleason told him. "She only has one motor."

"Engine."

"There's a difference?"

"Can she land?"

"Yes," answered the scientist after a pause. "She, uh, she wants to loop back, I think."

"She wants to land into the wind," said Smith. "Oh, wait—she's not trying to land on the main runway, is she?"

"How would I ask that?" said Gleason.

"She is. Okay. Hold on." Smith radioed the control tower, mapping out the situation for them. All traffic had been cleared and emergency vehicles were standing by.

"She's worried about the Soviet Kronos satellite," he explained to his backseater. "It's due overhead in twenty-five minutes. If she lands anywhere but close to the hangars, the satellite will catch her on the ground. She's being a jackass," he added.

"Why?"

"Ridiculous risk. She was ready to pancake in without gear a second ago. Now she's flying like she's out for a Sunday stroll in the park."

"What would you have done?" Gleason snapped.

Knife didn't answer. He'd have done the same thing.

"She's pointing to the ground," said Gleason. "She's rolling her hands."

"She wants us to make sure the gear is locked," he said. "All right, look, do a little loop with your finger, like we're swooping beneath her, then hang on."

"Okay."

As soon as Knife heard that Breanna gave the thumbs-up, he tipped the Eagle down, sailing under the large warbird.

"Gear extended and locked," he said.

"I gave them an okay."

Knife pulled off, trying to give Fort Two more room for its turn as it came around to line up for final approach. The plane was waddling now, its lone engine straining. It burped downward, caught itself, steadied into a bank.

"Is she going to make it?" Gleason asked.

"I don't know," he said honestly.

SMITH POPPED UP ON HER RIGHT SIDE, EASING THE F-15E away. It would have been a hell of a lot more convenient to have a working radio, but Knife's backseater gave them a thumbs-up. The wheels were locked for landing.

"Gear set," said Chris. "We can trust the idiot lights and HUDs."

"I'd rather not," Breanna told him. "Temp's critical in our one good engine."

"Maybe we can get Parsons to crawl out on the wing and fix that," said Chris.

"If we asked, he probably would." Breanna pushed Fort Two into a shallow bank. It began shaking like hell. She eased off, gently negotiating the maneuver.

Wonder of wonders, she came out of the turn lined up perfectly with the main runway.

"You're lucky today," said her copilot.

"I was going to blame that one on you."

"Two miles," said Chris. "We're redlining Engine Three."

"I can glide from here," she lied.

A very small percentage of people in the world were born to be pilots. Some fluke of genetics, some mystery of biochemistry, enabled them to fly by sheer instinct. They had some sort of sense about them, could tell exactly where they were and what the plane was doing without consulting instruments.

Breanna wasn't one of those people. She had to work at it, struggling for everything. She'd flown umpteen hours in B-52Gs and Hs, done more than four thousand in a simulator rigged to work like the Megafortress. Somewhere buried in that experience were situations somewhat similar to the one she found herself in now.

Somewhat similar, not exactly the same. There was no way to duplicate the whining complaint of the one good engine as it dragged more than 200,000 pounds of plastic, steel, and flesh through the thin desert air.

And no way to duplicate the flutter in her stomach as she passed the point of no return.

"We're going to make it," Chris yelled as they came down. "Oh, yeah."

"With extra frosting," she said, sensing she was right at stall speed, sensing she had it, sensing the wheels were about to slap against the cement. She felt good; she was in control.

Had Jeff felt that way right before the Flighthawk clipped his wing?

The thought evaporated as the big bomber's wheels hit against the surface of Runway One. They sprang upward, but she had it, she was on top of it, letting the plane roll as she applied the brakes gently, not wanting to blow the tires, knowing there was more than enough runway to stop safely, and in one piece.

ZEN SAT IN THE SHADOW OF THE HANGAR, EYES planted firmly on the ground as the sirens wailed. He could hear the support vehicles roaring out to Runway One as the stricken Megafortress came in. Everyone on the base was watching.

"She's down! She's down! They landed okay!" someone yelled. Zen rolled his chair forward to see, then followed as everyone started running toward the apron area where the Megafortress was headed.

Had they done this when he'd gone down?

No. That had been a tragedy. This—this had somehow turned instantly into a triumph. People were yelling and shouting and high-fiving. The big EB-52 was rolling free and easy.

Anyone who thought Ken James, the bastard Russian traitor, had killed this place would be stunned to see the spontaneous celebration out on the runway as Fort Two turned and taxied toward the hangars. Demoralized?

Downtrodden? Like hell. These were the best of the best, and when shit went down they pulled together. Zen found his adrenaline surging as he raced with the others, caught up in the jubilation. Vehicles were all over the place, blaring horns, wailing their sirens. Two or three hundred people, all buzzed with excitement, rallied to celebrate Dreamland's survival. For somehow, Breanna's successful landing of the stricken plane had turned into a metaphor for the base and its future. Zen could feel it.

She was alive, thank God.

He was relieved. More than that. He did still love her. He hadn't stopped.

The Megafortress stopped just short of the hangar area, mobbed by the crowd. The ventral entry hatch and ladder snapped open.

"Make them walk the gangplank!" somebody yelled.

They cheered as the first passenger, a staff sergeant from the motor pool, ducked out from under the plane. The President wouldn't have gotten a warmer welcome than Breanna when she finally emerged.

Zen started to wheel forward. He was about five yards from the bottom of the stairs when Mack Smith ran up. Smith had escorted Fort Two down in his Eagle, landing moments after her.

Zen stopped. Smith caught Breanna a step from the plane. He twirled her off her feet and then they embraced like lovers.

One or two people near Zen turned and stared at him. He pretended not to notice.

He'd managed to unclench his teeth by the time she appeared before him. She was smiling, unaware of what he'd seen.

"Jeff," she said.

"I'm glad you're safe," he told her as she put her arm

around his neck. He realized as he pulled back that his mouth tasted of metal again.

"YOU DID A HELL OF A JOB LANDING THAT PLANE," Breanna's father told her a few hours later in his office. Her clothes were soaked with sweat. Between the impromptu celebration and all the debriefings, she hadn't had a chance to shower yet. "A hell of a job."

She felt a shudder of cold run through her body, as if the air conditioner had just kicked on high. Everything was starting to hit her now.

"I think Sergeant Parsons saved us," she said softly. "Him and Rubeo. They figured out how to bypass the blown circuitry."

"Funny, Parsons didn't take any credit at all. Neither did that blowhard Rubeo. Captain Ferris says you took control the instant the computer went down. We're investigating," the colonel added quickly as a slight tremor swept into his voice. "There's a possibility a spike from the Army tests disrupted your gear, but some of the engineers say they've had trouble with computer interfacing throwing voltage around for the past week. I expect this is the sort of thing that will take, uh, a while to work out. The planes are grounded until we have a definitive answer."

Breanna nodded. She thought of saying something to her father, something corny, but the words stayed in her throat. She knew how he would react.

"I'll tell you, Bree," he started. "I'll tell you—"

He obviously intended to go on, but the words simply died.

"You did a hell of a job, Captain," he said finally.

"Thanks, Daddy," she said, spinning quickly and leav-

ing his office, wanting to take no chance he would see
her cry.

Washington, D.C.
10 October, 2030

JED BARCLAY PULLED HIS ARMS AROUND HIS THIN
jacket, trying to keep warm as he waited outside the posh
Georgetown restaurant. He contemplated going and waiting inside, but realized that his presence might inadvertently tip off any number of D.C. denizens that something
serious was up. His boss, National Security Advisor Deborah O'Day, wouldn't like that.

Barclay had spent the last two winters in New En-
gland—Harvard, to be exact—and told himself he
shouldn't feel cold at all; October in Washington was
balmy by Massachusetts standards. But his twenty-two-
year-old frame was practically trembling with the cold.

Finally, O'Day's Marine Corps bodyguard emerged
from the restaurant. The woman tensed as she spotted
him, then gave him a disapproving frown.

"Jed, what are you doing here?" said Ms. O'Day,
emerging behind her.

"I, uh—you're going to want to see this," he said.

He unfolded his hands to reveal a yellow manila envelope. O'Day took the envelope and moved over to the
yellowish light thrown by a faux-antique streetlight.
Meanwhile, her date—Brad Elliot, a recently retired three-
star Air Force general—emerged from the building. Jed
nodded at the general, who nodded back semi-affably.

"That's the Iranian base," Jed said helpfully.

"Yes, thank you, Jed. What the hell are you doing with
this outside of the basement?" his boss added.

"It's not classified," he said. "It's off the Russian satellite."

O'Day frowned deeply at his dodge. The Russians

made a limited number of satellite images available through a public European service, which, of course, the NSC had a subscription to. Primarily useful for agricultural purposes, the images did not precisely duplicate U.S. optical spy coverage—nor were they anywhere near as precise—but they were close enough. Since they were open-source, there was no prescription against carrying them off campus, as it were.

"The launchers have been dismantled," said O'Day.

"Yes, ma'am. The image is two days old."

"And they're where?"

"We're not sure. I mean, CIA isn't sure, and the Pentagon, well, they say not to worry. But I—well, I don't know."

"You're not on my staff to keep your opinions to yourself. Come on. It's cold out here."

"Yes, ma'am. Well, it's difficult to be definitive. I mean, since we took our main satellite off-line for repairs two weeks ago, we've been cobbling things over Northeastern Africa together. Between that and the clouds—"

"Jed," she said sternly.

"There were two tankers off Bandar three days ago. They're approaching Somalia now."

O'Day didn't bother asking for any other information.

"Contact Madcap Magician," she told him. "Have them put Ironweed into action. Whatever units they need. Fullbore. I'll be back at the NSC in an hour."

"Yes, ma'am," he said, glancing at the general before retreating back toward the Metro stop.

Dreamland
10 October, 1730 local

THE THICK DOOR TO THE HANDHELD WEAPONS LAB opened and Danny Freah found himself staring down at a white-haired woman old enough to be his mother's mother.

"Hi," he said. "I'm Captain Freah. I have an appointment with one of the engineers, Dr. Klondike. I may be a little late," he added apologetically.

"You're two hours late, Captain," said the old lady, shuffling back to let him in. She wore an ancient gray lab coat that looked a great deal like a housedress on her. "Fortunately, we were told that was your MO unless you were under fire. Come in."

Danny gave her an embarrassed smile and stepped into the long, narrow hallway as the steel door slid quietly shut on its gliders behind him. He had a tough time forcing himself to go slow enough to keep from running down the old lady.

Over the past few days, Danny had learned that Brad Elliot had run Dreamland with an iron fist, not only recruiting the best of the best but allowing almost no chaff—no political appointments, few "favors" to the contractors. But this old lady was obviously an exception; she had to be somebody's relative, given a job either to keep her off food stamps or fill out a pension requirement. Captain Freah liked that—it was good to know that even a tough three-star like Elliot had a little compassion.

"This way now, Captain," said the old lady, showing him into an immense, cement-walled room. There was a long firing range with a target track at the far end. She walked toward a large metal box that looked like an over-sized mechanic's tool chest, with double-keyed pullout drawers.

"Thanks," said Danny. "When's Dr. Klondike getting here? Maybe I'll get some target practice in while I'm waiting for him."

"I'm Klondike," said the old lady.

Danny watched in disbelief as she retrieved a set of keys from her pocket, examining each one slowly before finding the right combination to open a thick drawer near the bottom. She pulled out a Marine-issue M40A rifle, sans scope, from the drawer.

"And incidentally, I am not a doctor. My name is Anna."

"Is this for real?" he asked as she presented the gun to him.

"Whatever you may think of the Marine Corps, Captain, let me assure you that they have no peers when it comes to selecting rifles," she said, apparently thinking that he had been referring to the weapon, not her. "You will find the Remington Model 700 one of the finest chassis for a precision firearm available. You may indeed quibble with the use of fiberglass instead of wood for the furniture, but remember that the Marines operate in an environment typically humid, if not downright wet."

Still not sure whether he might be the victim of an elaborate gag cooked up by one of his men—or maybe Hal Briggs—Danny took the rifle in his hands. He had no questions about the gun. At roughly fourteen and a half pounds, with a twenty-four-inch stainless-steel barrel, it was absolutely a Remington, albeit one that had been hand-selected and finished.

"So where's the scope?" he said.

"You're impatient for one who keeps his own schedule," said Klondike, closing the drawer. She toddled over to a second set of cabinets, eventually removing a small, torpedo-shaped sight. At a third cabinet, she produced a visor set with a cord.

"How does this work? Laser?" asked Danny, examining the sight.

"Hardly," said the old lady, taking it from his hand and mounting it on the gun. She fiddled with a pair of set screws on the side, held the visor out, squinted, frowned, fiddled some more, then smacked the top. "Here," she said finally. "I'll get you some cartridges. The range is over there. I assume you can find it on your own."

Fitted with a Redfield telescopic sight, the sixties-era M40 was at least arguably among the best sniping rifles of all time. Simple yet highly reliable in adverse conditions, it could not turn a mediocre shooter into a marksman. But it could turn a highly trained marksman into a deadly and efficient killer. The sight was perfectly mated to the weapon, allowing the usual adjustments for wind and range and providing a remarkable amount of light to the viewer.

The visor doodad, on the other hand, was dim.

"It can be adjusted to your tastes," said Klondike, returning as Freah frowned and played with the LED visor screen. "Try it before you dismiss it, Captain. You said you wanted an advanced sniping weapon."

Still doubtful, Danny steadied the weapon against his shoulder, firing from a standing position. The visor projected an image similar to the view in a scope, though it was spread in an oval rather than a circle. A legend below the firing circle declared the target precisely one hundred meters away. He braced himself and fired.

He nailed the bull's-eye dead-on.

"Wow," he said.

"Oh, please." Klondike went to the panel controlling the target location on the wall. The target piece jerked back another hundred yards. "Go," she said.

He nailed it again.

She pushed the button and the target sped backward, this time nearly disappearing deep within the tunnel.

"Touch the lower edge of the visor," Klondike told him.

"Here?"

"Captain, please." She reached up and touched the very edge of the plastic panel near his cheekbone. Instantly, a range-to-target legend appeared next to the crosshatch.

Five hundred yards.

He missed.

By a centimeter.

Klondike frowned. "Perhaps the weapon takes getting used to. Ordinarily, you should get to seven hundred yards before beginning to lose some accuracy. It is, of course, a matter of skill, and choosing the right ammunition. No offense, Captain."

"How the hell does this work?" Danny asked. "Is it a laser?"

She shook her head. "A focused magnetic pulse, two signals with a Doppler effect. If it were a laser you would have optical problems shooting through glass or water."

"You can aim through glass?"

"Without manual correction. There are limitations, of course. The device cannot read two-dimensional shapes, and has difficulty with thin surfaces. You could not read a sign with it beyond sixty-two meters. The distance has to do with the harmonics of the different radar waves," she added. "The sight would also be theoretically vulnerable to a system such as the HARM, which can home in on it. Still, until we perfect smart bullets—*if* we perfect smart bullets—it's the most accurate handheld ballistic device available. I've done a little work on the barrel," she added. "And, of course, the bullets are mine."

"I have six guys on the Whiplash response team," Danny told her. "I'd like to qualify each one of them on the gun."

"It is a sniper's weapon, Captain. At some point in the future, perhaps, we will be able to mass-produce it. For now there is exactly one available for use."

"All the same, I want them checked out on it, if possible." Freah's Whiplash response team was an elite subgroup of his air commandos, cross-trained for a variety of jobs. Organized only in the last six months, they hadn't been called into action yet, with the exception of one training detail. But it was accepted that each member would be trained and expected to take on any other member's job at a moment's notice.

"As you wish. I suppose you'll be wanting body armor as well," said Klondike.

"We have flak vests."

"Captain, please." She shook her head. "Your vests are made from KM2, correct?"

"Well—"

"They weigh more than twenty-five pounds, and I doubt that half your men wear them half the time, no matter what the standing orders or situation may be. Our armor, on the other hand, is made of boron carbide plates and a thinner, stronger Kevlar derivative. Unfortunately, there's some loss of flexibility in our version, and we've only fashioned vests so far. Nonetheless, you'll find they weigh less than ten pounds, and can stop a 30mm shell fired from point-blank range."

"I'm in your hands, Annie," said Danny.

"Yes, well, don't get fresh," said Klondike, leading him out of the room.

Dreamland
11 October

COLONEL BASTIAN WALKED AROUND THE CHUNKY AIRframe that sat in the middle of Development Shed B/3, trying to hide some of his displeasure from Rubeo and the others he had gathered on the tarmac for this impromptu brainstorming session. To him, the F-119 looked like a flying tugboat.

A barely flying one, given its performance specs. Mike Janlock, an aeronautical engineer who specialized in BMI resin airfoils, had just finished saying that a handful of alterations would turn the aircraft into a robust attack weapon. But those changes would make it unusable aboard aircraft carriers, as well as highly unlikely to meet the Marine Corps requirement for vertical landing at forward combat weight.

Janlock and the others had said over and over that there were three pretty good planes locked inside the F-119 airframe. Choose one—hell, even two—and America would have a cutting-edge aircraft capable of filling a wide variety of attack roles for the next two decades.

But Dog's mandate was clear. He had to proceed with all three. Congress was so high on the project that yesterday afternoon a Congressional committee had voted to increase F-119 funding three hundred percent.

The same committee had postponed a decision on Dreamland, per the recommendation of the Joint Chiefs and Ms. O'Day.

If Dreamland survived, it would get a good hunk of the F-119 development money. Bastian's new "all ranks" mess halls—already a hit—could dish out all the fancy food they wanted for the next ten years.

But damn. The plane was a flying tugboat. Hell, it was one of those five-hundred-dollar hammers the media claimed the Pentagon was always buying.

"Colonel, you were saying?" prompted Rubeo.

"A survivable tanker," repeated Bastian. "The thinking is to replace KC-10 Extenders and HC-130's at the same time. It would be connected to the JSF project."

"So it has to be fast and slow," said Janlock.

He didn't mean it as a joke, but everyone laughed. Except Rubeo, of course.

"Seriously, if we did have one aircraft that could refuel helicopters as efficiently as CAP aircraft, in combat situations as well as on ferry flights, it would be a hell of an asset," said Bastian, reining them in. "I can tell you from experience, a fighter with battle damage can have trouble reaching normal tanking altitude and speed. KC-135 and KC-10 tankers did a hell of a job during the Gulf War, doing things they weren't technically capable of. I'd say more than a dozen lives were saved. At least. And ten times that number of planes. So what we're talking about, if you guys could pull it off—the potential would translate into a lot less orphans and widows. I realize it's not the conventional thinking, but I've seen what you guys can do."

With the exception of Rubeo, who was wearing his customary scowl, the engineers and officers nodded their heads. They hadn't thought about the problem in those terms before.

"What if we take the C-17 apart?" asked Jeremy Winters, a tall engineer with a hawk's nose and thick, wire-rimmed glasses. "Good capacity, short takeoff so we can use forward bases."

"Piffle," said Rubeo.

"All right, Doc," snapped Bastian, who'd had enough of the scientist's chronic pessimism. "What do you suggest?"

"It depends on our goal," said the scientist. He pursed his lips as if he had just bit into a lemon. "If our goal is simply to sustain funding, I suggest we take any aircraft we're interested in and claim that it should be studied as a tanker."

"All right, that's enough," said Bastian. "I'll deal with the politics. I want real ideas here, not fodder for Congress."

"Colonel, you and I both know that the JSF is our lifeline," said Rubeo, refusing to back down. "And charitably put, it's a camel. So the most optimum solution would be another camel. But as for a survivable tanker"—the scientist's voice rose an octave as he finally made a serious point—"the C-17 is a large and easily hit target. There is no way to change that."

"Escorts could protect it," said Smith. "Going to need them for the JSF."

Uncharacteristically, Smith hadn't said much at all.

Dog suspected that he had decided to say as little as possible about the JSF now that he was leaving; probably he was watching his political backside.

Smart, even though it pissed Bastian off.

"We already have a project study for a survivable, deep-penetration tanker on the shelf," said Major Nancy Cheshire. "It would need some work for low-speed refueling, but it would certainly meet the requirements for near-Mach speed, high-altitude regimes."

"What are we talking about?" Bastian asked, still glaring at Rubeo.

"The Megafortress KC."

Rubeo opened his mouth to object, but Cheshire cut him off.

"Some studies were done two years ago, but they never went anywhere. The idea was that we would need something that could keep up with the flying battleship concept, refueling it in a hostile environment," she explained. "Survivability was an important consideration and on that score, I know the plane got high marks."

"Megafortress, back from the dead," said Rubeo.

"What's your objection to that idea?" Bastian asked the scientist.

"None as far as the specific plane goes," said Rubeo, surprising Bastian. "My objection is one of principle. The Megafortress—all manned aircraft are redundant." He folded his arms in front of his chest. "Colonel, if you're looking to tie a project to the F-119's tail, tie the Flighthawks. They're the future."

"We've been down that road," said Bastian. "And in any event, the robots can't even refuel themselves."

"Piffle. We simply haven't thought about it properly."

Dog wanted his people to feel that they could speak freely; he didn't want a group of yes-men and suck-ups around him. And he knew that for a place like Dreamland to succeed, discipline had to be pretty loose.

But Rubeo really pushed the envelope.

"I appreciate your comments, if not your tone," Dog told him. "The debate about robot planes isn't relevant at the moment." He turned back to Cheshire. "How far along was the tanker project?"

"I don't know that it got beyond one or two proof-of-concept flights," she said. "But I'm sure it wouldn't take much to dust it off."

"The plane kicks out some fierce vortices," said Janlock. "We barely have them controlled enough for stable flight. We all saw how difficult it was to handle without the flight computer. If anyone other than Rap was at the controls when the gear crashed, we would have lost the plane."

"Okay," said Bastian. "Let's find out."

"Even though Fort Two and the others have been cleared for operations, we're not one hundred percent sure the voltage spikes were due to the Army tests," said Jennifer Gleason, one of the computer scientists. Her main assignment was the Flighthawks, but she had also had a hand in designing the advanced flight-computer components Fort Two was testing. "There are at least three other possibilities. We really ought to work through the test regimes to make sure."

"I'm confident that was the problem," said Cheshire. "And with the shielding and the backups, I think we're fine. Fort Two is due for a check ride this afternoon."

Bastian glanced at his watch. It was a little past ten o'clock. "I need to know by 1800. Doable?"

"Absolutely, sir," said Cheshire. "Rap should be getting suited up as we speak." She turned to Gleason. "We can run through some of your tests—all of them—at the same time."

Gleason nodded—clearly reluctant, but nonetheless in agreement.

"So this our first choice," said Bastian. "Choice number

two, I take it, would be to study the C-17."

"Not our project," hissed Rubeo. The implication was clear—a C-17 tanker wouldn't help keep Dreamland alive.

"Yes, well, there's nothing we can do about that," said Dog. "Anyone has any other ideas, let me know ASAP. In the meantime, let's get this done."

SEVERAL HOURS LATER, KNIFE SAT IN THE HANGAR where the conference had been, staring down from the F-119 cockpit. He was waiting for the security officer to green-light the plane from the hangar. A Russian optical satellite was just completing its overhead tour. The satellite was an old Kronos model incapable of resolutions greater than a meter in diameter, but Dreamland's operating protocols strictly prohibited the F-119 from being on the runway while it was overhead.

Ordinarily, Smith would be more than a little impatient to get going. But this afternoon he was feeling almost a little nostalgic. He'd gotten word just before suiting up that he was to expedite reporting to Wing A; an Air Force transport due to take off from Nellis at ten that evening was holding a seat. So this would be his last flight at Dreamland, as well as in the F-119.

The Congressional committee's decision on the F-119 didn't particularly surprise him; the project's various contractors had plants in over 150 Congressional districts, which added up to a hell of a lot of muscle, if not brains. That was the way appropriations went these days.

Smith had decided he was in a no-lose position on the JSF. If the program continued and the F-119 was finally cleared as a production model, his resume would note that he had helped develop it. If it was killed as an ill-conceived project—which, in his opinion, it was—he could point to the fact that he had seen this and gotten out. His final reports on the project would be worded so vaguely that they could be used to support either scenario. In the meantime, he'd be doing some real flying, and probably—though admittedly not definitely—adding good notes to his career folder.

He was learning this political game well.

The lieutenant at the front of the hangar said something into his walkie-talkie, then gave the up-and-at-'em wave to the crew. The tractor sitting in front of the F-119 cranked her engine; Knife let off the brakes and he began to roll out onto the tarmac. The fighter's engines had to be started from an external power cart or "puffer." Three crewmen had the cart in place almost as soon as the plane and its tow truck stopped in front of the hangar. They moved quickly; the crew chief pumped his arm in the air and, bam, Knife had his engines up and running.

Mack ran through his instrument checks, working swiftly with the no-nonsense rhythm he'd perfected during his days flying combat air patrol in the Gulf. With the systems at Dash-One spec, he asked for and received clearance from the tower. He tapped the top of his helmet for good luck—a necessary part of his preflight ritual—then began trundling toward Lakebed Runway 34. A black Hummer and a Jimmy, both with blue security lights and yellow "Follow Me" signs, led the way. Off to the east a temporary aboveground control tower and observation deck had been erected to monitor the flight.

Knife narrowed his attention to the small bubble around him as the vehicles peeled off. He pushed the F-119 to its mark, setting his brakes for one last systems check before takeoff. The right panel of his trio of multi-use displays was entirely given over to flight details. His eyes scanned the graphical readouts deliberately. Satisfied, he turned his eyes toward the left MUD, where he had the GPS system selected. The enhanced God's-eye-view screen rendered his plane as a blue dot on the color-coded terrain—in this case a brownish topo map overlaid by a gray rectangle signifying the limits of the test range. Groom Mountain's seven-thousand-foot-high peak lurked at the far end, drawn in sharp black lines. Smith shifted his thumb on the Hostas stick, adding radar input to the display; the shading changed to indicate that it was working, though it couldn't properly paint anything until he was over four hundred feet above ground, and couldn't really be trusted until about eight or nine hundred.

Something for the engineers to work on.

Ready, Knife thought. His left hand moved the throttle to maximum military power. The plane trembled as the turbines spooled, the brakes straining.

Temp, RPM, pressures perfect. Good to go. He backed to idle, took another breath, gave himself another good-luck pat.

Not that he needed it, of course.

"Tower, Playboy One, I'm ready for one last fling," he said.

"Playboy One," acknowledged the controller stiffly.

Knife released the brakes and spooled takeoff power, his mount rumbling forward.

BREANNA BANKED NORTHWARD, HEADING TOWARD Range F where the rendezvous was supposed to take place. The check flight and tests had gone well, but she could feel her stomach pinching her as they got ready for the rendezvous.

Maybe it was just the ham sandwich she'd managed while they orbited out of the Russian satellite's view, waiting for Smith and the F-119 to take off. Mustard always gave her indigestion. Everyone else was raving about her father's decision to spread the expertise of the executive chef among all of the base's cafeterias, but in her opinion the food at Dreamland still rated among the worst in the world.

"Optimum, optimum, optimum," sang her copilot as he ran through his check of the flight systems. Two of Dreamland's top techies were performing similar checks in the former radar and navigation suite below. The weapons bay was unoccupied, except by the computers.

Sitting behind Breanna and Chris on the flight deck was Major Cheshire, who was overseeing the refueling exercise. The Megafortress's synthetic bird's-eye view, created from radar inputs, was projected on one of her monitors. Another carried the input from a video cam installed at the rear of the plane, roughly where a refueling boom would be. With her com unit set to Playboy's frequency, Cheshire would pretend to be a boomer, talking the attack plane in for a tank. It was ad hoc, of course—there was no boom, and Major Smith had no lights to guide him under Fort Two's belly. But they just needed a rough approximation to make sure the concept was sound.

Breanna reached Range F at twenty thousand feet, precisely as planned for the first track. It bothered the hell out of her that the world's most versatile bomber might only survive as a milk cow. But as Cheshire had said when she explained the mission, better a live cow than a dead dream.

"We're ready any time you are, Major," she told her boss.

KNIFE STOMPED THE RUDDER PEDAL IN A LAST, DESperate effort to close in to the target cone below Fort Two. His right wing pulled up, propelled by a nasty eddy of air from the Megafortress's fuselage. He steadied it for a second, then felt the plane starting to lose speed and got a stall warning.

"Shit," he said, out loud and over the open circuit as he ducked the plane off the EB-52's tail.

"Okay, let's take a break," said Major Cheshire.

"Roger that," he snapped.

They'd been trying for nearly thirty minutes to get the F-119 under the Megafortress's belly. The vortices and wind sheers coming off the bigger plane's wings, fuselage, and tail were just too much for the F-119, even with its constantly correcting fly-by-wire controls.

Knife thought the controls themselves might be the problem. In his opinion, having a computer between him and the plane's control surfaces dampened the edge he needed to put the plane precisely where he wanted. It was like the difference between driving an automatic-shift and a standard-shift car; being able to flutter the clutch or hold the revs above redline without shifting could make all the difference.

But it wasn't like he could turn the system off. Like other inherently unstable craft such as the F-117, the fly-by-wire system was an integral part of the design, not an enhancement like in the EB-52. The JSF couldn't fly without it.

What had Bastian called it? A flying bathtub? Have to give Dog his due—he had that nailed.

"Let's move on to the drogue routine off the left wing," Knife radioed. "Stay at twenty thousand feet."

"You sure?" asked Cheshire.

"Look, you guys just follow the script, all right?"

"You okay, Major?" asked Cheshire.

Smith reminded himself the project was being monitored down in the tower.

"Yeah, okay. Let's go," said Smith. He began closing in on the Megafortress's left wing, now nearly a half mile ahead. He came in ever so slowly, drawing even with the tail—then found the plane sheering off to the left into a rapid spin.

His master warning panel freaked. He fell to nearly fifteen thousand feet before he could manage a recovery.

"Playboy, you have visible damage to the leading-edge aileron on the right wing," said Cheshire. "Copy? Knife, are you okay? Are you with us?"

"Roger that," he said. The plane's high-flying position— the pilot sat in what looked like a glass bulb at the top of the plane—gave him a good view of the wings. Finally sure he had it back under control, he twisted back and forth, doing a visual inspection to confirm Cheshire's warning and the legion of problem codes on the systems screen. The leading-edge surface was bent, and he could see a piece of metal extending out from behind it. He guessed that was part of one of the motors that worked it, which the screen warned had failed. Now he had to admit that the FBW system was useful—it was compensating so smoothly for the damaged wing that he barely noticed it. Undoubtedly the flight-control system had played a big role in helping him regain control of the craft.

Though serious, the damage wasn't fatal. But his gauges showed the temperature in his right engine had shot up to the redline; there must be a problem there as well.

Stinking F-119. What a way to go out.

Appropriate, though, considering the plane.

"Dream Tower, this is Playboy One. Emergency declared. I have a slight situation with my wing and engine. Looks like it's time to land," Mack said, adding his altitude, position, and heading, though they would already be projected by Dreamland's powerful sensors. He and Fort Two had the sky to themselves; all he had to do was line up, pop his wheels, and land.

"Tower acknowledges, Playboy. Copy your flying emergency."

"Mack?"

Breanna's voice seemed to come at him from the

clouds, breaking through the outside fuzz of his consciousness as he pushed toward Runway Two. He felt the kiss again, then returned to the matter at hand.

"I'm okay, beautiful," he told her. "I can't even tell there's a problem. But listen, do I get a kiss if I land in one piece?"

COLONEL BASTIAN STOOD BACK FROM THE MONITOR, nudging next to the air-conditioning unit in the cramped quarters of Dreamland's mobile test tower. He could see Smith's plane coasting toward the hangars in the distance. Obviously, the damage to the plane had been minimal.

The damage to the idea of using the Megafortress as a tanker, however, was another story.

But he had decided this morning that he definitely wanted to keep the Megafortress project alive. It wasn't just the fact that he believed in McLanahan's Air Battleship scenario. Even as a "simple" bomber, the Megafortress made sense. With a few tweaks, it could be as survivable as an F-15E while carrying several times the payload two or three times as far. Get into a low-intensity war in a hot climate—say, the Middle East, as McLanahan had hinted, or Southeast Asia—and a few Megafortresses might just turn the tide. And it would be cheap; the Air Force had literally hundreds of B-52's available for conversion.

At the moment, though, that was a drawback. There weren't enough jobs at stake to easily apply political pressure and keep it alive. But attach it to the F-119 as a survivable tanker, and there'd be plenty of pols. A few months of demonstration flights, maybe some careful work with contractors, and they'd have enough political support to revive the battleship concept.

But it was dead now.

Bastian listened as the controller exchanged information with an aircraft conducting a test near Range F.

"What's going on?" he asked Mickey Colgan, the flight officer coordinating the day's tests.

"Oh, that's just a drone taking off," said the captain. "Unpiloted Green Phantom doing IR testing. Pretty straightforward. It's got a JSF suit on. It has to catch another drone."

"I'm not following you."

"I'm sorry, Colonel. There are two Phantoms. One's just a stock drone. The other, Green Phantom, has some wing baffles and a few other mods to simulate the F-119's flight characteristics. They're controlled out of the Flight-hawk hangar. We're running checks on the nitrogen-cooling system for the gear in the IR's eye. It has to be kept at a constant temperature or—"

"You think Green Phantom could rendezvous with Fort Two?"

Colgan blinked. "Well, if the F-119 can't do it, that old Phantom, I mean, it's at least as bad a flier as the JSF itself."

"Who's the pilot?" asked Bastian.

"That would be Major Stockard, sir." Colgan seemed to bristle a bit. "They, uh, they're trying to get him back into the swing of things."

"How good a pilot is he?"

"Sir?"

"I mean with the drone."

"Well, before his accident, there was no one near as good as him," said Colgan. "But . . ."

"But what?"

"I don't know if he's back up to speed, Colonel. And he, uh, he's in a wheelchair."

"What's the frequency to the Flighthawk bunker?" said Bastian, moving back to the com panel.

*   *   *

TO SAY HE'D FLOWN THE QF-4 DRONE TEN THOUSAND times wasn't an exaggeration; Zen had learned to control the Flighthawks with the exact airplanes he was flying. He'd gotten so he could work them with his eyes closed before moving up to the much-more-difficult-to-control Flighthawks.

He closed his eyes now in frustration. The gig was simple—all he had to do was fly Green Phantom behind Phantom One-Zero-Mike at fifteen thousand feet with three miles of separation. Piece of cake.

Except his heart was pounding and there was sweat pouring from his wrists, and if it weren't for the automated flight computer fail-safe, he would have smacked Green Phantom into the ground on takeoff.

Things had gone badly yesterday, but that at least could be attributed to rust; he'd gotten better as the exercises wore on.

He wasn't sure what to blame this on. Maybe the F-119 mods. JSF wasn't exactly the world's most flyable plane, and Green Phantom was a pig's pig.

It was easier to handle than two Flighthawks at supersonic speed, though. So why was he sweating like a bull being chased by toreadors?

If he couldn't make this simple intercept, how could he ever control the U/MFs?

Zen rolled his neck around on his spine, the vertebrae cracking. He'd forgotten how heavy the control helmet was. He could actually take it off, since the console he was sitting at in Hanger B was basically a flight simulator on steroids. Arranged like a cockpit and developed for the Flighthawk, its standard multi-use displays were augmented by dedicated control and sensor displays, along with banks of specific system overrides and data collectors. They'd nicknamed it Frankenstein's Control Pod.

But if he was going to get back in the program, he had to do it right, and that meant using the helmet and the

Flighthawk flight sticks. It meant sucking it up and hanging in there, kinks, sweat, and all.

Zen checked the altitude on Green Phantom, nudging up to 15,500 feet. He was five miles away, closing on One-Zero-Mike's left wing. Though he had his left hand wrapped around Mike's control stick, the computer was actually flying the plane in its preprogrammed orbit. Zen nudged his right hand back slightly, gently climbing.

Piece of cake. Two miles to go. He moved his thumb to the center of the stick's oval top, keying the view screen from optical to FLIR input. The view at the top of his screen changed to a greenish tint, the world shading according to heat sources.

Driven by his preprogrammed flight plan, One-Zero-Mike began to bank. Zen started to follow, jerked his hand too hard, cursed, and then almost lost Green Phantom. The muscles in his fingers froze. He pushed the computer-assist lever at the base of the assembly, too embarrassed to use the voice command and acknowledge that he had blown it. The computer immediately grabbed the plane, putting it onto the preprogrammed course.

"Zen?"

"What?" he snapped over the headset.

"I have Colonel Bastian on the circuit," replied Fred Remington, one of the civilians helping run the tests. "Something's up."

"Yeah, okay." Zen's pinkie stretched to click down the lever at the front base of his right stick; it automatically engaged computer control for Green Phantom. "Let me talk to him."

"Major Stockard, do you think you can do me a favor?" said Bastian as soon as the line snapped open.

"Colonel?"

"I wonder if you have enough fuel in Green Phantom to try a rendezvous with Fort Two on Range F. We'd like to see if you can get close enough for a refuel."

Zen glanced at the gauge. The Phantom had plenty of fuel.

But getting close to a Megafortress was not exactly easy. Even the Flighthawks had trouble.

A Phantom with JSF mods? Ha.

And forget about the plane—he'd just blown an easy run at a drone.

Zen didn't know what to say. "You're looking for that to happen right now?"

"Can you do it?"

"Green Phantom simulates the F-119."

"That's exactly the point. We want to mock up a refuel off a Megafortress. Mack Smith had some trouble," added the colonel. "I'd like a second opinion."

"I'm on it," snapped Zen.

BREANNA TOOK FORT TWO OUT OF ITS ORBIT AT 25,000 feet, gliding gently on its left wing to twenty thousand smack in the middle of the range where the new exercise would take place. She pushed the big plane into place, gingerly nudging its nose so it slotted exactly along the three-dimensional flight line the computer was projecting in the HUD navigation screen. They were mimicking a standard tanker track, flying a long oval in the sky as if they were a KC-10 Extender or a KC-135 Stratotanker on its anchor near a war zone, waiting for attack planes and fighters returning from action. Neither Chris nor Major Cheshire had said anything since the colonel ordered the new trial.

Zen had said exactly four words over the radio, but the tension in his voice practically drilled a hole through her skull.

"Green Phantom, we have you at eighteen thousand feet, on beam, closure rate at two hundred knots," Cheshire told Jeff.

The robot Phantom was going approximately a hundred miles an hour faster than it should have been. Breanna flipped her HUD plot that showed the plane approaching behind them. Its speed abruptly slowed, but Green Phantom was still flying too fast to get into the refueling cone. She resisted the temptation to hit the gas, knowing that would only make things more confusing for Zen.

"Three miles," Cheshire said. "He's not going to make it."

Breanna could feel Chris staring at her. She continued to hold her position.

GREEN PHANTOM JUST WOULDN'T SLOW DOWN. ZEN nudged the throttle push-bar on the underside of the one-handed stick control. The thrust-indicator graph at the right side of the screen obstinately refused to budge.

He could tell the computer to lower power. He could tell it precisely how many pounds of thrust to produce—or, for that matter, what indicated airspeed he wanted. But using verbal commands, relying on the computer—it seemed like giving up. And he wasn't giving up. He was doing this, and he was doing it himself.

Partly because Smith had failed. And partly just because.

He tapped the glider with his finger. Finally the robot's speed began to drop, but it was too late.

"Breakaway, breakaway, breakaway," Zen said calmly on the interplane frequency. The "breakaway" call mandated full military throttle and an immediate one-thousand-foot climb by the tanker aircraft, and idle power and a one-thousand-foot descent by the receiver. Zen purposely used a calm tone of voice instead of an excited one to communicate to Bree and Cheshire that there was no imminent danger. When he was level, he said, "Let me try another shot."

"Copy that."

Tanker pukes would be laughing their butts off if this had been the real thing. Stockard pulled the computer-engage switch at the base of the stick, then gave the system verbal instructions to pull Green Phantom around. The C³ flight computer helping fly the plane was like a two-level brain. The basic level handled inputs from the stick and worked to keep the aircraft stable. For example, it knew that pulling back on the stick meant that the pilot wanted the plane to climb, and adjusted the control surfaces accordingly. This level was always on, and was very similar to what happened in a stock fly-by-wire system, such as the one in the JSF.

The upper level of the brain, which could be invoked verbally or by pulling the engage-disengage toggle that rose like a weed in front of the stick, was more an advanced copilot or even wingman. It translated verbal instructions, monitored sensors, and could plot and follow courses. It had a limited ability to plot and suggest strategy.

C³ could probably attempt the tanking demo on its own, with only some verbal prodding from Zen. But Jeff was determined to nail it himself.

If he could. Flying a remote-controlled plane under a tanker was a difficult task. Even without the odd wind eddies and vortices coming off the target plane, you were too far away. You were projecting feel and perspective literally across miles, imagining how it would be in the cockpit rather than really being there. You couldn't feel the plane buck or sense it starting to wallow, or know just how the detent on the throttle was going to nudge under your wrist. You couldn't slide your foot on the rudder pedal just so, moving your butt on the seat that infinitesimal inch to nail the hookup just so.

Jeff couldn't slide his foot anywhere.

Get over it, he told himself. Just fucking get over it.

Jeff took back control as the Phantom came out of its orbit behind the Megafortress. "Pilot," he said.

"Pilot," confirmed the computer.

He nudged the throttle down. He was three miles behind the Megafortress, closing at a rate of roughly two miles a minute, easing in.

"You're a little high," said Cheshire.

"Roger that," said Zen, stubbornly holding his position for a few seconds. The Megafortress had nudged down to eighteen thousand feet, speed nailed precisely at 350 knots.

A half mile off the tail of the big bomber, Zen took a deep breath, ready to go for it. He felt like he was crawling in, a thief sneaking in the back door.

"Looking good," said Cheshire.

Zen pasted his eyes on the V of the bomber's tail. Nice to have some director lights there.

Computer could give him some cues. Shit—why hadn't he thought of that?

Rust, rust, rust. Stubborn rust.

"Inside the cone in ten seconds," said Cheshire. "Nine, eight—"

The tail suddenly flashed large and then began moving to the right. The computer buzzed, but something inside Zen had taken over; he didn't hear the warnings or Cheshire's transmission. He nudged the stick to the right, thumb on the trim button as he corrected to compensate for the vortex. Then he gave the stick a quick shock forward, finessing the eddy of wind pushing Green Phantom backward. He nudged throttle, closed again, but the wind whipping off the bigger plane was beating hell out of his wings. He tried again, pushing in; again the computer screamed and Cheshire yelped, and he felt sweat soaking his zipper suit. Green Phantom's nose poked upward and it was over; he rolled downward, breaking off the attempt.

"Shit," said Cheshire.

"Copy that," he told her. "Let's go again."

"Zen, we're at the end of the range," said Breanna. "We have to take our turn."

Her voice sounded far away, the way it had the first night in the hospital, when he came to.

"Yeah," he said.

She didn't respond. The Megafortress had already begun a shallow bank, turning through the air.

"We briefed twenty thousand feet," he said testily, as if the two thousand feet might actually have made a difference.

Again she didn't respond.

Why was he so mad? Why did he feel humiliated? Smith had blown exactly this test, and he'd had the real stinking airplane. He'd been in the goddamn cockpit.

And he had two legs.

COLONEL BASTIAN LOOKED AT COLGAN.

"They were pretty close," said Colgan. "A hundred yards."

"That's an awfully long hose," said Bastian dryly.

"Between the wings and the engines, the Megafortress beats the hell out of the air," said Colgan. "The engineers used the vortexes to increase lift and flying characteristics. They were trying to maximize them, not smooth them out. I'm not an expert, but I don't think there's any question they can be eased off with some work."

No question, but many dollar signs. And in good conscience, he couldn't recommend proceeding with a project that showed no evidence it would succeed.

Why the hell not? What was the F-119?

A political plane. A horn of plenty.

A cow and a bathtub.

Did that justify lying about the Megafortress?

"Time's getting tight," said Colgan. "Want me to tell them to knock it off?"

Bastian looked up at the large round clock above the controller's console. The hands counted off time until the Russian satellite would be overhead.

Thirty minutes. They had to be back in the hangar by then, since the satellite would be overhead for several hours.

"If they want to try again, that's fine. Just don't get caught on the ground by that satellite."

"CONTROL ADVISES WE HAVE TIME FOR ONE MORE RUN around the track due to satellite coverage," Cheshire told Zen.

He had heard the tower transmission. It took every ounce of self-control not to snap back that he might not be able to walk but he could still hear as well as anyone.

Banking Green Phantom to start the approach, he realized he'd done his best flying in those few seconds after the alarms sounded. He'd slipped into a different mode, flying instead of tiptoeing.

He was too damn worried about everything—about not having legs, about who was watching, about how jittery Green Phantom and its JSF suit got under Fort Two. He'd been thinking instead of flying. He had to get beyond all that.

Just stinking fly.

Easy to say, harder to do.

"Fort Two," he said, "proceed around the track and take your speed up to five-fifty. Hold it there."

"Jeff?" said Breanna. "Five-fifty?"

"Do you copy, Fort Two?" he snapped.

There was a pause.

"Roger that," she said finally.

"Major, what exactly do you have in mind?" Cheshire asked.

It was a legitimate question. So why was he pissed at Bree?

He still loved her, even though he couldn't have her.

Don't let that screw you up. Of all things.

"The low-speed vortices the Megafortress throws off are pretty wicked," Jeff said, his lips and tongue pausing over each word. "We had trouble doing formations with the Flighthawks at low speed, but once we brought it up we were fine. You remember those tests, Major?"

"Affirmative," snapped Cheshire. "You may be right, Zen. I think you are."

"It's worth a try," added Breanna.

"Last one we have today," said Cheshire.

"Copy that," said Zen. "But there's always tomorrow," he added, the words suddenly bubbling into his mouth.

BREANNA STUDIED THE HUD CUE, HER SPEED PRE-cisely at 550 knots. Green Phantom came on steadily. She guessed that Zen had decided to let the computer handle the throttle speed this time, concentrating on his joystick controls. Going from the Flighthawks to the kludgy Phantom must be like going from a hand-built racing bike to a tricycle. She suspected the QF-4's engines were at the firewall.

He was coming in smoothly, though. Cheshire called out the distances—a half mile, five hundred yards, a hundred yards, fifty yards.

God, please let him do it, thought Breanna. Please. Whatever it takes from me, just give him this today.

"You're in! You're in!" Cheshire couldn't contain her excitement.

"Copy that," said Zen blandly.

Thank you, God, thought Breanna. Thank you.

* * *

ZEN STARTED TO FEEL A LITTLE COCKY AS HE SLIPPED
Green Phantom over to what would be a drogue position
on the left wing. An immense eddy of air flowing beneath
the number-one engine brought him back to reality, pushing the drone's nose downward. He fought it through,
hanging tough as he pushed toward the imaginary cone
that would signal success.

"Approaching my turn in zero-one," warned Breanna.

Zen grunted. He moved his hand to the throttle, intending to take over from the computer. As he did, the
robot began falling off to the right. He fought it back, but
by the time he had the plane level Megafortress was starting her turn. That made it more difficult; he poked in and
held it for a few seconds, then found the speed backing
down despite his nudging on the control. He slipped
back—had he been doing a real tank, fuel would have
splashed in his face.

"Pumpkin time," declared the controller.

"I can do it," he said, poking up his speed.

Colonel Bastian broke in. "Major Stockard, you've already accomplished your mission," he told him. "Let's
just get the cows back in the barn. I appreciate your ef-
forts. A damn good show. You too, Fort Two. You all
may have just saved the Megafortress project from ex-
tinction."

ZEN LET HIS ARMS DROOP OVER THE SIDES OF THE
wheelchair as Green Phantom rolled to a stop at the end
of its landing range. The control link snapped off; the
plane was now under the command of the ground crew,
which was busily arranging its front end under the special
hoist unit at the back of its trailer. The airmen would have
it tarped within seconds, just in case the Kronos satellite

managed somehow to slip its orbit and arrive ahead of schedule.

"Want to get something to eat before we debrief?" asked Remington. He'd left his control booth and was standing next to Zen. "You look like you could use a beer."

"Why?" Zen snapped.

"You need an excuse to have a beer?" asked the dumbfounded engineer.

"I'm on duty," said Jeff. He tried to make his voice sound less harsh, but it was clear from Remington's face that he had failed.

"Hey, suit yourself," said the engineer. "I'll feed back the video."

"Fred. Wait." Zen pulled off his headset, tossing it onto the console panel. He wheeled around, slowed by the industrial carpet. He remembered the day they had put that down, how good it had felt beneath his feet after standing for hours, watching one of the other pilots work with the drones.

Remington stood near the monitoring area, arms stiff, frowning at him.

"I didn't mean that," said Zen. "I mean, shit, yeah, I'd love a beer. But, uh, I haven't had any since, I don't know when."

"Well, if you're looking for an excuse," said the civilian, "I'd say that was a damn good one. We can snag a beer in Lounge B. I've already prepared the report on the refuel," he added quickly. "The colonel will have everything he needs."

Preparing the report was Zen's job. His anger twinged.

Had Remington done the work out of pity? Or was that just Remington, super-efficient nerd boy, always on top of things?

Not to mention thirsty.

Would he have done it before the accident? Zen couldn't be sure.

"I should look at it," he told the engineer.

Remington smiled. "My laptop's in the briefcase, with the report and video," he said, pointing. "We'll check it out while we're waiting for the bartender to pour some frosty ones."

Zen laughed. If he remembered correctly, Lounge B was self-serve. Come to think of it, last time he'd been here, it hadn't offered beer.

JEFF WASN'T IN THE FLIGHTHAWK CONTROL ROOM BY the time Breanna finished with the Megafortress. He didn't seem to be anywhere in Bunker B, the underground suite of offices used as the Flighthawk development center. Breanna began walking toward their dormitory suite, which was located in Yellow Two at the far end of the base.

The suite had belonged to her before they'd gotten married. Approximately 250 square feet were divided between two bedrooms, a central living room-kitchenette-utility space, and a bathroom. The decor was early pressboard, augmented by some posters of Impressionist prints inherited from the previous occupant, a chemist working in one of the weapons sections. Breanna greatly preferred the condo near Las Vegas she and Jeff had bought, but they had held onto the suite because it was convenient to have a place to crash on the base. Unlike many military facilities, Dreamland had a surplus of housing; while you couldn't count on the shower pressure in the morning, at least the price was right.

Breanna could tell Jeff wasn't in the suite as soon as she pushed open the door. She went to the bedroom and cranked open the windows, trying to remove the musty smell that had accumulated since she'd last been here a few days before. She sat down on the bed, found herself leaning back and sinking into the pillow. Despite the success of the test—despite Jeff's success—she felt depressed and drained. Things between them weren't going well at all. She had known there would be trouble adjusting; she had known it would be a long process, the most difficult thing they'd ever done together by far. But that didn't make her feel any better.

Bree got up and went to fill the tub. Baths always made her feel better.

Steam rose quickly from the tub, the water so hot she nearly scalded her fingers just pushing the stopper closed. Definitely a good-luck omen—truly hot water was as rare as good water pressure.

Straightening, Breanna began to undress. The steamy air softened her skin and sweat beaded from her face, running down the sides of her cheeks. She felt the poisons and worries that had accumulated in her body beginning to escape. She flattened her hands over her face, pushing her fingers back over her hair and then down over her chest to her hips and thighs, stretching slowly, relaxing after the stressful day.

Breanna slipped into the tub even though the water was still running. The knots in her muscles gave way; her legs slid limp against the sides of the narrow tub, the close confines somehow reassuring.

They had showered here together, many times. To be able to do that again, just once—

But those were distracting thoughts. She had to live in the present, not the past. She still loved Jeff. She might love him more, in fact—he was brave and determined and he could be stubborn, but that was attractive too. He'd nailed the test when the best pilot on the base—the *next*-best pilot on the base—had failed.

Jeff would never walk again. His back was broken. She could deal with that; she could survive that. And as soon as he was sure of that, as soon as he saw that she wasn't just pitying him, it would get better. She knew it would.

It would.

Breanna lowered her head to the surface of the water, feeling the tingle. She wanted to reduce her consciousness to just that feel, to just the hot tickle on her skin. Her face and breasts and legs fuzzed with the warmth.

Many times before they were married she sat in this very tub like this, thinking of Jeff. She believed she could will him there with ESP, close her eyes and he would magically appear at the door.

A knock in the hallway startled her.

Imagination?

No, there it was again.

"Jeff?" she called.

"Hey, anyone in there?"

Breanna jumped out of the tub. She grabbed the small towel from the bar, anxious to let him in.

It wasn't until she started to turn the knob that she realized it hadn't been his voice.

"No, it's Mack," said Major Smith.

Bree pushed the door shut quickly. "I'll—I was in the bath," she said. "Wait just a second."

Smith laughed when she reopened the door a minute later.

"You didn't have to get dressed for me, Rap," he told her.

"Major."

"My, we're formal today," said Smith. "Can I come in?"

"Sure," said Breanna, who'd jumped into her flight suit. As she closed the door behind him she glanced toward the bathroom, noticing her underwear on the floor where she'd left it. She went and closed the bathroom door.

"Expecting Jeff?"

"Well, he is my husband," she told Smith. "Can I get you something? A Coors?"

"Sure."

Breanna squatted down in front of the fridge, retrieving two beers from the bottom compartment.

"I figured I'd stop by and say good-bye." Smith told her, taking the beer.

"Good-bye?"

"Assignment came through."

"Oh?"

Smith shook his head. "Can't tell you about it." He grinned, obviously pleased with himself. "If you want, I'll try and get you transferred too."

"Thanks, Mack," she said.

"I'm serious. They'll be closing this place soon. A few months. Nothing against your dad," he added, sipping the beer.

Smith was attractive; good-looking and damn smart, he was also obviously bound for bigger and better things. He could play the political game and clearly wanted to be a general. She liked him, even though his ego was bigger than the room they were sitting in.

"How's the JSF?" she asked.

"An access panel flew off and jammed one of the rods in the leading-edge assembly," said the pilot. "The panel wasn't secured properly. Mechanics ought to be shot."

"That sounds a little harsh."

"You can't do your job, there's no excuse. I could have augured in," said Smith, who didn't seem very concerned. "Anyway, I'm glad to be rid of the F-119. I just wish—"

He let his gaze drift into hers. Breanna felt her heartbeat double.

"I'm not really attracted to you, Mack," she heard herself say softly. She knew instantly it was a lie, and he must have too. Breanna stared down at the floor.

"Bree."

His hand felt warm on her face, reassuring like the bath had been.

She forced herself to shake her head no.

ZEN ACTUALLY ENJOYED THE BEER, EVEN THOUGH HE drank only a quarter of it. Remington and the others seemed genuinely happy about the day's tests, and at least pretended not to notice that he was in a wheelchair.

He knew they weren't oblivious, and there were a few awkward silences and glances. Still, the test had gone well, and Remington's new laptop had some cool video extensions that replayed the flight videos very sharply, and the report was perfect. And what the hell. Between the beer and the day, he actually felt damn good. He even joined in the good-natured kidding of Lou DeFalco, the civilian who'd been acting as lead Flighthawk pilot in Zen's absence. They called DeFalco "Rock"—not exactly a flattering nickname for a pilot.

"You think I'm bad in the Flighthawks," said DeFalco with a laugh, "you should see me in Aurora. There I'm Big Rock."

"I heard you put one of the Flighthawks through the hangar door," said Zen.

"No way," said DeFalco. "It was the side of the hangar."

"True." Remington laughed. "We just barely missed. He came, I'm not exaggerating, within an inch. Damn computer protocols don't always lock out on proximity."

"Hey, if they did, Rock would never get off the ground," said Paul Kardon, one of the weapons engineers.

"Hey, Zen," said Nancy Cheshire, walking in. "Your wife's looking for you."

"Uh-oh," groaned the others in unison.

"The ball and chain beckons," deadpanned Remington.

Zen laughed along with the others.

"You better go run her down, Major," said Kardon. "And don't take any guff. Remember—you outrank her."

"Yeah, but she's connected." DeFalco laughed.

Zen tried Bree at the Megafortress bunker, and then over at the Taj, before one of the security sergeants said he'd seen her heading toward Yellow Two, the dorm building where she had her apartment.

Their apartment.

She was trying. Shouldn't he let her make the attempt? There was a chance that she might be able to get over the fact that he was a cripple.

Was that fair? Let her waste her life on him?

Even though the entrance to the dorm building was ramped, Jeff had trouble negotiating the bumps. He had to jiggle his wheels sideways on one, and that killed his momentum. Finally he reached the exterior hall, only to find it nearly impossible to pull the heavy door while rolling backward.

"Hey, Major, let me grab that sucker for you," said Captain Danny Freah.

"Thanks," said Zen, rolling backward as the big Air Force security officer pulled open the door.

"Ought to have an electronic eye on it," said Freah as Zen rolled into the foyer.

"That's not necessary," said Zen, fighting against his embarrassment.

Freah seemed to sense the awkwardness, and opened the inside door quickly.

"Heard you nailed that tanker sim this afternoon," said Freah. "Good going."

"I didn't realize that'd be big news," said Zen.

"Hey, Major, relax," said Freah. He pulled his hands back as if he'd touched a hot stove. "I happened to be in the control tower when you got it. They were applauding."

"Yeah," said Zen. He hadn't meant to snarl. He pulled

his wheelchair around, starting down the hallway for the room. It was automatic—he didn't think about the stairs at the far end of the hall.

The flight down was only six steps deep, the suite door barely ten feet beyond that. But there was no way he could get down the steps without help. He'd have to go back through the lobby and around through the back wing, where there was a ramp. As he started to wheel backward, he saw the door to the suite open.

Mack Smith popped his head out, then turned back to say something before leaving.

SMITH SKIPPED UP THE STEPS, DISAPPOINTED WITH Breanna and maybe with himself. He hadn't gone there to seduce her.

So why had he gone then?

He hadn't found an answer before he reached the lobby. Coincidence of coincidences, who was just arriving but Bree's husband Zen.

That was close.

"Hey," said Knife, grabbing Zen's chair as he was rolling down the back hallway. "Hey, Zen, what are you up to?"

"What are *you* up to?" snapped Stockard furiously.

Smith let go of the wheelchair. Captain Freah and a Spec Ops security guard were standing near the front door a few yards away.

"I'm sorry," said Smith.

Paralyzed and all, Stockard looked like he was going to bolt out of the chair and strangle him. Mack knew better than to say anything about Rap, even though nothing had happened, but he wasn't exactly sure what to say.

"I was just making the rounds, saying good-bye," said Mack, taking a step back. He hadn't had a chance to say anything about Zen's legs, but this sure as hell wasn't the time.

And anyway, what the hell could he say? Tough break? He'd already said something like that in the hospital.

"I'm saying good-bye," Mack repeated.

"Good-bye for what?"

"Hell, Zen, what's up your ass?" Smith took a step backward and stuck his hands on his hips. For a second he thought Stockard was going to put his head down and ram forward with his chair.

"Uh, Majors," said Freah, coming toward them with the air of a kindergarten teacher. "Can I be of some assistance?"

"I'm fine," said Zen.

"Me too," said Knife, starting for the door. "Good-bye, Zen. Tell your wife I said hello."

"Tell her yourself," said Stockard.

Smith spun around and headed through the lobby door, letting it slam shut behind him.

III
A matter of conscience

Two weeks later

Ethiopia
21 October, 0400

"ALL RIGHT MARINES, LISTEN THE FUCK UP." GUNNERY Sergeant James Ricardo Melfi gave the small handpicked platoon one of his best sneers, even though it was difficult for them to see in the dim light from the nearby flare. "That means you too, Goosehead," he told one of his sergeants. "Jack, you close your fuckin' mouth or I'm puttin' a boot in it. You want to yawn, you go to the dentist. All right, girls, here's the deal. We come off the Chinook, we split into two squads, we hit the buildings the way we laid it out. We take out missile one and missile two, we call in the fuckin' Air Force. We give the weenies two minutes to get here because they're not Marine aviators." He paused to allow his men the appropriate contemptuous snort, then continued. "At that point, we take the administration building, which should be defenseless, assuming the Air Force has done its job. If they have not, then Fire Team B, following my lead, will do it for them, wiping out the tank with their bare hands if they have to."

Actually, they would be using a Russian-made SPG-9 piece of shit. The light antitank gun fired a 73mm missile that had a fairly good chance of destroying the ancient M47—but only if it hit it. The weapon wasn't particularly known for its accuracy.

"Team A, meanwhile, will be taking care of the machine guns on the east side of the building. Prisoners and wounded to be evacuated to the Chinook rendezvous point, blah-blah-blah. You girls got that?"

"Oh, we got it, Sergeant Honey," said the Team B point man, Jerry Jackson.

"Listen, Swishboy, you just make sure you don't trip going out of the helicopter," Melfi told him. "I'll boot your black ass right into the sandbag post."

"Oh, I wish you would, Gunny."

The others laughed, and so did the sergeant, even as he shook his head. He thumbed toward the two green, unmarked Chinooks standing on the dirt pad behind him. The flare he'd lit behind him made the aircraft look almost purple in the early morning twilight. Looming beyond them were jagged hills, their sharp shadows and shapes making the place look like the far side of the moon, rather than the ragged hinterland of northeastern Ethiopia.

"Okay, let's run this like we're under fire, all right?" said Gunny. "Check your gear and move out."

The Marines quickly gave their rifles and gear the once-over as they silently lined up to board the helicopters. They'd been issued plain-Jane M-16A1 rifles that had been bought on the black market. Besides the Russian antitank gun, they were carrying two French machine guns—AA52's, which were actually quite good, though they used odd-sized bullets. The Chinooks that were to carry the Marines ostensibly belonged to Zaire. Their uniforms, which had an Army puke-green tint to them, bore no insignias or markings.

In Gunny's opinion, these and a dozen other elaborate precautions designed to camouflage the group's identity weren't going to fool anyone if the Marines were actually called on to do the job they were practicing to do. In Gunny's opinion, they'd be better off admitting they were Americans and, hot damn, taking a real Marine Expeditionary Force—Cobras, Harriers, CH-53's, SAWs,

M240's, the whole shebang—against the damn Somalian SAM site and blowing the living shit out of it, foreign politics be damned.

But of course, Gunnery Sergeant James Melfi had been in the Marines long enough to not have an opinion in these matters. If Madcap Magician wanted to pretend they were merely pissed-off mercenaries hired by a pissed-off and jealous African dictator who wanted to get back in power in Somalia, so be it.

"All right, girls, let's move it out," said Melfi, prodding his men to board the double-bladed Chinook transport. Captain Peter Gordon, who'd been conferring with the pilots, frowned at him—he'd already bawled Melfi out twice today for using "inappropriate language."

"Sergeant?" snapped the captain.

"Pussies are all hot and wet for you, Captain," said Gunny with as straight a face as he could manage.

"HELOS BEARING THREE-NINER."

"Confirmed." Mack Smith glanced at the way marker on his INS and put his plane into a bank away from the path the two helicopters were taking. "Poison Flight, prepare to break. Let's do this the way we drew it up."

"Three."

"Four."

The four F-16's now split into two different flights, Mack and his wingman staying southeast of the helicopters while the others flew north. Mack scanned the glow of instruments in the Viper cockpit, then snapped his APG-68 radar into ground-attack mode. He was ahead of schedule, but had had trouble picking out the target during last night's exercise and wanted to take no chances this time.

"Helicopters should be putting down now," he told his wingman, Captain Kevin Sullivan. Sullivan acknowl-

edged. Packing a pair of HARM missiles, Sullivan was to
watch for any radar indication that would indicate SAM
activity. The HARMs, or High-speed Anti-Radiation Missiles, were designed to home in on the powerful radar
systems used by SAMs. In this particular scenario, they
were looking for an SA-3 battery, a medium-altitude,
medium-range missile system protecting an installation on
the northern coast of Somalia.

The simulated coast of Somalia. They were actually
flying over Ethiopia.

"Ground team inbound," snapped the Chinook pilot on
cue. The secure, coded KY-58 com system rendered the
voice almost metallic. "Taking fire. LZ is hot."

"Poison One riding in," said Mack. He snapped the
sidestick hard, rolling into a dive from 18,500 feet. Mack
gave a quick glance toward his radar-warning receiver,
making sure he was not being tracked. He mimed hitting
his master arm switch, working through his routine as if
he were actually carrying the four GBU-24 laser-guided
bombs and six five-hundred-pound "dumb" or unguided
bombs they planned to use on the mission.

"SA-3 site is up," said Sullivan. "Dotted. HARM away.
You're clean."

In theory, the most serious antiair site Mack would face
had just been taken care of before it could launch missiles.

Knife, meanwhile, had put his Viper into a steep dive
toward the target. His targeting system in the HUD projected a diamond smack on the long wall at the base below; the wall was simulating a tank.

"Bombs away," he said, pretending to pickle the iron
off his wings. He jostled the wings up and down, as if
simulating the g forces as three thousand pounds fell off,
beginning to recover and position himself to fire the laser-
designated GBUs on the ground team's cue.

*   *   *

GUNNY FELT HIS KNEE TWINGE AS HE TROTTED TOWARD his two-man SPG team. He tried to ignore it, grumbling as the F-16 banked above.

"All right, tank is wiped out," he told the men. "Get the machine gun. Come on, let's go, let's go. This ain't a pleasure cruise. Move it!"

"Bam," said the loader after the gunner mimed the weapon firing.

"Good, okay, okay," shouted Gunny. The men were leaping over the wall, firing live rounds at the empty warehouse.

A fresh flare rose in the distance. Captain Gordon trotted up, a nightscope in his hand. There were only three night-vision binoculars assigned to the entire thirty-member assault team.

"Looking good, Sergeant," said Gordon.

"Uh-huh," said Melfi. His knee was really screaming now, but there was no time to baby it. With the first and second ring of ground defenses now wiped out, the six men on his right were supposed to move in and take out the surface-to-ship batteries installed along the railhead. The Silkworm missile launchers were being simulated by a pair of old Land Rovers at the far end of the warehouse complex. Gunny half-trotted, half-walked behind the fire team as they scrambled forward. As they bolted over the wall that had played the role of the tank, they suddenly stopped.

"What's going on?" he yelled at them over the wall.

"Supposed to be an armored car," hissed one of the men, reminding him of the scenario. "We're hitting it with the LANTIRN for the F-16."

"Shit. Right. Sorry," said Gunny, taking advantage of the break to walk around to the edge of the wall rather than struggling over it. Meanwhile, the fire team leader illuminated the pretend target so the F-16 above could hit it with GBU-24's.

"Destroyed!" yelped the team's com specialist, who was communicating with the plane.

Gunny followed along as the team proceeded to the parking area where the Silkworms were supposed to be. The Marines moved quickly—a little too quickly, of course, since there was no one actually in front of them. The two demolition specialists set their charges on the Land Rovers.

"Move out, move out!" called the team leader.

Gunny retreated with the others. He barely made it back to the wall before the cars blew up.

"Okay, into the helicopter!" Captain Gordon screamed.

Gunny permitted himself a moment's worth of satisfaction, staring at the flaming trucks. They'd made sure the gas tanks were full—might as well have one big boom. Then he walked back toward the LZ, where the helicopter was winding its props.

"HELO OUTBOUND," SMITH TOLD HIS FLIGHT.

The other pilots checked in as the four F-16's proceeded to their postattack rendezvous point. In theory, two HARM missiles, six five-hundred-pound iron bombs, and a total of eight GBU-24's had been fired at the ground installation on the coast of Somalia, all scoring hits. Destroyed were two SA-2 and four SA-3 ground-to-air launchers, along with their radar vans and specialized crews. More importantly, two batteries of Silkworm antiship missiles had also been wiped out. Not to mention one tank, one armored car, and an unspecified number of Somies.

Fantastic. Now if the Iranians and Somalians would cooperate, the operation could proceed.

Smith squirmed in the F-16 seat. Canted back at thirty degrees to make it more comfortable in high-g maneuvers, it felt awkward to him, almost as if he were sitting in a dentist's chair. He knew that eventually he'd get used to it, but that didn't soothe the kinks in his shoulders.

Mack checked the time. Four-forty. They had plenty of time to go again, as planned. But before he could signal the helicopter, their ground controller broke in.

"Poison Flight, this is Madcap Magician. Return to base. Repeat, return to base."

"One copies," he said, recognizing the voice of ISA commander Major Hal Briggs.

Briggs ordinarily wasn't up this early, let alone working the radio. And Mack knew the major was supposed to be in Saudi Arabia today, overseeing another operation only tangentially related to the crisis in Somalia.

Smith's heart started double-pumping. "Okay, guys," he told the others. "Let's get back to base pronto."

The White House
21 October, 0700 local

IN HIS SEVEN MONTHS AS SPECIAL ASSISTANT TO THE National Security Council, Jed Barclay had seen—seen, not met, not talked to—the President of the United States of America exactly twice before. And now today—now, this instant—he was giving him a personal briefing in the upstairs residence of the White House on the most important and dangerous international development since the Gulf War.

Hell, this was twenty times more dangerous, as he was endeavoring to point out between his nervous coughs and tremors.

The President's Chief of Staff frowned as the word "hell" escaped from Jed's mouth. Neither the President nor Ms. O'Day reacted. Jed pushed on.

"The Iranian mullahs have decided that the time is right for their Greater Islamic League. That is, of course, Islam as they interpret it, not as most of the rest of the world or even Iranians interpret it. But you're all aware of that. The takeover of the Somalian government was the first step. Locating the Silkworm antiship missiles there was the second. They have a credible threat to shipping, and their ultimatum must be taken seriously. In a few months, they'll have the aircraft carrier they're building with the Chinese. Either the West—us basically—adds a one-hundred-percent tax to the price of oil and divides it among members of their alliance, or they will attack shipping. They've menaced two ships already."

Jed paused, sensing that he was starting to hyperventilate. He had prepared a short sidebar to his presentation outlining the origins of some of the weapons systems known or suspected to have been shipped to Somalia and southern Iran, including a dozen improved SA-2Bs that seemed to have come from Yugoslavia. But it was superfluous and his audience was anxious; he took a long breath and moved on.

"We have several options. The first, of course, is negotiation—"

President Lloyd Taylor shifted in his seat. "Cut to the chase, son. The election will be over before your report is. What are the odds of the covert action working?"

Jed literally gulped as his mind shifted gears. He had prepared long arguments for and against each option, including the Madcap Magician operation the President had just referred to. That plan—removing the surface-to-ship and surface-to-air missiles in Somalia with a "sanitized" covert-action team—was, in fact, his recommendation. But he'd come expecting to have to argue for it, and only now realized that the President might actually already have discussed and considered it in great detail with Ms. O'Day.

He coughed, then jumped to what he had planned as the conclusion to his presentation.

"By knocking out the missiles we can demonstrate a

firm hand. Resolve, I mean," said Jed. "At the same time, the diplomatic solution can proceed. The covert, I mean, Madcap Magician, is preferable because it can move quickly and provides at least a veneer of deniability. In any event, full military intervention would take days if not weeks to pull together, by which time the price of oil will have risen catastrophically. Madcap Magician has positioned and trained units under the Ironweed contingency; they need only a few hours' notice. As far as negatives go, we're working without real-time satellite coverage and the intel—"

"Odds of success," prompted Ms. O'Day in a stage whisper.

"The simulations," he said, "have shown a seventy percent chance of success."

"Seventy percent?" said the President's Chief of Staff.

"I think it's worth the risk," said O'Day.

"What does our Harvard whiz kid think?" asked the President. He said Harvard the way someone who had graduated from Yale would.

"Well, sir." Jed fumbled with his tie. He'd spent nearly as much time choosing the tie as memorizing the speech. "I, uh—I concur with Ms. O'Day. However, we have to—"

"However, you feel that the possibility of failure is higher than the models indicate," said the President. "But that we should proceed anyway."

"Well, see, it depends on what you're measuring. There's a built-in prejudice in any such model. I mean, I tried to keep it out of this one, but you have at least a three percent coefficient." Jed gulped—Ms. O'Day had warned him, above all else, not to use the word "coefficient." "But the real issue here goes beyond the computer model."

"I agree. Computer modeling of political situations is absurd," said Taylor's Chief of Staff.

"Well, that's a bit far," snapped Jed, momentarily forgetting where he was. "I mean, the thing is, we do need tools to quantify certain factors. See, my point is, Mr. President, we have to meet this aggressively. To a certain extent, we have to be willing to risk partial military failure. And we also have to anticipate adverse reaction from the other Arab states. Saudi Arabia will feel particularly vulnerable, as will Egypt. They'll definitely bar their bases to us. We'll end up having to rely on Israel for the military buildup, and that will have even more consequences. But if we do nothing—if we fold—the results will be disastrous. We should be prepared for a measured but aggressive response. When Libya joins the coalition—and I say when, not if—we should attack with everything we've got. There are a dozen contingency plans drawn up for that. At that point, the Greater Islamic League folds. I'm certain of that."

"Where'd you get this punk kid?" Taylor growled to O'Day. "Excuse us," he said harshly, dismissing Jed.

Confused and impotent, Jed slipped out of the room. He felt like he had been punched in the stomach.

Worse. Maybe hit in the head with a baseball bat.

He walked down the hallway in a daze. Ms. O'Day somehow materialized behind him. With a stern look, she motioned for him to follow her downstairs. He did so, despite the searing pain of his insides. Never in his life had he screwed up so badly.

And the thing was, he wasn't even sure precisely how he had screwed up.

Too many coughs and stutters. Not enough respect. Mentioning the computer simulations, even though they were one of the reasons he was here. And above all, using that damn word "coefficient."

Neither Jed nor his boss spoke until they were back in the NSC basement, walking toward her office.

"I'm sorry," he said.

"Sorry? For what?"

"I didn't mean to, uh, make the President angry."

O'Day laughed. "Jed, you may be a genius at foreign policy and computer science, but you have a lot to learn about Washington."

"Washington?"

"There's an election in three weeks, remember?"

"Well, yeah."

Ms. O'Day shook her head.

"Was I supposed to check this with polls or something?" Jed asked. He had a vague notion that military action would hurt the President's chances at getting reelected. On the other hand, rising gas prices would effectively kill them.

Wouldn't they?

"Jed, Ironweed is proceeding," said O'Day. "Madcap Magician has already gotten the okay to move. We're ratcheting up for the reaction. Two carrier groups are moving into the Mediterranean for training missions. Everything you suggested is proceeding. Hopefully, it won't be needed," she added. The National Security Advisor pursed her lips. "But if it is, we'll deal with it the only way possible—aggressively, but with a measured response. In the meantime, Cascade is being detailed to the Middle East to keep an eye on things."

"Cascade?"

"My personal representative. Unofficially, of course. His assignment is to observe the routine training procedures, familiarizing himself with them."

"But the President was angry. And he certainly didn't authorize—"

"Keep that in mind," she said sternly. "And forget about the election, okay?"

She glanced at her watch. "Your flight leaves from Andrews in a half hour. If you hustle, you may be able to hitch a ride on Marine One with the President's wife."

"The President's wife?"

"Don't be surprised if she doesn't make the flight," added O'Day, "even though she's the only one on the passenger list. Probably just as well. She would definitely want you to change that tie. Good God, Jed. We have to go shopping when you get back."

Dreamland
21 October, 0700 local

ORDINARILY, COLONEL BASTIAN DIDN'T HAVE MUCH USE for donuts, especially the crème-covered, choke-your-arteries kind. But Ax had insisted that they were manda-tory morale boosters for early morning staff meetings, especially when the people gathering were going to hear things they didn't like hearing. And so he'd let the ser-geant go ahead and bring the damn things to the confer-ence room, along with the coffee tankers and an oversupply of semi-hard bagels. It was a good thing too—they'd been going at this now for nearly an hour without letup.

Long enough for Dog to concede, if only to himself, that the donuts weren't that bad an idea.

"Colonel, I've gone over the numbers at least ten times with the contractors," pleaded Major Cheshire. "There's just no way we can sustain the EB-52 project with this little money. The flight-computer system for the three new planes alone will cost ten million dollars."

"There's got to be a way," said Bastian. "The budget committee is reluctant even to grant that much."

"What's another ten million to them?" groused Rubeo. "They probably spend more than that on lunch."

"Each computer has to be designed specifically for the individual plane," explained Cheshire. "The gallium-arsenic chips that control flight functions are made by the NSA plant, which sets the price. That's where the expense comes in. It's absurd, I know, but they're padding their own budget."

"Then do it another way," said Bastian. "Can't you use off-the-shelf parts?"

Cheshire shook her head.

"Can we make the chips ourselves?" he asked.

"Not without a fab," said Rubeo, "which will cost billions. Colonel, you can't nickel and dime Dreamland. It won't work."

"I wouldn't call ten million dollars nickels and dimes," said Bastian. "That's a hell of a lot of money."

"Colonel, wouldn't it make more sense to tell the Congressmen these are the weapons systems that we need?" asked Cheshire.

Bastian sighed. She was right. On the other hand, that wasn't the way this was going to work. The Air Force and DOD had already done that.

And under their scenario, Dreamland hadn't made the cut.

O'Day wanted program figures and a new base budget so she could reinstate HAWC on a black line, with help from her Congressional allies. If Bastian had had more leverage—if he'd been a three-star general instead of a lowly lieutenant colonel—he'd be able to fight on a few other fronts and maybe get Dreamland back in the big game. But he simply didn't have enough weight to counteract the generals who wanted Dreamland closed down because of the Ken James affair; O'Day's strategy was the only play.

"Look, I'm recommending we proceed with the Megafortress program, which calls for developmental trials of several models," Bastian told them. "But realistically, the only portion of the program that we can count on will be the tanker, because of JSF."

"That's the project that should be discontinued," said Rubeo.

"Well, Professor," Dog said, "if you want to call your local Congressman and tell him that, be my guest."

"One Megafortress could do the job of four JSFs," said Cheshire.

"Can it land on an aircraft carrier?" Bastian said.

"It wouldn't have to. Its unrefueled range—"

"Look, I'm not going to argue about the JSF design. I agree with everything that's been said. But I have to deal with reality." Dog pushed himself back in his chair. "Now let's get back to our agenda."

ZEN TURNED THE CORNER INTO THE FLIGHTHAWK ground-level hangar so sharply he practically ran down Jennifer Gleason, who was making some adjustments to the on-board computer in the Hawk Two. She was bending over the front of the aircraft, her back to him; he found himself gazing at the soft, perfect curve of her hips.

"Hey, Zen," she said, still bent over the U/MF-3. His chariot made it impossible to arrive anywhere incognito.

"Hey, yourself," he said.

"Back from the colonel's meeting so soon?"

"I sent Mike," he told her.

"Poor Mike."

"Yeah." Mike Janlock, the resident BMI resins and airfoil-design specialist, was the senior scientist on the Flighthawk project and had been in charge of it before Bastian's reorganization. Even if Zen hadn't begged out of the colonel's budget session because of the morning's test flight, he probably would have asked Janlock to go along in his place. Jeff didn't want to spend the time ducking the pitying glances everyone else would be throwing toward him. Besides, word was Bastian had already made his final decision on the Flighthawks—they weren't making the cut. No amount of meetings or reports or well-reasoned arguments or even pity would change his mind about "robot" planes.

"Well, we're not closed down yet," said Gleason.

"No, not yet." Jeff grabbed the wheels of his chair. "You're blowing off the preflight briefing?"

"No, sir," said the young computer scientist. She glanced back at him. "We had the discrete-burst module reengineered last night, and I'm getting it in place. I'm almost finished."

"You did it *again*?"

"The last one failed the shock test after you, uh, went home."

"You should have called me."

"Well, as a matter of fact, we did."

"I was over in the visiting officers' hall. I didn't feel like going all the way out to Ewen," he added lamely.

"Anyway, I'm just about done. Everybody else is inside." Jennifer smiled at him, then went back to whatever it was she was doing. She'd tucked her long hair up under a white smock cap; a single strand draped down across her neck, hanging down over her shoulder. Her breasts pushed against her lab coat as she leaned into the machine; he could see the outline of her nipple against the fabric.

Stop, he warned himself, rolling forward to the small room they used to brief their missions.

Everyone was there—including Breanna, who was sitting at the far end of the table talking to Lee Ong. Ong was responsible for the Flighthawks' physical systems and acted as the "mission boss," coordinating the many details involved in the airborne tests.

So why was Bree here?

"Good morning," said Zen, wheeling himself toward the front of the room. "Jennifer should be in shortly."

He glanced around the room, carefully avoiding

Breanna's gaze. "Where's Bobby?" he asked, referring to the usual pilot of the E-3 mother ship.

"Captain Fernandez has the flu," said Breanna. "So does Kathy. I volunteered to fly Boeing in their place."

Zen snapped his head toward her.

"You don't have a problem with that, do you?" she said defensively. "Pete Brinks is coming over to copilot."

"No, of course not, Captain," he said. He turned to the others. "Captain Stockard flew Rivet intercept flights in RC-135's when she was a teenager," he told them. "Maybe she'll entertain us with stories about eavesdropping on Russian air defenses if things get boring."

"Maybe I'll just roll Boeing through an invert if things get boring," she said.

Zen felt his face starting to flush as the others laughed. He turned the floor over to Ong, then rolled along the far side of the room toward the coffeepot at the back. Coffee was one of the things he'd all but given up since the accident, but he didn't want to sit out at the front where Breanna could stare at him.

It was possible that the two pilots assigned to fly Boeing were actually sick. And Breanna was at least arguably the next best choice on the base to take the mission; she had a lot of experience in the large jets. But it seemed to him like a hell of a coincidence.

Not to mention the fact that he should have been consulted about who would replace the other pilots. He hadn't seen Mike this morning, nor had he talked to Ong. One of them must have made the call.

If Zen asked—*when* Zen asked—undoubtedly they'd give him the same line Jennifer had used. They'd tried calling him at home, blah-blah-blah.

And maybe they had. They could have called and gotten Bree. She would have instantly volunteered. That was Bree.

So maybe they weren't conspiring against him. Even if it seemed that way.

He hadn't gone home last night, and in fact hadn't gone home for the past few nights. He was, in fact, avoiding her, trying to figure out what to do—or rather, how to do it.

Ong laid out the mission succinctly, setting the overall objective. They were going to put the Flighthawk through a series of low-altitude maneuvers to simulate a low-level penetration during an attack mission. The mother ship would follow behind it, first at five miles, then ten miles, then fifteen, and finally twenty. The extended distances were the point of the exercise; the Flighthawks had never been successfully controlled beyond seven miles while operating in Combat One, the secure communications mode.

Breanna then stood and reviewed her flight plan. Ordinarily this was, at best, a perfunctory part of the session. But Rap gave a precise, detailed briefing that covered everything from expected wind to fuel burn to radio rescue frequencies. She even included information about simulating an airdrop launch for the U/MFs, which the Boeing could not in fact handle. Jeff could tell the others were impressed that she'd done her homework.

Tough act to follow. He put down his coffee and began wheeling himself toward the front as she finished. With all the details already presented, his job was basically to ask if there were any questions and then give them a rah-rah to hit the door with.

He didn't feel very rah-rah, though.

"We've gone over the courses and the distances," he told them, faltering. "We, uh, we have complete satellite clearance through the morning. The Devil Canyon portion at the end of the flight is trickiest, because at twenty miles we have physical obstructions between the Boeing and the Flighthawk, assuming we're at proper altitude—which of course we will be," he added quickly, glancing toward Bree.

She was looking at him attentively, not glaring, not accusing, just watching.

"Look, I know it's likely the project is going to be cut," he said, looking back at the others. "There's no reason to bullshit you guys. You're too damn smart. There's no political backing for the Flighthawks. You guys have been dealing with it for a hell of a lot longer than I have."

He noticed one or two heads going up and down, saw a few frowns. Jennifer put her hands in front of her face as if she were going to cry.

"The thing is, we're right. I know we're right. The Flighthawks, UM/Fs, are the way of the future," Jeff said. "There's a lot of work to be done, as we all know, but somewhere down the line, these guys are going to be saving a hell of a lot of lives. They're going to keep pilots from getting their butts blown off." He laughed. "Not every pilot. But a lot of them. And this is what's going to happen. They'll mothball us, close us down. We'll all go on to better jobs. Me, I'm thinking McDonald's. Can I supersize that for you, sir?" he mocked.

They laughed.

"But I'll tell you what's going to happen," Zen continued. "Few years from now, maybe two, maybe ten, maybe twenty—hell, I don't know, the future. Somebody's going to find our work on a shelf somewhere, and they're going to realize we were right. They're going to pull our reports out and they are going to save themselves a ton of work. Probably enough work to save one or two pilots in the process. So we have to get as much done before they pull the plug. Bastian's going to save Dreamland," he added, "by doing what he has to do. So we have to hang tough and do what we have to do." Zen wheeled backward, starting for the door. "Let's go kick some butt out there today, huh?"

Zen left them in silence, wheeling out the door before they could react. He continued across the hangar and out onto the tarmac where the modified 707, "Boeing," waited.

The Flighthawk remote systems had grown even bigger since Zen's accident. The UM/Fs had been grounded for nearly nine months while the entire project was reviewed; computer capacity had been increased on the controlling end, adding to the stored emergency procedures and routines. In the interim, and unrelated to the accident, the cooling mechanisms for the secure communications gear had been "improved." These increased the remote controlling computer pallet from the size of a Honda Accord to that of a Chevy Suburban with a weight problem. Not only did it no longer fit in an F-15E, it was a squeeze to make the rear of the Boeing.

The scientists swore the gear would be miniaturized in the future—but they kept coming up with "improvements" that added to its bulk. Near-room-temperature superconducting chips and circuitry promised great advances in speed and much smaller sizes, but the gear was still too sensitive to be relied on. Not to mention expensive.

Zen's accident had led the Air Force to abandon an important part of the original concept—having a combat pilot fly the robots along with his own plane. There were proposals to fit the gear into a B-2, but the guidance telemetry could theoretically alert next-generation sensors to the invisible bomber. The B-1 fuselage needed extensive modifications to fit the controlling unit. Neither plane's wings could easily handle both UM/Fs, though the B-2's could be reinforced to do so.

The Megafortress EB-52, on the other hand, was big and strong enough to handle the job. And in fact they had conducted several airdrops and test runs from the Megafortress before Zen's accident. They'd managed one last week, just to make sure some of the modifications to the computer worked properly. Zen would have liked to do more, but the only Megafortress currently plumbed for airdrops was being used as a test bed for next-generation radar and communications-jamming equipment. Those tests were running behind and had very high priority. By the time the plane—nicknamed "Raven"—was free for real feasibility work, the Flighthawks would be history.

"Hey, Major. Ready for blastoff?" asked Pete Connors out on the concrete apron.

"I've been ready all my life," Zen told him, following Connors out toward the Boeing. The airman had parked a forklift near the rear crew door. They'd perfected this method of boarding the plane several days before. It was a hell of a lot easier than crawling down the stairs on his butt—which he had done on Raven.

"I ought to get one of these built into my wheelchair," Stockard told him as he maneuvered under the large forks. Connors had played with the blades so he could easily lock them beneath Zen's chair.

"Gee, Major, I'm surprised you haven't gone for the Version 2.0 Upgraded Wheelchair," joked Connors. "Has your TV, your satellite dish, your come-along cooler."

"No sauna?" Jeff braced his arms as the metal forks clicked into the bottom of his chair.

"That's in 3.0. You should sign up for beta-testing," said the airman. "Ready?"

"Blastoff."

It took Connors two attempts to get him lined up and through the special equipment bay in the rear of the plane. But that was a vast improvement over the first day, when it had taken eight or nine and he'd nearly fallen to the ground. Zen gave the airman a thumbs-up before rolling forward into the test-crew area.

"Great speech, Major," said Ong, who'd sprinted out to oversee one of the engineering crew's most important preflight tasks—brewing coffee in their zero-gravity Mr. Coffee.

"I thought you guys fell asleep on me," said Zen. "I heard some snores."

"No, seriously. Thanks." Ong tapped his shoulder. "You're damn right."

"Thanks," said Zen.

"Oooo, Mr. Coffee is smiling," said Jennifer, climbing in. "Smells like we should use that for fuel."

"Too corrosive," said Ong.

Zen wheeled over to the Flighthawk station, carefully setting the brake on his wheelchair before snapping the special restraints that locked it in place. The mechanics had cleared a pair of seats and reworked the control area so his seat could be locked in place.

Zen reviewed the hard-copy mission data Ong had left for him before getting ready for takeoff. Placing the Flighthawk computer in static test mode, he took hold of the mirror-image flight sticks, working quickly through the tests with the dedicated mission video tube at the center of the console. He limbered his fingers—they were always cramping like hell—and then pulled on the heavy flight helmet for a new round of checks.

The ground crew, meanwhile, had wheeled the Flighthawk and its portable power cart out onto the runway. With the control systems operational, Jeff and the computer began yet another round of tests, making sure that both sets of flight computers and the link between them were optimal. Only when this new round of tests was finished did the ground crew fire up the Flighthawk engine, powering the small plane with a "puffer," or power cart specially designed for it. The Flighthawk's miniature engine needed a large burst of air running through its turbines before it caught fire.

The UM/F purred like a contented kitten. Impatient to get going, Jeff ran through the control surfaces quickly, flexing the flaps and sliding the rudder back and forth. He split the top screen of the visor into feeds from the forward and tail cams for the test, confirming visually the computers' signal that all the surfaces were responding properly. He revved the engine one last time, checking temps and pressures.

Preflight finally complete, he put his visor screens back into their standard configuration. Blue sky filled the top half, with a ghosted HUD-like display in the middle and engine and flight data in color graphs to either side. The bottom was divided in three, with radar, flight-information, and instrument screens left to right. If he were flying two Hawks, the typical layout would feature the second plane's optical or FLIR view on the left, and a God's-eye of both planes and the mother ship in the middle.

"Let's get this show on the road, Captain," he told Bree.

"Acknowledged, Hawk Commander," she said. "Hell of a speech, Jeff. Everybody appreciated it."

"Uh-huh."

The jerk of the aircraft as it moved toward the main runway always took him by surprise; he was so absorbed by the Flighthawk's stationary view that the sensation was momentarily disorienting.

"Fly the prebriefed orbit," he told Breanna as they waited for the tower to give them final takeoff clearance.

"I wouldn't do otherwise," said his wife.

"Anything else you want to say?"

"No," replied Bree.

"I stayed in the officers' guest suite. I was too tired to come home."

"I wasn't asking," said Bree.

Zen waited silently as Boeing lifted off and began to circle across the range. Hawk One continued to idle, waiting for its mother ship to hit its first way marker before coming up.

"Point Alpha reached," said Breanna finally.

"We're good, Jeff," said Jennifer, monitoring the systems a few feet away from him. "It's your show."

"Flighthawk Control to Dream Tower, request Clearance B for Hawk One, takeoff on Lake Runway D, per filed plans," he snapped.

"Tower confirms, Hawk Control. Hawk One, you are clear for takeoff," said the controller. "Unlimited skies, we have no wind at the present time. Not a bad day for a picnic. Good aviating, Major."

"Thanks, Straw," Zen told the controller. He brought the Flighthawk to takeoff power and let off the brake. The slope graph indicating speed galloped upward as the ground flew by in Jeff's visor view. By 120 knots the Flighthawk was already starting to strain upward. Zen pulled back on the joystick and the aircraft darted into the sky, eager to fly.

How could they kill this plane? he thought. It needs less room to take off than a Piper, is harder to find than a Raptor, and can turn twists around an F/A-18.

Hawk One's speed and altitude built exponentially as the P&W powering it reached its operating norms. Zen flew to five thousand feet, steadying his speed at five hundred knots. He began banking into an orbit approximately three miles south of the mother ship, Boeing's tail appearing in the top of his screen. The techies would run through a series of signal tests here before proceeding with more difficult maneuvers.

"Data flow is good," reported Ong. "Ninety seconds more," said the engineer. Physically, he was somewhere to Zen's left, but he seemed a thousand miles away, back on the ground.

God, to be flying again, Jeff thought. To feel the g's hitting you in the face as you yanked and banked, to hear the roar of the engines as you went for the afterburners and shot straight upward, to gag on the kerosene as the smell of jet fuel somehow managed to permeate the cockpit.

Okay, some things he could do without.

"We're ready to push it," said Gleason.

"Pilot, proceed to second stage," Zen told his wife.

"Proceeding," said Breanna.

Smith was gone. Jeff hadn't said anything to her about the SOB that night—what was there to say? Who could blame her for going somewhere else?

He would have preferred anyone else in the world. But you didn't get to choose who your wife had an affair with.

"Major, we're ready. If you can bring your altitude up to ten thousand—"

"I'm on it," he told Ong, pulling back on the flight stick and nudging the throttle slide.

They were going to simulate an air launch with a roll and tumble beneath the mother ship—not the preferred, smooth method, but a necessary test to make sure the improvements to the communications system held. Jeff pushed away the extraneous thoughts, pushed his head into the cockpit, into the unlimited sky around Hawk One. He *was* flying again, and if he didn't smell the kerosene in his face or maybe feel the g's kicking against his chest, his head was there, his mind rolling with the wings as his eyes fought for some sort of reference, his sense of balance shifting and almost coming undone as the small plane inverted beneath Boeing to kick off the test pattern.

"Good, good, good," sang Jennifer. "Oh, Mama, we're good."

"Yes!" said Ong. "Solid."

"Hawk One copies," said Jeff, swinging around and heading into a trail pattern behind Boeing as briefed.

"Drop simulation was perfect," added Ong.

"I got that impression."

"You want to push it? We can try that penetration test

we put off yesterday," added the engineer. "I think our game plan was way too conservative."

"Copy. Bree?"

"I'm game, if you tell me what you want."

"Circle back and just begin again. I'll take it from there."

"Roger that," she said.

Jeff took the Flighthawk off toward the west end of the range, zooming near Groom Mountain before heading back on a high-speed intercept with the mother ship. As he came around, the search-and-scan radar bleeped out a big, fat target for him, painting Boeing as if she were an enemy bomber trying to sneak in for an attack.

Fit this sucker with some decent missiles and it would be a front-line interceptor.

"Beginning Test Phase," Jeff told the others as he closed behind the Boeing at a rate of roughly fifty miles an hour. "Ten seconds."

"Go for it," said Ong.

"Copy," said Bree.

Why was he avoiding her? It was more than Smith. Hell, Smith had nothing, or almost nothing, to do with it.

Zen pushed the Flighthawk into a dive as it flew under the tail area of the mother ship. He mashed the throttle and rolled inverted, swooping down and around in the direction of the mountains. The plane swooped through a thousand feet before he leveled off at five hundred feet, cranking at just over five hundred knots.

"Computer, ground terrain plot in left MUD," he said. Immediately a radar image appeared. Zen pushed the Flighthawk lower, running toward the mountain range.

Attack planes often flew at low altitude to avoid radar. The reflected ground clutter made it difficult to detect planes when they were close to the ground. Something as small and stealthy as the Flighthawk would be invisible.

Zen flew Hawk One into a long canyon at the far end of the test range, gradually lowering his altitude to three hundred feet above ground level. The floor of the canyon was irregular; he went through one pass with only fifty feet between the UM/F and the side of narrow ridge.

The image in the main viewfinder was breathtaking. He could see the sides of the mountains towering above him as he raced down the long corridor. He flicked his wrist right, pulling the small plane on its wing as he took a turn into a pass. The radar plot in the lower quadrant flashed with a warning of an upcoming plateau, but Zen was on it, gently pulling back and then nailing the throttle for more speed. The exercise didn't call for him to break the sound barrier, but what the hell. He felt the shudder, then eased back as the image steadied—there was no longer a line between him and the robot plane; the distance had been erased.

"Looking good," said Ong somewhere behind him.

"Mama!" yelled Jennifer.

"I'm having trouble keeping up," reported Breanna.

A complaint? A compliment?

The Flighthawk was at nearly top speed, flying at less than a hundred feet over the ground. Zen began his turn, starting to lose speed as the wings dragged through the air. The UM/F's flight surfaces adapted to minimize some of the loss, the forward canards pushing upward as he made the turn. He was down to 550 knots, pretty damn good, the plane having taken nearly nine g's. The maneuver would probably have blacked out a "real" pilot.

"We're still hot," said Ong. "Okay, Major, Captain— knock off and return to holding track. Series One, Two, and I guess we'll call Three complete. We need a few minutes to dump the data, but it looked impressive."

"Full communications gear and functions," reported Gleason.

"I had some trouble at the end," said Breanna. "You pulled out to about eight miles."

"Yeah, well, you just have to keep up," Zen told her.

"Doing my best, love," she snapped.

Zen could feel the others in the control area around him bristling. They used to banter back and forth like this all the time—but then it had been joking fun; now it seemed to stick, to wound.

"Sorry, Captain," he said. "I guess I was feeling my oats. I'm still getting the kinks out."

"No apology necessary."

He couldn't remember how they'd been. He couldn't remember the past and didn't want to—the past was poison now.

"Let's try the same test, only at twenty-five miles," suggested Ong. "You think you can work the track out, Zen?"

Twenty-five miles was twice as far as their improvements were supposed to be good for, and beyond the theoretical limit of the communications and control system. But Jeff just snapped back, "Copy," and began pushing the Flighthawk to its starting point.

This time he took the initial dive a little easier, letting his wings sweep out as he found the thicker air. Boeing swept south, widening the distance between itself and Hawk One. Zen concentrated on the virtual windshield, moving with the small plane as it sailed over the mountain slopes at five hundred knots. His altitude over ground level dipped to a bare fifty feet.

He could go lower. He nudged the stick, more brown flooding into the view screen.

He was fifteen miles from the mother ship, forty feet AGL.

Thirty-five.

He felt like he was there. The dirt-alert buzzer sounded, warning him of an upcoming ridge.

Zen leaned his body with the stick, sliding around the obstruction.

Oh baby.

"Hawk connection lost," scolded the computer suddenly.

"Hold present course. Override safety procedure. Reacquire," Zen demanded. He still had live visuals, and in fact thought he was in control.

"Out of range," said the computer. *"Safety Routine Two."*

"Shit. Bree."

"We're where you put us," she said defensively.

"Reacquire," Zen repeated. He jerked the stick, but nothing happened.

Then the view screen went blank.

Behind him, the engineers were scrambling.

"It went into fail-safe mode," said Ong. "Sorry. Once it's in Routine Two it's impossible to override. That was added."

He stopped short of saying, "After your accident."

"We did really good, though," insisted Gleason. "We were at seventeen miles before the signal began degrading."

"Once it did, it went like shit," added Ong.

"Com modules are off-line," reported Jennifer.

"Hawk One is returning to the lake bed," said Ong. He broadcast a generic "Knock it off" alert over the Dreamland frequencies, even though the skies were clear.

"Well, at least we know the fail-safe is working," said Breanna.

If Jeff hadn't known how expensive the helmet was, he probably would have thrown it through the Boeing's fuselage.

*   *   *

DANNY DIDN'T GET AROUND TO CHECKING HIS SECURE e-mail until mid-morning. Hal had gotten back to him— but not with the football prediction he'd expected.

"Danny, won't be talking to you for a while," read the message. "Having too much fun. Wish you were here."

He leaned back on the hard metal chair in his security commander's office. He wasn't sure where "here" was, but he had a pretty good guess. CNN that morning had reported that the Iranian Navy had stopped a tanker off the northern African coast. It had also reported that the President had been "in close consultation" with his security advisors and other world leaders all night.

If Danny hadn't taken the Dreamland assignment, Hal probably would have asked him to join whatever he was putting together. He'd be in the middle of things.

He might still end up there, if Whiplash was called out.

For just a second, the young captain allowed himself the luxury of fantasy. He saw—felt—himself on a big Pave Low, zooming into a firefight, bullets and missiles flying through the air. He saw himself in a Hollywood zoom, dashing into the smoke, a wide grin on his face.

It wasn't really like that. It was dirty and it was messy and you never knew exactly where the hell you were, or whether you were going to live or die.

But he loved it anyway. Or at least, loved having survived it. Nothing could beat that rush.

Danny jumped to his feet and went to attend to one of the million things that needed attending to.

WITH MACK SMITH GONE, MAJOR RICKI MENDOZA WAS the ranking officer on the F-119 test project. Colonel Bastian found her in the JSF project hangar, an underground complex directly below Hangar Three, an hour after his conference broke up.

"Colonel, glad you could come over," she said as if she

had been hoping he'd come. Her voice echoed off the polished concrete floor. "I was just about to discuss the testing schedule for the new avionics suite with Greg Desitio, the vender rep. Want to join in?"

Bastian grinned at Desitio, who'd told him earlier that the avionics suite had been delayed another six months because of "unspecifiable contingencies." Then he turned back to Mendoza. "Actually, Major, I wanted to take one of the fighters out for a spin."

"For a spin, sir?"

"You think you can arrange a test flight?"

Mendoza's cheery manner vaporized. "Well, we'd have to check for the satellite window and—"

"I looked at the satellite window already," Dog told her. "It's clear until three."

"And then the prep time involved—"

"I understand there were some landing gear issues to be gone over, and you had slotted a test flight."

"Well, yes, but we've already prepped that mission."

"You don't think I can handle it?" Dog asked.

Mendoza narrowed her eyes. With Mack's departure, her stock had skyrocketed; clearly she didn't want to be bothered by a puny lieutenant colonel.

Bastian struggled to keep his poker face.

"Of course you can handle it, sir," said Mendoza. "The JSF is a pleasure to fly. It's just that Captain Jones is already upstairs and ready to go."

"Jonesy doesn't mind," Bastian said, enjoying the sight of the air deflating from her cheeks. "I already had him brief me on the flight. He's flying chase in my F-16."

While Dog felt pretty full of himself as he hustled into his flight gear, he hadn't pulled rank just to annoy Mendoza and upset the flight-test crew. He had decided that if Dreamland's future was tied to the JSF, he should at least feel how the seat felt beneath his fanny.

It felt fairly good, actually. Stonewall One—one of the

three F-119 testers—had a newly modified ejection seat that featured a form-molded back and bottom. It wasn't possible to make the padding on an ejection seat very thick; the force of the seat as it rocketed out of the craft would bruise a pilot's butt, if not break his bones. But this was by the far the most comfortable pilot's chair Dog had ever sat in.

Unfortunately, that was about the only superlative the plane deserved. The sideseat control stick, familiar from the F-16, felt sloppy from the get-go. The plane was supposed to be optimized for short-field takeoffs, but the engines were sluggish. Even with a reduced fuel load and no payload, Dog found himself struggling to get into the air.

Airborne, things seemed even worse. The plane lumbered rather than zoomed. In a turn, the wings acted as if there were five-thousand-pound bombs strapped below them—and maybe one or two above. Worst of all, the AC wasn't working properly; Bastian kept glancing around the cockpit to double-check that he wasn't on fire.

All of these things could and would be fixed. An uprated engine was under development, though its weight and some maintenance issues made it unattractive to the Navy. The present avionics system—stolen from an F-16—would be replaced *eventually* by a cutting-edge system that would do everything but fly the mission for the pilot. And on and on.

Still, the plane itself seemed like a tugboat. Dog tried yanking and banking as he completed his first orbit around the test range at six thousand feet. The F-119 moved like a toddler with a load in his pants, waddling through maneuvers that would be essential to avoid heavy flak while egressing a target.

Not good.

It did somewhat better at fifteen thousand feet, but it took him forever to get there. Dog thought back to the complaints of the A-10A pilots during the Gulf War, when standing orders required them to take their heavily laden aircraft well above the effective range of flak as they crossed the border. Those guys hated going over five hundred feet, and they had a point—their airplanes were built like tanks and carried more explosives than the typical World War II bomber.

The JSF, on the other hand . . .

Dog sighed. The politicians were in love with the idea of a one-size-fits-all-services-and-every-mission airplane. The military had to suck it up and make do.

Did they, though? And what would those politicians say when the people who flew the F-119 were coming back in body bags?

He checked his instruments and position, then radioed in that he was ready to check the landing gear.

"WE WERE NEVER OFF THE BRIEFED COURSE," BREANNA repeated. She folded her arms and stared across the make-shift conference room. Zen continued to glare at her; she felt sure that if she turned she'd find the plasterboard wall behind her on fire.

"I didn't say you were off course," he said.

"Well, you implied it."

"I think we did fairly well," said Ong, clearly as uncomfortable as the other techies in the room debriefing the mission. "We have to go through the downloads and everything else, but we were out at seventeen miles before the connection snapped."

"I think I can tweak the com module some more," said Jennifer. "We're definitely on the right track."

The scientists continued to talk. To Breanna, it was as if they were speaking in a room down the hall. She could feel Jeff's anger; it was the only thing that mattered.

But why? The scientists were saying they'd just kicked butt on the test.

That was what they were saying, wasn't it?

So why was Jeff frowning?

He was pissed at the world because of his legs.

"We keep bumping up against the limits of the bandwidth," said Jennifer, talking to Bree with what was probably intended as a sympathetic smile. "The degradation of the secure signal is difficult to deal with in real time. If we didn't have to encode it and make it so redundant, we'd be fine."

"We are making progress," said Jeff. "The changes you made worked."

It seemed to Breanna that his manner changed as he spoke to the computer scientist. He was more like himself.

"We can make it better." The young scientist twirled her finger through one of the long strands of her light hair. Maybe she did it absentmindedly, but the way she leaned against the table at the same time irked Breanna. Her shirt was at least a size too small.

Why didn't she just yank it off and be obvious?

"What's the big deal whether it's ten miles or twenty?" said Breanna.

"Because the mother ship is a sitting duck," snapped Jeff, turning on the glare again. "A MiG or a Sukhoi at ten miles could crisp Boeing before it even knew it was there. We need to push out to fifty at least."

"You're supposed to be flying with combat planes," said Breanna.

Ong started to explain about the size of the computer equipment, but Breanna cut him off.

"Yes, I know. Right now you need a lot of space in the mother ship for the control computer and the communications equipment," she said. "What I'm suggesting is, you make the mother ship survivable."

"A JSF with a trailer," joked one of the engineers.

No one laughed.

"Megafortress," said Breanna. "Twenty miles, even ten, would be fine."

"Yeah, well, get us the flight time," said Jeff. "We've had a total of two hours with Raven in two weeks. And before I got here, there had been two drops in three months."

"I'll try."

Zen nodded. For an instant, maybe half an instant, his anger melted away. Breanna thought she saw something in his eyes, something she hadn't seen in a long time.

She might have imagined it. She knew in that second that she truly loved him, that she wanted to help him past this—past everything. She loved more than his legs. She loved his mind, his spirit, the way he laughed, the way he said everything was bullshit when it was. The way he actually listened to her—listened to anyone, no matter what he felt toward them.

Breanna felt more and more like an outsider as the debriefing session continued, the crew and engineers picking over different possibilities for improving their connection. Jeff was very businesslike, rarely joking; it seemed to her he'd become colder since the accident, and not just to her.

She followed him into the hall as the meeting broke up. "Jeff" she called as he started into the men's room.

"I got to pee. It's full," he told her. He pointed to the small pouch he carried at the side of the chair—a piddle-pack.

"Tonight?" It was all she could manage as her throat started to close.

"Yeah. No sweat. I'll be home. Sorry about last night. I was just too beat to deal with getting back. And it was late."

"Sure," she said, but by the time she got the word out of her mouth, he'd pushed into the rest room.

*   *   *

W HEN C OLONEL B ASTIAN RETURNED TO HIS OFFICE AF- ter his test flight, he found himself walking around, re- arranging things on his desk that didn't need to be rearranged. He went through Ax's two piles of papers that needed attention—left pile, immediate attention; right pile, sooner-than-immediate attention—got up from his chair, sat back down, got up again.

Dreamland had been included as a direct line item in the F-119 program. In the past few days he had received calls from several generals above him, including the three- star Air Force "liaison" for the interservice project. He'd also spoken to two admirals, three DOD budget analysts, no less than five Congressmen, and a Senator. All had congratulated him, assuring him that Dreamland's future was now set. While other facilities were trying to wrestle some of the JSF tests, it was clear that Dreamland was the best suited for the project.

Part of the reason for this, Bastian knew, was the fact that everyone figured they could keep a puny lieutenant colonel under their thumb. And while there had been hints of a promotion "in the wind," as one Congressman put it, even a full bird colonel or brigadier general would be a long way down the pecking order.

In the wind. It was a foul wind. By hitching himself and Dreamland to the JSF, he was saddling the Air Force with a turkey.

Worse, he was going against his conscience and his duty.

Was he? Was telling other people what they wanted to hear such a sin?

The JSF wasn't *that* bad a design. Hell, the people here knew how to fix it. They could too—though the necessary changes would turn it into two or three different planes, with less than forty percent interchangeable parts. Each plane would be excellent, well suited for its job. The only drawback would be the expense.

No, the only drawback would be the fact that DOD and the Joint Chiefs and Congress and the President wanted a Joint Services airplane, one size fits all.

How many men would die because of that?

None—there'd be excellent CAP and AWACS and the SAMs would be suppressed, and everything would snap together clean and to spec every day. What could go wrong?

"Hey, Colonel, why are you messing up my system?" asked Ax, standing in the doorway. "You're making one pile out of two."

"Jeez, Ax, did you knock?"

"Sir, yes, sir," snapped the sergeant, momentarily coming to full drill-master attention.

"Come on in, Sergeant Ballbuster," said Bastian. "What the hell are you up to?"

"Just looking after my papers, Colonel," said Ax, fishing the signed documents from Bastian's desk. "How was your flight?"

"Uneventful, thanks," said Dog. "Who's my next appointment?"

"Nothing on your agenda rest of the day." Gibbs smiled. "I believe there was some sort of scheduling snafu that indicated your test flight was continuing until tomorrow and that you couldn't be disturbed."

"You're a piece of work, Ax."

"Thank you, sir." The sergeant smiled again. "I do actually have a question for you."

"Shoot."

"Well, I've been thinking. I have this friend who has this problem. He's an executor for a trust. All the people connected with the trust, they want him to buy some stock. He thinks the stock is lousy, but he knows that if he doesn't buy it, they'll can his sorry ass and hire someone who will. He kinda needs the job, and he figures if they fire him he'll be bagging groceries. On the other hand, he likes to look himself in the mirror every morning when he's shaving."

Bastian shook his head. "Thanks, Ax."

Gibbs's face was the very model of innocence. "Sir?"

"Tell your friend to do what he thinks is right, and damn what everyone else wants," said Bastian, getting up. "I'll check in with you later."

"Thank you, sir," snapped the sergeant as Bastian snuck out the side door.

BREANNA HAD TIMED IT ALL OUT WITH THE PRECISION of a deep-strike mission against a well-fortified enemy city. The five-disc CD player had been armed with Earl Klugh and Keiko Matsui—jazz artists admittedly more to her taste than his, but definitely capable of establishing a preemptive romantic mood. Two long tapers of pure bees-wax sat in candleholders in the middle of the freshly polished dinette table, ready to cast their flickering soft light over the borrowed china place settings with their elegant flower patterns. A bottle of Clos Du Bois merlot sat nearby, with a six-pack of Anchor Steam Beer on standby in the refrigerator. Two salad plates—with fancy baby lettuce and fresh tomatoes from a helpful neighbor's garden—were lined up for the initial assault. A light carrot soup would follow, with waves of seafood crepes and lamb chops to administer the coup de grâce. The lamb was running a little behind, but otherwise everything was perfect, including the long, silky dress Breanna hadn't worn in more than a year. She glanced at herself in the hall mirror, bending and twisting to make sure she'd gotten rid of the flour that had spilled on the side. The dress was very loose now on the top and in the back; she'd lost a bit of weight since Zen's accident, but figured that was better than the opposite.

So where was he? He had boarded the Dolphin helicopter shuttle from Dreamland for Nellis precisely an hour and a half before; she had promised dibs on the leftovers to the pilot so he'd call with the heads-up. At Nellis, Jeff would have boarded the public bus—it was a "kneeler," dipping down to ground level to allow wheelchairs to access an onboard elevator—and ought to have arrived at the end of their condo development's cul-de-sac ten minutes ago.

If he blows me off tonight, I'll kill him, Breanna thought to herself.

And just on cue, she heard his key in the door.

She jumped into action, lighting the candles with the small Bic lighter, hitting the stereo, killing the lights, relighting the burner under the asparagus. Rap made it out to the foyer just as Jeff closed the door behind him.

"Hey," she said.

"Hey," he said. "What's going on?"

"I thought you'd like some dinner," she said, reaching toward him. He held his briefcase out in front of him; she took it from him and then leaned forward and gave him a peck on the cheek.

"Hungry?" she asked.

"Well, kinda."

"Come on," Breanna said, backing away. "Dinner is served."

"I guess I can't suggest we send out for pizza," said Jeff.

"Not if you want to live."

He rolled forward to the table in the seating area between the kitchen and living room. Breanna rushed to unfurl his napkin, placing it gently on his lap. She let her cheek brush against his as she did.

In her fantasy about how this would go, Jeff turned his

mouth toward hers and they began a long and passionate kiss, interrupted only by the buzzer announcing that dinner was ready.

In reality, the buzzer rang as soon as their cheeks met. She pecked his cheek, cursed to herself, and went and got the soup.

"Wow," said Jeff.

"We had this at the first restaurant you took me to. Remember?"

"The first restaurant I took you to was Cafeteria Four at Dreamland."

"Restaurant," she said, sitting down. "Cafe Auberge."

"Oui, oui," he said.

"Oh, God, wine. You want wine? I have merlot. Or beer—I found a six-pack of Anchor Steam."

"Either's fine."

"Why don't we start with wine?" she suggested. "It will go with the main course."

"There's a main course?"

"Dahling, *I* am the main course." She fluttered her eyes, laughing as she retreated to the kitchen.

DOG WROTE OUT THE DRAFT OF HIS FORMAL REPORT on a lined yellow pad as he sat at a back table in Cafeteria Four. He made a few false starts, pausing to listen as a pair of engine technicians debated whether the meat loaf or open-faced turkey was better. He considered walking over to say hello, but their embarrassed waves somehow reminded him that he was just avoiding the work at hand. He nodded, then began writing in earnest, his Papermate disposable pencil squeaking over the paper.

"Despite the great weight of politics and certain outrage that I'm sure will meet this report, I cannot in good conscience recommend that the F-119 project as currently constituted proceed," he wrote. "I have carefully reviewed the data on the project, and have personally flown the aircraft."

He paused, wondering if that might not sound a little conceited. Before he could decide, Danny Freah's deep voice bellowed behind him.

"Letter home, sir?"

Bastian looked over his shoulder to find Freah grinning. "Not exactly," he said.

"Probably not a classified document," said the base's security officer, pulling up a chair.

"Probably is," said Bastian. "But I figure you'll bounce anyone who gets close enough to steal it."

Freah laughed. "I'm raring for a fight."

"How are things doing?"

"Security checks have come back clean. Hal left things in good shape."

"I imagine he would," said Dog.

"He's up to his ears about now," added Freah.

"In what sense?"

"I was watching CNN a while ago. The Iranians sound like they're going to make a play to cut off shipping in the Gulf. Increase the price of oil."

"Another attempt at wrecking my budget," said Dog. He jostled his pen back and forth. "You miss the action end, Danny?"

"This is a big job, Colonel. I'm grateful for the assignment."

"That wasn't my question."

"I didn't realize it was a question."

"I guess not," said Bastian. "In a way, I guess I miss the action too. Not losing kids, though."

"No, sir," said Freah, suddenly serious. "That part sucks."

"Yeah."

"Well, as long as everything's secure," said Freah, standing up.

"Looks like it."

Dog watched Danny go to the cafeteria line. He emerged with an orange juice carton, then disappeared out the side door.

Losing kids sucked. If his concept of Dreamland were ever implemented—if it truly became a cutting-edge unit assigned to covert and non-covert actions where high-tech could leverage a favorable result—he'd be sending plenty of kids into harm's way.

Including his daughter.

Bastian put his pencil back to the pad. He reviewed what he'd written, letting the sentence about his flying the plane stand. Then he added, "I have appended some of the relevant reports. Because of the political nature of this project, I have taken the precaution of removing the names of the authors. This recommendation is my responsibility and my responsibility only."

Would that save them, though? It wouldn't exactly be difficult to figure out who had done what.

"You look like you're trying to untie the Gordian knot."

Surprised, Dog looked up to find Jennifer Gleason, the young computer scientist who worked primarily on the Flighthawk project, smiling down at him.

"The Gordian knot?" he asked. "You know, I've always wondered what that was."

"The Gordian knot was a complicated knot tied by King Gordius of Phrygia," said Gleason. "Supposedly, anyway. The oracles claimed that whoever could undo it would rule Asia. So along comes Alexander the Great. He hears about it, goes over to it, and without wasting a blink of his eye, slices it with his sword."

Bastian laughed.

"Probably not a true story," said Gleason. She flicked her head back so her long reddish-blond hair glistened at her shoulders. "But it has a certain charm."

"Especially if you're trying to work out a budget," said Bastian.

"I'm sorry, I didn't mean to interrupt."

"No, I need interruption," he told her, flipping the top page back over his pad so the writing couldn't be read. "Sit down."

She slid in across from him and took the top off her yogurt container.

"Dinner?" he asked.

"More like a late lunch."

"No wonder you're so skinny."

"I hope that was meant in a professional way."

"Touché, Doc."

"Most people call me Jennifer or Jen, Colonel." Gleason smiled and then spooned some of the vanilla-flavored yogurt into her mouth. "I always thought doctors were the people who were sticking stethoscopes in your face and thermometers in your chest."

"I think that goes the other way around."

She smirked. Dog searched for something else to say, but all he could think of was the Flighthawk project—not a good topic, since he'd already decided to recommend cutting it. And in fact he half-expected she'd sat down to make a pitch for keeping it.

"You run every morning?" she asked.

"I do actually."

"I saw you this morning. I was going to ask if I could join you, but I chickened out."

"I don't bite," said Bastian.

"I was a little worried about your pace. I only run to keep in shape for climbing. I rock-climb on weekends," she added.

"You rock-climb nearby?"

"There are some great climbs in the mountains at the end of F Range," she said.

"I always wanted to try it."

The words slipped from his mouth before he could stop them, but she didn't laugh.

"It's easy. I'll show you sometime. As long as you don't mind taking orders from a civilian."

"I don't think I'd mind at all."

"Good."

"You can run with me anytime you want," he said.

"I'll see you in the morning then," said Jennifer, finishing her yogurt.

He watched her walk away, then went back to work.

JEFF HADN'T EATEN LIKE THIS IN YEARS, NOT EVEN IN A restaurant. Breanna had knocked herself out for him, and he appreciated it.

But it only made him more determined.

The truth was, he'd come to this conclusion months ago. Seeing her with Smith just brought him back to his senses.

So why didn't he feel calm about it?

Dessert was the only course she hadn't cooked herself, homemade cannolis from the only Italian bakery within five hundred miles. As Jeff finished his, he leaned back in the chair and watched her sip her wine.

"You're beautiful, Bree. Really, truly, beautiful," he told her.

"Nice of you to notice," she said. The line had once been a joke between them, usually applied to something like doing the dishes or vacuuming without being asked. Now it sounded off-key, almost sorrowful. "You want some more wine?"

He shook his head. "Maybe that beer."

"Fine."

A twinge ran through him. He didn't really want the beer. He was stalling. Damn, he'd become good at that, hadn't he?

Still, he waited until she came back, the beer in a frosted pilsner glass.

"You thought of everything," he told her.

Stall, stall, stall.

Just go for it.

Bree seemed to sense what was coming. "Jeff, I want us to work," she said, her voice beginning to tremble. "I know it's been hard. I know it's going to be tough—"

Something deep inside him took over, a calm forcefulness that pushed him to take care of things as he knew they had to be taken care of. Jeff held his finger up to her lips. "Bree—"

"D-don't—" she stuttered.

"I saw you the other night with Mack Smith."

"You saw me where?" She straightened, suddenly stiff.

"I saw him come out of your suite at Dreamland. Our suite."

"No—"

"It's okay, Bree. It really has nothing to do with anything."

"But—"

"Look, I've been thinking about this a lot. I decided a long time ago—six months maybe. You don't need me, Rap. I'm going to hold you back."

"That's bullshit. It's all bullshit," she said. Her face was flushed; she practically spat as she spoke.

Wine or blood?

"No, listen to me," he said calmly. "It's not your fault. I understand. Totally. This wasn't part of the deal."

His hands started to tremble. He reached to put the glass of beer on the table in front of him; it slipped halfway, falling to the floor.

"Oh, Jeff, no," she said, throwing her arms around him.

"I want a divorce," he told her. "For your sake. For mine too. It'll help us move on."

"No, Jeff, no." Breanna buried her head in his lap, sob-bing. He bent over, fingers running through her hair, his eyes blurry with the leaping flame of the candles on the table.

Ethiopia
22 October, 0350

SERGEANT MELFI SETTLED INTO THE CANVAS SEAT AS the Chinook jerked into the sky. The large engines on the big-hulled Boeing helicopter had a distinctive whomp that seemed to push the twenty Marines down between the tubular supports of their seats. Gunny scanned the row of men toward the front of the chopper. The dim red interior lights added more shadows to the darkened camo faces, making the unit look like a collection of ghosts riding in the night.

If the operation went smoothly, it would seem as if ghosts had carried it out. Within two hours, the Iranians would lose most of their ability to launch a preemptive strike against Gulf shipping.

Assuming everything went off as planned. The intelligence bothered Gunny; they'd been given satellite information that was several hours old. That might be okay for the big stuff—blowing up another Silkworm missile battery wasn't a big deal. But the Iranians could easily have airdropped some light armor, or added more machine guns near the bluffs overlooking the Silkworm battery.

Too late to worry about it now.

"Zero-five to LZ," barked the helicopter crew chief.

"Hang tough, girls," said Gunny, cinching his helmet strap. "We do this dance the way we rehearsed it."

KNIFE NOTED THE WAY MARKER AND DID A QUICK SCAN of his instruments. He had the volume on his radar-warning receiver near max; his air-to-air radar was set at wide scan. The sky was clear ahead, the sea and coastline peaceful.

Not for long, he thought. The helo was cutting a course bare inches from the scrub trees and jagged hilltops twenty miles to the west. Further along the coast, a flight of F-117's was cutting over the Gulf of Aden, aiming for another secret Iranian base on the Somalian coast. All hell was about to break loose.

"Poison Flight, time to twist," said Smith to his F-16 wingmen.

"Three."

"Four."

The two F-16's peeled off, their exhaust nozzles swelling red in the dark sky as they accelerated northward. Knife pushed his nose down, beginning a glide toward their target area. His wingman fell in behind him.

The Chinook would broadcast a signal when it was ten seconds from the LZ. Anything before that was trouble. Smith made sure his radio was set, then quickly checked his GPS page, double-checking to make sure his navigational gear was functioning properly. The INS would conjure a diamond in his HUD to show the target area when he rolled in; he wanted to make sure it would be accurate if he had to roll in with the dumb bombs in a hurry.

His heart beat like a snare drum. He was swimming in sweat. He jerked his head back and forth, practically screwing it out of its socket, checking for other fighters, for missiles that had somehow managed to defy or trick his gear.

Wasn't going to happen. But knowing that didn't relax him, and certainly didn't stop the sweat or the drumbeat.

He'd felt this way in the Gulf, though not on his first mission. His first mission—the first three or four, really— had been tremendous blurs. He was so consumed with the minutiae, the tankings, the radio calls, simply checking six, that he hadn't had a chance to get nervous.

Mack had also lost about ten pounds in three days, so obviously he'd been sweating a little.

His first kill came on the first patrol he flew, a fluke.

Not a fluke. A product of a zillion hours of training. It was a push-button, beyond-visual-range kill with a Sparrow radar missile. He'd ID'd, locked, and launched in the space of maybe three seconds.

Skill. That was definitely how he nailed splash two—though the F-15's tape had screwed up, depriving him of credit.

He wasn't getting a shoot-down tonight. The Somalians didn't have an air force and the nearest Iranians were well over two hundred miles away. And besides, he was driving an F-16 configured for ground-pounding.

"Bad Boys to Poison Leader, we are one-zero, repeat, one-zero. All calm."

Before Smith could acknowledge, his RWR began bleating and an icon appeared in the middle of his receiver scope. An instant later, his wing mate yelled a warning over the short-range radio circuit.

"SA-2 battery up! And two more. Shit. There's four batteries there, not two. Sixes! SA-6's! Shit-fuck! Where did those bastards come from?"

GUNNY HAD RUN TWENTY FEET FROM THE REAR DOOR of the Chinook when the flare ignited overhead. He began cursing, immediately understanding what had happened.

"Team One, Team One!" he shouted, pushing his old legs hard as he ran forward. "Listen up! The defenses are on the south end of the field. They moved everything beyond the ditches. Come on, come on—everybody move it! Let's go!"

As he ran forward, Melfi caught sight of the first muzzle flash from the enemy lines: a streak of red that flared oblong in the black smear. The ground shook, but the explosion was at least a half mile away from the LZ. The Somalians had zeroed their weapons in on the highway, obviously expecting the attack would be there. They had fired the flare as well.

"They don't know where we are!" shouted Gunny to his men. "Come on, come on, they can't see us. Let's go. We got about ten seconds to get across their ditch. Mine team! Mines! Come the fuck on! Blow the field so we can advance. *Come on!*"

The different elements of his assault team began fanning out, remembering the instructions for this contingency. They were sluggish, weighed down by their equipment and hampered by the dark.

Or maybe it just seemed to Gunny like they were moving in slow motion. The two buildings where they'd expected resistance lay twenty feet ahead, across a large ditch lined with antitank obstacles. The buildings were quiet.

Which didn't mean they were empty, of course.

The missile launchers had apparently been moved closer to the water, nearly four hundred yards further south of the spot briefed. Small-arms fire was coming from that direction. The finicky light from the Somalian flare showed pointed shadows around the slight rise there, but they were too far away to see anything, let alone attack it.

There was a thud, then a series of thuds.

Nothing.

No mines.

"Let's go, let's go," shouted Gunny. "They moved everything to Purple site."

"Incoming!" yelled someone ahead. "Tank!"

Gunny threw himself to the ground. A large-caliber shell, possibly from an M47, splashed through the trees at the right. The sergeant pushed himself back to his knees, and for the first time realized all hell was breaking loose at the north end of the site, where Captain Gordon and his team had gone.

"Get the SPG on that tank," yelled Gunny. "Com! Com!" he added, calling for the radio specialist. "Where the hell are the F-16's?"

As if to answer, a tongue of fire lit from behind the Somalian lines and two huge fists leaped from the earth.

"TWO LAUNCHES, ELEVEN O'CLOCK!" SHOUTED SMITH AS he saw the missiles flare off their launchers. His RWR skipped out warning bleats as he jinked hard and kicked out tinsel, metal chaff designed to fool the radar of the acquiring missile.

In some respects, the Somalians had done them a favor by turning on their radars and firing the missiles. Powering up his HARM missiles, the pilot of Poison Two calmly dotted the offending radar van on his threat scope and released the antiradar missiles. With the targeting information downloaded into their miniature onboard computers, the radiation-seeking missiles were in can't-miss mode—even if the radars were to turn themselves off, the missiles would fly directly to the target points and obliterate the gear.

But that didn't account for the surface-to-air missiles that had been fired, or pure bad luck. The SA-2's were equipped with terminal guidance devices that allowed them to home in on an enemy even if their ground units were wiped out. Worse, as far as Knife was concerned, were the SA-6's—nasty medium-range missiles that weren't supposed to be here, but were now sending his warning gear into a high-pitched shriek.

And the SA-3. Not to mention triple-A, which erupted with a red cloud to the northeast.

Knife's head swirled in a tempest of colors and sweat. The warning receiver was still bleating. He pulled the

Fighting Falcon over, yanking the F-16 nearly backward in the air, altitude dropping abruptly as he fired off more chaff.

Pulling back on the sidestick at fifteen thousand feet, he found the target area in his windshield. Someone had even fired a flare to show him where everything was.

Thoughtful.

Knife forgot about the SAMs and the antiair and the RWR as he saw the muzzle flash of an ancient M47 tank foam red about three o'clock in his screen. The tank was his primary target if the ground team ran into trouble.

Which obviously it had.

"Poison One, targeting tank," he said. His pipper slid over the dark shadow of the turret before he realized he hadn't had any communication from the ground team at all since the helo had called with their time-to-landing.

It was too late to worry about that now. Red fingers jabbed out toward his eyes; he ignored the flak and pushed the trigger on his stick, pickling two five-hundred-pound bombs into the tank. As he started to pull out he saw another ground missile launch; he nudged his stick to the right and called the launch, at the same time riding forward to dump iron on the launcher. If Poison Two acknowledged, its broadcast was lost in the blur of gravity and the roar of his F-16A's GE F-110 turbofan as he pickled, then jerked hard to get away from the new missiles.

THEY HAD JUST TARGETED THE TANK WHEN A LOUD whistle sounded above them. Before Gunny could shield his eyes, the night flashed white. The tank erupted in a two-fisted swirl of fire, dirt, and metal sailing in every direction.

"About fucking time," growled Melfi, picking himself up. "Forward, forward! Tank's history. Go, girls!"

One of his men began screaming on his right. Gunny ran up and found Lance Corporal Gaston curled over a large splash of tangled uniform, half his side blown open by bomb fragments. The medic reached him in the next second; Gunny saw him wince and realized Gaston wasn't going to make it. He straightened, saw that half the kid's arm was lying on the ground.

"Get those fucking ship missiles," Melfi yelled, pulling his M-16 to his side. He ignored the complaint from his knee and began to run toward the heaviest gunfire.

SMITH WHIPPED BACK TOWARD THE TARGET AREA, FInally satisfied that he had ducked the SAMs. A wall of tracers illuminated the coastline, thrown up by four or five Russian-built ZSU-23 antiaircraft guns. It occurred to him that he was only seeing a fourth or a fifth of the actual bullets being fired, since only the tracers showed in the dark. A shitload of lead was being propelled into the sky.

Fired blindly, but dangerous nonetheless. Knife clicked his radio, asking Poison Two for his position.

No answer.

"Two, this is Poison Leader, posit?"

Nothing.

"Two? Give me your position. Two? Posit?"

"Poison Two blind," his wingman finally replied. "Two-one-one for one-three off egress."

Smith blew a long sigh into his mask before plotting his wingman's position with the bearings he'd broadcast. He thought he'd gone down.

"All right, you're five, six miles south of me, due south," Knife told him.

"Poison One, copy. I have you on radar. I'm Angels twenty-five. Out of arrows, Knife. I took some flak but I'm okay. Engine's fine. Controls responding."

"You're hit?"

"Roger. Fuel's fine. Nothing bad, but I can see burn marks on the wing and I felt it."

Knife glanced at his own fuel gauge, calculating that he had enough for perhaps five more minutes' worth of action before hitting bingo, the theoretical turnaround point. He was still carrying four GBUs under his wings.

They were intended for the Silkworms. But the ground team still hadn't checked in, which meant that they weren't in position to illuminate the targets with their laser designators.

He'd have to do it himself. No big deal, as long as he could find the targets beyond the wall of flak.

Assuming his wingman was okay.

"Two, if you can hold an orbit, I'm going to mop up."

"Copy. Go for it, Knife. I'm fine."

Smith tried hailing the ground team as he plotted a course toward the Silkworms. He climbed to just over twenty thousand feet, well out of reach of the flak. But the air seemed to percolate with it, his Viper shuddering as he came up on the dirt landing strip that marked the western end of the target zone.

The radio static cleared as he eyeballed the master arm panel.

"Poison One, we are sparking the target. Repeat, sparking your target."

About fucking time, he thought, acknowledging and leaning slightly on his right wing. He was ten miles from the site. Eyes pasted on the video screen, he hunted for his target. There were vague blurs, but no cues, no nothing. The LANTIRN targeting gear was having a hell of a time sorting through the battlefield smoke. In the meantime, the cloud of flak had moved in his direction.

"Poison One, have you acquired?"

"Negative," he groused. "Just make sure you got it on."

"We're taking fire."

Yeah, no shit. Join the party.

He was less than five miles from the target and running over a minefield of antiaircraft fire before the target finally crystallized in his monitor. The sparkle had a big, fat Chinese-made SS-N-2 missile dead on; he goosed off one GBU, then released another, just to be sure.

"Find me another target," he barked.

The magic flashlight moved to a new target. As he was about to launch he realized he was about to overfly his target. He pickled anyway, got messed up, confused, lost himself for a second pulling around to retarget. His RWR screamed a fresh warning and for a half second Mack Smith fell completely apart, lost his concentration and the plane, fell behind himself in a whirl of gravity-fed vertigo, the F-16 responding to his sharp jerk on its fly-by-wire stick.

Jesus, he thought. Oh, God, I'm screwed.

THE ANTISHIP MISSILE SITE ERUPTED WITH A CASCADE of secondary explosions, each bigger than the last, as if a series of larger and larger gas cans had been ignited with a pack of firecrackers.

"That's it, let's go, let's go!" Gunny shouted. The explosions were so intense he could feel their heat on his face, and he was nearly a half mile away.

"The pilot wants more targets!" shouted the com specialist.

"Tell him he's blown everything to hell," shouted Gunny, grabbing the man with the target designator and yanking him backward. "We're going while the going is good! Come on, girls! Come the *fuck* on!"

His men finally snapped to behind him as he trotted back toward the LZ. The explosions at the missile-launching pad had shocked the defenders silent, but Gunny knew that wasn't going to last. He fanned his arms through the air, urging his men back toward the waiting Chinook.

He found himself standing at the spot where Gaston had been hit.

He glanced down, looking for the remains of the poor kid's lost arm, thinking to give it a decent burial.

Wasn't there.

A fresh explosion snapped him back to life. He whirled around, saw his point man trotting toward him, a grin on his face. Jerry Jackson was first in and last out.

"Hey, Sarge."

"Jackson, knock that fucking watermelon grin off your face and get moving," Gunny yelled.

"Gee, sweetheart, I didn't know you cared," mocked the corporal as he caught up.

"We got everybody?"

"Didn't see no one," said Jackson. "Better check around for Gaston, though. You know how he likes to jerk off in the bushes."

"Yeah," was all Gunny could manage.

KNIFE'S STOMACH PITCHED TOWARD HIS MOUTH. HE clamped his teeth shut, holding steady on the control stick as the dark, oxygen-deprived cowl slipped back from over his face. The F-16 could withstand more than nine g's, at least one more than its pilot under the best of circumstances, and this was hardly the best. The plane was pointing nearly straight down, shrapnel streaking all around, an SA-3 somewhere in the air, hunting for his belly. He could escape it—he'd been in more difficult spots—but only if he could keep his head clear. And right now that seemed damn impossible.

Gravity clamped its thick fingers around his temples. Squeezing with all its might, it began to mash his skull into powder. The wind ran from his chest, and a long, jagged sword began ripping up his stomach.

An image shot into his head—Zen Stockard, his body being propelled from the F-15 cockpit, hurled sideways in a tumble.

Poor bastard.

Just not good enough. Not as good as me.

I am not getting fried here.

Smith regained control of himself as well as the plane, rolling through an invert and now tracking to the north, the RWR still bleating. Even so, he began hunting for a target. Everything was on fire below, everything; he couldn't find anything to hit.

Knife jinked and saw a large shape passing through the air maybe four hundred yards away. It was the missile the Somalians had fired, but to Knife it seemed like the demon that had tormented him all through the attack, the panic that had tried to sneak up on him, panic and rust and doubt.

"No fucking way," he screamed. He pulled himself up in the slant-back seat, straining against the restraints. The enemy missile shot clear, unguided, lost, no longer a threat.

The ground team's Chinook was two miles away and taking fire; there were armored cars approaching from behind the buildings. He took a quick breath, switching the mode on the LANTIRN bomb-guidance system to allow him to designate the target himself. The targeting cue instantly zeroed in on the lead vehicle.

"Good night, motherfucker," he said, loosing the GBU from his wing.

GUNNY AND JACKSON WERE TWO HUNDRED YARDS from the helicopter when the ground began percolating with heavy machine-gun fire. The two Marines dove into a ditch, where they found themselves pinned down with half a dozen other Marines. They could hear but not see the helicopter beyond a row of low trees or bushes. An armored car or personnel carrier, maybe two, rounded out from behind the near building and began firing.

"We have to move!" yelled Gunny. "Move!"

"Move!" echoed Jackson, trying to urge the others to stop returning fire and retreat to the Chinook. "We'll cover you."

The far end of the ditch burst with an explosion. Gunny cursed, falling forward and hitting his chin on Jackson's boot.

"Damn it," he said, starting to pull himself up.

"Down! Down! Incoming!" yelled Jackson.

Something roared above them and the armored car hissed. Red metal flew through the air.

"The Chinook's moving!" yelped Jackson.

"Go! Go!" yelled Gunny. Above them one of the F-16's was wheeling through the sky, trying to cover their retreat. The Somalians had temporarily turned their attention to it, throwing everything they had into the sky.

"You got balls," Gunny told the F-16 as he burned a clip in the direction of the Somies. "Even if you are a pansy-ass Air Force pilot."

KNIFE WAS OUT OF GBUs AND ABOUT HALFWAY through his store of cannon shells, slashing and dashing the Somalian forces as the Chinook tried desperately to round up the last members of its fire team. The helicopter pilot's aircraft had been hit and he was worried about making it back to Ethiopia, but the man didn't want to leave without every one of his passengers aboard.

Somewhere in the past two and a half minutes, Knife had told the pilot that he'd hang in there as long as needed. Somewhere in the past two and a half minutes, Mack had decided he had to stay close and help keep some of his guys alive. And somewhere in the past two and a half minutes, Major Mack "Knife" Smith had realized that he was flying maybe twenty feet over the trees and taking a hell of a lot of risk with all this metal flying through the air, not to mention the damn fireworks from the still-exploding missile stores.

Flames from the two vehicles he had smashed gave him a clear view of the remaining troops firing on his Marines. Smith swooped in for a low-level cannon attack. The Chinook stuttered to his left as he rode in, the barrels on his M61 beginning to churn. He cut a swath through the Somalians, then picked up his nose to bank around for another pass. As he did, he saw a pair of wheeled vehicles moving forward behind the far building. He couldn't be sure, but he thought he saw an H-shaped shadow at the top of one of the vehicles—a missile launcher maybe, but he was beyond it too fast. His RWR stayed clean.

"Poison One, this is Poison Three, we are moving to engage four bogies at this time," snapped the lead pilot of the second group of F-16's. "Repeat, we have company. MiGs. Possibly Libyan. They're coming south and they are hot!"

"Copy," said Knife. It was past time to call it a day. "Pelican, get the hell out of there," he told the Chinook pilot. "Go! Now! Go!"

He banked around to cover the helicopter's retreat. He hunted the shadows for the two vehicles he'd seen, his forward airspeed dropping toward two hundred knots. He saw something loom on his left; by the time he got his nose on it a tongue of fire ignited from the top.

Missile launcher. Probably an antitank weapon or something similar, but he felt sucker-punched as the missile sailed toward the helicopter. He began to fire his cannon, even though he wasn't lined up right; he pushed his rudder to swing into the shot, but was too high and then too far to the right. He thought he heard a stall warning and went for throttle; rocketing upward, he realized he was low on gas.

The helo was still hovering. The missile had missed.

His RWR bleeped. The MiGs were on them already. Shit.

"Pelican! Get the fuck out of here!" he screamed.

He plunged his aircraft back toward the remaining vehicle, again firing before he had a definitive target. Meanwhile, Poison Three called a missile launch; things were getting beyond hot and heavy.

Knife reached to put the throttle to the redline, already plotting his escape southwest toward Poison Two.

Something thudded directly behind his seat. He felt the Viper's tail jerk upward, and in the next instant realized the control stick had stopped responding.

"I'm hit," he snapped. And in the next instant he pulled the eject handles, just before the plane tore into a spin, its back broken by not one but two shoulder-fired SA-16's.

GUNNY AND JACKSON WERE STILL FIFTEEN YARDS FROM the Chinook when it started to pull upward. But the old sergeant had been prepared for this—he'd removed the flare pistol from his vest pocket to signal them.

Before he could fire, something exploded above him. He jerked his head back and saw the plane that had been covering their escape erupt in a fireball. Something shot into the air; a second or two later he realized it was the pilot.

Gunny turned around.

"Gunny, Sarge, shit. Helo's this way," said Jackson, grabbing his arm. "Come on."

"We got to go get that pilot," Gunny said.

"Fuck that."

"Here," Gunny said, pressing the flare gun into his point man's hand. "I'll catch up."

"The hell you will," said Jackson. The corporal tugged the older man around.

"I'm giving you an order to get the hell out of here," said Gunny.

"If you're stayin', I'm stayin'. I got point," said the Marine, pushing past in the direction of the parachute blossoming in the firelit sky. It was falling over the low hill to his right, away from the Gulf of Aden.

It was probably a moot point by now, since the Chinook was thundering off in the distance. Still, Gunny appreciated the sentiment.

"I hope to hell that pansy-ass pilot's got a radio," he grunted, following up the hillside.

IV
Whiplash

COLONEL BASTIAN WALKED THE TWO MILES FROM HIS office to the base commander's "hut," the wind chilling his face. He'd shipped the summary of his report via the secure e-mail link and packed off the full package, committing himself before he could change his mind. You were supposed to feel good when you followed your conscience, but he felt as if he'd just stabbed a friend.

A lot of friends. Not to mention himself.

Dog paused near the entrance to the low-slung adobe structure that was his temporary home at Dreamland. The guard assigned to his premises had taken shelter in a blue government Lumina parked a few yards away; Dog nodded in his direction, then turned his eyes toward the old boneyard that began twenty or thirty yards away. Surplused aircraft and failed experiments sulked in the darkness, watching him with steely eyes. Among the planes were craft once considered the nation's finest—a B-58 Hustler, some ancient B-50 Superfortress upgrades, three or four F-86 Sabres. They were indistinguishable in the shadows, tarped and in various stages of disrepair. But Dog felt their presence like living things, animals driven to cover.

Time moves on, he thought to himself.

He waited for something more profound before finally

shaking his head, realizing he was freezing out here. The desert turned cold once the sun was gone. He trotted toward his front door, deciding to throw himself into bed and rest up for the inevitable storm tomorrow.

The phone was ringing inside as he opened the fiberglass faux-wood door. He picked up the handset, bracing himself for an angry blast from one of the many generals and government officials connected with the F-119 project.

But the caller was his own Sergeant Gibbs.

"Colonel, we need you back at the office," said Ax.

"What's going on?"

"You need to make a secure call back to D.C.," said the sergeant. "Whiplash has been activated."

"Does Danny know?"

"Captain Freah is on his way here," said the sergeant. "He had to round up his men."

"Send a car."

"It should be there in about ten seconds," said Ax.

Dog put down the phone. While in theory the team could be headed anywhere, even a training mission, Dog realized it must mean things had popped in Somalia. More than likely, that was why Washington wanted to talk to him.

Better that than the JSF.

He took a moment to pull on his old leather flight jacket, then went back outside, where a Humvee was waiting for him.

Danny Freah was at the wheel.

"Whiplash has been activated," said Freah as Dog pulled himself into the seat.

"Ax just told me. You have transport?"

"I was hoping you could expedite something. They want us in Africa yesterday. There's a C-5 en route from back East."

"A C-5?"

Freah smiled and shrugged. His team consisted of only

six men; they carried their forty pounds of equipment on their backs. The big Lockheed transport planes could move the better part of a company.

Freah quickly lost his smile. "Word is, two of our pilots went down in Somalia. And two or three Marines stayed back to help them. One of the pilots was Major Smith."

"Shit."

"A rescue operation is being planned."

"That C-5 will take eighteen hours to get you there."

"At least," said Danny.

Bastian folded his arms across his chest. ISA and Madcap Magician would have its own units nearby, but obviously they were anticipating serious trouble.

"Maybe we can wedge your boys into the backseats of our SR-71s," he joked.

"We only have one on the base," said Freah, who didn't seem to be joking. He pulled the Humvee in front of the Taj. "What about a Megafortress?"

"An EB-52?"

"Major Cheshire says Fort Two could make the run in less than twelve hours."

"Fort Two is a test bed. They nearly crashed a week ago."

"I know that," said Freah. "I also know the Somalians have this thing about dragging soldiers through the streets after they kill them."

Dog got out of the truck and walked into the building, barely pausing for the security scan. Danny caught up in the elevator; neither said anything as the car began its slow descent.

Africa was a damn long way to go in a plane that typically never left the protected airspace over Dreamland.

On the other hand, there was at least a rough precedent. Another EB-52 had been used in Central America during the Maraklov/James fiasco some months before. The plane had acquitted itself quite well.

But it had also been flying with a full crew.

Fort Two was more than a transport. If he was going to send it halfway around the world, he should send it with a full weapons load. It'd be invaluable.

Hell, it'd be the star of the show. Demonstrate what Dreamland could do.

That wasn't what this was about. They had to get Smith and the others out.

"Ax, get Major Cheshire over here right away," he said as he stormed into his office.

"She called a few minutes ago to say she's on her way," said the sergeant. "ETA in zero-five. Your burger should be here by then as well," added Ax. "Fries too. Got one for Captain Freah as well. Coffee's on the boil."

Northern Somalia
22 October, 0525 local

MACK SWAM MINDLESSLY, EYES CLOSED, BODY BUF-feted by the waves. A fish or something had attached itself to his chest, clamping powerful jaws around his ribs. He gasped for air, then realized he wasn't swimming at all—he was hanging by his parachute harness. Every part of his body ached, but his ribs hurt most of all; he guessed some were broken.

He'd lost his helmet somewhere. Undoubtedly he'd taken it off himself, but he couldn't remember doing so. He was suspended about thirty feet up the side of a jagged hill, the top of his chute snagged around a tree or rock. One of his hands had somehow tangled in his lines, and his legs were roped against each other. He faced a sheer cliff.

There was a knife in his speed pants. He tried to bend his body, and felt himself starting to fall. Desperately he tried to grab the rock; he rolled sideways, still caught.

Smith tried leaning toward his leg, but found he was

stuck. As he craned his head upward he saw someone else on the hill above him.

It was a woman. Her dress fluttered.

No. The parachute.

He was in shock, close to losing it. He was going to die here.

Mack told himself to calm down. All he had to do was get off the hill, get his radio. They'd be looking for him by now. The sun was already up.

Shit. His wingman hadn't been nearby. They'd have only the vaguest idea of where he was.

Not like when Zen went down.

He felt a twinge in his legs. They hurt, but nowhere near as bad as his ribs. A good sign, right?

Smith had a pocketknife beneath his vest, secured there by a lanyard clip. Steadying himself against the rock face with his left hand, he managed to thread his other arm free from the tangle. Then he slid his fingers beneath the vest to feel for the knife. He had to lever his elbow around, and felt a fresh twinge from his ribs as he grasped the clip and worked the knife free. He brought it back and pulled it open, only to have it slip from his hand. Dirt and small rocks slid all around him as he grabbed helplessly for it.

Shitfuckinhell. This can't be happening to me. Not me, goddamn it. I'm too fuckinggoddamngood a pilot to have my fanny waxed and end up snagged on a stinkinggoddamnfuckinghell hillside. It's a goddamn joke.

Smith took as deep a breath as his injured chest would allow, then pushed his right arm in the direction of his tangled legs. He felt himself start to slip, but kept going; he tumbled sideways again, but snagged, crashing against the rocks as he grabbed his leg with his right hand. He got the knife, then realized his legs were pinned together, not by the parachute line, but by the metal buckles on the lower straps, which snugged the pant legs above his boots.

He levered the long knife blade behind one of the straps and freed himself, carefully gripping the knife this time. As he straightened out he began to drop again; he managed to swing his elbow against the rocks as he slipped down about five or six feet before the chute once more snagged. As he stopped he smacked the side of his face, scraping his cheek and nose.

When the burn subsided, he realized he could simply slip himself out of the harness and drop free. Problem was, the ground was still a fair distance.

Twenty-five feet? Maybe only twenty. There were bushes at the bottom of the ravine.

Long way to fall, even if the pigmy trees broke his fall. Better to slip down some more, even though the scrapes hurt like hell.

Knife swung his legs forward and back, gently at first, then harder, trying to nudge himself down. A sharp knob on the rock poked his forearm. Dirt and pebbles shot down the hill, but he stayed put.

His gut began to retch. Bile came up into his mouth and his ribs screamed with pain.

Stinkingfuckshithell. How the hell can this be happening to me? Me!

Knife clawed at the wall next to him. Maybe it would be easier to climb up it. He lodged his knife into the webbing of his vest, then tried digging his feet into the cliff side. He levered himself up a few feet, one step, two steps, a third. He managed to pull himself up enough so that the lines hung free. He stepped to the right, trying to avoid getting tangled. He took one step, then slipped and fell, sliding two or three feet before managing to grab on and stop.

Nothing to do but let himself fall.

But as he reached to unclasp his harness restraints, the rock or tree or whatever it was holding him began to give way. He pushed himself close to the face of the hill, trying to squeeze into the dirt and rocks as he slid. He clawed and slipped the whole fifteen feet to the ground, crashing through foliage so sharp he thought he had fallen into a spear pit.

Finally on the ground, Mack lay back, trying to blink away the pain—trying, in fact, to blink away everything: Africa, the mission, the shoulder-fired SAMs that had hit him.

Had to be shoulder-fired SAMs. He'd had no warning and they'd gotten his tailpipe. But Mack Smith wasn't supposed to be the kind of pilot who got his fanny nailed like that, was he?

Finally, Knife rolled over and got to his feet. He removed his Beretta from the vest, checking to make sure the weapon was loaded. It felt heavy in his hand, a little greasy, as if it were covered with oil.

The ejection-seat survival kit and life raft sat at the very base of the hill a few yards away, looking as if someone had come and set them out for him. Besides flares, water, some candy bars, and other odds and ends, the kit included a PRC-90 survival radio, backing up the one he carried in his vest.

As he bent to open the kit, he heard something crashing through the bushes a few yards away. He slid to one knee, slowly raising the pistol to eye level.

Something moved and he fired.

There was a squealing, subhuman noise, a half growl.

"I'm sure as hell glad that wasn't me," said a voice behind him.

As Smith jumped back, something grabbed his pistol hand. He began to fight back, found himself wrestled to the ground.

"Relax, pilot, we're on your side."

A green and black mask contorted over him.

It wasn't until the teeth flashed white and gold that Knife was certain the figure was human.

"I'm Sergeant Melfi. My point man Jackson is around here somewhere. We're Marines. Come on, Captain, let's get the fuck out of here. Shooting that pig may have felt good, but it's gonna bring a bunch of Somies runnin'."

"Pig?"

"Whatever. Fuck, maybe it was a lion," said Melfi. "Come on, Captain, let's go."

"I'm Major Smith."

"Whatever. Come the fuck on. We have to get on the other side of these hills and find some real cover."

Dreamland
21 October, 2030 local

DOG STOOD OVER HIS DESK, STUDIOUSLY IGNORING THE blinking light on his telephone. The light indicated that someone from Deborah O'Day's office was holding—and had been holding now for at least ten minutes.

"The thing to do is split the Whiplash team between two planes," he told Cheshire and Freah. "This way we can crew them. They'll arrive loaded for bear."

"We don't have two planes ready," said Cheshire. "Only Fort Two is in shape to fly. Raven's computer and fly-by-wire systems are still being upgraded to take care of the problems Fort Two encountered. We should have them on-line by tomorrow night."

"What about Plus?" Bastian asked, using the nickname for Megafortress One, officially carried on the books as EB-52-DT1A Megafortress Plus. Plus had been used a few months before to help recapture the stolen DreamStar experimental aircraft, flying all the way to Nicaragua.

"The wings are still being refitted. It will be at least a week before it's ready. Raven's the one to go. The ECMs will blast out anything the Iranians have."

"They'll overheat first," said Rubeo.

Proposed as the next-generation electronic-warfare set,

the xAQ-299 admittedly had some heating issues. But having decided to send the Megafortresses, Bastian was in no mood to let Rubeo's dour puss derail him.

"All right, let's do this," he said. "Use Fort Two to take Whiplash to Africa. We'll expedite the work on Raven, pack the two other crew members and more weapons in it, and ship it out as soon as it's done. How soon can you take off?"

"Actually, Colonel, I think it would be better if I take the Raven," Cheshire told him. "I've been flying it and its voice-command system has been trained for my voice. Besides, given the ECMs, it's more likely to be the one that would see action."

"Who flies Fort Two?"

"I took the liberty of alerting Captain Stockard," Cheshire said. "She should be on base within a half hour."

Dog nodded, then glanced at his phone.

"Danny, this sound good to go?"

Freah nodded.

"Let's do it," said Bastian.

"Colonel, I must note that you're sending a test aircraft into a war zone," said Rubeo.

"I don't believe it's an official war zone yet," said Bastian dryly. "I'm sending it as a transport. Both planes are going as transports."

"Semantics—"

"Doc, I appreciate your coming, truly I do," said Bastian. "I don't know why you thought it important to show up, but I appreciate it."

Dog held up his hand, cutting off himself as well as the scientist.

"Out, everyone," he said as he picked up his phone. "This is a classified call. Go!"

*   *   *

BREANNA URGED THE SMALL HONDA FASTER, PLUNGING through the desert night toward the base. She was glad to escape, glad to run from the disaster that had become her life. On some level she knew Jeff's attitude was just a phase, a plateau on his way to coping with his disability, adjusting to his new life. But on another level, she was starting not to care. There was only so much she could take.

The counselors had tried to prepare her for this; they'd been hopeful, predicting that it would soon pass. They all felt Zen would come back stronger than ever, his true nature winning out.

But how did they know? They all had perfect spines, working legs. None of them had been top-dog test pilots with blue-sky careers ahead of them.

He suspected her of seeing Knife? *Jesus.* Where the hell did that come from?

Major Cheshire hadn't said what was up, but she did promise a helicopter would be waiting to whisk Bree from Nellis to Dreamland. Obviously something big was brewing.

Thank God. She needed a diversion.

MS. O'DAY HERSELF WAS ON THE LINE WHEN DOG picked up the phone.

"Colonel, I think you've lost your mind."

"Sorry to keep you waiting, Madame Advisor," he replied.

"Don't *Madame Advisor* me. I read your e-mail. Do you know what you're up against on the JSF?"

"Yes, ma'am."

He heard a loud sigh from the other end of the line. He imagined the petite woman shaking her head back in her office, rolling her eyes before scrunching herself over the desk. She'd pull up the sleeves of her white blouse—

O'Day always wore white blouses to work.

"Dog, are you damn sure about this?"

"The F-119 is not a workable design as presently configured," said Bastian, repeating the bullet line of his memo. "It can be, but the changes it needs will mean missing the interservice target."

"They're going to come after you on this, Tecumseh," O'Day said. Rarely if ever did she—or anyone, for that matter—use his given name. "Wait until morning."

"I know."

"I'll back you up, if this is your considered opinion."

"It is."

"It may mean Dreamland closes."

"I weighed the consequences."

"All right. You've heard about Somalia?"

"Yes. We have a team getting ready for transport." Dog debated whether to tell her exactly how he intended on supplying that transport, but decided it was best not to. If she didn't know, she couldn't order him not to.

Not that she could order him to do anything, at least not directly.

If he was so afraid of telling her, why do it in the first place?

"I may call on you to look over some estimates. It will have to be back-channel," she said.

"Understood."

"This is going to dominate things around here for a few days," she added. "It will take some of the heat off you and the JSF. I suggest you use it to line up the ducks."

"The ducks?"

"And next time my office calls, Colonel, don't keep me on hold," she said, hanging up.

DANNY FREAH CAUGHT A RIDE OUT TO THE MEGAFORtress hangar with Lieutenant Greenbaum, whom he was leaving in charge of base security in his absence. He spat out directions machine-gun style, warning Greenbaum about a dozen details that could snap up and bite him in the butt if he didn't watch them. But all the time he talked, Danny was shaping his mission plan in his head. He had his go-bag in the back, along with a silenced MP-5 equipped with a laser sight. Four other members of his team would be similarly equipped; the other two carried M-16A2/M203 grenade-launcher combos.

The M40A sniper outfit had a special metal box all to itself. Along with a set of custom-tailored carbon-boron protective vests, it was waiting with the team in the hangar. There was also a line-of-sight discrete-burst com set developed by another of Dreamland's experimental labs. While the gear technically wasn't cleared for operational use, Klondike had cleared it for "field testing."

She'd also warned there'd be hell to pay if they lost it. But Danny didn't plan on letting that happen.

According to the orders he'd received, Whiplash's prime duty would be to crew a Pave Low tasked to transport and support a Delta assault team. But the Whiplash operators were trained to crew everything Air Force Special Operations flew; they could eat snakes, jump from planes, and leap tall buildings with a single rappelling line. They might be called on to do any or all of those once the fun started.

Greenbaum pulled up in front of the hangar. A ground crew was already working furiously on the big black bomber inside.

"Okay, now as far the duty rosters go," Danny told his lieutenant, "you do have some flexibility."

"Captain, no offense, but you've gone over the rosters maybe five times already? Seriously, sir, I do think I can handle it. The only tough part is going to be controlling my jealousy."

Freah laughed. "I hope you'll still feel that way in a week."

"I'm sure we will, sir."

Freah looked at the young man's face. Greenbaum looked like a jayvee kid who'd been told he wasn't making the trip to the big bowl game. He also looked to be all of fifteen, not twenty-three.

Of course, Freah wasn't much older. He just felt like he was.

"Okay, Greenie. Kick some ass."

Freah's men were waiting in the hangar. Lee "Nurse" Liu and Kevin Bison were at the entrance, copping smokes, while the others huddled near the big black plane's tail, watching as the ground crew prepped the aircraft.

Freah had selected the Whiplash response team himself. All of the men were qualified as parajumpers with extensive SAR experience, cross-trained to handle each others' responsibilities. Freah had organized them roughly along the lines of a Green Beret "A" team for ground operations.

"Looks like they lost two planes about twenty miles apart," Perse "Powder" Talcom told him. Powder was the team point man and intel specialist; he had gathered satellite maps and some briefing information before reporting to the hangar. "One to MiGs and the other to ground fire. Roughly, they went down here."

Talcom pointed to large swatches of the Somalian coast.

"Got to figure they got SAR units out there already," he added. "Navy task force coming up from this direction. Few days away, though."

Freah nodded. Talcom had recently been promoted to tech sergeant—obviously because he had relatives in the Pentagon, according to the others, who were all staff sergeants.

"What you're saying is, fun's going to be over before

we get there," said Bison, coming in from his smoke.

"There's a lot of other shit going down," said Freah. "Libya's getting involved. There's talk of Saudi Arabia being declared a no-fly zone."

"Good," said Jack "Pretty Boy" Floyd, the team com specialist. "I'm getting bored around here."

"What's a no-fly zone mean to us?" asked Liu.

"It means you don't fly there, Nurse," said Powder.

"Nurse was thinking of strapping on a rocket pack and taking on the ragheads by himself," said Bison. Liu had earned the nickname "Nurse" because he was the team medic.

"I'd like to try a rocket pack someday," said Geraldo "Blow" Hernandez. Hernandez was the tail gunner and supply specialist, as well as the team's jumpmaster.

"Yeah, Blow, I bet you would," said Freddy "Egg" Reagan, adjusting the elastic that held his thick eyeglasses in place around his bald head. Reagan was the squad weapons specialist, and could handle everything from a Beretta to an M-1 tank. Rumor had it he was learning to fly an Apache helicopter on the side.

"All right, we may end up with something important to do, but at the moment our assignment is straightforward," Freah told them. "There's a Pave Low en route from Germany. We take over for the regular crew, yada-yada-yada. You guys know the drill."

"Hey, Captain, we invented the drill," said Blow.

"Is it a DeWalt or a Bosch?" said Powder.

"That's supposed to be a joke, right?" asked Liu.

"If I have to explain it, it's not," said Powder.

"No shit, Sherlock," said Egg.

"Captain, what are we really doing?" asked Blow.

"Whatever they tell us to do," said Freah. "That good enough for you?"

"They wouldn't call us out if they didn't want us playing snake-eaters, right?"

"Maybe," said Freah, who suspected that Madcap Magician did have some covert ground action—aka "snake eating"—in mind.

"Captain Freah?"

Freah turned to find Captain Breanna "Rap" Stockard standing in full flight gear behind him. She extended her hand and he took it.

She had her old man's grip. "Looks like we have a problem here."

"What would that be?"

"You have one man too many. I was told your team had six members."

"It does."

"I count seven."

"Six and me."

"We have only six seats in this aircraft, besides mine and my copilot's," she said. "And frankly, that's not a particularly comfortable configuration, since it means I'm flying without a crew."

"Major Cheshire said it wouldn't be a problem."

"I didn't say it was a *problem*," said Breanna. She had her old man's snap as well. "I said it wasn't comfortable. I'm traveling without a navigator or a weapons specialist a damn long way into a particularly difficult environment. What that means is—I'm in a pissy mood. Now, who's staying behind?"

She was in a pissy mood, Freah thought, but there was no way he was backing down.

"Everyone's coming," he told her. "I'll sit on the floor."

"This isn't a 707," said Breanna.

"A plane this big can't fit another person?"

"He could sit in the nav jump seat," said one of the crewmen nearby.

Breanna shot him a drop-dead glance, then turned back to Freah.

He couldn't resist smiling. "See?"

"If we were to set you up in a jump seat, there'd be no way to egress the plane," she told him.

"You can't just walk out the door?" asked Powder.

"If there's an emergency, there's no way to eject," Breanna told the sergeant. She had her father's anger, all right—it was barely under control. "Captain, come here a minute."

Freah followed her outside the hangar.

"Look, I'm not trying to give you a hard time," she said. "Just pick one of your men to stay behind."

"Major Cheshire said it was doable."

"I'm sure Major Cheshire thought six meant six, not seven."

"Look, I'll take the jump seat," said Freah. "The nav thing. I can bail out if there's a problem."

Breanna rolled her eyes. "You're talking about a folding seat in the bottom of the plane. If there's a problem, you're going out a tiny hatch—or the bomb bay. And that's if I can slow the plane to 275 knots. You know how fast that is?"

"It's slower than I've done HALO jumps," said Danny.

Breanna looked at him. HALO stood for High Altitude, Low Opening; it was typically done from C-141's. He'd actually only done it three or four times, but at this point he wasn't admitting anything that might argue against him.

"Good fucking luck," she said.

"I'm willing to take the risk, Captain."

"It's a hell of a lot simpler to leave one of your men on the ground. He can come later with Raven or find another ride."

"We get there with five men, I may not be able to do my job," Freah said. "That may mean Smith doesn't come back. You want to take that responsibility?"

Breanna's face turned red.

"Hey, listen," said Freah, "your dad approved this."

"Fuck my dad," said Breanna, spinning away.

"Lady is pissed," said Blow when Freah returned to the group.

"Let's get going, no screwin' around," Danny told them, ignoring the titters. "We're not flying fuckin' TWA."

Somalia
22 October 1996, 0620 local

MACK BIT HIS SLEEVE AGAINST THE THROB IN HIS RIBS as he slid to his knees. His heart pounded in his ears and his chest throbbed. He barely managed to stifle a cough.

They were in scrubland on the side of a hill, maybe a mile or two south of where he had landed. Where exactly that placed them in the larger world Knife had no idea. There were people nearby, though it wasn't clear whether they were soldiers or even exactly where they were. Sergeant Melfi had just hit the dirt a few yards ahead and lay motionless, studying something nearby.

Knife reached his right hand to his holster. Something moved behind him and he realized it must be Jackson, catching up.

At least, he hoped it was Jackson. He managed not to jump as the Marine touched his shoulder.

"What's up?"

"He just stopped," Smith said, nodding toward Melfi.

"He's not too bad at point," said the Marine. Then he added, "You want that morphine?"

Smith shook his head as vigorously as he could without jostling his ribs.

"You look pretty bad."

"Drugs'll put me out," Knife told him. "You'll have to carry me."

Mack wasn't even tempted. The pain told him he was alive.

They watched Gunny crane his neck upward, then duck back down. Finally, the sergeant came back to them.

"Village maybe twenty yards away from where I was," hissed Melfi when he returned. "Damn shacks are built out of old trucks and steel signs mostly. Damn. People live like that?"

Neither Smith nor Jackson spoke.

"Ground's nice and flat," added Gunny. "I think there's a road beyond it."

"Helicopter could use the village as a locator," Smith told them. "If there is a road, it could land there."

"Yeah." Gunny, balanced on his haunches, considered it. "Let's move that way, try and flank it," he said finally. He threw his head around suddenly. Jackson quickly brought his gun up.

"Getting paranoid," said Gunny when nothing appeared. "How much time until the next transmission, Major?"

Smith looked at his watch. "Five minutes."

"All right. Let's get a little further back, make it harder for them to see or hear us, then we'll move around that way. See where I'm pointing to?"

Knife nodded.

"You know what? Let's get behind those trees and you make your radio call now," said Gunny. "Yeah. We can all take a break. For one thing, I got to pee. Getting too old for this shit. Go for it, Jackson. You got the point again."

Melfi gently rested his hand on Smith's shoulder, holding him back as Jackson moved out. The two Marines had emphasized battle separation several times, but while Knife wasn't exactly unfamiliar with the concept—fighter aircraft practiced it, after all—something innate wanted him to keep close to the two men and their M-16's.

When Gunny finally released him, Mack heaved himself forward. He waddled low at first, moving sideways and then finding a stride that kept him balanced as well as close to the ground. The point man was moving a bit quicker, the distance between them gradually spreading from five to ten and then fifteen yards. All things considered, Smith was pretty damn lucky—not only had he managed to avoid capture after bailing out, but he had a Marine escort to help lead him to safety.

Going to take a hell of a lot of ribbing about that.

Jackson had almost reached the copse ahead when Knife caught the sound of a prop-driven plane approaching from the south. He grabbed the Prick ninety, cursing himself as he realized he'd neglected to turn the radio's dial back to off after his last transmission. There was no time to worry if that might have hurt the battery or not— he held it up and began broadcasting, starting with the call sign he had used while flying.

"Poison One to Project Command, to any allied aircraft. Do you read me?"

He snapped off the transmit button, looking upward. The plane he had heard was nearly overhead, relatively low, though he couldn't see it yet. From the sound, it was driven by a prop. That could mean it was a Bronco-type observation craft—Madcap Magician had at least one of the ancient but dependable OV-10's in its stable.

On the other hand, it could be nearly anything else.

"Poison One to all aircraft, do you read me?"

He flipped over to the second rescue band and retransmitted. There was no response.

The airplane above passed without him being able to see it. He guessed it was between one and two thousand feet. But it seemed to be flying in a straight line.

"What do you think?" Jackson asked, crawling next to him.

"If it's one of ours, it should have heard us," said Smith. He pressed the radio to his ear. It was also equipped with a small earphone, but he thought he got more volume without it. Smith tried broadcasting again, this time pointing the antenna in the direction of the plane.

"Nothing?" asked Gunny when he came back.

Knife shook his head.

"I didn't see it," said the sergeant.

"Me neither," said Jackson. Knife shook his head too.

"Maybe they're not on our side," suggested Melfi.

"Somalians don't have much of an air force," said Smith. "And the Iranians would be running a MiG down here. But you're right. There's no way of knowing. Could be a civilian they pressed into duty. It didn't seem like it was moving in a search pattern, but it's hard to tell. I mean, I've never been on this end of one." He meant it as a joke, but the others didn't laugh. "How far are we from the coast?"

"Maybe another half mile this way," said Gunny.

"I think we should go back to our plan then," said Knife. "We go out to the ocean and broadcast from there. If that was the Somalians, then they'd have an easier time with us near the village."

Gunny ran his finger back and forth across his chin, thinking. "See, if I'm a soldier, I come here, ask these villagers if they saw anything. They say no, I move on. I don't waste my time searching around here, not unless these folks have seen or heard something. Besides, the ocean's a good hike back that way, and that's where they'll be looking, I'd guess."

"Hey, Gunny," hissed Jackson.

Smith and Knife turned. Jackson crouched down, pointing his gun back in the direction of the village.

"Something big moved."

"Another pig, I hope," said Smith.

"Wasn't a pig before," said Gunny, pushing away toward a low ridge to their right.

Knife returned his radio to his pocket, making sure it was off this time. He took out his gun.

Melfi and Jackson froze. So did he.

He couldn't hear anything. He couldn't see anything, either. He blew a long, slow, deep breath from his mouth, waiting.

Gunny put his hand up, then began waving it, as if he wanted Knife to move backward. Mack took a long step backward, then another. The trees they'd been aiming for were less than ten yards away. Just beyond them were some low bushes and what seemed to be another clearing of tall grass.

Jackson was sprawled on the ground, crawling forward.

Knife took a half step toward the copse, watching as the Marine worked toward a trio of bushes no more than a foot high. He had reached into his pants pocket for something.

Gunny stood straight up. Relieved, Knife let his pistol hand drop to his side.

As he did, Jackson whipped something from his hand, a baseball or a rock.

A grenade.

Smith threw himself to the ground as Gunny opened fire. Bullets ripped overhead and there was an explosion, then another, then something acrid burned his nose.

Smoke. A smoke grenade, meant to confuse the enemy.

Real grenades as well.

There were shouts and more gunfire. Knife ignored the pain in his ribs as he pushed himself back to his feet and began to run, heading for the trees, unsure exactly what he was supposed to do next. He glanced at the Beretta in his hand, then nearly tripped as he reached the first tree. He flew behind the narrow trunk, gun-first, reminding himself that the first figure he saw emerging from the thick fog of smoke would be one of his own men.

He waited, saw nothing. He heard nothing.

The best thing to do, he thought, was to transmit their position. He reached his left hand to take out the radio, felt the pull in his ribs. Somehow he managed to ignore it, taking out the PRC-90 and dialing it to beacon, not wanting to take his attention from the ground in front of him. Smoke curled around the trees and branches, as if a massive cloud bank had descended to earth.

Nothing.

Knife shifted behind the tree, then turned his attention to the radio.

"Poison One to allied command," he said. "Team is under attack. Repeat, we are taking fire."

He stopped, listening for a response.

The airplane again, in the distance, coming from the north.

Maybe it could hear him but not the other way around.

Or maybe it was directing ground forces against them.

At this point, that didn't matter. They knew where they were.

Allied command. Shit. Like he was in the Gulf or something?

"Smith to whoever," he said, his heart pounding wildly. It felt as if it were smashing itself against his injured rib bones. "We are two and a half miles from the coast, maybe more. We're southwest of the Silkworm site."

There was a scream and more gunfire. Knife dialed the radio back to beacon, then spun around.

Nothing to shoot at.

The airplane roared overhead, barely at treetop level.

He'd have to gamble that it was on his side. Mack began to run toward the open field. With his first step the ground behind him erupted with a massive shell burst. Thrown off his feet, he dropped both the radio and his pistol, but somehow managed to land on his good side. Tumbling head over heels, he crashed into a bush and got up. He could see, or thought he could see, the shadow of a plane passing at the edge of the yellow grass just ahead. He threw himself toward it, running and breathing and feeling his ribs like a sharp ax ripping through his skin. He began waving his arms, then felt some force pulling him around, lassoing him like a steer. He swung sideways and found himself on the ground, tackled. A Somalian soldier pushed an AK-47 into his face and said something he couldn't hear, though his meaning was pretty damn plain.

Dreamland
21 October, 2130 local

BREE FOUGHT THE BILE BACK AS SHE COMPLETED THE last-second checks before heading off the Dreamland runway. There were any number of reasons for her to be angry, starting with the Spec Ops captain's in-her-face attitude. The jerkoff thought it was macho to sit on the floor.

Jump seat, whatever. Asshole.

"Good to go, Rap," said Chris.

"Yeah," she grunted.

It was Jeff she was mad at, though. This was just a milk run—admittedly a long, long, long one, but still just a milk run. Assuming she made the refuels without any problem.

Piece of cake. Even with a mix of missiles in the belly.

Jackass Spec Ops captain. Just because he was her father's friend didn't mean shit. She was in charge of the plane—she had a good mind to march downstairs and tell the fucker to strap himself onto the rotating missile launcher in the bomb bay.

See how macho he thought *that* was.

She had debated going to Cheshire and demanding that Freah delete someone from his team. She had every right to do that—she probably *should* have done that.

But she hadn't. In her mind, and maybe only in her mind, it was the sort of thing a woman couldn't do. A woman couldn't afford to be less brave, less macho, than a guy.

How was watching out for her crew—strike that, her *passengers*—not being brave?

Freah would have to cut a stinking hole with a blow-torch to get his sorry ass out of the plane if there was a problem. Because she sure as shit wasn't going to slow down so he could crawl over to the hatch.

Maybe he'd move the computer equipment in the weap-ons area, find a way to squeeze through the bulkhead spars and crawl back to the bomb bay. Ride a cruise missile down to earth like what's his name in that whatchama-callit movie.

Asshole!

"Rap?"

"Dream Tower, this is Fort Two. Request clearance for takeoff."

"Tower. Uh, Captain, didn't we do this already?"

Another fucking wise-ass, Bree thought, pushing the throttle bar to get the hell out of there.

COLONEL BASTIAN WATCHED FROM THE TARMAC AS THE immense black plane lifted itself into the night, a dark shadow shuddering into the air.

It would be an exaggeration to say he'd thought more about his daughter in the past hour than in her whole life, but it was probably true that it was the longest sustained stretch in quite a while. He'd tried concentrating on other things, and even taking a nap, but couldn't; finally he'd decided to go out to the hangar area and wish her luck.

But he'd stopped short. He told himself that he didn't want to embarrass her in front of her crew, but he knew that was a lie. He'd stopped because he didn't know what to say.

Or rather, he didn't think he could say what he wanted

to say. Which was a lifetime of apologies, maybe.

He hadn't been there when she was born. He hadn't been there when she was growing up. It was partly her mother's fault, partly a question of circumstances, partly his career. Her mother had asked for a divorce even before she was pregnant, and then taken off, just disappeared. Ravena's wild streak had attracted him in the first place, the edge of danger in their relationship. Her unpredictability fired him up; he liked the edge, or had, or thought he had, when he was a young fighter jock on top of the world.

The jock eventually grew up. Ravena hadn't.

Breanna had, though.

It was his fault he hadn't been there. No one else's but his.

Dog folded his arms around his chest, eyes straining to see the disappearing shadow in the distance. She was a damn good pilot; he should be proud.

He was. He was also worried about her, an anxious father who'd just sent his daughter off on her first date.

If only it were that, he thought, finally losing track of the plane in the vast, overwhelming sky.

Dreamland
22 October, 0600

"WHAT DO YOU CALL A CRIPPLE TRYING TO CROSS A road?"

The two airmen looked at each other as if they'd just caught their parents in a foursome in Times Square.

"Roadkill," Zen said. "What do you call a one-legged bank robber?"

The airman on the left shrugged. The other laughed nervously. "What, Captain?" he asked.

"Misunderstood."

The roar of the helicopter approaching the Nellis landing pad made it possible for the two airmen to escape. The Dolphin shuttle—a French-made Aerospatiale SA.366 Dauphin adapted by the Air Force as a transport and occasional SAR craft—whipped in as if dropping into a hot LZ. The men bolted for it as it touched down a few yards away. A ground crewman pushed forward the access ramp that had been specially built for Zen. Stockard wheeled slowly, methodically building momentum as he sidled and bumped through the wide side door. Because of its SAR function, this Dolphin had a large open bay in the rear; it was easier to get in and out of than the other, which was a dedicated ferry generally reserved for—and preferred by—officers.

"Morning, Captain," said the copilot, trotting back as Zen wheeled himself into the bird. "You in for this week's football pool?" He pulled a sheet of paper from his pocket.

"I ought to get cripple's odds," Zen said, taking the sheet.

"Man, you're in a strange mood this morning, sir," said one of the airmen he'd been tormenting with his jokes.

"I'm just a strange guy, I guess," said Zen, reaching around to strap his chair to the helicopter's restraints. Greasy Hands had had someone install the quick-release hookup, making it easy for him to secure himself. Maybe next week they'd put in a special window.

"All aboard what's coming aboard," yelled the copilot out the rear door before pulling it shut. There was, of course, no one else waiting in the off-limits and well-guarded shuttle area. The pilot whipped the engine into a fury and the helicopter shot upward.

He *was* in a strange mood, Zen conceded to himself. Maybe it was because he thought he'd made a mistake with Bree last night.

He still knew he was right, that they had to end their

marriage. But his stomach hurt, and it wasn't just because of the heavy meal.

They'd sat there for an hour or more after he told her. Neither one of them spoke. Then she got up to go to the bathroom. He flipped on the TV.

Someone from Dreamland called her in. Bree left without explaining what was up. He assumed there was some sort of problem with the Megafortress; she had that kind of look on her face. He could tell.

At least he thought he could.

He glanced at the list of football games on the pool sheet, but the light was dim and he didn't really feel like going through it now. He folded it into his pocket.

Jeff had spent quite a lot of time last night thinking about using the Megafortress as the Flighthawk mother ship. He thought it might just be possible to save the project by tying the UM/Fs to the KC configuration, which itself was hitching a ride on the JSF. The Flighthawks would be perfect escorts over hostile territory.

The JSF was a joke, so what the hell. Might as well get something useful out of the program.

Stockard mulled how to best present the idea to his father-in-law during the short flight to Dreamland. He was still thinking about it as he made his way over to Cafeteria Four for breakfast.

"Ham 'n' Swiss bagel," he told Maggie, the counterperson, as he took his customary bottle of water.

"A bagel today? My, oh, my. Living on the edge, aren't we, Captain?" said Maggie.

"Cripples have to," Zen told her.

"Don't you ever use that word in front of me," she said, nearly throwing herself over the steam tray that separated them. "My son is in a wheelchair. He ain't no cripple."

"I didn't mean anything. I, uh . . ." Zen held out his hands apologetically. "I mean, shit, look at *me*."

"Well, you ain't no cripple." Her face was red and

her voice was shaking. "That damn chair doesn't give you the right to make fun of nobody."

"I'm not making fun of anyone. I didn't know about your son. I'm sorry."

She flipped the bagel together and plopped it on a plate with a harsh slap.

"I'm sorry," Zen said. "Really."

"Yeah," she said. Maggie pushed her lips together; finally, she nodded slowly.

He wanted to say something else, but all he could manage was another "sorry." Maggie turned quickly to greet a newcomer. Zen took the tray and wheeled himself out into the nearly empty room.

Nancy Cheshire was sitting at a table a short distance from the doorway. She waved at him to come over; he moved toward her slowly, the coffee lapping at the top of the cup on his precariously balanced tray.

"Hey, Jeff. Sorry if I woke you up last night," she said as he slid his tray in.

"No, I was up," he told her. He sipped his coffee, thinking how he could make it up to Maggie. She'd always been one of the few people who'd treated him like a regular person.

"Ought to be nearly there by now," said Cheshire.

"There *where*?"

"You haven't heard what's going on?"

"No. Where's Bree? You called her last night?" he added, finally catching up to what she'd been saying.

"Two planes got shot down in Somalia," Cheshire told him. "They're putting together an operation to rescue the pilots. Madcap Magician has an operation under way. They've called in Whiplash, one of our Spec Op security units. Danny Freah packed up the team in Fort Two and took off for Africa a few hours ago."

"In a Megafortress?"

Cheshire nodded. "We're sending Raven out as soon as

the control systems are tested. We're carrying Fort Two's crew members, and some more weapons. I should be sleeping," she added, shrugging.

"Weapons?"

"If they're needed."

"I'm coming with you," Zen told her. "With the Flighthawks."

"Don't be ridiculous."

"Raven's already set up for us. We can load the computer gear back in on the pallets and be ready to rock in an hour," he told her. "It won't take a half hour."

"Jeff, the Flighthawks aren't ready for combat."

"And Raven is?"

Cheshire shook her head. "The Megafortress has already seen action."

"Raven hasn't. And the Flighthawks have been flying for as long as Fort Two has."

"That doesn't mean anything."

"We can provide escort and act as scouts," said Jeff.

"We've only done two airdrops."

"That's in the past week and a half. We did maybe a million before my accident."

She frowned, not even bothering to refute his exaggeration. Jeff kept talking, convinced he was right—convinced that not only would the Flighthawks do a great job, but that they would prove their worth to everyone and the project would live on.

He would live on. Or fly on.

"Raven and Fort Two are too valuable to risk anyplace where somebody else got shot down. The Flighthawks can take chances you can't."

"Maybe five years from now. Three years if we're lucky," said Cheshire. "After a hell of a lot more work and practice."

"You think the pilots who got shot down are going to be alive in three years?"

"I didn't think you cared that much for Mack Smith after, uh, the accident," she said.

"Smith was one of the pilots?"

Cheshire nodded.

"Yeah, well, I'm still going."

SHAVING, COLONEL BASTIAN CONSIDERED WHETHER HE might just escape for a few hours—pull the phone out of the wall, or better yet, steal away to a Vegas hotel and sleep for twenty-four hours.

Wouldn't that go over big with the F-119 junta?

But hiding wasn't exactly his style. And besides, he needed to stay available in case O'Day wanted his input on Somalia. So he fortified himself with a quick, very hot shower, and headed back to the Taj.

By now Bastian had learned it was much faster to avoid the elevator's security systems and go down the stairways, which "merely" required a second retina scan, magnetic strip card, and a nod to the security detail at each floor. He had just burst out into the hallway down from his office when Major Stockard yelled to him from the elevator area.

"Colonel, just the man I was looking for," said Jeff, wheeling his chair at breakneck speed. "Can we talk for a second?"

"Sure, Zen," said Bastian, pushing open the door to his outer office. The room was jammed with a dozen other people waiting to see him. Dog gave the room a quick glance, though he could tell from the chaos that Ax was temporarily AWOL. "Sergeant Gibbs will be with you all shortly," he said, waving off any interruptions as he plunged into his personal office. He held the door open as Stockard wheeled through, then closed it quickly.

"Colonel—"

"I'm sure she's fine," said Bastian quickly.

"I'm not worried about Bree, Colonel," said Jeff. "I know she's fine. I want to get the Flighthawks on Raven."

"What?"

"The Flighthawks. If you're sending a second Mega-fortress to Africa, you should send the Flighthawks along too. They can act as escorts and scouts," he added. "We'll have real-time surveillance and CAP."

"I don't know, Jeff." Dog pulled out his desk chair and sat down. "For one thing, I don't have approval to send the first Megafortress, let alone the second. I'm only authorizing it on the grounds that the first one doesn't have a full crew aboard. In theory, the two planes are supposed to come back."

"Come on, Dog. You're stuffing the Raven with air-to-ground weapons. I agree with you. We should be in this."

"You're getting ahead of yourself. The weapons are for defensive purposes only."

"JSOWs?"

"If there are ground installations targeting them," said Bastian. It was, at best, a thin veneer—but that was all he needed.

"So they'll need up-to-date intelligence. I've flown the Flighthawks off Raven before. I know it will work."

The phone on his desk buzzed. Bastian looked at it angrily.

"You know I'm right about this, Colonel," said Zen. "If you're sending another Megafortress, the Flighthawks should go too. They're proven. They're expendable escorts."

"You haven't proven anything yet," Bastian told him. He snapped up the phone. "Bastian."

"Couple a dozen people waiting to talk to you, Colonel," said Ax. "And Washington—"

"Start a list. Tell Washington I'll get back to them," he snapped, hanging up the phone. He turned back to Stockard. "You think aircraft that cost a half a billion dollars to build are expendable?"

"That's the whole program cost," said Jeff. "But even if it were the cost of one plane, it's a hell of a lot cheaper than someone's life."

As mad as he was, Bastian couldn't quite disagree with that.

Especially since one of the lives they were talking about was Rap's.

"Have you used the Megafortress as a mother ship?" he asked.

"Absolutely," said Jeff. "Once they're off the wings, flying them from the Megafortress is like flying them from anywhere. Come on, Dog. You know it makes sense. Send them."

"You're asking me to send an untested flight system into a war zone."

"You already did that. Shit." Zen nudged his wheelchair forward. "You want to prove Dreamland will work, don't you? I know the whole concept—cutting-edge technology in the hands of an elite force. I have a copy of your paper. You're right. That's why this makes so much goddamn sense."

"Where did you get a copy of that?"

"My cousin works for the NSC," said Zen, realizing he'd gone too far.

"Which cousin is that?"

"Off the record?"

"No."

"Well, I don't want to get my cousin fired." Jeff pushed on, obviously hoping to skirt the question. "The bottom line here is, I want to put into practice what you've been preaching. Cutting-edge weapons on the firing line, where they belong."

He was right—or at least he was making a damn strong

argument. How could he not? It was exactly what Bastian himself believed.

But was Bastian right? He'd written that paper in an air-conditioned Washington, D.C., office over a few quiet afternoons. It was summer, and his evenings had been ·spent on a golf course, learning to play.

The report, and the man who wrote it, had been far removed from the realities of command, let alone combat. He hadn't had to worry about the consequences of failure.

"Zen, I'm going to forget that claim to have seen an eyes-only code-word report that I doubt you're cleared to read," he told him. "What do we do if one of the Flight-hawks crashes?"

"I hit self-destruct." Jeff shrugged. "God, Colonel, they're killing us anyway, right? What do we have to lose? I'm not asking you to send the JSF. You know this will work."

Ax's short double rap on the door interrupted them. The sergeant appeared with two cups of coffee and a stack of folders beneath his arm.

"Intel report you want to look at, Colonel," said the sergeant, setting the folders down. "Courtesy of Centcom Planning."

"Centcom?" Dog took the folder in his hand. It contained a short, undated memo accessing antiair defenses possessed by Iran. The emphasis was on mobile systems purchased from the former Soviet Union. According to the report, the Iranians were suspected of possessing a "sizable" number—"more than twenty"—of SA-3's, SA-6's, and man-portable SA-16's.

Serious weapons, all. There were also improved SA-2's, old but reliable SAMs. Though their systems were well known, their old-style radar could take advantage of some deficiencies in stealth technology—in other words, they could "see" F-117's in some circumstances.

They could also see the Megafortress.

Not the Flighthawks, though. Or at least not quite as soon.

A pair of the robots could extend the scouting range, take the risks. Keep his people safe. That was his mission, no?

No. This wasn't his mission at all. He'd taken a hell of a risk using Fort Two as a transport. He knew—he strongly suspected, at least—that once the Megafortress was available, it would be used. And that would certainly hold true for Raven, with its ECMs.

And the Flighthawks. Damn straight.

Who would resist the temptation to use them?

Didn't he want that, though? Didn't he want to demonstrate how right he was?

No, it wasn't a matter of him being right. It was a matter of getting the job done. And saving lives.

Bree's.

"Ax—who sent this report?" he asked his sergeant.

"Came eyes-only, without any ID," replied the sergeant. "I thought Ms. O'Day had forwarded it."

"I find that hard to believe."

"Don't know what to tell you, Colonel," said the sergeant, slipping out the door.

"You put him up to this?" Bastian asked Zen.

"I haven't a clue what that paper says," said Zen.

"All right. See if it's doable. I haven't approved anything yet," he added harshly as Stockard started to smile. "I want to talk to Cheshire and Rubeo about this first."

"No sweat. I'll round them up," said Zen, spinning around.

Picking up the phone to ask Ax to come back in, Bastian couldn't help but wonder if he would have said something different if Bree weren't piloting Fort Two.

*   *   *

WAITING FOR THE ELEVATOR TO ARRIVE, ZEN WONdered if he ought to get word to his cousin Jed Barclay that he had inadvertently squealed on him. But it might be easier for Jed if he didn't know—Jed had a natural deer-in-the-headlights look about him, except when he tried to lie.

Then the boy genius who'd gone to Columbia at sixteen and moved on to take two doctorates at Harvard looked like a third-rate car thief.

Slotting himself inside the elevator car, Zen felt a twinge of doubt—not about the Flighthawks, not even about himself, but Bree. If the Colonel *was* willing to send the Flighthawks, what did it say about what was going on over there?

Better to focus on his own problems, he thought, worrying about how long it would take to get the Flighthawks on the Megafortress.

Somalia
22 October 1996, 1900 local

SOMEWHERE ALONG THE WAY, MACK HAD LOST TRACK not only of where he was and what time it was, but of how many people were swirling above him. In the past few hours, Smith had been carried beneath a pole suspended between two soldiers like a piece of game, packed into the back of a pickup, shoved into the back of a sedan, placed gently in another pickup, and marched several miles—more or less in that order. Manacled and blindfolded the whole time, he had been offered water but no food, and three times allowed to pee. He hadn't been beaten, not even at first. In fact, he'd probably give his captors three stars in the Mobil Guide to African Kidnappers.

Actually, they weren't kidnappers. Third World or not, they were members of a serious army. They had a command structure and obvious discipline. Smith was the intruder and criminal; it was very possible that they had legal grounds to execute him.

Not that they needed legal grounds. They had more than enough weapons, one of which poked itself now into the side of his neck.

"You, Captain, you will come this way," said a voice with what sounded to him like a British accent. Smith followed the prods, quickening his pace as a hand gripped his sleeve. He tripped over a low riser and heard his feet echoing over a porch of some sort. A door opened ahead of him. Two men shouldered him down a hall to a set of carpeted stairs. They started him upward slowly, but then another hand pushed from behind. With his legs chained, he flailed for balance; the guards on either side picked him up by his elbows and carried him to a landing.

Down another hall, into a room, into a seat—hands grabbed at his face and his eyes flooded with light.

"You will tell me your name," said the blur in front of him.

"Why?" said Smith, trying to focus.

"Because at the moment your status is quite in doubt. Spies are shot without trial."

The man was short, a bit on the round side. He wore a long, coatlike gray garment. He had a beard; his face was white. A small turban, gray, topped his head.

"I'm a prisoner of war," said Knife.

"Then you will tell me your name and rank, and we will go on from there," said the man, his English softened by a vaguely Middle Eastern accent. He did not smile, but he spoke matter-of-factly, as if he were dealing with a young child.

"Major Mack Smith."

"You are with the U.S. Air Force," said the man. "You were flying an F-16. What is the name of your unit?"

Smith didn't answer.

"Your call sign was Poison," continued the man. "You bombed an installation of the Somalian government."

"It was an Iranian base."

The man finally smiled. It was faint and brief.

"Major, the base is under the control of the Somalian government. The men who captured you and brought you here were Somalian. I assure you, there are no Iranian soldiers in Somalia, or anywhere in Africa."

"What about you?"

"I am an ambassador," said the man. "An advisor. Nothing more."

"I'm your prisoner?"

"No. You are no one's prisoner. You don't exist."

"I'm free to go then," said Smith. The pain in his ribs stoked up as he mockingly jerked his body upright.

"If you were to leave here now, you would be shot."

Middle-aged and obviously a cleric of some sort, the Iranian exuded calmness, as if he were projecting a physical aura of considered peacefulness. Two men stood in plain brown uniforms behind him; neither uniform had insignias or other marks of rank, and they were not carrying weapons. About a dozen troops, Somalians apparently, stood near the door and the sides of the room. It seemed to be a classroom; a blackboard filled the wall in front, its shiny surface glaring with the reflected overhead lights. There were several rows of seats, though no desks that he could see, behind him.

"Are you hungry?" asked the Iranian.

"No," lied Smith.

"I would suggest it is in your interest to be truthful," said his captor. He turned to one of the men in the uniforms and said something. The man nodded, then left.

Knife gazed around the room, trying to memorize details. Yellow parchmentlike shades were drawn down over the windows on his right. The floor was covered with seemingly new linoleum, the kind that might be used in the kitchen of a modest American home. A crucifix was mounted above the middle of the blackboard.

Maybe he was in an old mission school? Or certainly some building that didn't specifically belong to the government.

Or maybe it did. He wasn't in Boise.

The aide returned with a tray. A large bowl of rice and some sort of vegetable sat in the middle. There were no eating utensils. Smith looked at it doubtfully as the tray was placed on a wooden chair and set down in front of him. A thick reddish brown liquid covered the rice.

His manacled hands moved toward the bowl. Stopping them seemed to require more energy than he had. Smith scooped a few fingers' worth of food into his mouth, then quickly consumed the contents. The liquid was sweet and sticky in his throat; the rest of the food was bland.

"And get him some water," added the Iranian.

Two other Iranians in plain brown uniforms came in with the man with the water. One of the men had a small Sony video cam, the kind a family might use to record their child's first steps. Smith held his head upright, staring blankly into the lens.

"State your name, please," said the Iranian cleric.

"Mack Smith," he said, taking the metal cup of water.

"Are you injured?"

He considered what to say. "I think one of my ribs is broken."

"How did that happen?"

He hesitated again. If he said they had beaten him, they would simply erase that portion of the tape. Besides, it wasn't true.

"I'm not sure," he said.

"Where are you?"

"Good question."

The Iranian cleric smiled and nodded. Finally he said

something to the man with the camera, apparently telling him to turn it off, since he did so.

"The bruises on your face—did they come from the ejection?" asked the Iranian.

"What bruises?" asked Knife. He hadn't realized his face was injured.

"The force of the ejection would have been severe. Your parachute was found near where you landed, on the side of a sheer cliff. You are fortunate that your legs were not broken."

"Yeah, I'm one lucky dog."

"You will find in time, Major, that that is very true." The Iranian motioned to the guards behind him. Two strong arms levered him upward from his chair; caught by surprise, Mack dropped the water, splashing it on his uniform and the floor. The two men behind his interrogator bristled, stepping forward quickly as if he had made a threat.

"An accident, I'm sure," said the Iranian, holding them back with a subtle gesture of his hand. He looked at Knife the way an older relative might, as if he had known him all his life, as if he were comparing the man before him with a mental image of the child he had been. "I must attend to some business, Major Smith."

The Iranian started to leave.

"What's going to happen to me?" Smith asked.

"Possibly, you will be put on trial. If that happens, I will be your advocate."

"Who are you?"

"You may call me Iman or Teacher. I am your advocate," said the Iranian. He swept from the room, the two brown uniforms and half a dozen Somalians in tow.

"GODDAMN FAGGOT IRANIANS," MELFI TOLD JACKSON. "Least they could have done was beat the shit out of us."

"Yeah," said Jackson.

He'd been shot in the leg and Gunny could see the pain hit him in waves. Worried Jackson might pass out, the sergeant continued to talk and joke, hoping to keep him going.

"Stinkin' pilot's probably making a deal for us right now, what do you think?" said Gunny. "Bet we'll get dancing girls and blow jobs."

Jackson snorted. His eyes started to close.

Gunny jumped up from the bench. Ignoring the two Somalians standing near the basement steps, he grabbed Jackson by the shirt and shook him.

"Yo, stay with me, boy. Yo. You're mine, shithead. Don't go nowhere."

"I'm okay, Gunny. I'm just tired."

"Hey, you douche bags—get me a fucking doctor here, okay?" Gunny yelled to the men. "You faggot bastards, don't you understand English? Hey! Hey!"

The door to the basement opened. Still holding Jackson, Gunny watched as a man in a long robe descended the stairs. It was the Iranian who had questioned them earlier. Several other Iranians and Somalians followed him down.

"Hey, Ayatollah, where the fuck is that doctor?"

The others rushed around the two Americans. One grabbed Gunny; before he could slug the SOB, his arms were pinned behind him.

"We need a fucking doctor," Melfi told the Imam.

"Your soldier will receive what attention is available," said the Iranian. He nodded, and two of his men lifted Jackson up and carried him away. The Marine's head flopped to the side. "The wound does not appear serious."

"I'll tell you what. Give me a fuckin' AK-47 and you can find out how serious it is."

"Your false bravado is hardly appropriate."

The Imam nodded again. Gunny was thrown to the

floor. Before he could manage to get up, his arms and groin were pinned by heavy boots.

"This ain't exactly Geneva Convention style," growled Gunny.

"This isn't Geneva, Sergeant," said the Imam.

A man with a video camera appeared from behind the cleric. A red light flashed on near the lens; Melfi spat and stuck his tongue out. The videographer continued for a few more moments, then snapped off the camera.

"Thank you, Sergeant," said the Imam, seemingly amused. He said something to the others. One or two of the men grinned.

"You're a real fuckin' comedian, Ayatollah," said Gunny as the others released him. He rolled up and sat on the floor, watching as the Imam walked back up the stairs. Most of the others followed. A young soldier came down with a tray of rice mush similar to what they'd given him a few hours before. Gunny took the bowl, made a show of sniffing it, even though he figured they wouldn't bother poisoning him—they'd just shoot him and be done with it.

Grub wasn't as bad as some of the crap the Navy served on their aircraft carriers. He spooned it quickly into his mouth with his fingers. Like before, the soldier waited for the bowl quietly a few feet away.

"Here ya go, Sport," Gunny said, tossing the bowl back. The kid was skinny; he'd be easy to overpower. But he didn't have a weapon, and the Somalians near the stairs did. Odds were they'd be too jumpy to hold their fire, even if he had their comrade around the neck.

"You find a beer up there, you let me know, huh?" Gunny said as the soldier disappeared up the steps.

Hell of a jail, he thought. Reminded him of the storage room in an old NCO club in Florida. Guys used to help one of the waitresses rearrange the boxes downstairs.

Ooo-la-la.

The door above opened once more. A pair of black boots appeared, followed by the Somalians in their beat-up sneakers.

Major Smith.

Gunny tried to keep his expression blank as Smith was prodded down to the basement. Unlike Gunny and Jackson, Smith was wearing a set of manacles on his hands and legs. He walked slowly, then stood at attention a few feet away. Neither man spoke as the soldiers turned back and went up the stairs.

The instant the door closed, Smith collapsed on the floor.

"Jesus, Major, you all right?" said Gunny, not quite in time to keep Smith's head from slamming on the hard-packed dirt.

"Yeah, I'm okay," said Smith. His eyes were closed. "Where the fuck are we?"

"Jail, I think," said Gunny.

"Upstairs looks like a school or something. We still in Somalia?"

"They had us in the back of a van the whole time," Gunny told him. "I'm not sure. I think so. We were headed west, maybe northwest, I figure. Near the coast, but not on it. Some Iranian guy's in charge. Raghead."

"The Imam," said Smith.

"Looks like Khomeni," said Gunny.

"This guy's our lawyer or something." Smith groaned. "Or he's pretending to be, so we trust him."

"Lawyer?"

Smith pulled himself forward, finally opening his eyes. "Ribs are killing me," said the major apologetically.

"Yeah. They beat you up?"

"Haven't touched me."

"Us neither. Strange. They must be scared."

"No. They're going to put us on trial. They don't want us hurt before then. We're propaganda." Smith glanced toward the two Somalians standing at the foot of the stairs. They were holding South African 9mm BXPs, Uzi-like weapons with telescoping stocks and air-cooled muzzles. "What happened to Jackson?"

"They took him upstairs. He got shot in the leg."

"How about you?"

"Head hurts like shit," said Gunny. He pointed to the scrape on his scalp where he'd been nicked by a bullet. "Otherwise only thing that smarts is my pride."

Gunny told Smith how Jackson got hit and went down right after they were spotted. Gunny tossed a smoke grenade and went to get him. Somewhere around there another grenade went off, tossed by Jackson or the Somalians, he wasn't sure. Either it was a concussion grenade or a dud; in any event, all it had done was slam the sergeant to the ground. When he tried to get up he found half a dozen Somalians in his face.

"I guess I got shot somewhere along the way," added Gunny. "Lucky for me it hit my head and bounced off. Hit me anywhere else and it would have gone right through."

"Let me see it."

Melfi bent down and let Smith examine the wound, even though Jackson had already said the bullet had only grazed him. The major agreed, describing it as the sort of red singe a barber's razor might make.

"What happens next, you figure?" Gunny asked.

"Take us to wherever the trial is."

"If we don't get rescued first," said the sergeant. "Or bust out first."

Smith gave him a weak smile. "Yeah, we'll just have to bust out."

"I got a knife blade in my buckle," whispered Gunny.

The major didn't understand at first. Finally he nodded. "My radio," he told Gunny. "Somebody should have got the signal."

"They'll come for us," said Melfi. "Don't worry, Major. Hell, Jackson and me are expendable. But you're a fuckin' officer. You bet your ass they're going to come and get you back."

Smith groaned in reply, then sank to the floor, starting to nod off.

MACK FOUGHT TO KEEP HIS EYES OPEN. THE BASEMENT smelled like a cross between a biology lab and the kitchen of an Indian restaurant that hadn't been cleaned in a week. Knife held his elbow right below his injured rib, pushing it in to keep himself from puking.

A medical attendant—the man clearly had not been a doctor—had roughly taped the rib after prodding him harshly a few times upstairs. He'd also offered some pain-killers, but Smith hadn't dared to take them.

Knife knew he should be coordinating strategy or planning what they would and wouldn't say with the Marine sergeant. But the pain and his fatigue and the stench were overwhelming. Thoughts flew in and out of his head like dreams. He saw himself running at the two men near the stairs with their guns, saw their bullets tearing him apart. It might be a relief.

The door opened. He saw three men coming down, carrying a fourth. They seemed to float over him.

The fourth man was dumped on the ground.

It was Jackson. Melfi went to him as the others retreated back upstairs.

"I feel better," Jackson was saying on the ground. Sergeant Melfi helped him upright. "They gave me morphine. I don't feel shit."

"You fuckin' druggie," said Melfi. He flashed a grin to Mack, letting him know it was a joke.

"There's another pilot," said Jackson. "They're going to move us soon. Tonight."

"That'll be our chance," said Gunny. "We'll break out then."

"Oh, yeah, sure. We'll kill them all," said Mack, feeling his head slip back as darkness fell over him.

Naples, Italy
22 October, 1405 local

TO JED BARCLAY'S UNTRAINED EYE, THE PLANE LOOKED like a 707. And in fact, the JSTARS E-8C was indeed a former commercial airliner that had been almost completely rebuilt. It had extensive command and control equipment, not to mention heavy security. The NSC staffer had been issued special code-word clearance just to board the craft.

Which impressed the Army major standing and barring his way at the entrance not a whit.

"But I'm *Cascade*," Jed repeated.

"Good for you," said the major. "You're also too young to shave."

"I get a lot of that," said Jed. "If you just let me take the retina scan—"

"What makes you think there's a retina scanner aboard?" said the major.

Two Navy officers trotted up the steps. The major nodded at them and let them pass into the interior of the plane.

"You didn't even ask for their creds," said Jed.

"This is a Navy operation," said the major. "I'm only providing tactical assistance. Besides, they beat the pants off me in a poker game last night."

"Actually, this isn't a Navy operation at all," Jed told him, momentarily wondering if he might get further by suggesting he played poker as well. "We're still working with Madcap Magician."

Jed was fudging—overall command of the operation

was due to shift to the Navy as soon as the command staff could arrive, which wouldn't be for a few hours.

"And you think that's going to make a difference?" said the Army officer.

"To be honest, it makes no difference," said Jed. "Listen, Major, no offense, but I spent several hours this morning talking to the ambassadors of Egypt and Saudi Arabia about their refusal to allow U.S. planes to use their bases. Then I had to listen to an Iranian cleric, obviously a madman, denounce me for a half hour. Even more frustrating was talking to the State Department's Middle Eastern desk, trying to explain to them why quick military action and not diplomacy was required. To be honest with you, I'm in a really pissy mood."

The major frowned at him, but finally moved back from the door. There was no retina scan—in fact, there was no security device at all.

"You don't want my NSC card at least?" Jed asked him.

"I'll throw you in the ocean if you don't check out," said the major, pushing him into the operations area. "Don't touch anything. These monitors here—"

"Are slaved to different parts of the SAR, which gives you approximately a sixty-degree view of a selected battlefield area. Smearing of the image is countered through interferometry calibration, as well as the Litton LR-85A Inertial Measurement System. There are a total of eighteen consoles aboard this craft, which is an upgrade from the original twelve and the seventeen powered stations in the first production models, though of course one could argue that there are never enough. Frankly, the main concern with JSTARS is not the physical operation of the battlefield view and coordination system, which demonstrated its potential in the Gulf War, but rather the temptation to use the craft to micromanage the battlefield, robbing individual officers, ground- and air-based, of their decision-making role. The same concern was raised—and to some degree remains valid—with AWACS operations. And I'd be up for any poker games you do manage to organize. I assume we're not taking off for hours, right?"

The major frowned, but said, "You'll do," before turning and walking away.

Northeastern Ethiopia
22 October 1996, 2000 local

"WE'RE NOT STOPPING."

"I know that," Bree snapped, working to hold the Megafortress on the rain-slicked tarmac. Flaps, brakes, reverse thrust, and a hurried Hail Mary seemed to have little effect as the big plane hurtled rapidly toward the end of the runway. Shapes loomed left and right, lights streaming with the rain. Breanna's arm locked as the Megafortress's nose bounced harshly across the poorly maintained concrete. A jumble of low buildings lay ahead; the Megafortress threatened to slide into them sideways, her left side trying to jerk forward.

Finally the plane's forward momentum eased, the brakes or maybe the prayer catching. Breanna eased the big plane back to the center of the runway, managing a full stop three yards from a large puddle that marked the end of the concrete.

"That wasn't four thousand feet," said Chris. "Let alone six. And I thought it never rained in Ethiopia before January."

Breanna edged her throttles carefully, turning the EB-52 toward the side access ramp on her right. As she did, a Hummer with its lights on approached from the right, driving along the apron. She guessed that it had been sent to show them where to go. Rolling slowly, her heart returning to normal, she turned the Megafortress onto the path. The truck pulled a 180 and began speeding away toward a hangar area.

The runway had had minimal lighting, and this access ramp had none; Fort Two's lights provided a narrow co-coon for her to steer through. Breanna saw another plane standing at the far end of the ramp—a parked MC-130 Hercules.

"Must be the place," said Chris, spotting the military transport. "We're going to have a hell of a time taking off in this rain," he added.

"We'll round up some volunteers to push," she told him, watching their guide truck disappear to the right. Breanna leaned back in her seat, the exhaustion of the long flight finally taking its toll. They had pushed Fort Two about as fast as it had ever gone for much longer than it had ever flown. While she and Chris had switched on and off—and the computer autopilot had helped con-siderably—Bree's brain was crispy and her legs and arms felt as if they had been run over by a steamroller. She hadn't slept now in more than twenty-four hours, and had needed three caffeine pills—she didn't like anything stronger—en route.

Four large Pave Lows and a civilian DC-8 airliner were parked at the far end of a group of buildings that looked more like warehouses than hangars. The Hummer spun off and blinked its lights; Bree began to swing the plane around into the designated parking area. Two Marines with M-16-and-grenade-launcher combos appeared from one of the buildings, sauntering up as if they landed Megafortresses here all the time.

"Gee, where's the brass band?" asked Chris.

CAPTAIN FREAH WAITED IMPATIENTLY AS THE BOMBER trundled toward its parking area. He'd been able to sleep only a few hours, but felt a burst of energy and excitement as the big plane finally stopped. Undoing his restraints, he bolted up from the uncomfortable jump seat and grabbed his gear. Squeezing into the hatch area, he pulled down the handle to open and lower the access ladder. It sounded like a bus tire puncturing as it burst open; Danny took it two steps at a time, ducking his head and scooting out from beneath the plane. A pair of rain-soaked Marines waved him toward a nearby pickup. After the cramped quarters of the Megafortress navigational bay, even the warm but heavy rain felt good. Danny stood out on the tarmac getting soaked while the rest of his team disembarked. Leaving Hernandez behind to wrestle with their gear in the storage bay, they hopped into the rear of the pickup. The rain surged as the truck started, but it seemed to be a final burst, for by the time they reached the low-slung building at the far end of the base it had slowed to a drizzle.

Freah jumped over the side of the truck, walking double-time inside. Hal Briggs greeted him in the hallway.

"Look what the cat dragged in," said Briggs, slamming Danny with a shoulder chuck. "Damn. I thought the ETA you gave was a typo."

"You didn't think I'd let you have fun without me, did you?" asked Freah. His men filed in behind him; Danny introduced them.

"Grub's that way," said Briggs, pointing down the hall. "You'll find a cafeteria, whole nine yards. You have a half hour," added Briggs, glancing at his watch.

"Just a half hour?"

"Ospreys should be here by then."

"Ospreys?"

"Since you busted your hump to get here, we'll give you something real to do," said Briggs. "Come on. Let me fill you in over at the terminal building. It's our command bunker."

"What is this place?" Danny asked.

"Russkies built it as a commercial strip place back in the seventies, then abandoned it when they realized the area was too rugged to support any sort of industry. Thank God for Commies with money, or at least bulldozers and cement, huh?"

Freah followed the major back outside. They walked around the side of the building to a Humvee. Briggs got in and Danny followed; they drove back toward the area where the Megafortress had parked.

"Shit. You came in a Megafortress?" said Briggs as they passed the plane.

"How do you think we got here so fast?"

"They had room to land?"

"I guess."

Briggs turned right between the last and next-to-last buildings, then made a sharp right onto a long access road. They followed it as it circled around a row of small hangars; they looked more like sheds.

Three F-117 Nighthawks and three F-16 Vipers were parked beyond the sheds, guarded by a dozen air commandos. Briggs slowed just enough to let the guards know it was him, then sped on toward a large terminal building. Even in the dark it was obvious the building had been abandoned for some time. Lights shone eerily inside, and shadows seemed to leak from the broken windows. Two more Air Force Special Ops guards with M-16's met them as Briggs pulled to a stop. Danny recognized one of the men, but barely had a chance to nod as Hal walked briskly inside.

A group of men clustered inside the empty reception hall, examining a series of maps spread over a trio of tables. The maps spilled over the sides; there were clutches of satellite pictures and a few rough sketches arranged around them.

"This is Danny Freah," said Briggs, introducing him around. Quickly, Briggs filled him in on the situation. A

Marine assault team supported by four F-16's had attempted to take out several batteries of SAM missiles and a Silkworm base on the Somalian coast, while a flight of four F-117's went after a pair of Silkworm bases a few miles to the northwest. Both of these bases were more extensive and better defended than had been thought, and the team came under heavy fire. An F-16 and one of the F-117 stealth fighters were downed. The F-117 was apparently lost to an SA-2; the long-wave radar was able to detect the vortices caused by the plane, and it was especially vulnerable while launching its missiles.

"We don't jam the radars—or I should say we didn't—since that costs us the element of surprise. Our targets were destroyed," Briggs added. "Frankly, the SAM had only about a one-in-a-hundred chance of getting the plane. It was an acceptable risk." He jabbed his finger at the map, pinpointing a spot on the hilly plains just south of the coast. "We have a strong suspicion that the pilot was alive because we have radio intercepts from an Iranian MiG about a parachute in this area. His name's Stephen Howland. Captain. Twenty-six. From Carroll Gardens, Brooklyn."

Danny nodded.

"Our intelligence is limited," admitted Briggs, "but we think that the Somalians have already recovered at least the plane. CIA has a source saying he saw an airplane on a flatbed truck out on this road. It's not really a highway; more like a dirt road with pretensions that runs through these mountains and hills. Anyway, it would make sense, because this road goes right to Bosaso, on the northern coast, which is within five miles of where we think the plane went down. From Bosaso they might go down to Mogadishu. Or maybe they'll try for Libya, heading west on this highway here. It's been improved recently; we think the Iranians have helped widen and repave it. It hooks up with Burao. From there they would have a highway, a real highway, through Ethiopia, the Sudan, Libya, wherever they want to go."

"Why Libya?"

"Libya has signed up for the Greater Islamic League," said Hal. "So bringing the prisoners there might be one way of guaranteeing that their partner is involved. The Iranians may also figure that with a Presidential election coming up, pounding Tehran will be an enormously popular thing to do."

"Would it?" asked Danny.

"I don't know about the politics," said Hal. He quickly went on. "They also know we're sending ships up from the Indian Ocean. They also suspect that we could base forces in Kenya. So to the Iranians it might seem safer to go by ground. They might not think we're watching."

Briggs slid one of the satellite pictures around and pointed at it. It covered an area near the northeastern coast of Somalia. "One of our satellites is being repaired by the shuttle, and the remaining birds aren't positioned very well for coverage. We're also having a hell of a lot of trouble because of the weather and the clouds," said Briggs. "This image is several hours old. We're trying to arrange an overflight in the morning. We have a Delta Force team ready to go in as soon as we have a target. But we're talking several hundred square miles to cover. And it's nearly four hundred miles from here. We'd like to get the stealth fighter back, or at least blow up the wreckage. As soon as it's located, we go. Same thing on the pilot."

"What about the F-16?" asked Danny.

"You may know him—Mack Smith. He was at Dreamland. Tall guy. Typical pilot ego."

"Sure."

"He went out over here, a few miles away. Mack seems to have stayed around to help the Marines. The Marines credit him with saving their necks, because their helicopter was under fire. Two members of the assault team apparently saw it get hit and left their helicopter to help Smith."

"No shit."

"Yeah. Like I said, their helo was getting hit and in the confusion the pilot decided his best course of action was to get out," Briggs said. "He didn't know he was missing two men. In any event, he did manage to save the rest of the team and the helicopter."

Briggs slid the satellite image away, jabbing his finger at a yellow blotch on the map. "We're getting an intermittent signal beacon from this spot here, about two, two-and-a-half miles south of the Silkworm base, back in these hills here. We haven't been able to raise the pilot. We sent a rented Cessna and managed to get this," he added, moving around the papers to find some sketchy photocopies of snapshots.

"We think it's the wreckage of the plane. Satellite will survey this area as well," said Briggs. "We're sending a team at first light. Worst case, we can destroy the wreckage. We'll also have a team overfly the area of the radio transmission. If Smith's down there and can work the radio, they'll grab him."

"That our job?"

"No. We want you to help secure this site here. Your team and a small group of Delta operators, hitting them from two sides, airlifted by Ospreys. It's a village about ten kilometers further west that the Iranians have been using to train the Somalians. The feeling is that if Smith and the Marines were captured, they'd be held there." Briggs pulled a pair of reconnaissance photographs and some hand-drawn sketches from the other side of the table and showed them to Danny. "These were taken a few hours ago. They give the general layout. This school here used to belong to a Catholic missionary order. You see the gun emplacements. And this here is a SAM site."

Danny strained his eyes to make out the small blotch beneath Major Briggs's finger. It looked like a microscopic Brillo pad.

"We think it's an SA-6, which comes on a mobile launcher. It's likely that there are now more, since the defenses at the Silkworm site were beefed up," said Briggs.

"Where the hell are they getting all this hardware?" Freah asked.

"Where aren't they?" said Briggs. "The Silkworms come from China, where they may also have bought some fighters. There's been a large inflow of weapons into Libya from Russia. Some of that has disappeared, which we think means it's headed here. There have also been some small boats slipping into Mogadishu in the south, with or without help from the Yemenis; it's unclear."

Briggs continued laying out the situation. The antiaircraft defenses posed a serious problem. The F-117's and F-16's would be needed to help the other operations. The Ospreys would arrive without escort or backup, traveling quickly at treetop level. Though that was under the detection envelope of the missiles' ground radars, it would be dicey.

"We're short on air support," said Hal apologetically. "The *Eisenhower* is heading up from the Indian Ocean, but they won't be close enough to help us for at least two days. We'd like to have Smith and the others out by then. If we don't, this thing is likely to escalate even further."

"We have the Megafortress," suggested Danny, who'd been waiting for an opportunity to offer the plane. "They're packing cruise missiles and four JSOWs fresh out of the development lab. They can cover us going in."

"Are you talking about my airplane?" said Captain Stockard, walking toward them from the door. She was still in her flight gear, wearing a deep scowl.

"Captain Stockard," said Briggs. "How are you, Bree?"

Breanna ignored him, speaking to Danny instead. "That's my aircraft. With all due respect, Captain, I'll discuss its capabilities."

"I was just pointing out that it carried weapons," said Freah.

"Did you mention the runway's about five hundred feet too short to take off from?" said Breanna. She turned back to Briggs. "And I don't want to talk about landing. Why the hell didn't you give us a heads-up on that, Hal?"

"I wasn't aware you were flying a Megafortress in to begin with," said Briggs. "How are you, Rap?"

"I've been better. My butt's sore and I came this close to blowing out my tires."

"We're installing mesh," said Briggs. "We can push that up. I can't do anything about your butt while you're in uniform," he added.

"Very funny. When's the mesh going on?"

"ASAP. A thousand feet okay?"

"I'll have to do the math," Breanna said. "Major Cheshire has to be told. Raven's heavier than Fort Two because of the older engines. If it's wet and she's carrying fuel, she's going to have a hard time stopping."

"Raven? Another Megafortress?"

"We made the flight without a crew," said Breanna. "Cheshire's following with a weapons officer and a navigator. She should be here within twelve hours, maybe less."

"Shit. We can use her."

"Damn straight," said Danny. "The plane has jamming gear."

"It's the next-generation ECMs," said Rap, throwing a glare at Freah. "I doubt they'll have time to remove it all. Just as there wasn't time to remove the air-to-ground missiles we were carrying. Officially, we're only here as transports."

Briggs shook his head slowly, but he had the start of a grin on his face.

"Of course, local conditions prevail. Assuming we do get airborne," Breanna added, "I'm going to need as much target data as possible. The computer's persnickety and my copilot's a real whiner. Personally, I'd trade them both for a good weapons officer, or even a halfway decent radar navigator."

Dreamland
22 October, 1200 local

"COLONEL, I THOUGHT WE HAD A DATE!"

Dog jerked his head up from his desk. Jennifer Gleason was standing in the doorway.

"I had to run by myself," said the scientist, striding into his office. She plopped herself down in a chair.

"I'm sorry, Doc," said Dog. "I got tied up."

"So I heard." Jennifer glanced back at the office door. Dog looked in time to see Sergeant Gibbs closing it.

He'll get his, Dog thought.

"Want to do lunch?" asked the scientist.

"I can't. I'm sorry," said Bastian. "I've been handling the fallout, from, uh, some recommendations I had to make."

"You mean killing JSF, right?" She flicked her hair back impishly.

"That's supposed to be classified."

"Come on, Colonel. You can't fart on this base without everyone catching a whiff. Not that colonels fart."

For some reason, the word "fart" and her beautiful mouth didn't seem to go together.

"I actually didn't come here to ask you to lunch," said the scientist quickly. She leaned forward, somehow metamorphosing from a beautiful if slightly insolent young woman to a senior scientist. "I came to make a recommendation regarding the Flighthawk program. I feel the mission to Somalia should go forward."

"It's not a mission," said Dog, angered that the flight was being openly discussed.

"I understand, Colonel. I also feel that I should be along in case something goes wrong."

"Doc—"

"First of all, call me Jennifer. Or Jen." She favored him with the briefest of brief smiles. "Second of all, there is no one in the world who knows that computer system better than I do. That's not a brag, that's a fact. If you're sending those planes halfway around the world, I should be there with them."

"I don't know that there's enough room for you," said Dog.

"I checked with Major Cheshire. She says there is."

"Major Cheshire only reluctantly approved carrying the Flighthawks," said Bastian, who'd spoken with Cheshire only a short while before.

"She was worried about not having enough support. I'm the support."

Dog shook his head. It was one thing to send the Mega-fortresses; while they were definitely still in the experimental stage, an early version had already seen some action. Justifying the Flighthawks was much more difficult, especially since they'd lack the veneer of a "transport" mission. And sending a civilian into a war zone was potentially a hanging offense. Her loss would be a serious embarrassment, and not just to him.

"I'm afraid it's not possible," he told her.

"If you lose the U/MFs," she told him, "they'll hang you out to dry."

"If I lose you, they'll grind me up into little pieces."

"You're not going to lose me. Between me and Parsons—"

"Parsons? Sergeant Parsons?"

"He's waiting in the outer office to talk to you. We drew straws to see who would go first," she added.

"No way."

"Colonel, if I were a man, you'd let me go. You need support personnel for the UM/Fs. Shit, the only other person who's qualified to fix that fucking computer and the com system is Rubeo. You want to send him?"

"You talk like a sailor, you know that?" Dog said.

Jennifer shrugged. "My bag is packed."

If she were a man—hell, that was impossible to even imagine.

They did need a support staff. But a girl?

She wasn't a girl, damn it.

"I want to talk to Cheshire before I make a decision," said Bastian finally.

"Good," said Jennifer, jumping up. "Should I send her in right now, along with Major Stockard, or do you want us to keep going the way we planned?"

Shaking his head, Bastian went to the office door and looked out into the reception area. Cheshire and Parsons were there, along with three other Flighthawk specialists.

"Where's Stockard?"

"Making sure the Flighthawks are prepped," said Cheshire.

"Everyone in here," he told the conspirators.

In the end, Dog had no choice but to agree that if it made sense to send the Flighthawks, it was logical to send a support team as well. Parsons could probably build the damn things from balsa wood and speaker wire. Gleason made the most sense as a technical expert, since she knew both the software and the hardware used by the Flighthawks' control system. No way he was sending Rubeo—it would undoubtedly be too tempting for him to be left behind.

Sending a high-tech team halfway around the world with untested weapons was exactly what he had called for in the white paper he'd written so many years ago. So why did his stomach feel so queasy?

"You're good with this, Major?" he asked Cheshire.

"If the Flighthawks are going, and I think they should, we have to support them."

He nodded. "This is my responsibility," he told her. "I'm ordering you to do this."

Her face flushed, probably because she knew that the Band-Aid he'd just applied to her culpability wouldn't cover much of anything if things went wrong.

"I have some phone calls to return," he said. "I'll try to be there for your takeoff."

"Fourteen hundred hours sharp," said Parsons as they exited.

"That soon?"

"We'll kick some butt for you, sir," said the sergeant.

Bastian returned the wily old crew dog's grin, then pulled over his mountain of pink phone-message sheets. Every member of the JSF Mafia wanted to take a shot at chewing off his ear today; might as well let them have a go.

"Lieutenant General Magnus, please," he said, connecting with the first person on his list. "This is Colonel Bastian."

"Oh," said the voice on the other end of the line.

Dog was more than familiar with the tone. It meant, "Oh, so this is the idiot my boss has been screaming about all day."

As he waited for the connection to go through, Dog fingered the official Whiplash implementation order, which had come through earlier in the day.

YOU ARE HEREBY ORDERED TO IMPLEMENT WHIP-LASH AND SUPPORT SAME WITH ALL APPROPRIATE VIGOR.

"Appropriate vigor" could mean Megafortresses. It could mean Flighthawks.

Not if people like General Magnus didn't want it to. Magnus was close to the Air Force Secretary; word was he was being groomed to be Chief of Staff. Dog knew him largely by reputation. An able officer, Magnus was a good man, unless you disagreed with him.

Then he was the devil's own bastard.

"Bastian, what the hell are you doing out there in Dreamland? You sleeping?"

"No, sir, General," said Dog.

"I understand you've been there for two weeks."

"It's about that."

"You took your goddamned time."

Well, thought Dog, at least he has a sense of humor.

"Well, I do my best, General, as pitiful as it may be."

"I don't think it's pitiful at all, Colonel. I think it's goddamn time somebody had the balls to say what a piece of shit this JSF crate is."

Dog looked at the phone, waiting for the punch line.

"You still there, Bastian?"

"Yes, sir," said the colonel.

"Good. We're going to take a hell of a lot of shit on this, I guarantee. But I'm behind you. You bet your ass. I read the whole damn report. Ms. O'Day made sure I got a copy. And a friend of hers. Brad Elliott. I didn't think you and Brad were pals."

"We're not."

"Oh? He talks about you like you're his son. Says you're right on the mark."

"Well, uh, I'm flattered. To be candid, General, I thought you were a supporter of the JSF."

"What? Did you read that in the *Washington Post*?"

"No, sir."

"I expect you're taking a lot of shit," said Magnus.

"That's an understatement," said Dog, not entirely convinced that Magnus was on the level.

"Well, hold tight. And keep your nose clean. Some of these pricks will use anything they can against you. The Congressmen are the worst."

"Yes, sir," said Dog. "Thank you, sir." But his line had already gone dead.

Somalia
23 October, 0100 local

MACK WOKE TO FIND THE IMAM STARING AT HIM. SERgeant Melfi and Jackson were gone; perhaps he'd only dreamed they were here with him alive.

"Major, very good," said the Iranian. "Come now. We must meet our fate."

The Imam straightened, then gestured at him to rise. Though still groggy, Smith felt almost powerless to resist.

"What's going on?" Mack asked.

"You are going to stand trial," said the Imam. "Justice will be swift."

He turned and walked back to the steps. Someone behind Mack pushed him; he stumbled over his chains, but managed to keep his balance.

Goddamn. Mack Smith. The hottest stick on the patch. Damn Iranians were going to make him the star of "don't let this happen to you" lectures for the next hundred years.

The man behind him pushed again. Knife's anger leaped inside him; he spun and grabbed the startled soldier by the throat, pushing him to the floor with surprising ease. He smashed the bastard's head against the concrete. The chain of his handcuffs clanked against the man's chest as he grabbed the guard's ears, pulling them upward to smash him again, then again, feeling the thud of the floor reverberating across the Somalian's skull.

He knew he was being foolish. The best thing to do

was go along, resist, yes, but not so overtly, not so crazily. Doing this was like committing suicide, or worse.

And yet he couldn't stop himself. Blood spread out behind the man's face as Mack pounded again and again, screaming, shrieking his anger.

Then a sharp light erupted from behind his ears. Then his head seemed to collapse. He blanked out.

"YOU SCREWED UP THEIR PLANS, MAJOR," GUNNY WAS saying. "You really threw them for a loop. I don't know what you did, but it messed them up. Kept us here for hours. And they didn't want that, I can tell you."

Mack waited for the hunched shadow to come into focus. They were moving, in a train—no, a bus, an old school bus with half of its seats removed. Gunny, the Marine Corps sergeant, was kneeling next to him in the back aisle. There were stretchers on the wall of the bus next to him, empty.

"What do you think, Sarge?" said another Marine.

Jackson. He was leaning over a seat a few feet away.

"I don't know. I'd say he took a slam to the noggin. You with us, Major?"

"Yeah," groaned Knife.

"You have blood on your flight suit," said Gunny. "Don't look like yours."

"No?"

Mack struggled to sit up. He was still chained at the hands and the feet. "I hit somebody," he told them.

"No shit?" said Gunny. "Way to go, Major. Dumb, but way to go."

"Yeah, it was dumb," agreed Mack.

"You messed them up," added the sergeant. "Put them on notice that we're no pushovers."

The bus lurched off the side of the road, coming to a stop.

"City," said Jackson, looking out the window. "By their standards anyway."

"Where are we?" Mack asked.

"Damned if I know," said Gunny. He went to the window and looked outside. "Pretty damn dark."

"Think it's Mogadishu, Sarge?" asked Jackson. A few years before, several U.S. soldiers had died there in an ill-fated relief operation.

"Nah. Wrong direction. We're still way north. We've been heading west." Gunny returned, hovering over Mack. "Damned if I know where the hell we're going. Can you get up, Major?"

"Maybe," he said. He let Melfi pull him up; he sat on the floor, waiting for the blood to stop rushing to his head.

"Did he die?" Mack asked.

"Did who die?" Gunny asked.

"The guy I hit."

"Don't know," said the sergeant. "The raghead guy's still alive, if that's who you're talking about."

"I didn't hit him," said Mack. "I hit one of the guards. A Somalian."

The door to the bus opened up front. Two Somalian soldiers came up the steps, followed by an American in a flight suit—Captain Stephen Howland, one of the F-117 pilots. The Imam was behind him. The soldiers stepped aside and let the pilot pass. He walked toward them slowly, eyes fixed on the floor. He didn't seem to be injured, beyond some bruises to his eyes.

"I see Major Smith has recovered," said the Imam mildly. "There will be no more episodes, Major. They make our task that much more difficult. Our hosts get bothered."

"You could just let us go," said Gunny. "Then we'll go easy on you."

The Iranian had already started off the bus. The others

followed, leaving them to the two Somalian guards and driver at the front.

"They're taking us to Libya," said the pilot as the driver started the bus.

"Libya?" asked Johnson.

"Yeah. The Iranians have declared a Muslim coalition against the West," said Howland. "Libya, Sudan, Iran, now Somalia. Iraq is cheering them on."

"The usual shitheads," said Gunny. "They won't get anywhere."

"I don't know," said Howland. He sat in the seat opposite Johnson. "They're gloating about Saudi Arabia and Egypt. They think they're coming in with them. Something about air bases. Probably they didn't give our planes permission to land." The pilot shook his head. "There's a whole lot of shit going down and we're right in the middle of it."

"Aw, come on," said Gunny, trying to cheer him up. "If you're standing in shit, at least it can't rain on your head."

"Unless you slip and fall in it," said Howland.

"Jeez, Gunny, look at that." Jackson pointed out the back window. A flatbed truck had pulled up behind them. A huge scrap of black metal was lashed to the rear; Somalians clustered all over the wreckage as well as the roof of the vehicle's cab.

"My plane," said Howland. He looked down at Mack. "They must have been waiting for me to open the bay and pickle. I got the warning and started doing evasive maneuvers, but like an idiot I flamed out."

"You were just unlucky," said Mack.

"What happened to you?"

"I fucked up," said Knife.

"Ah, bullshit on that," said Gunny, his voice almost vicious as he turned from the back window. "Fuckin' major saved our asses is what he did. That wasn't no fuck-up. And it wasn't bad luck."

"Wasn't good luck," said Mack.

"No, sir. No fuckin' sir," said the sergeant as the bus lurched forward. "But it sure as shit wasn't a fuck-up."

Mack fought off the swelling pain in his head to acknowledge the thank-you with a nod.

Northeastern Ethiopia
23 October, 0300

BREANNA PULLED BACK ON THE CONTROL STICK DESPITE the warning from the computer that they hadn't yet reached optimum takeoff speed. She pushed down on the throttle bar with her other hand, as if the extra force might somehow squeeze more oomph out of the four power plants, which were already at max.

She was also mumbling a Hail Mary. Couldn't hurt.

Despite the computer's disapproval, Fort Two caught a stiff wind in her chin and lifted off the mesh runway extension, clearing the trees at the far end of the runway with a good two inches to spare. Breanna gave herself a second to exhale, then began banking to swing onto the course north. They would fly at five hundred feet above ground level all the way to the border. At that point, she would take the plane even lower and goose the engines; they would be on their target in precisely five minutes. Chris would unleash the two cruise missiles on the known SAMs.

What happened next depended on the Somalians and the Iranians who were helping them. According to the satellite photos, a ZSU-23 antiaircraft gun sat at the northwestern corner of the complex. It would be nice to eliminate the gun before the MHV-22 Ospreys arrived with their assault teams. On the other hand, the Zeus had a limited line of sight toward that end of the base, so attacking it wasn't a priority if other defenses had been installed along the southern edge of the old school grounds.

Unfortunately, there was only one sure way to discover if there were additional defenses there—the Megafortress would have to show itself and see if anyone took a potshot at it. It could then use its JSOWs on them.

The EB-52's ECMs could automatically ID all known Soviet-era detection and targeting radars, buzzing bands from Jaybird to DesiLu, as Chris liked to joke. At the same time, it could automatically note the source of the radars, supplying the data for the targeting lobe of its multifaceted brain. On the other hand, Fort Two could not preemptively wipe out radars and signal radios like Raven, for example, nor was it equipped to deal with the next-generation gear found in more sophisticated Western systems. They'd have to punt if they came up against any.

"Vector One and Vector Two are airborne," said Chris. Pushed to top speed, the tilt-wing rotorcraft transports could approach four hundred knots, more than twice as fast as "normal" helicopters. They were coming in right behind the Megafortress.

Breanna checked her instruments, scanning the glass panels of the cockpit as slowly as she could manage. Time was starting to blur by as quickly as her heart was pounding.

Jeff had told her about the first time he'd been in combat, flying over Iraq. He'd tried to keep calm by counting slowly to himself as he looked at each instrument in his F-15C, counting it off.

That was Mack Smith who'd told her that. Jeff hadn't flown Eagles in the Gulf.

"Interceptor radar ahead," said Chris.

Breanna looked at the left MUD, which painted the sky ahead with different colors, indicating the presence of enemy radars. A green blob hung halfway down the screen, dripping and fading. The computer was processing signals received by the enemy and plotting them in real time on the screen, color-coding the seriousness of the threat. Green meant that the enemy could not detect them, generally because it was out of range due to the Megafortress's stealthy configuration or, as in this case, low altitude. Yellow meant that they could potentially be detected but hadn't been. Red meant that they were being actively targeted.

"We have a MiG-29, two MiG-29's," said Chris, working with the computer to ID the threats. At this point they used only passive sensors—active radar would be like using a flashlight in a darkened room. "They're well out of range. Seem to be tracking north. Thirty miles. Thirty-two. Other side of the border."

"Keep an eye on them for the Ospreys," Bree told him.

"Gotcha, Captain."

Breanna hit her way-point just south of the Somalian border, adjusting her course to track northeastward.

"Lost the MiGs," said Chris. "Think they were from A-1?"

"A-1's supposed to be too small for anything bigger than a Piper Cherokee," said Breanna. The airstrip was located about twenty miles northwest of their target area, right on the coast.

"Maybe from Sudan then. Or Yemen. They have to be working at the very edge of their range." Chris checked through the paperwork, double-checking their intelligence reports and satellite maps, making sure the MiGs couldn't have landed anywhere nearby.

"Mark Two in zero-one minutes. Border in zero-one minutes," the computer told Breanna. It also gave her a cue on the HUD that they were nearing the danger zone, spitting back the flight data they had programmed before.

"Stand by to contact Vector flight," she told Chris. "We're looking good."

"Hell of a moon," he said.

Breanna had no time to admire the scenery. She edged the Megafortress lower toward the ragged steppes and jagged rocks of the African Horn, glancing quickly at the MUD to make sure no enemy radars had suddenly snapped to life. The Megafortress was now skimming over the rocky savanna at a blistering 558 nautical miles an hour. She had to be careful and alert—the EB-52 lacked terrain-following radar. Even with the improved power plants the Megafortress lacked the oomph of, say, an F-111, which could pull up instantly if an obstacle loomed. The computer and sensors helped her stay low along a carefully mapped route.

"Border," said Breanna. They passed into Somalia, apparently undetected. Their target lay approximately 150 miles dead ahead.

"Preparing to launch cruise missiles," said Chris, selecting the weapons-control module on his computer display. "Bay."

The Megafortress was equipped with a rotary launcher in the bomb bay similar to the devices installed in B-52Hs. In a stock B-52, up to eight cruise missiles could be mounted, rotated into position, and then launched. Fort Two's launcher allowed for a variety of weapons besides the cruise missiles; in this case, two Scorpion AMRAAM-plus air-to-air missiles and four JSOW weapons, which had imaging infrared target seekers. The AGM-86c cruise missiles had to be preprogrammed, a relatively laborious task for someone like Chris who wasn't used to doing it. But once they were launched they did all the work.

"Bomb bay is open," the computer reported to Breanna. The open bay made them visible to radar, though their low altitude made it extremely unlikely they would be spotted.

"Launch at will," Breanna told Chris.

The computer made the process almost idiot-proof, but

Chris worked through the procedure carefully, making sure they were at the preprogrammed launch points and altitudes before pushing each of the large missiles off. The twenty-foot-long flying bombs lit their engines as they slipped below the Megafortress, popping up briefly before descending even lower, guided by radar altimeters and sophisticated on-board maps.

"No turning back now," said Chris as he closed the bomb bay door.

"We can always turn back," said Bree. "Let's hope we don't have to."

DANNY FELT THE REST OF HIS ASSAULT TEAM STARTING to tense as the Osprey passed over the border into Somalia. Talk had gotten sparser and sparser since takeoff; no one had spoken now for at least five minutes.

No matter how much you trained for combat, or thought about it, or dreamed about it, you were never ready for it when it arrived. You punched the buttons like you were trained to, reacted the way you'd taught your body to react. But that didn't mean you were really, truly ready. There was no way to erase the millisecond of fear, the quick surge of adrenaline that leaped at you the instant you came under fire.

These guys knew it. They'd been there before.

"Vector One has peeled off. We're ten minutes from our target," said the pilot.

Some of the others tried peering out the windows, craning their heads toward the front. The cruise missiles would be finding their targets any second now; in theory they'd see the flashes.

Danny steadied his eyes on his MP-5, double-checking it to make sure it was ready. He had two clips ready in each vest pocket, along with a grenade, the pin taped so it couldn't accidentally get snagged.

Good to go.

*   *   *

CHRIS HAD HIS FACE PRACTICALLY PASTED TO THE
screen, which was projecting an infrared image of the Somalian base, now just over twelve miles away.

"Nothing," he said. "I see the SA-6's, that's all. But
we're still a good way off."

"No Zeus?"

"No antiair guns at all. No other defenses."

"AGMs to target, ten seconds," said Bree. "Nine, eight,
seven—"

"Wow, I see it!" shouted Chris, and in the next second
the horizon lit with a yellow-red explosion. "Got him!"

The second cruise missile splashed five seconds later.
Both completely obliterated their targets.

Breanna tensed, waiting for the RWR to warn her that
the Somalians had belatedly turned on their antiaircraft
radars.

Nada.

She activated the nightscope viewer panel. The view
was limited to twelve degrees and Breanna never felt particularly comfortable with it, preferring the radar and IR
scans. But the synthetic view didn't mind the humid conditions caused by the recent rain, couldn't be jammed, and
was easy to sort when things got hot—pun intended.

"We're going to be overhead in about sixty seconds,"
she told Chris. "What do you think?"

"I don't have a target," he said. "Looks like the place
is deserted. Shit, there are no secondaries. I think those
SAMs were decoys."

"Or we missed."

"No." Chris played with the resolutions on the screen.
"I saw them. They're gone. No related vehicles. I'm thinking decoys, Bree. Or they left. Place is deserted."

"Vector Leader, this is Fort Two," said Breanna, alerting the assault team. "SAMs have been splashed. No live defenses. Copy?"

"Roger, copy," returned the ground mission commander from the Osprey. "We'll proceed as planned."

"Fort Two," said Bree. She turned to her copilot. "Chris, pull out the satellite maps. Give me the heading of that east-west road."

"I can see it on the screen," he told her. "What are you thinking?"

"Let's see where it goes," said Bree. She selected the FLIR imaging for her MUD, then banked the Megafortress to follow along the roadway. It rose through the hills toward northern Ethiopia, with a new leg skirting Hargyesa, a relative megalopolis. The road seemed deserted—or at least there were no warm engines or bodies on it, according to the FLIR.

"They could be anywhere, Bree," said Chris. "We don't want to get out too far from Vector, in case they run into problems."

"I'm not intending on getting too far away, Chris," she told him. "Relax."

"I'm relaxed," he said defensively. He checked his screen. "They're thirty seconds away."

Breanna swung out of the south leg of her orbit, heading back toward the center of the target area. She selected the starscope input for her screen, and saw two dark shadows leap into the green, wings tilting upward as they swept into a landing.

"Dead as a doornail," said Chris, who was using the infrared to monitor the scene. "Nothing moving. Nothing hot."

"You're ready with the JSOWs just in case?"

"Now who's getting tense?" asked Chris.

"Let's open the bay doors just to be sure."

"Roger that," he snapped. She couldn't quite tell if he was being sarcastic.

*   *   *

THEY'D PLANNED TO RAPPEL, SO HITTING THE GROUND behind the swirling motors was a bit of a letdown, but Danny could live with it. He and the rest of the Whiplash team spread out quickly, moving to cover the first team's assault of the main building.

It wasn't much of an assault. The Delta troopers had lowered themselves from their Osprey to the roof of the main building, working down to the main floor in about a fifth of the time a training exercise would have taken— less actually, since any training exercise would have used another Spec Ops team as enemies.

"We're clear, Captain," said the Delta commander over the com set. The lightweight Dreamland gear made him sound as if he were standing at Danny's side. "We have blood on the floor in the basement, and some flight gear."

"Shit. We're too late."

"All right. We'll search and secure," said the commander.

Danny cursed, then relayed the information to his men.

AS SOON AS THE GROUND TEAM CONFIRMED THAT THE school was deserted, Breanna pointed Fort Two toward A-1, the airstrip close to the Gulf of Aden.

"I don't know, Bree," said Chris. "They could be anywhere. I'm thinking Mogadishu."

"Mogadishu's five hundred miles southeast of here."

"My point exactly."

Breanna didn't think that they would be lucky enough to find them on the ground. But she did want to see if her theory was at least possible. A-1 was a little more than seventy-five miles away, a straight line back toward the northwest. While they didn't have particularly fat fuel reserves, she figured they could get close enough to get a look at the airstrip before turning back to shepherd the Ospreys home.

"We'll be within FLIR range in five minutes," she told her copilot.

"Four and a half. I've already computed it," he told her. "Man, I could go for a cigarette right about now."

"I thought you gave up smoking."

"Stuff like this tickles my throat," he said. "Shit, we got something in the air."

Chris seemed to be operating on a sixth sense, picking up something before the high-powered detectors had sniffed out the radar. But he was right—a Jay Bird radar had flicked on ahead. The computer poked a green puff in the radar-warning screen. It was below them, which seemed impossible since they were at only a thousand feet.

"The source is far off," said Chris, hunkering over the screen and working the computer to refine the read. "This is on the ground, Bree. Shit, this has to be a MiG-21. Off, it's off."

"On the ground? Has to be A-1."

"Yeah. Like it was a maintenance check or something. Or a decoy."

"We'll be close enough to find out pretty soon."

"Be nice to have a pair of fighters covering our butts about now," Chris said.

"We can deal with a MiG-21 ourselves," said Breanna. "Ground radar?"

"Negative. Scope's clean. No ground stations. Nothing. Of course, they could take off and turn it on once they were in the air. We're sitting ducks here."

"The MiG radar can't find a standard B-52 at twenty miles," said Bree.

"What I'm worried about are those MiG-29's we saw before," said Chris. "Maybe they're Libyan fighters. Qaddafi's got a bunch of them."

For once, his fear was well-founded. The passive sensors on the MiGs could theoretically allow the interceptors to target Fort Two from long range, possibly even before being detected by Fort Two's own passive arrays.

"I think those MiGs we saw before are out there," said Chris. "I thinking they're waiting to ambush the Ospreys. They could be in those mountain ranges to the west."

"If they came from Libya, they'd never have the range to linger," said Bree.

"What if they launched from A-1? If it's long enough for a MiG-21, they'd have no problem."

Breanna leaned closer to her stick. They were about thirty miles from the airstrip.

"I think there's something stalking us, maybe twelve miles off," said Chris. "What do you think of turning on the active radar?"

"If there is something out there, it'll tell them we're here," said Bree. "And it's expressly against orders."

"Well, there is that," said Chris. "But getting shot down is too. If we hit the radar we can get a clear picture. We see something, we launch the Scorpions. I swear something's watching for us, Bree. They're to the west, right there." He pointed across the cockpit. "I can feel it."

"We'll see them first," said Breanna.

"Maybe not. They could circle out through the hills, duck around us, go for the Ospreys. The rotor engines are monster signals for any IR seeker. They'll be sitting ducks."

Less than sixty seconds now separated them from the small airstrip where Breanna believed Smith and the others had been taken. Turn on the radar and they might never reach it.

On the other hand, if the MiGs were where Chris thought, the Ospreys would be sitting ducks.

"Go to search and scan," she ordered.

"On it."

Chris was wrong. The MiGs weren't in the mountains to the west.

They were hugging the ground forty miles to the east, running south like all hell. There were four of them, and while two were within striking distance of Vector, they didn't seem to be interested in the Ospreys—they were going for the F-117's, just arriving on target with their Paveways as Breanna clicked the radio to broadcast a warning.

Northern Somalia
23 October, 0430

AS THE BUS WOUND DOWN OUT OF THE HILLS, THEY could smell the scent of the sea through the open window. The moon and the stars were fading, the sky blending into the early dawn.

"There's an air base down there," said Gunny, who was at the window. "Shit, Major, come tell me what I'm looking at."

Smith pulled himself up from his seat and stepped over Jackson, who was sleeping in the aisle. Howland was hunched two rows back, snoring into the seat back. Mack's head had stopped hurting, but his ribs throbbed worse than ever. He slid in the seat behind Melfi, his leg irons clanking as he pushed his face to the window.

A long strip of black jutted roughly parallel to the sea, lit by the full moon. A phalanx of heavy earthmovers worked on one end, pushing and leveling. On the other, crews were erecting a shelter of some sort; from here it looked like a curved pizza box. There were planes lined in a neat row near the middle. They were far away and the light was poor, but one was definitely an airliner or similar transport. There were at least two others, smaller military jets, possibly MiG-21's. The bus bounced and turned around the road, its path taking them out of view.

"The strip's being extended. They've paved it pretty recently," Mack told Gunny. "We had a small airstrip on the map up north here somewhere when we briefed the mission; I think we had it pegged as a dirt strip. It's a lot bigger than that now."

One of the guards at the front of the bus grunted an instruction to keep quiet. Mack held up his hand as if he would, then leaned close to Gunny.

"There's a transport down there, an airliner. I can't tell in the dark what it is, but I'd bet they're going to fly us out."

"I say we don't," hissed Gunny. "I don't think they're going to be taking us home. And I don't want to star in this trial the raghead is talking about."

"I agree," Mack said. He felt his ribs tug at him, as if to remind him they weren't exactly loaded with options. "I don't know what sort of chance we're going to have, though."

"Were you thinking of that when you slugged the raghead's guard?"

"No," said Mack. "But I should have."

"You make a move, we'll follow," said Melfi solemnly. "Should we stall getting off the bus?"

What would that get them? A few more minutes? For what?

Odds were the Iranian would just shoot them and be done.

Preferable to being turned into cowards and traitors. That was where this was headed.

Mack grunted noncommittally, unsure what to say, much less do. He put his head back against the stiff seat top. The anger that had exploded inside him had disappeared; it seemed foreign now, as if it belonged to someone else—Melfi most likely. He was a pilot—logical, careful, precise.

Except when he let himself get shot down. That had

been a fuck-up, despite what Gunny had said.

Unlike him. He was too damn good to get whacked so easy. Too damn good to do something stupid.

So what the hell was he doing sitting here?

As the bus started down the winding road, the moon stabbed his eyes. Mack sighed, but didn't close them.

Northern Somalia
23 October, 0430

FORT TWO SQUEALED AS IT TUCKED AND ROLLED through the air, almost as if the Megafortress welcomed the seven-g back flip. Breanna felt her world narrow to a small cone as she rolled into a dive and recovered in the opposite direction. She had become the plane, pushing through the air like a force of nature, turbines spinning, wings slicked back. It took several seconds for them to gain momentum in the new direction; she rode the air current gracefully, plunging her nose down and picking up speed. By the time the MiGs reacted to their radar, they had narrowed the gap to thirty miles, the outer edge of the AMRAAMs' range.

"Open bay doors, prepare to launch," she told Chris.

"Bay. They're taking evasive maneuvers."

Breanna's HUD showed the radar's air-combat-mode projection, with the enemy bandits displayed as triangles with directional and speed vectors. Confident that it could nail each of the aircraft, the combat computer displayed red hatch marks over each plane.

"Which ones are near the F-117's?"

"Good question. Hold on."

The stealth fighters were too far away to be detected directly; Chris set the computer to look for atmospheric anomalies—essentially canceling some of the correction it normally did to erase interference from the wind. He managed to find two of the F-117's, just starting their attacks.

"One MiG within theoretical visual range," said Chris. "Targeting."

A box appeared around the triangle. The tiny symbol blinked, as if the computer were jumping up and down, yelling at them to nail it.

"Fire," said Breanna.

The Scorpion AMRAAM missile slipped out of its launcher so easily that only the launch indicator told Breanna it was gone. With a one-hundred-pound explosive warhead, the Scorpion packed roughly twice the explosive power of a standard AMRAAM, while retaining its high speed and superb active radar capabilities. Once launched, the missile took care of itself.

"Tracking," said Chris. "F-117's have buttoned up. I can't see them at all. Okay. One MiG heading north. They're out of it. More evasive maneuvers. They're looking for us. SAMs are up! Shit. We're spiked by that MiG. They're targeting us for air-to-air."

"Vector One to Fort Two, what's your situation?"

"Hold tight, Vector," said Breanna. The threat screen painted the sky ahead yellow, overlapping radars probing for them. Two fingers of red appeared at the sides; Breanna snapped the Megafortress ninety degrees, trying to beam the MiG that was now targeting them. The computer, meanwhile, began emitting electronic fuzz to confuse the ground-intercept radar that had snapped on.

"The open bay's going to give us away," Breanna reminded Chris.

"Having trouble picking out the MiG that's spiking us," he replied.

"Can we get the SAMs?"

"Two MiGs heading for us. Twenty miles, dead-on. They'll nail Vector if they take off."

"Get the lead MiG," Breanna directed. "Then we'll go for the SAMs."

"He's too low. They're firing."

"Missile type?"

"No ID. No radar."

"Impossible. They wasted heat-seekers from that range head-on?"

"Lost the missiles. We're still being spiked. Missile launch."

The RWR buzzed a warning; the second MiG had fired an AA-10 Alamo radar missile at them. Breanna pulled the Megafortress into a hard bank, unleashing tinsel and then pushing the plane into a dive. The strategy essentially provided the enemy missile with an easy—but nonexistent—target.

She sensed what the Iranians were doing, and fired diversionary flares as she cut a series of zigs in the sky.

"Yeah," said Chris, catching on. "Three missiles tracking. The first must have been long-range heat-seekers, looking for our butts when we turned. I have a target."

"Fire!" Breanna steadied the Megafortress as the missile dropped from the bay.

"We're boxed. Damn it," said Chris. His voice went up several octaves. "Okay, I'm firing. Shit. Here's another Alamo—"

"Close bay. Hold on," said Breanna calmly. She nailed the Megafortress nearly straight down, goosing off chaff and flares. At a thousand feet she rolled inverted and turned ninety degrees into the Doppler radar, in effect making the plane invisible in the eddy of the radar waves. The carbon fiber wings strained at their design tolerance as the massive plane twisted.

The Russian missiles realized they had missed, and blew up a thousand feet overhead. Shaking off the shock waves, Breanna rolled the mammoth plane upright, nudging her even lower.

"Splash one MiG!" said Chris. "Scorpion got it."

Breanna grinned, then went back to trying to sort out their location as well as that of their enemies. They were north, heading in the direction of A-1. One of the MiG-29's was running north toward the Red Sea.

"F-117's got something," blurted Chris. "Shit. Lots of secondaries. Wow! Big-time explosions. Nailed those mothers!"

"What happened to that SAM that was tracking us?" Bree asked.

"Lost it. Nighthawks got it or it just turned itself off without firing anything." Chris clicked the radar into long-distance scan, searching for the MiGs. "We may have splashed that first MiG too," he said. "I don't have it on the scope. I have two, moving out at warp speed into the Red Sea. Spooked 'em good."

"Go back to passive systems."

"Damn straight."

Breanna checked the bearing and speed that ghosted in the screen against the instrument readings in the MUD. She punched the Megafortress's self-test circuits, having the computer run its diagnostics as if they'd been tooling around Dreamland for the past hour.

The computer congratulated itself with perfect scores. All systems green and growing. Time to go back to the barn.

Almost.

"Let's make it hard for the SOB to land," she told Chris.

"Bree?"

"We still have the JSOWs in the bay. We'll be within range of A-1 in zero-two."

"What about that MiG-21 on the ground?"

"Something to aim at," said Breanna.

Chris sighed deeply, but turned back to his displays without saying anything. He had meant that they were out of air-to-air weapons, which Breanna already knew.

"We have plenty of fuel," she told him.

"We'll be into reserves on the trip home," he said.

"You're not going after A-1 because of Mack, are you?"

"What?"

"I mean, you're not getting emotionally involved here?"

"Screw you, Chris. I'm trying to do my job."

"Yes, Captain."

"Fort Two, this is Vector. Situation."

"We've chased a flight of MiGs away," Chris told the Delta leader. "We're proceeding north to check on A-1. We believe it may be their base."

Breanna stared at the terrain ahead, rendered green and gray by the starscope panel. Mountains gave way to a dark black that would turn into the sea in about ten seconds. There was a road through the hills on the left. The base should be beyond that, over the next set of ridges just before the water.

"Fort Two, this is Vector. Advise us on the situation at A-1. Are our passengers there?"

"They're nuts too," said Chris over the interplane circuit. "We're pushing this too far."

"Vector, this is Fort Two," said Breanna. "Stand by."

She glanced quickly at the threat indicator. No radars.

"Chris, are you just nervous?"

"I'm not nervous, I'm sane," he told her. "We've been flying for a shitload of time, just getting here. We're flying over a base that launched four MiGs at us. You don't think there are ground defenses?"

"We'll see what defenses there are in a second," said Breanna. "I won't take unnecessary risks."

She could practically hear his teeth grinding. But he nonetheless hunkered toward his display screen, where he selected the FLIR and began a close scan of the base, which was just now appearing beyond the hills.

"One Zeus antiair gun, right on the coastline. Machine guns, something, I don't know, light, near the road. There's a ship offshore. Tanker or something. No, no, I'm wrong—patrol boat. Has a gun. Bulldozers—man, this looks nothing like that satellite photo we saw."

That was an understatement. The Iranians had expanded and widened the strip, making it nearly three times as long as it had been, undoubtedly strengthening it as well. They were building hangars at the far end. Three aircraft—two older MiG-21's and one DC-8 or 707—sat on a ramp area, their tails almost hanging over the water.

"Bus, other vehicles. I'm switching from the FLIR to the starscope. Shit—I have the F-117!" said Chris. "It's moving. Shit, they're loading it off a truck at the far end—no, they're sliding down into a bunker. Shit. Shit. See it?"

"No," said Breanna. "Can you target it?"

"Bay," said Chris. "No, wait. No. They're in the hangar. I can't tell whether it's concrete or not. I don't think so. I don't have a target point."

Breanna nudged the stick to bank.

"I can't be sure what that hangar's made of," said Chris. "It looks like it's cement-reinforced."

"Can you fly the JSOW into the hangar?"

"Maybe," said her copilot. "The angle's tough. I can hit it, but the missiles might not penetrate. I don't know what's inside, whether it's all on the surface or if it's like Dreamland's hangars, with ramps and elevators."

"That's unlikely."

"Yeah. But what do you figure the odds are our guys are with the plane?"

Instead of answering, Breanna checked the threat scope again. There were no radars active. The Megafortress was slipping through the night undetected.

They might never have a chance like this again. If the wrecked plane was there, odds were their men were too.

On the other hand, there was no telling what sort of defenses the Iranians and Somalians had waiting.

Her instinct said go for it. She clicked the transmit button.

"Vector leader, here's our situation," she said, laying it out.

"We're en route," snapped the Delta commander. He patched in the pilots as Breanna had Chris sketch the base and approach.

"We'll take out the Zeus as you come in," Breanna said. "The hangar with the aircraft will be three thousand meters beyond it, close to the water."

"We'll hit it, take out the plane, and look for our guys."

"Roger that."

"ETA five minutes," said the lead pilot. The two Ospreys were rushing through the mountain passes, heading for their target. "We're going silent com."

"Fort Two," acknowledged Bree. She turned toward her copilot. "Hold one missile in reserve for the hangar if they can't reach it."

"Yeah. That's what I was thinking." Chris nodded, then sighed so loud her earphones practically shattered. He sounded like a horse that had just lost its chance to run in the Derby. "Listen, I'm sorry about that emotion thing I said. I didn't mean it."

"We're both tired," she said, worried that his crack had been all too true.

Northern Somalia
23 October, 0445

THE OSPREY WHEELED OUT OF THE HILLS JUST AS THE big antiaircraft gun at the edge of the base exploded. Skipping forward, the MHV-22 plopped herself down a few feet from the DC-8 at the edge of the ramp. Danny jumped from the rear of the plane behind Powder, and saw two figures running toward him; he pushed the trigger on his sub-submachine gun and the men crumpled immediately.

"Fuel truck! Fuel truck!" Liu yelled behind him. Danny saw the tanker under the airliner's wing. Bison had thrown himself in a crouch, aiming his SAW grenade launcher at the easy target.

"Don't blow it! Don't blow it!" Freah yelled. They were tasked with searching the plane before destroying it, in case the pilots and Marines were aboard already.

"Somebody in the cockpit!" shouted Hernandez.

Gunfire erupted to his right, a short burst of automatic fire. Danny threw himself down as a flare ignited overhead. He heard the rumble of a heavy machine gun at the far end, saw the silhouette of an Osprey, the other Osprey, descending near the hangar.

There was a boarding ladder near the fuselage of the DC-8 less than twenty yards away. The door was open and there didn't appear to be any soldiers or guards between them and the aircraft.

"On the plane! On the plane!" screamed Danny, jumping to his feet. Talcom and Hernandez were already at the ladder cart, exchanging gunfire with someone at the top. "Use the concussion grenades!" he shouted as he ran. "Knock them out! Don't hurt our guys!"

His men didn't need to be reminded of such basic procedures, but Danny yelled them anyway. Talcom and Hernandez had managed to get inside the plane in the few seconds it took for him to reach the ladder. He took the rungs two at a time, a concussion grenade in his hand. He slipped his thumbnail beneath the tape, ready to toss it in.

"We're clean! We're clean!" Talcom was yelling. "Somebody's in the cockpit!"

Danny threw himself into the airliner, rolling on the rubber-matted floor. The plane shook with a nearby explosion. Something burned on the other side of the base, faint red flickers mixing with the predawn twilight. Danny pulled out his small penlike flashlight, playing its narrow tungsten-lit beam carefully across the interior. The airliner was configured as a bare-bones passenger transport with fifteen or sixteen rows of seats between the boarding door and the flight deck. Talcom and Hernandez were huddled near the cockpit, their heads next to the closed door, listening to see what was happening on the other side. Freah spun around, checking the rear of the plane. There were maybe another dozen rows of seats back to a curtain. He got to his feet and ran back, ducking into the last row of seats.

He took the concussion grenade from his pocket, held it up so the others could see.

Talcom gave him a thumbs-up. Freah pulled the pin and rolled the grenade under the curtain. In the next moment his men at the front fired off the lock on the cockpit door. Danny waited for the boom of the grenades, then dove up and over the seats, rolling into the galley.

No one was there. A cargo compartment lay beyond the galley. He tried the door, found it locked. He stood back, fired at the recessed handle. It still wouldn't budge. He threw himself against it, his flashlight slipping from his hand and clanking so loudly against the counter that for a split second he thought it was a gunfire.

"Captain! Captain!" yelled Hernandez.

Danny spun back to see a dazed man with vaguely Middle Eastern features being herded down the aisle by his two sergeants.

"Guy's the pilot. They were just ready to take off, I think," said Hernandez. "Head's scrambled or maybe I just can't understand what the hell he's saying."

"APC coming up from the other end of the base," added Talcom. "Egg's holding him off."

Freah grabbed the pilot. "Where are our men?"

The man shook his head as if he didn't understand. Freah tightened his grip and pushed him against the seat.

"My people!" he demanded.

The man said something unintelligible.

"Captain, our grenade probably beat shit out of his eardrums," said Powder. "Even if he understands English, he probably can't hear. Sucker's lucky he wasn't killed."

The plane rocked with a fresh explosion.

"That APC's going to nail us, whether they're aiming to or not," yelled Hernandez from the doorway.

A moment later the front of the plane exploded.

Northern Somalia
23 October, 0445

THE FOUR-BARRELED ZSU-23 VAPORIZED AS THE WAR-head of the JSOW exploded. Flames lit the night as Breanna continued through her orbit, one eye on the blank RWR screen.

"Vector aircraft are in. They're at the hangar and on the airliner," said Chris, who was monitoring the radio transmissions as well as scanning the site with the infrared. "Vehicles back near the terminal building."

"Patrol boat?"

"I have it designated. We can take it out at will. Machine-gun fire on the north side of the base. I think they're shooting at us. No SAMs. No radar."

Breanna continued around, edging the Megafortress over the water. They were within the lethal envelope of a shoulder-fired missile like a Stinger or the SA-16, the Russian equivalent; she had to be ready to pull evasive maneuvers at any second. Still, she found her thoughts wandering, drifting down to the assault teams, wondering if they had found Mack.

Why did she care? Why had Jeff accused her of having an affair with him?

"Bree?"

"Take it out," she snapped, her unconscious alerting her to the fact that the patrol boat had snapped on a scanning radar. Her hands were already prodding the Megafortress away.

"Missile away," said Chris. "Scope is now clean."

The boat had turned off its radar, but nonetheless began firing its weapon, a large-bore cannon. The air below them crackled and popped with the explosions.

Suddenly it smoothed out and the horizon glowed.

"Got the motherfucker," said Chris. "Big fucking burn. Go baby, go baby."

"Good one." Breanna checked her warning screens, making sure Fort Two hadn't been hit. They were clean, systems in the green.

"APCs launching an attack," said Chris, back on the FLIR.

"Can you take them out?"

"I can get one, if you can spin us back so I can get a better look. After that, we're down to our last missile. You still want to save it?"

"Yeah," she said, beginning the bank.

"APC near the hangar or the airliner?"

"Hangar," said Breanna.

"Here's something for you to take home to the Ayatollah," said Chris as he pickled the missile off.

Breanna's laugh was interrupted by the RWR buzzer. The two MiG-29's they'd scared off earlier were on their way back.

Northern Somalia
23 October, 0445

THE BUS STOPPED NEAR THE GATE, ALLOWING THE flatbed with the plane to get by. As the Imam walked up the steps, something exploded about a mile away.

"We are under attack," the Iranian said calmly. "You will follow me off the bus."

"No, we won't," said Mack. This was a gift—now it made sense to stall.

"You will follow me off the bus." A trio of fresh explosions rocked the vehicle even as he spoke, though they did not affect his manner.

"Maybe we better," said Howland. "We're going to get blown up here."

As if to underline his words, the top of the bus was perforated by machine-gun fire. Outside, men were yelling and screaming. Smith heard the sound of tank and truck motors roaring nearby. The whomp of descending helos—or maybe Ospreys—filled the air.

"You will follow me now," said the Iranian, disappearing out the front. The two Somalians trained their weapons on the Americans.

"What do you think?" Gunny asked.

Bullets sprayed nearby, sending dirt and rocks against the side of the bus.

"I say let's move," said Howland. "And at least get ourselves out in the open where we can make a run for it."

"Yeah," said Mack finally.

They didn't move fast enough for the Somalians—one of them raised his rifle and sent a quick burst through the roof of the bus. The four Americans flinched, but kept moving, walking deliberately to the front and then down the steps. Somalian soldiers crouched nearby; one or two men ran and others yelled, though they seemed confused, perhaps panicked. It was unclear where the attack was coming from or even what was attacking them. A large jet zoomed overhead, its hull dark against the moon. One of the soldiers stood and emptied his AK-47 at it.

Idiots might just as well shoot at the stars, Mack thought.

The Imam had begun walking toward the back of the terminal building a few feet away. One of the guards went to Mack and prodded him to follow, pushing with the barrel end of his rifle. As Mack began to walk, there was a fresh burst of gunfire behind him. A machine gun began firing nearby, shaking the ground and air with a jackhammer thud.

Mack felt something sharp flick him in the face. He thought it was a bug at first; reaching up, he found his face wet with blood. A bullet had chipped a piece of cement up and nicked him below the cheekbone.

The guards pushed the Americans toward a knot of soldiers at the side of the terminal building, urging them to run and occasionally firing into the air. It wasn't clear whether they were shooting at the plane or planes attacking, or just trying to scare them; neither made much sense.

Mack was only vaguely aware of the others following behind him. Despite his chains and his resolve to go slow and look for a chance to escape, he was trotting, moving quicker than he wanted.

The Imam was waiting at the back corner of the building.

"Into the plane," the Iranian commanded. A few yards away, three soldiers pulled a black tarp off a small, high-winged aircraft in the field behind the building. The twin-engined, boom-tailed craft was an ancient Antonov An-14 "Clod"—a Soviet-era transport used mostly as a civilian plane thirty years ago. As the cover was removed, a man ran to the rear of the fuselage, yanking open a set of clamshell doors and ducking inside. The small plane rocked with his footsteps as he leapt into the cockpit; the engines started almost instantly, revving with a high-pitched grumble.

"Quickly," said Imam.

"No," said Mack.

"You will come now," said the Iranian. He raised his hand, revealing a pistol. Before any of the Americans could react, he fired point-blank into Jackson's forehead. The Marine's head snapped back and then seemed to disintegrate; his body fell almost straight down beneath it.

"The sergeant will be next," the Imam added, quickly

pushing his gun into Gunny's face. One of the guards had already grabbed the Marine from behind.

"Into the plane, Major, or your sergeant will die," said the Imam. "You and the captain will be dragged aboard anyway. I will not kill you, even though that is plainly what you desire."

Meekly, Mack bowed his head and started for the plane.

Northern Somalia
23 October, 0455

DANNY FELL HEADFIRST OVER THE SEAT, BARELY HANGING on to his submachine gun. A hurricane seemed to descend around him; his nostrils burned with the smell of plastic and metal burning.

"Captain! Captain! Captain!"

He couldn't locate the voice. He tried to stand, felt his throat revolting. He threw himself down to the floor. Instead of landing against the carpet, he kept going, his head and shoulders falling into the open air.

The side of the plane next to him had been blown away. Hanging on by his feet, he flailed back toward the aircraft. Then he saw that the skin of the plane had been twisted into something like a ramp; it would be easier to climb down. As he turned around and began to try to do so, an arm came out of the thick smoke in the plane. He yanked it over him, pulling a man out of the hole, pushing him to climb down. He only realized it was the Iranian pilot as the body slipped and then rolled to the ground.

Another explosion erupted to his left. Danny felt a surge of air against his face, found another body rolling against his. He grabbed it and pushed it toward the tarmac. He rolled down after it, saw it was Talcom.

"Where's Hernandez? Where the fuck is Hernandez?" he screamed.

Powder, dazed, maybe unconscious, didn't answer.

Danny clambered back up the jagged side of the plane, prodding through the acrid brown stench. He reached the floor of the passenger compartment, got to his feet, and then nearly fell backward as flames erupted in his face. The heat was so intense he could only retreat, tumbling over backward and falling out of the plane headfirst. He managed to grab a piece of metal, slowing himself but ripping his uniform and cutting his arm as he pirouetted around. He fell next to Talcom, who was trying to stand; both men slammed down and flattened the still-dazed Iranian pilot.

It would have been comical had the fuel truck nearby not erupted.

Somehow, Danny managed to pull Talcom and the pilot away. All three collapsed about twenty yards from the jetliner, gasping for breath and feeling the hot flame of the tanker truck.

"Hernandez, we lost Hernandez," said Freah when Liu grabbed him.

"No, he's in the Osprey," said the medic. "Come on. We have to go. Fighters are coming. Let's go. They blew the hangar."

Danny shook his head clear, bolting to his feet. He'd lost his MP-5, but he seemed okay; he didn't think he'd been hurt.

Sunburned maybe. Damn fire was hot.

"My team," he shouted, twisting back.

"We're all here!" yelled Liu. "Come on, Captain."

A massive black cloud hung over the hangar at the other end of the field. The Delta Osprey was taxiing away from it, toward them. An APC was rumbling thirty yards away.

Danny stood motionless as the armored personnel carrier's turret began to revolve in the direction of the Delta Osprey. Then he started to run toward the APC with all his strength.

"Captain! Captain!" shouted Liu.

As Danny ran, he reached into his pocket for the grenade.

Nothing but MP-5 clips.

Cursing, he kept running. He remembered he'd used the grenade in the airplane, and reached for the other pocket, retrieving a stun grenade. The grenade wasn't powerful enough to do anything to the exterior of the vehicle; it would have to be thrown inside.

He fumbled with the taped pin as he bolted atop the APC. It was an ancient vehicle, a BTR-60P with an eight-wheeled chassis and a 12.7mm gun mounted in a turret at the front. The gun barrel lurched back, firing toward the Osprey. Danny grappled with the hatch, but there was no way to open it once locked from the inside. He threw himself on top of the gun turret, thinking he might stuff the grenade through the gun opening. But he saw there'd be no chance of that as the gun fired again; desperate, he pulled his Beretta out and stuffed the barrel against the small viewing slot at the side of the front of the truck. He fired several times as the APC lurched to the side; Danny fell to the ground. The Osprey was revving its rotors furiously, pulling away. Danny rolled the grenade beneath the APC and ran back for his own craft, expecting at any moment to be shot. The ground rippled near him and he felt himself flying into the air.

Liu and Hernandez caught him just before he hit the ground, stumbling but managing to keep their balance as their Osprey lurched backward toward them. The others grabbed them and Danny felt himself suddenly pulled upward, the rotorcraft taking off with its bay open.

"We're in! We're in!" yelped Talcom.

Bison stood near the open doorway, firing his SAW. The APC continued to fire at them.

"Shit," said Freah.

"They got away," said Liu. "They got off okay. Vector One."

"Good."

"We got the Iranian, he's alive," added the medic. "We're all here. Scratch the airliner. Hangar's gone. F-117's toast."

"Pilots?"

Liu shook his head.

"Pair of MiGs gunning for us," said Reagan, who was back near the cockpit. "We're not home free yet."

Danny pulled himself to his haunches, then lifted himself to the canvas rack that served as a seat in the battle-rigged MHV-22.

"What'd you do, Captain, try and blow up an APC with a smoke grenade?" asked Bison, turning around now that he'd gone through his clip. The rear doorway began to close behind him.

"I think it was a concussion grenade," said Freah.

"Oh, that's different," said Bison.

"Probably gave them a good headache," said Danny. And he began to laugh.

So did the others. They must have laughed for a good ten minutes.

When the pilot called back that they had eluded the MiGs, the laughs just got louder.

Northern Somalia
23 October, 0505

"LEAD MIG HAS US SPIKED."

"Yeah," said Bree. She held her course steady. They had to suck the MiGs away from the Ospreys before the enemy fights saw the defenseless aircraft.

"They're buying it. Both of them coming for us."

Breanna glanced at the radar screen. The MiGs were

about twenty miles out to sea, closing fast. The Ospreys were just getting off the ground.

"Be ready with the Stinger air mines," Bree said.

"Max range of the Stingers is three miles," warned Chris. The Stinger air mines were the Megafortress's last remaining defensive weapons. In place of the standard B-52's tail guns, the Megafortress had a cannon that fired small explosive rockets. The cannon was steered by an aft-scanning radar and the missiles fired in an attacking fighter's flight path. At a proper range determined by the fire-control computer, the rockets detonated, creating a cloud of shrapnel in the enemy fighter's face several dozen meters wide.

The problem was, the air mines were short-range weapons. An enemy fighter had to close within knife-fighting range before they were effective. The Megafortress's stealth characteristics usually forced an enemy fighter to forgo radar-guided missiles and use short-range heat-seeking missiles or cannons, and that was when the air mines worked the best. Bree and Chris would have to survive a long-range attack before they'd be close enough to use the weapons.

As long as the Ospreys got away, she thought, her fingers cramping tight on the flight controls.

"We're in range," said Chris. "They haven't locked us, though. Shit. The Ospreys will be on their scopes any second. They're going to think we're a blip or a ghost and go for the Ospreys."

Breanna cursed. If only she still had two AMRAAMs in the weapons bay.

"Switch on the targeting radar," she said. "Lock them."

"Rap?"

"Do it!"

"Okay, okay." Chris worked the controls quickly, not quite realizing what Bree was up to. "They have us. They're locked. Shit, the MiGs are launching!"

"Kill the radar. Batten down the hatches," she said. Breanna splashed out chaff and pushed the plane over. The air was filled with electronic fuzz as the Megafortress shot downward, Breanna yanking and banking for dear life. The MiGs and their missiles flashed somewhere overhead as the Megafortress continued her evasive maneuvers, turning back in the opposite direction, then pulling five or six g's through a fresh set of zags. If a standard B-52 could have somehow found the momentum to make the maneuvers, its wings would have sheared off at the roots.

"We're clean. MiGs have turned. They bought it—they thought we were targeting them. Good call, Bree. Shit, I should have thought of that."

"Take out the runway—now," she ordered.

"Bay," warned Chris, dialing up the final air-to-surface missile. While not optimized for runway-crashing, the large hunk of explosive molded into the front of the missile would create a rather large and hopefully unavoidable hole in the middle of the Somalian field.

"Airliner is smashed. Another plane down there, off to the side," warned Chris.

"The runway. Now," demanded Breanna. The computer warned that one of the MiG radars had again targeted them, measuring their distance for a fresh attack.

"Launching. Gone. Good. Buttoning up."

The radar-warning tone blipped. "Tail radar warning," said Bree. "Here they come."

"Air mines ready," said Chris.

Breanna fired off her last flares and tinsels and inverted the big plane, rolling her down toward the ground like she was an F-16 on a practice range, yipping and yawing to get away from some frisky students.

"Two MiGs within range . . . Stingers firing!" Chris shouted. The fire-control computer began launching Stinger air mine rockets at their pursuers, one every three seconds, sowing clouds of deadly tungsten chips in the MiGs' flight path.

One of her "students" launched a heat-seeker toward their tailpipe. The other let go of his last radar missile.

Gravity slapped Breanna hard across the face as she slid the Megafortress a hairbreadth above the waves of the Gulf of Aden. Lights flickered in her eyes, stars or a Christmas light or the sun peeking through the hills. The stall warning yelped, but she was on top of it; one of the engines coughed loudly from a compressor stall, but she compensated beautifully. Chris monitored the computer's automatic clearing procedure.

Bree recovered, picking the big plane up by its wing roots. She banked south, lost the MiGs on the FLIR as they searched to the north.

The air mines were just as effective against air-to-air missiles as they were against fighters. As the MiGs' missiles closed in on the Megafortress's hot exhausts, they were shredded by the air mines' deadly debris. As the MiG pilots tried to close the distance for one last try at their quarry, they too fell prey to the silent, invisible invaders. Without warning, the tiny tungsten chips splintered turbine compressor blades, cut fuel lines, and shattered windscreens. Crippled and almost out of fuel, both MiGs broke off their attacks and headed for the closest emergency runway.

"That was close," Breanna admitted.

"I think you went out to ten g's on that last yank," said her copilot. "A-1 dead ahead."

"Yeah."

"Jeez, I nailed the runway. No way those MiGs are landing there. They'll end up ditching."

"I'll send a sympathy card."

It seemed like the entire countryside, dirt and all, was on fire.

"Plane!" Chris yelled.

Breanna jerked the Megafortress upward as a dark shadow lumbered across their path. A small two-engined propeller craft pulled up from the grass near the terminal, barely making it into the air ahead of them. It edged toward the hills to the west.

"I got a bad feeling about that," said Chris.

Breanna looked at him.

"We don't have enough fuel," he said. "We may not even make it back as it is."

They didn't have any weapons left on board.

"I could clip its wings," said Breanna, even though she knew that was wildly improbable.

"Go to the radar and track it?" suggested Chris.

"They'll be lost in the ground clutter," she said. She banked to the west; even with the FLIR at maximum resolution, the small plane was difficult to make out in the hills.

"Due west. Going to the Sudan," said Chris. "Or Libya."

"Alert Madcap Magician," she said. "Maybe they can scramble something to follow it."

Breanna leaned back against her ejector seat, the last vestiges of her energy starting to drain out. "All this way, and we missed them."

"If it was them," said Chris.

"Aw, come on," she said, trying to force a smile into her voice. "I trust your woman's intuition."

"Plotting new course," was his only reply.

V
TV time

Ethiopia
23 October, 1540

YOU COULD SMELL A COMBAT BASE. PART OF IT WAS the sweat in the air. Part of it was spent fuel, and the ammo being packed.

Another part was fear.

Zen smelled it as he worked his way down the Megafortress's stair ramp, levering himself sideways down each step, aware that he was being stared at—or actually, that people were pretending not to stare at him. He used his arms and shifted his weight carefully as he lowered his butt; he wanted to come down on his own power, but he also didn't want to fall on his face.

It had been more than five years now since he'd been on a combat base, not counting his brief rotation in Turkey to enforce the no-fly zone in Iraq. This felt different for all kinds of reasons. For one thing, he'd probably had more sleep on his flight over than his whole time during the Air War.

And for another, well, he hadn't had to use his arms quite so much.

Sergeant Parsons held the wheelchair for him on the tarmac. Zen came off the side into it, managing to swing himself upward and fall perfectly—almost perfectly—onto the chair.

"I'm getting too heavy," he told Parsons. "Have to lay off the ice cream."

"You find ice cream here, you let me know," said the sergeant. "Let me go check our birds."

Parsons ducked under the wing to examine the Flighthawks, which were attached to the inner wing spars of Raven. Zen pushed himself a few feet away, taking stock of the crowded air base. Tensions had continued to escalate during the night. There had been raids against bases in northern Somalia. The Iranians had sunk a ship in the Red Sea. Two U.S. aircraft carriers were steaming from the western end of Mediterranean. The Saudis and Egyptians were furious about U.S. overflights and reconnaissance missions, to say nothing of the President's decision to use Israeli airports as refueling stops.

Four C-130 Hercules, two painted black and two in dark green jungle camouflage schemes, were lined up near the Megafortress. Beyond them were a parcel of Blackhawk and Huey helicopters, along with a pair of large Pave Lows. Three F-117's and five F-16's were also lined up at the edge of the strip, parked dangerously close together.

The runway had been expanded, but Cheshire had still had to dump fuel before landing. Taking off was going to be a bitch; Jeff wondered how the F-117's managed it, since the bat planes typically needed a good long run to get off the ground.

"God, Zen, is that you?"

Zen spun his chair around and saw Hal Briggs, hands on hips, frown on face, standing behind him.

"Hey, Major."

"You brought the Flighthawks?" said Briggs. "You're here to fly them?"

"Who'd you think would fly them? Rubeo?"

Briggs frowned, but at least he didn't offer the usual "sorry about your legs" routine. Zen waited while Briggs greeted Sergeant Parsons and the others. Major Cheshire came down onto the runway; Hal began filling her in on the situation, walking with her toward his Humvee. Zen followed, listening to Briggs explain why he believed the captured Americans were in the Sudan. They were mounting a comprehensive search mission, he told her; Raven would be an invaluable part. Briggs and Cheshire got into the vehicle. Zen pushed to follow.

"Whoa! Whoa!" he yelled as Briggs started without him. "Yo! I'm not in yet."

"Uh, sorry, Major," said Briggs. "There's food and a lounge inside this building here. We're going over to our command center."

"Yeah, no shit. That's where I'm going." Jeff pulled open the rear door, working the wheelchair as close as possible. It was too long a stretch, but at this point he didn't care.

"Well," started Briggs. "No offense, but—"

"I'm in charge of the Flighthawks," Zen told him. "Since I'm going to be working the major part of the mission, I sure as shit ought to be in on the planning, don't you think?"

"First of all, the drones aren't in the game plan."

"They're not drones," said Zen. "They're scouts and escorts."

"I agree that Major Stockard ought to be involved," said Cheshire.

Briggs, obviously pissed, said nothing. Zen pulled himself up into the Hummer, pushing and yanking his body along. Major Cheshire got out of the Humvee and folded his wheelchair for him, handing it inside. Zen answered her weak, apologetic smile with a curt nod, pulling the chair nearly on top of himself. He wasn't exactly comfortable, but he would be goddamned if he was going to admit it.

This is better than pity, he thought to himself. *I can deal with this.*

When they stopped, Jeff managed to slam the chair out

and then slide into it without any help. Not that it was pretty.

Nor was it easy getting into the building. Fortunately, there was only one step and it was barely two inches high. Zen managed to get up by coming sideways, building a little momentum, and practically jumping upward. For a moment he thought he was going to land on his head.

He took the fact that he didn't as a good sign. He wheeled through the door, teeth grinding but determined to get past the frowns and stares. Moving quickly, Jeff followed Cheshire toward the large map tables where the commanders of the operation were clustered. Briggs introduced them, then turned over the briefing to a Navy commander, who was coordinating the search components.

"The Antonov was tracked approximately to this point," he said, dispensing with preliminaries as he poked his thumb on a topo map of northeastern Africa. "We estimate the plane's range before refueling at one thousand miles, which gives us this semicircle here. You'll note that's a wide area. A lot of Sudan is involved. We have relatively high confidence that the aircraft did not take off after landing. We believe they're waiting for nightfall. F/A-18's and a Hawkeye from the *Kennedy* will be responsible for this area here," he added, his pinkie circling a crosshatched swatch of northern Sudan near Egypt. "Another flight will patrol Libya. That leaves southern Sudan, below the Libyan Desert. It's a low-probability area, but it has to be covered."

"What about Egypt?" said Zen.

The commander made a face. "We don't have permission for overflights."

"All the more reason to watch it."

"Zen, please," said Briggs.

"We're aware of the possibility," said the Navy commander. "We're compensating to some degree, but obviously there are limits. We have some under-the-table help from the Israelis."

"Where's the *Kennedy*?" Cheshire asked.

"That's one of our problems," admitted the commander. "All of these planes are operating at the far end of their range. It's dicey, I don't deny that."

"Major Cheshire, you have this swatch here," said Briggs, pointing to the southernmost area of the Sudan. He then turned to the F-16 commander. "Havoc Flight's F-16's will patrol here and here. We're waiting for a KC-135 inbound to refuel you."

"Excuse me," said Cheshire, "but with our range, it would make a hell of a lot more sense for us to take that area. Then Havoc won't need to tank." She grinned at the F-16 flight leader. "Unless you want to try refueling off a C-130."

"We've done it," he said.

"I've pissed in my pants, but I wouldn't want to repeat it," said Zen. The C-130 in question was rigged for helicopter refueling. The type's extreme versatility and the pilots' attitudes couldn't make up for the fact that the Herky Bird was considerably slower than the F-16.

"We may have the KC-135 on board by then," said Briggs. "In any event, I don't want to risk the Megafortress anywhere near Libya."

"That's a good six hundred miles south of Libya," said Zen. "And with all due respect to the F-16's, they'd be ten times as vulnerable as Raven and the Flighthawks."

"We're not sending the Flighthawks," said Briggs.

"What are Flighthawks?" asked the Navy commander.

"UM/F-3's," said Zen. "They're unmanned fighters that can be used as reconnaissance craft. They'll widen the search cone exponentially."

"They're experimental drones," said Briggs. "Unpiloted craft."

"They are piloted. They fly by remote control. They're

as capable as F-22's," Stockard told the naval officer, aware that he was violating the protocol about the program's classified status. "The Flighthawks can beam real-time video and electronics back to Raven. They're armed with cannons and can shoot down anything Qaddafi can throw at them. The only difference between sending them and the F/A-18's is that no one's risking their life."

"If we have unmanned aircraft that we can use, I'm all for it," said the naval officer. "That is serious Indian country out there."

"Those are experimental aircraft," said Briggs.

"No, they're *developmental* aircraft," said Jeff. "There's a big difference."

"I think they can do the job," said Cheshire.

"What do we do if one goes down?" Briggs's voice made it seem more a certainty than a question.

"It's not going down," Zen said.

"I can't afford to be optimistic."

"If there are problems, I blow it up. Look, the classified stuff is all aboard Raven anyway. That's the plane we have to worry about. The fact that it's here—shit, don't you think we have to use the best stuff we have? Why let anyone—anything, I mean—go to waste?"

"I don't think there's much of an argument," said the Navy commander. "If you're confident these craft can do the job, I say go for it. I've seen what Pioneers—"

"These are nothing like Pioneers," snorted Zen.

"I'm on your side, Major," the commander snapped. "I say we slot them north, Hal."

"Agreed," said Briggs finally. He looked up at Cheshire. "Major, we'd like you off the runway as soon as possible. We want you in the area before dark."

"We'll be there," said Cheshire.

Zen followed her out of the conference area. "Hey, Nancy," he said as she reached the door. "Thanks."

"No problem, Jeff. I agree with you—it's safer to risk the Flighthawks than a pilot."

"I meant thanks for standing up for me."

"Oh, you stand up for yourself just fine. Where do you figure the rest rooms are around this place?"

"I don't know, but I'm going to guess they won't be handicapped-accessible."

"And I won't be surprised if there's only a men's room."

"I'll guard the door for you, if you do the same for me."

"Deal." Cheshire grinned.

SINCE SHE WAS A WOMAN, THE SPEC OPS SUPPORT team had offered Breanna a separate room to sleep in— a closet down the hall from the large, open warehouse room that had become an ad hoc dormitory. She'd turned them down. Not because she didn't want to be treated any differently than anyone else, but because she was so damn tired she couldn't contemplate taking one more footstep than necessary. She took off her boots and dropped onto the narrow cot fully dressed, hunkering under a blanket without a pillow. She fell right to sleep.

And woke less than two hours later. The place was quiet, except for Chris, snoring several cots away. A dull blue light filtered through the windows high on the wall, but it wasn't the light or the snores that distracted her. The mission kept playing over and over in her head, bits and pieces of it swelling her mind with ideas of what she might have done differently. She felt the hard seat of the Megafortress pinching her butt as she took the g's ducking from the MiGs. She saw the flames on the ground, felt the air rumbling with the cannon fire. She saw the small airplane they'd all missed until it was too late.

So close. She could have rescued Mack and the others.

After an hour of tossing and turning, Breanna finally gave up and went in search of food. Besides MREs, the makeshift kitchen was offering two specials of the day: instant oatmeal and fresh boar.

"Boar?" Bree asked the Green Beret sergeant who was standing over the tin pots.

"Boar, ma'am. I caught it, I skinned it, I cooked it."

"You bullshitting me, Sergeant?"

"Ma'am?"

"Okay. I'll take some."

"You won't be sorry." He removed a steel lid on one of the pots, sending an acrid smell into the air. "And you can trust the water too. Treated and boiled for good measure. Sweet potato?"

"Why not?" said Bree, momentarily wondering if she should resort to the MREs.

"Full complement of your vitamins, ma'am. Nice flyin', by the way. Heard you did a kick-ass job."

"Thank you, Sergeant," she said, still dubious about the food as she walked to the nearby table area.

Her opinion remained in flux through three or four bites. The meat had a taste somewhere between fresh pork and week-old beef. And the sweet potatoes: Forget about it.

The water, at least, was good. She took a long sip—then almost spat it out as her husband wheeled into the room.

"Jeff?"

"Hey, Bree," said Zen, rolling toward her. "How you doing?"

"I'm fine. What the hell are you doing here?"

"The Flighthawks are going to join in the search."

"You're crazy," said Breanna.

Major Cheshire appeared at the front the room with the rest of the crew from Raven, as well as her navigator and weapons operator. Breanna managed to hold her disbelief in check while the others went for food.

"Jeff? The Flighthawks?"

"Yeah?"

"You're pushing them past the limit. Not to mention yourself."

"I don't think so," he snapped. "I slept the whole way over."

"That's not what I meant."

"I heard you were in action."

"Don't change the subject."

"Listen, Captain." Jeff had his major's face on, and it wasn't pretty. "You're cute and all, but I don't answer to you."

"Jeff. Come on, be realistic."

"This chair has nothing to do with my abilities."

"I'm not talking about your abilities." Breanna heard her words echoing harshly in the room. Her face flushing hot, she repeated the sentence, though softer this time. "I'm not talking about your abilities."

"I'm hungry. That was a great dinner, by the way. We'll have to do it again sometime."

ZEN WHEELED UP TO THE END OF THE LINE, SMIRKING at the Green Beret chef's obvious discomfort. Hell, he was starting to like being a one-man freak show attraction.

Breanna's attitude didn't surprise him. At least she'd finally come out and admitted it.

One of the Delta operators had told him while he was waiting to use the john that she'd kicked butt on her mission. He was happy for her, damn proud in a way, even if she hadn't given him a chance to tell her so.

They could be friends. He wanted that maybe, or something like that.

"Wild boar," the Green Beret behind the makeshift

lunch counter was saying. "I caught it, I skinned it, I cooked it. Of course, you could have an MRE. Or oatmeal."

"That boar. You catch it with your bare hands?" asked Zen.

"Sir? You think I'm nuts?"

"No, just making sure it's sanitary," said Zen. "Dish me up a heap. Come on, let's go," he added. "I have some planes to fly."

"You fly planes?"

"Two," said Zen. "At the same time."

The sergeant spooned the food onto the dish carefully, undoubtedly convinced he was dealing with a psycho.

Which, Zen thought, might not be too far from the truth.

Sudan
23 October, 1540 local

THE RUSSIANS CALLED THE ANTONOV AN-14 "PCHEL-ka," which meant, "Little Bee." NATO called it "Clod."

Both names were equally appropriate. The small but sturdy aircraft flew at just over a hundred knots, skimming the hills and rugged valleys of eastern Sudan. There were eight seats, including the pilot's, but the Iranians had crammed seven soldiers in along with the prisoners, the pilot, and the Imam. The plane lumbered through the air, obviously complaining about its heavy load—which was all the heavier because it had been outfitted with bladder tanks in metal rigs that looked like blisters on the fuselage. Mack's fatigue kept him from getting more than a rough idea of where they were; it was obvious they were flying west, but he couldn't be sure whether they had gone beyond Ethiopia, and if so, how far. He kept dozing off, jostled back to consciousness by his guards and the pain in his side, though by now his ribs had hurt so long he was almost used to the ache. Finally they reached wherever they were supposed to reach; six soldiers in light brown uniforms met them as they taxied along what seemed to be a dirt road in front of some tents on a flat plain well beyond the mountains they'd gone over. While Mack and the others were hustled out of the Antonov, brown camo netting was thrown over the plane. A nearby group of scraggly cattle were herded around. The emaciated animals—they weren't cows, exactly, at least not as Mack knew them—poked their noses toward the men curiously, but quickly lost interest.

The prisoners were led to a tent. Gunny and Howland lay down on the dirt floor, immediately curling up to sleep. Mack sat with his arms huddled around his knees, watching the shadows outside. Two guards sat in front of the tent; two others sat at the rear corners. Men and animals moved around them, seemingly at random.

Land this flat probably meant they were somewhere in Sudan. If what Howland had said was true, their next stop would be Libya. Most likely, they were hiding out until night, when the small, low-flying plane would be harder to detect.

Once they got to Libya, they'd be put on trial in an attempt to whip up public support for the Greater Islamic League, perhaps fomenting revolutions in Egypt and Saudi Arabia, or at least intimidating their governments sufficiently to get them to join the Iranians.

Damn unlikely.

Maybe not. Impossible for him to know. In any event, what happened in the wider world was largely irrelevant; what happened to him was what mattered.

Knife pulled his arms around his knees, digging the chain into the flesh. It made no sense to think about things he couldn't control. But what else was there to think about?

Dreamland. The JSF. His career. Breanna Stockard. Zen.

Poor dumb Zen. Crippled.

Maybe Stockard hadn't screwed up. Maybe he had been a good enough pilot, and just been nailed by bad luck.

Like Mack.

Was it just luck, though? He'd never put much stock in luck, preferring to trust ability and effort. What a shock now to find they might not matter at all.

"You should rest, Major," said the Imam. "You and I have a long journey ahead."

Startled, Knife jerked around. The Iranian had come into the tent without his guards. He'd moved so silently he seemed almost to have materialized there.

"We will be leaving at dusk," said the Iranian. His hands were folded in front of him; it was possible, probable, that he had his pistol in his sleeve, but it was not visible. In fact, he gave the impression not merely of being unarmed, but of being far removed from any conflict—far removed from here, as if he were in a mosque, preparing to pray or more likely to preach.

"How did it feel?" Smith asked.

The Imam's eyes gave nothing away, yet he obviously knew that Mack was talking about shooting Jackson, for he answered, "Within Allah's grasp, all is justified."

"How do you know you're in his grasp?"

"I know," said the Iranian confidently.

"Why him and not me?" Mack asked.

"Your role has been ordained." The Imam nodded, as if he had actually answered the question. He gazed at Mack as if he were a penitent seeking guidance. "You should not question your fate. You must learn to accept it."

"What the hell does that mean?"

"You are feeling guilty that your soldier died. But he would have died eventually."

"I'm not feeling guilty about anything."

"When you can say that truthfully, you will be at peace," said the Imam. He nodded again. "I pray the day will come."

Mack felt a surge of anger, but something seemed to hold him in place, fatigue or perhaps something else. He wanted to ask how a murderer could have the gall to cite God as his justification, to pretend to be holy and wise. But he stayed fixed in place, unable to move.

"Submit yourself to your fate, and to the will of Allah," said the Imam. "Then you will find peace."

He stepped backward, leaving the tent.

Dreamland
23 October, 0800 local

AS REAMINGS WENT, IT WAS FIRST CLASS. FOUR GENerals tag-teamed Bastian during the conference call, chewing him out relentlessly for sending the Megafortress to Africa.

And all he could say in his defense was—a second was on the way, with even more untested top-secret weaponry and a civilian scientist aboard.

Magnus especially was angry. "I spoke to you less than twenty-four hours ago," said the general who'd earlier congratulated him for his JSF report. Though influential, he was actually the junior member of the chew-out team. "You sure as hell could have given me a heads-up."

"I didn't think it was necessary."

"You, Colonel, should not think," Magnus snapped.

Bastian was being treated as if he were a green-gilled tadpole airman, not the commander of the country's most advanced weapons-testing facility. He bridled, but he kept his cool, holding his tongue as the generals continued to berate him. Because he knew—and they knew—that in the end, he'd been right. The Megafortress had made it possible for the downed F-117 to be destroyed. And, according to preliminary intelligence, Whiplash had just barely missed snatching the pilots back—again, thanks largely to the Megafortress. One major Somalian base had been smashed, two Iranian MiGs had been shot down, and two others apparently forced to ditch. The Iranian plan for a pan-Islamic rebellion against the West was falling apart, largely because he'd decided to send an "experimental" aircraft as a transport.

Well, more or less.

"The bottom line here, gentlemen," said Ms. O'Day, finally rejoining the conference call after the others had vented for nearly twenty minutes, "is that we have a continuing situation. Colonel Bastian has helped us considerably. You and I may not approve of what he has done— and undoubtedly we may consider sanctions in the future. But at the moment, well, let's make some lemonade here. His aircraft and personnel are under operational control of the Madcap Magician commander. I believe that's where they should stay—with the local commanders, who are in the best position to know what they need to get the job done. Now if you want to reverse that, it's possible. I will carry the recommendation personally to the President. I won't support it, but I will relay it."

"We can relay it ourselves," snapped General Gold, the Air Force Chief of Staff.

"Your call, Martin," said O'Day.

Dog wished the conference call had been made via video. He'd give anything to see his bosses fuming at O'Day.

On the other hand, they might see him gloating. And that would be fatal. Assuming he wasn't already cooked.

"I don't think we should reverse it," said Magnus. "Frankly, between you, me, and the lamppost, Tecumseh, I would have done the same thing."

"Then you'd be out of line," snapped General Alcane.

"In line, out of line, the bottom line is results. We've got them," said Magnus. "What we need now is for Madcap Magician to pull the pilots out. If that takes Megafortresses and robot planes, I'm all for it."

"What we need now is to nuke Iran," said Alcane.

"If that's your recommendation, I'm sure the President will want to hear it personally," said O'Day coolly.

"Gentlemen, Ms. O'Day, there's no need to discuss this further with Colonel Bastian," said Gold. "Colonel, you have a difficult assignment at Dreamland. You're trying your best and doing better than expected, but I realize that you may be slightly in over your head."

"I hope not," said Bastian.

"Brad Elliot is still well thought of around here," continued Gold. "And he supports you." Gold laughed. "Hell, he thinks you should have sent more. But—and this is an important *but*—we have a chain of command that must be followed. Granted, your situation is special. But from this moment on, you are to report directly to General Magnus. That pertains to everything—testing, operations, budget, latrines. Keep him informed. Understood?"

"Yes, sir," said Dog. Before he could say anything else, his end of the call was shut down.

"How'd you do?" asked Ax, barging in a millisecond after Bastian hung up.

"Well, I got my head chewed off and threatened with unspecified sanctions. Then about twelve layers of bureaucracy above us were cut away, and the only general in the Air Force who thinks I'm worth anything was just made my boss. The Chief even said I was doing a good job."

"Not bad," said Sergeant Gibbs. "You're learning. Keep going and in a couple of weeks you may be ready to take over for me when I go on vacation."

Ethiopia
23 October, 1820 local

THEY USED AN OLD SAC TRICK TO HELP RAVEN GET airborne with a full load of fuel, firing the Flighthawks in sequence with the main engines, as if the UM/Fs were rocket-assist packs. They then refilled the Flighthawks' fuel tanks in-flight, siphoning off fuel from the Megafortress. Between the takeoff and the tanking procedures, Jeff felt drained; fortunately they had a lull before he was due to drop the Flighthawks.

"It'll be easier next time," said Gleason as he pulled off his heavy helmet. She was sitting next to him in the converted weapons station.

"You think so, don't you?" Zen joked.

"I hope so." Briggs had tried to keep Jennifer from flying the mission because she was a civilian, but her protests and Cheshire's insistence had kept her aboard. Zen was glad she'd come.

"We are twenty minutes from Alpha," said Cheshire. "You want to break open your snacks, go for it."

"I thought I'd grab a brewski," said Zen.

"Make mine a Sam Adams."

"I'm in for a Chardonnay," said Gleason.

Zen reached for his mission folder, laying out the latest overhead photos and the grid map that showed the area they would be surveying. Their search pattern looked like an upside-down W with a backward Z on the last leg; they would start about ten miles northwest of Malakal, heading for the Libyan border. The Flighthawks would fly ahead roughly five miles, about seven miles apart. While the Flighthawks would vary their altitudes between six and twelve thousand feet depending on conditions, Raven herself would stay above 25,000 in a warm and dry layer of air unlikely to produce contrails. The altitude would give the plane a considerable buffer against triple-A and shoulder-fired SAMs likely to be in the area. Anything larger would have to be jammed once detected; until then, they would fly without the powerful radars activated, hoping to get in and out unnoticed.

"Zero-five to Alpha," announced Cheshire.

Zen looked up in shock—had he just dozed off? He glanced at his controls; they were indeed five minutes from the drop point.

"Initiate C^3 self-test sequence on Hawk One," he told the computer as he pulled on his helmet.

"Test sequence begun. Test sequence complete," announced the computer.

"Initiate C^3 self-test sequence on Hawk Two."

The computer came back quickly, showing all systems in the green. Cheshire had already pushed the nose of the Megafortress upward; they would launch in a shallow dive, the pilot initiating a zero-alpha maneuver at release. The wind shear across the Megafortress wing surface would help accentuate the separation. They'd then repeat the process again for the second plane. Although technically it was possible to launch both at the same time, Stockard had never done so.

Zen selected Hawk One's infrared view for his main visor screen, ghosting the flight instruments and data in it as if it were a HUD. The world looked dark and cold from the UM/F's nose.

"Alpha," said Cheshire.

"Computer, launch sequence on Hawk One. Countdown from five."

The computer took up the chant, counting down in its mechanical voice as the engine ignited. Prodded by the Megafortress's 480 knots of airspeed, the turbine spun hot and ready. Zen let the computer proceed as it automatically released Hawk One.

"Maintain programmed course," he said after a quick

review of the instrumentation indicated all systems were good. "Main viewer optical from Hawk Two. Begin Hawk Two launch sequence. Countdown from five."

Hawk Two's turbine stuttered. Zen nearly pulled the trigger button on his left joystick, which in launch mode automatically stopped the takeoff. But the graphics hit green and he let the Hawk go, this time maintaining personal control over the plane.

Good launches, quick and smooth. Better by far than either of his drops at Dreamland.

It was like flying, and it wasn't. It was like riding in the back of a roller coaster, imagining you had control.

In the dark, the total dark.

Plus with your left hand.

"Infrared view, Hawk Two," he said, staying in Hawk Two's cockpit. The screen snapped into a yellowish red haze. Hawk One's tailpipe glowed at the top of the left end of the screen. Zen prodded Hawk Two gently to the right, gliding and quickly building momentum. He checked the instruments, then gave control to the computer, skipping over to UM/F. It was easier there, maybe because he was right-handed. Like playing baseball and batting from the right side, even though you'd learned to switch-hit.

"Computer, split top viewer, add optic feed from Hawk Two on left."

The computer complied. He now had a panoramic view of the twilight. Both planes descended at near-Mach speed, running through clear, dry air.

"We're green and growing," he told Cheshire.

"Roger that."

"Feeding infrared views to flight deck," said Jennifer. The Flighthawk feeds came through the test system. She punched something on her console. "They'll get the FLIR no matter what you select. I can feed them radar and optics too, if they ask."

"Looking good back there," Cheshire told them.

Baseball. This was ten times more difficult than switch-hitting—you were going at it from both sides of the plate at once, facing two different pitchers. Zen felt as if his mind were splitting in half; sweat began creeping down his neck.

A Sudanese city—or what passed for one—loomed in the view projected from Hawk One as Zen began leveling the planes off at ten thousand feet. A group of low-slung concrete buildings sat above a shantytown of trailers, discarded metal containers, and ancient vehicles. The computer, working with parameters programmed by Jennifer, studied the different shapes for the possibility of an aircraft. Meanwhile, Raven's weapons officer scanned for transmissions that might indicate their quarry's presence.

"You have a shape on that northwest quadrant," Jennifer said. "The computer's not flagging it as hostile. Grid AA-4."

"Yeah, I have the quadrant," said Zen. Holding Hawk One steady toward the Sudanese city, he moved Two lower to check out the unexpected contact off its left wing. The sweat now began to pour in buckets as he rolled the plane into a tight dive, dropping it quickly to five thousand feet. The Hawk's radar transmitted a detailed image back to the mother ship; Jeff left it to Jennifer to examine as he flew the plane low and fast across the edge of a Sudanese settlement that apparently had been obscured by clouds on the photos. He brought the Hawk lower, picking up speed; he straightened his wings now at five hundred feet, three hundred, sensors blazing.

RWR clear. No SAMS, no defenses.

A building and a shed, if you could call them that. Neither was as big as a cottage back home.

A bus lumbered ahead. Zen began to pull off, then saw something flash to his left. Not sure what it was, he stayed on his course, accelerating.

Another vehicle, this one an ancient pickup. He nailed his throttle down, streaking past before rocketing back upward, hewing right. He pushed his left hand toward him, riding Hawk Two closer to the other half of his mind, which was just passing the Sudanese city.

"Whoo, that was fun," said Jennifer. "Initial analysis clean. I'm playing the optical sensors back to recheck those buildings."

Zen shut her out. It was difficult enough being in the Flighthawks.

It hadn't seemed this hard when he flew them before the accident. And yet he'd been controlling three planes then—his own as well as the two UM/Fs.

His head felt like it was going to break in half.

"Clean," announced Jennifer. "No visible life-forms, Dr. Spock."

When Zen didn't respond, she added, "Our ten-year mission, to explore new worlds—"

"Yeah, I got the joke," he snapped.

"Sorry."

Zen saw a small truck off the side of the road, then another.

Hawk One screen, right? They were starting to blur together, despite the purple separator line.

The trucks weren't significant, he decided. The Hawks crossed the Wadi al Madi, a trench that emptied into the Nile much further to the east. He couldn't tell if there was water in it or not as he passed, holding both Flighthawks at eight thousand feet.

They were invisible, dark birds in the desert night, riding the wind. He selected both FLIRs in the top screen, trying to get more comfortable. They came up toward the east-west railroad line that perforated Sudan; he took the Flighthawks down it to nearly the limit of their safe separation distance before edging back.

Maybe he shouldn't think of them as if they were two

planes. Maybe they were really one, a coordinated being, an extension of himself. Like his arms or eyes, working together.

There was a rhythm; once he found it he'd be fine.

Once he found it.

"We're coming to Bravo," Cheshire told him. "We'll follow your turn."

"Roger that, thank you, Raven," Jeff said.

"Hawk Two at Bravo," the computer told him.

Though a basic element of formation flying, coordinating a parallel turn was tricky, and even experienced pilots could have trouble doing it. It was not easy to hold position, and the pilots had to coordinate their maneuvers carefully. In some ways it was even harder with the Flighthawks, since he couldn't—or didn't want to—use the throttle to cover any mistake. But Zen didn't need to; he had the planes moving in tandem, perfectly balanced against each other, working like the hands of a prizefighter prodding his enemy. He came around to the new bearing southeastward with the Hawks nailed on beam precisely seven miles apart. He allowed himself a brief exhale of congratulations and relief.

A boxer probing his opponent. This one was a cipher, without noticeable weaknesses. The desert went on forever, admitting no secrets. Finding Smith in it would be impossible.

If it weren't for the fact that there were other people with Knife, Zen wouldn't mind missing him completely.

The idea snuck up from behind, curling around his spine as if it had risen through the sweat beneath his flight suit.

He hated Smith.

Because of the accident? Or because of Bree?

He wanted her back. And not to be friends. He was wrong about the divorce. He had to fight for her.

How the hell did you do that in a wheelchair? He

couldn't even do his goddamn job without sweating buckets.

A herd of cattle materialized on the right side of the viewer, crowding out his thoughts about his wife, bringing him back to the Hawks. The warm bodies milled back and forth in the rapidly cooling desert air. There were some tents, a vehicle.

"Nomads," said Jen.

"Yeah," he acknowledged.

Something moved in the far corner of the left end. Zen pushed his attention toward it, realized he was seeing a gun emplacement.

"Ground intercept radar active," warned the computer. Information spat at him—ID'ing a pair of twin 35mm GDF antiaircraft weapons controlled by a Contraves Skyguard system. The Swiss-built system was relatively sophisticated, though its maximum range was well under twenty thousand feet. According to the threat screen, the Flighthawks had not been locked, though the radar was active.

"I'm going to get close and personal," he told Cheshire after filling her in.

"Copy. We'll hold to our flight plan."

Zen looped Hawk Two into a turn about three miles from the radar source. He changed the main viewer from optics to FLIR. It was a military installation. The guns were mounted at the northern edge of a complex that included several dug-in shelters and four tanks. Several vehicles were parked at the southern end; the Flighthawk camera caught a soldier on guard duty smoking a cigarette. The UM/F passed within two miles of the radar unit without being detected.

"No aircraft," said Jennifer.

"Yeah," said Zen, concentrating on returning the Flighthawk to its briefed flight path. The fact that the antiaircraft weapons used a Western-made radar could mean that it

was a rebel unit opposed to the pro-Libyan government—
or not. In any event, their Anotonov didn't seem to be
there.

Exhausted, Zen returned to the programmed course. He
had to have a break; reluctantly he turned the controls
over to the computer and reached down for his Gatorade.
He was so thirsty he drained it and had to reach for his
backup, sitting in a case on the floor by his feet.

"Hard work, huh?" asked Jennifer.

"Yeah."

"You're doing good."

"Yeah."

"You want some advice?"

"Advice?"

"You're doing a lot of the routine stuff the computer
can handle," said Gleason.

Anger welled inside, but before he could say anything,
Gleason reached over and touched him on the shoulder.
It felt electric, almost unworldly—his mind was still out
with the Flighthawks, as if he were actually in their cock-
pits.

"You're doing fine, Major," she said. "Let the computer
do the routine stuff. That's what it was designed for. You
do what's important. You're trying to control both planes
at the same time."

Zen glanced at the instrument screens, making sure the
UM/Fs were operating fine, then pushed up the helmet to
see her.

"It's almost like you're afraid the computer's going to
take your job," Jennifer said. "I know we haven't had a
chance to run many flights with two planes since you've
been back, but you're getting twitchy. You're not letting
the computer fly like you used to."

"It's my job to fly them," he told her.

"Absolutely," said the scientist. "But you can't split
yourself in half. You can trust the computer."

"I do trust it," he said.

Jennifer smiled. Jeff wasn't sure what to say. In the old days, before the accident, had he let the computer do more?

Maybe.

Maybe he didn't trust it because of the accident. And maybe she was right—maybe he was worried it would take his job, leave him with nothing to do but sit in a corner and gather dust all day.

Wasn't going to happen. He wasn't a fucking cripple, legs be damned.

"Zero-ten to Delta," said Cheshire, announcing the upcoming turn.

"Flighthawks acknowledge," he told her, pulling the visor back on. "Zero-ten to Delta."

"Scopes are clean, everything is looking very good," said Cheshire. "Flighthawks are doing a slam-dunk job, Zen."

"Yeah."

"I know it's needle-in-a-haystack country down here," she added. "But the Navy planes have the most likely territory. Nothing lives down here except sand."

Zen got ready for the new turn. Cheshire was right—the ground they were covering hadn't seen rain in eons. Devoid of water, there were only a few sparse settlements, and no nomads to speak of.

Except for the ones they'd seen a short while before, who'd been parked in the middle of sand.

Grazing animals over sand?

"Bobby, do me a favor, would you?" he asked the navigator. "Look at where our nomads were. They over a water hole?"

The navigator took a few minutes to get back to him. "Not on the map, but maybe those guys know where the water is."

"Yeah. We got a satellite map that detects underground water sources?"

"What do you think this is, the library?" said the navigator with a laugh.

"Just checking."

"There's got to be water there," said Bobby. "The cattle have been there for at least two days."

"Two days?"

"More. They're on the U-2 photo and the satellite image Madcap Magician gave us, which is at least three or four."

Stationary nomads over a dry patch of land.

"Computer, hold Hawk One on the preset course," said Zen. "Hawk Two, power to ninety percent."

"What's up, Zen?" asked Major Cheshire, who'd heard his conversation with Bobby.

"Stationary nomads—sounds odd to me," Jeff told her. "I think I can just skirt close enough to them on your programmed course."

"I'll shift two degrees and it'll be easy."

"Make it one and I can keep Hawk One where it is."

"I told the computer to plot a new one," said Jennifer. "Just in case."

"Input it," Zen told her.

"I-Band interceptor-type airborne radar detected, active, source beyond range," yelped Bobby over the aircraft's interphone. The Megafortress's passive detectors had picked up two MiG-25's at nearly fifty thousand feet. "These babies are running, not walking," he warned. "Mach 2. We'll be within their theoretical detection envelope in thirty seconds. We can jam at will."

The Soviet-era active radars on the MiGs had a detection range of roughly fifty miles. But with its stealthy profile, it was likely—though not certain—that the MiGs wouldn't pick up the Megafortress until they were less than ten miles away.

Which would happen in two minutes at present course and speed. The Flighthawks, on the other hand, were too low and too small to be detected. Their own threat screens, powered by less capable sensors, were blank; they hadn't picked up the MiGs.

The I-band radars used by early models of the Soviet-era MiG-25 had been compromised years before; Raven's ECM gear would have no problem defeating them. But that would alert not only the MiGs, but potentially the people they were looking for, that they were in the air. It was better to try to pass undetected.

"Prepare for evasive maneuvers," ordered Cheshire. "We'll hold on to our ECMs and missiles until they're necessary. Bobby, watch their detection envelope for us."

"Bandits are positively ID'd as MiG-25's, probably with Acrid AA-6's," he reported. "They'll be in range to see us—let's call it ninety seconds. Ducking them's a crapshoot, Major."

"Hawk Leader?"

"I say duck them," Zen said. "Get down in the ground clutter and odds are they'll go right by. Even if they catch a sniff, it'll take them time to find us, let alone lock. In the meantime, I can check that camp."

"I agree. We'll chance it. Hang tight," said Cheshire, rolling the Megafortress. "Way down."

Zen told Hawk One to double back and initiate one of its preset routines, closing on Raven to fall into a trail off the mother plane's right wing. Then he concentrated on Hawk Two.

Nothing but desert showed in the FLIR screen. His body started to shove sideways with the Megafortress's evasive maneuvers; it felt odd with the Flighthawk flying level. His bearings started to slide out of whack, his equilibrium upset.

Zen fought the creeping dizziness, pushing the nose of the Flighthawk down. As he dropped below three thou-

sand feet, voices began shouting above and behind him—
Cheshire and the crew barking instructions back and forth,
the MiGs coming on. The UM/F's threat screen plotted
the I-band radar's detection envelope as a wavy line of
yellow floating above it.

An ocean of hot orange appeared in front of him, the
cattle or whatever in the camp moving around. The shadows moved like silent eddies.

A trio of tents sat to one side. Something else, relatively
hot, was half buried in the sand, or maybe behind the
sand.

Or sandbags with a tarp.

Optics. Nada.

Back to FLIR. A truck motor maybe?

He was past it. One of the MiGs was almost directly
overhead. The threat screen went completely red, then
blank.

He could pop up behind the SOB and nail him. The
Libyan would never know what hit him.

"Alert—approaching maximum operational range,"
warned the computer.

Zen pitched the Flighthawk back toward the Megafortress. He lost sight of the camp.

"They're turning. They're behind us," Bobby warned.
"They may know we're here. We were close. Suggest we
break and run."

"Negative," said Cheshire calmly. "Staying on course."

Zen pushed the others away, pushed himself back into
his own cockpit—he banked hard in the direction of his
target.

Nothing. The FLIR blanked with interference—sand or
something, a fog of some type, was being kicked up, and
that was all he could see.

An aircraft?

"Active radar," he ordered. "Ground-attack mode. Max
filter."

"Zen!"

Something edged out of the sandstorm, lumbering into the air.

He pushed to follow. He was the Flighthawk now, not its pilot—his body moved with the plane, his head, his eyes, his hands, even his dead legs.

"Alert—approaching maximum operational range," warned the computer.

"Radar to scan and search, low-altitude, maximum aperture," demanded Zen. "Synthetic radar view."

"Disconnect in five seconds at present course. Auto-recovery to mother ship. Fail-safe level one. Three seconds to level two."

He saw it for a second, the heat source hot now, then buried in the cloud of dust. An aircraft, definitely an aircraft.

"Two, one—"

Zen pulled the joystick back, ducking just close enough to the Megafortress to retain control. He lost the aircraft that had taken off from the Bedouin camp in the ground haze. The Flighthawk was barely twenty feet from the ground and the computer began spitting error codes.

"You have to get higher and closer," Jennifer broke in. "We've lost the laser-communications mode completely, and the radio error coefficient's climbing. Jeff! Jeff!"

He was out there with it, beyond the tether. He went back to the FLIR view screen and saw the Pchelka dead ahead, its two antiquated engines churning a whirlpool of dust as it lumbered over the dunes.

His thumb clicked on the weapon-select button, toggling over to arm, then designate.

He didn't want to shoot it down.

Fly over it. Force it down.

Zen eased back on the throttle, nudging the weapon-select toggle back to safe as he began to pull the stick back, gaining altitude even as his forward airspeed slowed.

And then everything went blank, the command link snapping.

"Shit!" he cursed.

"I know, I know," yelled Jennifer. "It's okay, it's okay; it dropped into fail-safe. Damn. We're maneuvering too violently at too far a distance. We're under attack."

Zen pushed his head back, realizing for the first time that they were under fire.

"TAKE THE SON OF A BITCH THAT FIRED THE MISSILES out," Cheshire ordered as she snapped the Megafortress onto a new course heading. The Libyans were somewhat better armed than they had been led to believe—semi-active radar missiles and Lark look-down radar. But they had no clue what they were up against; Raven's ECMs quickly jammed the four missiles that had been fired— and every radar within two hundred miles for good measure.

She still had her hands full. The interceptors could go nearly three times as fast as the Megafortress with its antique power plants. And they were behind her—if they closed fast enough, they could use their heat-seekers, which were immune to Raven's ECMs.

As the lead MiG closed, Cheshire swooped to the left, hoping to get the enemy planes to overtake her and provide an easy rear-quarter shot for her own weapons officer.

No dice. One of the MiGs dropped back while the other cut south. Cheshire tried turning into the second interceptor, only to nearly collide with one of the Flighthawks.

"Zen, Jesus!" she managed as she punched the plane lower.

"Targeting MiG. Bay," called the weapons officer. "Fox One!"

He'd launched a Scorpion radar missile.

ZEN CURSED TO HIMSELF AS HE BROUGHT HAWK ONE back under control. The flight computer had become confused by the mother ship's maneuverings, almost fatally. He had to go to bird's-eye view on the main screen to sort it all out, dropping speed on both planes. To make things worse, his left forefinger began to cramp; he went to voice control on the throttle for Hawk One. He needed the computer's help to get both planes in their set positions, a half mile behind the Raven's wings. By that time, the Pchelka was well off the screen.

"Splash one MiG!" declared the weapons officer. His nickname was "Deadeye," the kind of moniker often applied ironically. From today on, it'd be said with respect.

"Second MiG going west. He's running hot. My guess is he's turning tail back for Libya," reported the radar/navigator. "Whoo—looks like he's got some friends. More contacts, well north. Unidentified, but definitely not friendlies."

"Okay, folks, this is where we round up our horses and head out of town," said Cheshire.

"Major, that was the Pchelka," said Zen.

"I've already radioed their location and direction," replied Cheshire. "They're headed into the Navy search sectors."

"Shit. They're miles from the nearest patrol route."

"I have no control over that, Jeff."

"We can't leave them now."

Cheshire didn't answer. But he could tell she wasn't turning the plane around either.

"Nancy, damn it."

"Zen, at this point, there's nothing we can do. Now get

those UM/Fs in tow. They've got to be at bingo by now.
You run out of fuel and there'll be hell to pay."

"Don't talk to me like that," said Zen.

"Like what?"

Like I'm a moron and a fucking cripple, he thought—
but he kept his mouth shut. She was right about the planes
being at "bingo"—a theoretical turnaround point computed to give them enough fuel to return home without
running the fuel tanks dry.

"Bandits have turned around. They're going north. Still
looking for us. We're clean," reported Bobby. "That
Pchelka's off my screen too."

"Computer, combat trail, standard offset," Zen told the
Flighthawk computer.

Sudan
23 October, 2000 local

"SO, MAJOR, IT IS YOU AND I THEN," SAID THE IMAM,
standing at the edge of the camp. The Pchelka, with
Gunny and Howland, had vanished in the distance. Overhead, the warplanes rumbled; Mack saw a flash in the
distance.

"Have you ever been to Tripoli, Major?" asked the
Imam. "It is a beautiful city, looking out on the ocean."

"That where we're going?"

"Our journey is long," said the Imam. "That is but one
stop."

"I hope we're not walking."

The Imam said nothing. As the jets above cleared,
Mack heard the low drone of a helicopter approaching.

"What's going to happen to them?" Knife said.

"They will be put on trial, then shot."

"Same as me?"

"Not yet," the Imam said. "My superiors have taken an
interest in you."

"Why?" Knife's ears started to ring—this didn't sound good.

"At first it was suggested you be punished for attacking one of our soldiers while a prisoner in captivity, which, as you know under the Geneva Conventions, is attempted murder, a serious offense. But then we received some interesting information. For some unknown reason, Major Mack Smith, you seemed to disappear from the Air Force roster for a long time. You were flying F-15's for a time, then you disappeared, then you reappeared flying F-16's. Odd."

The Iranian delighted in seeing Knife swallow nervously.

"Well, Major, are you more than just another swaggering but incompetent fighter pilot?" he went on. "Perhaps you were involved in some secret activities? As you say in your insipid American television commercials, 'Inquiring minds want to know.' Inquiring minds in many nations in the Islamic brotherhood, and perhaps beyond. We shall find out what your official records do not tell us."

"What do the Geneva Conventions say about taking prisoners of war to another country?" Smith asked. "You seem to apply the law only when it suits you."

"And what of your country? An undeclared war against a peaceful nation? You forfeited your right to protection under the law when you accepted this unlawful mission."

"Do whatever you want with me. I'm not talking to you or your so-called brotherhood."

The Iranian smiled but said nothing.

Mack snorted with contempt. It was about all he could do—besides the manacles on his hands, there were four guards flanking him with their AK-47's.

He felt like making a run for it anyway. In the long run, it probably didn't matter—if anything, it was at least arguably better to be shot here, before they could use him for whatever propaganda extravaganza they were cooking up.

One thing was certain, this wasn't exactly helping his military career. So much for being part of the A team.

"Major, you find me amusing?"

"No. I'm laughing at myself."

"Good. That is the first step on the road to enlightenment. You will be assisted on the second step," he added, grinning at his joke as a Jet Ranger whipped in for a landing.

Ethiopia
24 October, 0400

FOR THE FIRST TIME SINCE HE'D BEGUN REHABILITATION, Jeff wished he had a self-propelled chair. As he rolled from Raven to the waiting truck, his arms began to feel like thin pieces of glass, ready to break; his shoulders became uncoordinated pieces of meat, barely able to propel them. The Ethiopian base drummed with activity. Army engineers had added nearly a thousand feet to the runway, as well a second parking area. Four new C-130's had arrived, and there were at least five times as many vehicles as when they'd left. Things were popping.

That was a bad sign. They were starting to plan for long-term operations, not quick-hit emergency actions.

He'd been so damn close.

The problem was that he couldn't use both planes together. It was too difficult to keep track of them. But the computer couldn't be trusted—it had nearly nailed Raven.

They could fix that. Jennifer was already working on the adjustments.

So he hadn't screwed up on the accident either. The computer had just gotten confused.

He knew that. He'd always known that.

Damn, his arms were beat.

An M44 six-by-six truck sat at the edge of the tarmac. Major Cheshire trotted ahead and asked the driver if they could have a lift to the terminal building, where she was due to brief Hal Briggs.

"Y'all hop on in," said the driver, an Army Ranger with a Texas accent that seemed to sprawl all the way back to the States.

"I'll take the back," said Zen. He pushed around toward the rear, where he spotted another Ranger.

"Yo, Corporal. Think you can boost me up?"

"Sir?" The kid looked a little like he was talking to a ghost. The driver had hopped from the cab; Jeff wheeled himself around to make it easier for them to hoist him.

"I'm thinking of losing weight," he said to the corporal, who hopped up after him.

"No problem, sir." The soldier threw his boot against the wheel as they started up, bracing his arm against the side.

"Human brake, huh?" Zen said to him.

"Yes, sir."

Zen started to laugh. A few weeks before—hell, yesterday—the man's seriousness would have convinced Jeff that he was being condescending, pitying him. Today, it just struck him as funny.

"I'm not going to roll off," he said.

"Yes, sir." The soldier kept his foot in place.

"You in the 10th Mountain Division?" Jeff asked, noticing the soldier's patch.

"Yes, sir."

"Damn good unit."

"Thank you, sir."

The corporal never cracked a smile.

Hal Briggs met them outside the terminal building.

"Good job," Hal boomed, helping the corporal lower Jeff to the pavement. "We were able to track the plane."

"Really?"

"The Hawkeye was waiting off the coast. It caught it coming north, thanks to your information," Briggs said. "We're ninety percent sure where they're taking them."

"Ninety percent?" said Major Cheshire.

"Navy likes numbers," said Briggs. He smiled and held his hands out apologetically. "This is their baby now; we're back to being, uh, consultants. Come on inside, I'll fill you in."

Madcap Magician and its associated Special Ops units were now a tiny part of an operation that included three aircraft carriers and a Marine Expeditionary Unit in the Mediterranean. The strikes on the Silkworm missiles had been successful. Two Iranian MiGs had been shot down; the Megafortress had accounted for one Libyan MiG-25. And as Hal had said outside, planes from the *JFK* had tracked the Pchelka believed to be carrying the pilots and Marines to a bunker site just outside Tripoli.

The situation room had been tidied up some; there were now neat clusters of men gathered around tables and laptop computers. Wires snaked everywhere. A thick pair led to the rear of the building, where portable generators the size of soda trucks were humming. Their vibrations played a mamba back through the building and up through the floor so violently one of the armrests on Zen's chair rattled.

Hal led them to a corner of the room that had been set off by sandbags. A large table with maps sat behind the bags; half a Satcom and a large laptop computer were tucked against its legs. There were no chairs.

"The President has authorized an operation to retrieve the hostages," Briggs told them. "But only if it can be launched within the next eight hours."

"Why eight hours?" Jeff asked.

Briggs nodded, agreeing with the implied criticism of the deadline. "The UN Security Council is due to meet then. Apparently, Washington wants to avoid any possibility of a condemnation—or worse, offers of mediation. They want a fait accompli. The Saudis and the Egyptians are up in arms, but the Iranians are hesitating. Retrieving our men will take their last cards away. Moderate elements in the Iranian government—"

"There are moderates in Iran?" said Cheshire.

"The politics really aren't my business," said Briggs. "But the way I read it, the Iranians and Libyans think their best bet is to hold a trial. The NSC analyst who's been helping us thinks the Islamic League is teetering on collapse and will fold if we prevent that. As far as that goes, I think he's right. The Iranians really have been the driving force here; Libya, Sudan, the Somalians—bottom line is they're followers. Now if Egypt were to get involved—that's a different story. In any event, we want to cut that all off. And we will. Or rather, the Navy will. With our help."

"You're not launching an assault from here," said Jeff, trying to shake off his fatigue. "We're twenty-five-hundred miles away."

"No. Two SEAL groups will make the actual assault from the Mediterranean. A Marine MEU is taking care of a diversionary raid. We're sending our Delta operators and Whiplash to man some SAR points in the mountains to the south. Both of them are loading up now. Nancy, if you'd brief the Osprey pilots on what's out there, I'm sure they'd appreciate it."

"Okay. We found an antiair battery that wasn't in our briefing. Beyond that, it was pretty clean. Except for the MiGs."

"Good," said Hal.

"Drop the other shoe," Zen told him.

Cheshire turned to Jeff.

"I've played poker with Hal too many times not to know he wants something else," Jeff explained. "He wants us to do more than brief the roto pilots. He's explained too much. He doesn't ante in on that last round unless he thinks he can win. Then he talks to you and tries to get you to help sweeten the pot."

"The SEALS need some real-time surveillance of the Tripoli bunker complex," said Briggs. His voice was flat—he could have been playing poker, sitting on a full house with nothing showing. "They're talking about using F/A-18's, but I think it's too damn risky. There's one Pioneer UAV with the MEU, but that bunker has more SAMs around it than the Kremlin. It won't last. And besides, the Pioneer would be useful for the diversion."

"We can do it," said Jeff. "We can use the test circuits to transmit optical and infrared views to a satellite uplink. If you've got a JSTARS on the other end, they can relay it."

"Zen, that's a damn long flight away," said Cheshire. "And we haven't slept."

"I slept on the way over. I'll be fine," said Jeff.

"You look like you're tired as shit," she answered. "And you're sweating buckets."

"Sorry if I stink," he said.

"That's not it."

"I don't want to push anybody beyond their limit," said Hal. Now he wasn't bluffing or playing poker—he was damn sincere. "But that bunker is a bitch. We have the plans from the Italian company that built it, because we were worried about the Libyans using it. There's a way in, but it's going to be tight. They need to know where the guards are sixty seconds before they land."

"Piece of cake," said Zen. "Show me the plans and a map."

"You okay with this, Major?" Hal said to Cheshire.

Cheshire hesitated, but then nodded her head. "Raven can wipe out the ground radars for the assault teams. It makes sense."

"You're not too tired?" Hal asked.

"No, damn it."

Briggs nodded, then reached for his Satcom. But as he started to click into the line, he looked up at Jeff. "I was wrong," he said. "I apologize."

"Not necessary," lied Zen. Then he added, "So you were sitting on four aces, huh?"

"Just two."

THEIR WELL-EARNED REST HAD DONE NOTHING TO LIFT the Whiplash team's mood. Danny's men were pissed that they had just missed the pilots and Marines. That they'd barely managed to escape without anything worse than a broken fingernail only added to the bitterness. And the fact that they were taking a decidedly secondary role in the new operation was about the last straw.

"SEALS just want the effin' glory," groused Bison as the Osprey lifted off. Freah could see it was going to be a long flight.

"I don't see why we don't take out the bunker ourselves," said Hernandez. "While they're going in the front door, we sneak in the back."

"Goddamn Navy's gonna screw it up."

"The bunker is about seventy-five miles from Eagles Nest," Talcom pointed out. "A hop, skip, and a jump. We can nail it in five minutes."

"We could have packed into a C-fucking-17 and dropped in," said Hernandez.

"You find a C-17 over here, you let me know," said Danny, settling into his seat.

"We also serve who sit and wait," said Liu.

"Screw you, Nurse," said Talcom.

"I suggest you guys either get some sleep or play some cards so *I* can get some sleep," said Danny finally. He snugged his pack beneath the seat, taking care not to unsafe the special quick-burn device. Besides a NOD and more ammunition than a normal platoon could use in a year, his rucksack contained maps and satellite photos of every Libyan base in the northern part of the country. As Hal had told him before they took off, it always paid to be prepared.

"YOU HAVE TO STAND DOWN," BREANNA TOLD MAJOR Cheshire as she gulped her coffee in the mess area. "You need a rest, Nancy. You're dead on your feet."

"Raven has to take the Flighthawks," insisted the pilot as she gulped her coffee. It was the second cup she'd had since walking into the cafeteria area a few minutes before. "Fort Two isn't set up for them."

"I can fly Raven. Chris too. We're both fresh."

"It's my responsibility," said Cheshire.

"It's going to be your responsibility if you crash the plane into the desert. Jeff, tell her." Breanna glanced toward her husband. He looked worn as well, with deep creases on his forehead. And his flight suit was soaked through around his neck and shoulders.

"I don't know," he said.

"What don't you know?" She wanted to scream at him—he was her husband, he should be supporting her.

But maybe that was why he wasn't.

"Nancy, you can't fly," she said, turning to Cheshire.

"I can and I will," said the major. Her eyes locked on Bree's, and suddenly Breanna understood.

It was the woman thing. No way she could back down or out. She had to be as tough as the men.

Even though she was exhausted.

Against her best judgment, against her will even, Bree nodded.

"But maybe we should rotate the crew a little," said Cheshire, eyes still locked on hers.

Bree jumped at it. "Yes. I'll take the copilot slot. Sibert

and Jones will fill the weapons and navigator positions."

Cheshire started to shake her head.

"No, Bree's right," said Zen, finally coming to her defense. He looked up into her eyes as he spoke. "She should fly Raven. You're beat."

"She'll fly copilot," said Cheshire. She jumped up quickly, draining her coffee. "We'll use Sibert and Jones. Rap is my copilot. That's it."

She marched off to get more coffee.

"Why the hell didn't you back me up?" Breanna said to Jeff as soon as Cheshire was out of earshot.

"I did."

"You don't think I can do it?"

"I don't know what you're talking about, Bree. I did back you up. Nancy's fine."

Her eyes caught his. He'd always believed in her before—encouraging her to pursue her career, to push herself into different planes. Now his faith had wavered. She could see doubt in his eyes.

"You're beat yourself," she told him.

"I'll take greenies if I need to stay awake," he said.

"Oh, and that'll make you real sharp," said Breanna, who knew even that was a lie—Jeff wouldn't take aspirin except at gunpoint. She got up and went to check on the plane.

Over the Mediterranean
24 October, 0600 local

"OKAY, KID, YOU WANT TO MAKE YOURSELF USEFUL?" asked the major.

Jed Barclay looked up from the bench chair in the "lounge" compartment, a bulkhead in front of the "business" area of the JSTARS jet. They'd been airborne now for nearly twelve hours—a routine assignment for the command and control aircraft, which had undergone ex-

tensive engine work following the Gulf War to make sure
it could fly for more than a full day without coming down.
The long gig had allowed them to keep track of devel-
opments in Libya and Egypt. Libya's armed forces were
now on full alert; Egypt remained on the fence, though
some of its air units seemed to be at a high degree of
readiness—a good or bad sign, depending on how you
wanted to interpret it.

"What do you need?" Jed asked.

"I need someone to handle communications with an Air
Force unit called Raven," said the major. "They're part
of Madcap Magician. My guys have enough to do with
the Navy end."

"Sure. They're F-111's?"

"From what I've been told, it's a B-52."

Jed nodded, guessing but not telling the Army officer
that the plane must be an EB-52—quite a different beast.
The Megafortress's existence was still technically classified. Hal Briggs had reported that two had been "loaned"
to him, ostensibly as high-speed transports. But Briggs
obviously had found their capabilities irresistible.

The planes originated from a base near Las Vegas
where he believed his cousin Jeff Stockard was stationed.
Small world.

"All you have to do is sit at a console and talk to them.
They won't be on station for two or three hours, at show
time," added the major. He sounded almost apologetic.
"And look, don't touch anything."

"Yes, sir."

"Hey, lighten up. I'm kidding. Besides, we got baby
locks on the medicine cabinets."

Near Tripoli
24 October, 0700 local

THE IRANIANS PUSHED GUNNY AND CAPTAIN HOWLAND
out of the small plane moments after it rolled to a stop.

They were hustled into the back of an open-bed truck. Large bags of shredded paper and cardboard were thrown on them. A tarp was pulled over the bed and the truck roared away.

"What the fuck do you think this is about?" Gunny asked the pilot.

"Damned if I can guess," answered Howland.

The truck took a sharp turn. Its wheels bumped over some harsh pavement, then hit a smooth patch. The driver floored it, sending them rolling backward.

"I think I'll reconnoiter," said Gunny when he regained his balance. He crawled toward the side of the truck and managed to poke his head up, but it was nearly impossible to see anything; not only was it dark, but they were moving extremely fast. He worked his way around to the tailgate. It didn't look like they were being followed.

"What do you think, Captain? We're not being guarded," said Gunny, sliding back next to the pilot.

"I find that hard to believe," said Howland. "Maybe we just can't see them."

"Yeah." Gunny pushed himself toward the front of the truck, trying to peek up through the covering there. But he couldn't find an opening and didn't want to risk alerting their captors.

"They're probably sneaking us into one of their prisons," said Howland. "Maybe they're staging something near the plane. Whatever that commotion was when we took off from Sudan probably tipped them that they're under surveillance."

Gunny wasn't particularly interested in theories. "We might be able to jump for it," he suggested.

"Then what do we do?"

"Then we escape."

"If we're in Libya," said Howland, who had worked out their direction en route, "we're also probably in the middle of the desert. We'll die of thirst inside a day."

"Better than dying on TV for them," said Gunny.

"Maybe," said the pilot.

Before either of them could say or do anything else, the truck veered sharply to the right. They rolled against each other and then the side. Gunny pushed himself upward just as the truck came to a stop.

"Shit," he said.

Men were shouting. The tarp and bags were whisked off. Two spotlights clicked on, blinding the Americans.

"This way. Out of the truck. Quickly," said a man holding a pistol. "Into the shelter or you will enter as dead men."

Gunny and the pilot were pulled down by three or four Libyan soldiers, who pushed them toward a set of cement stairs. Perhaps they were in the middle of a desert, but the stairway smelled like a swamp. At the bottom, two men without weapons but with arms the size of elephant trunks muscled them into a room barely the size of a closet. There was no furniture; two bare lightbulbs in steel cages shone down from the ceiling, eight feet above.

One of the men pointed to the floor, indicating they should sit. Gunny lowered himself reluctantly, wondering if he ought to fight. But even if they made it past these gorillas, there were at least six soldiers with automatic rifles in the hallway outside.

A soldier—this one short and frail-looking—entered carrying two trays of food. Each tray had a large bowl of fruit, another of mushy buckwheat, a third of grilled lamb. There were pitas and large bottles of cold water.

Howland picked up one of the bottles as the steel door slammed shut. They were alone.

"They'd just shoot us," the pilot told Gunny as he drained about half the bottle. "They wouldn't waste poison."

"Yeah. You're probably right," said Gunny, still eyeing the food. "Assuming this shit is edible."

"It's probably pretty good," said Howland, poking the meat with the bread. "The condemned always eat well."

"Yeah. That's one way of looking at it." Gunny picked up what seemed to be an orange, peeled away the skin, and took a bite.

It was an orange, or close enough. He devoured it. Then he ate some of the fruit and two pieces of the pita bread. Satiated, he put his head back against the cement wall. He'd caught some z's on the plane and didn't think he was particularly tired, but he began to drift off. At one point he woke to Howland's loud snore, then nodded off again.

At some point, he dreamed that the door reopened. The man who had brought them the food reappeared, taking the trays. Then the gorillas appeared and pulled both Gunny and Howland roughly to their feet, pushing them back into the hallway. Gunny seemed to fly to a narrow flight of stairs, descending down another passage covered on all four sides with a thick brown coir carpet.

At the end of the hall, Gunny saw that Howland was with him. They stepped into an eight-by-eight room with smooth whitewashed plaster walls and a thick tan wool carpet. The room had been turned into a television studio—two chairs were set up beneath a lighting bar. Two cameras with camera operators stood opposite them. Monitors were positioned so anyone sitting in the chairs could watch themselves. The six soldiers who had been escorting them filed in behind.

"You will sit in the chairs and respond when questioned," said a voice from above. "Your trial will begin shortly."

"Am I dreaming?" Gunny asked Howland.

"No. They're going to televise this," said the pilot. "This is happening."

"Shit," said Melfi, shaking his head, trying to get his wits back. He was truly awake; all of this was real. "And

I always wondered what it would be like to be on TV. Shit."

Libya
24 October, 0920

IT TOOK NEARLY FOUR HOURS TO COVER THE ROUGHLY two thousand miles from their base in Ethiopia to southern Libya, not counting the aerial refuel shortly after takeoff. Jennifer Gleason and Jeff spent the entire time running through a set of changes for the Flighthawk programming that would keep the UM/Fs separated from their mother ship during fail-safe mode. Jennifer's fingers dashed over the small keyboard at her station, stopping only so she could wade deeper into the notes she'd made on her yellow pads. Jeff helped read back some of the commands and numbers. Most of it was in machine-code assembler level; he didn't have a clue what he was reading.

Jennifer also had an idea about adding to the compression routines in the command system, in essence widening the communications bandwidth and lengthening the distance they could operate from the mother ship. At one point she started to explain it, but Jeff just waved her off.

"Tell me what to do," he said. "I don't have to understand it. There's no time."

She gave him a tap on the shoulder and went back to work. They completed the work with fifteen minutes to spare before the drop point.

Jeff climbed aboard the Hawks, running through the preflight checks. He was so tired now that fatigue felt like a piece of clothing around his upper body, heavy and warm.

"Drop point at zero-two," said Breanna over the Megafortress's interphone circuit.

"We're here already?" answered Jeff, honestly surprised.

"Looks like it."

They ran through the flight and weather data, following their launch protocol precisely. With everything dash-one, Cheshire put the plane into a zero-alpha maneuver, nosing in as she accelerated. The Flighthawks dropped off the wings on cue and Zen began working them onto their flight paths, roaring downward across the still-peaceful Libyan countryside. The sun glinted in his view screen as the planes picked up speed. They were at eighteen and twenty-two thousand feet respectively, well separated in the cloudless sky.

"SEAL commander on the circuit," advised Cheshire. "Along with Cascade."

"Hawks are green," said Zen.

"So's Big Bear," said the SEAL commander, using the SEAL team's call sign.

"Acknowledged." Jeff thought the voice sounded vaguely familiar, but it belonged to Cascade, a crewman aboard the JSTARS electronic command plane in the southern Mediterranean. Cascade was communicating with Raven and the SEALs through a secure satellite system, linking the feeds from the Flighthawks to the Navy commandos. "Silent com until zero-two."

The line snapped clear. The gear seemed to have a way of scrubbing sound right out of the wires, as if the airwaves were erased.

Jeff clicked the button to get back to his intercom circuit.

"Twenty minutes," he told the crew. "Smoke 'em if ya got 'em."

"As long as they're not your sneakers," answered Breanna.

Jeff laughed. She used to say that all the time.

*   *   *

THE OSPREY'S TILT WINGS BEGAN PITCHING UPWARD AS the craft banked toward the mountain pass. Danny could feel the heat of the desert through the skin of the plane as he waited for it to land. The plan had called for them to land on a small plateau on the other side of the hill, but the pilot had seen someone there as they approached.

Talcom gripped his SAW so tightly Danny thought he was going to snap his fingers through it. He reached over to the sergeant and gently put his hand on the machine gun.

"Nice and easy," he told Powder.

Sand and pebbles began whipping against the body of the Osprey. Talcom and some of the others winced, obviously thinking it was rifle fire.

"Nice and easy," Danny repeated to his men as the rear door began to open.

BREANNA KEPT ONE EYE ON HER INSTRUMENT PANEL and the other on her commander. Cheshire was definitely tired, but she was on top of her game. She'd held Raven steady through the Flighthawk release, performing the launch maneuvers flawlessly and without help from either Rap or the Megafortress's autopilot. She continued to work carefully, reviewing nav data and making a minute adjustment to her course.

The radar-warning receivers in Raven had several times the range and about ten times the selectivity of Fort Two's. They were now within a hundred miles of two large ground-intercept radars just south of Tripoli; the threat screen painted their rays bright green ahead. Toggling the screen showed that Raven could get within twenty miles and still look like a misplaced seagull to the ground radar; after that, the computer painted a "path of least observance" that would take the EB-52 to within about five miles before it was likely to be detected.

The real value of the fancy gear would come when the assault started. Raven would put its custom-made gallium arsenic chips to work jamming the sensors, adding its fuzz to the electronic noise from a pair of Navy EA-6 Prowlers. Every radar and most of the TVs in North Africa would be toast.

"Hawks are zero-five from commitment. We're green all around," said Jeff.

Breanna, who always had a hard time thinking of herself as a copilot, began to click her mike button to respond, then let go as Cheshire acknowledged. The major gave her a smile, then turned back ahead, studying the clear sky.

Jennifer Gleason said something to Jeff about one of the computer readings. Breanna felt the muscles in her back tense at the girlish lilt in the scientist's voice. If she ever washed out as a scientist, Gleason would have no trouble finding a job doing telephone sex.

"We're picking up some interesting transmissions," said the weapons officer. "Have something in grid B-2 just beyond the mountains."

"Radar?" asked Cheshire.

"No. Some sort of microwave, but I can't quite pin down the source from this distance. It's encrypted. Lot of data, like it's a video feed. It's coming from the middle of nowhere. You want me to record it?"

"Negative," said the pilot. "Don't waste your time."

"I'm also getting audio for a video feed that's being beamed out of Tripoli," he added. "I think it's our trial."

God, thought Bree. Poor Mack. His parents would hear him, probably see him, on CNN. The tape would be shown over and over and over.

"Yeah, shit. I have a sound track. Getting a location. I can pinpoint it. Hang on."

The sophisticated tracking gear in Raven allowed him to plot a radar source within .0003 meters—roughly a tenth of an inch—once he locked and tracked it. The process took anywhere from forty-five seconds to five minutes.

"You want to hear this? Damn, it *is* the trial. It's in English."

"No," snapped Breanna.

"Neither do I," said Cheshire. "Run through the emergency tanker locations and frequencies for me."

It took Bree a second to realize Cheshire was talking to her. She turned her eyes to the right instrument panel, where the fuel burn as well as the reserves were projected. Personally serviced by Greasy Hands before takeoff, the ancient TF33-P-3's were humming better than the day they left the shop in early 1962.

"We're running a few hundred pounds ahead," she told Cheshire. "So I don't think we need to—"

The major turned her head toward her without saying anything.

"I'm sorry," said Breanna, reaching for the data on the tankers.

DANNY HIT THE GROUND A FEW FEET BEHIND TALCOM, not sure whether his sergeant had seen something or was just being cautious. They were still a good twenty feet from the plateau, approaching from the blind side.

"Team, hold," he said, speaking softly but distinctly so the communicator pinned to his collar could pick up his command. Bison was about five yards behind him. Liu and Pretty Boy were working their way around the other side.

"Thought I saw something," whispered Talcom.

Danny had contemplated sending the Osprey around from the front to draw the attention of any Libyans while they came around from the flanks. He'd rejected the idea, however—if the aircraft was shot down they were in serious trouble.

"I'm coming to you," he told Talcom, raising his body. He took a crouching step toward the sergeant's chocolate-chip fatigues, then another, then trotted ahead and slid in.

"I can get over them," said Talcom, pointing upward. A jagged rock face rose above nearly fifty feet. There looked to be few if any handholds.

"Hell of a climb," said Freah.

"That's what I'm thinking," said the sergeant. "We'll trade weapons. You just cover my ass if they come for me."

Danny eyed the rock wall doubtfully, but then gave Talcom the MP-5, which was shorter and much lighter than the SAW. He helped him snug it against his back.

"Wish I brought my climbing shoes," said the sergeant, starting upward.

"Powder's going to try to get some height on them," Freah told the others. "Liu, you and Floyd hold on until Powder's up. Nurse, you on the circuit?"

No answer. The Dreamland-engineered radio system had a good range, but perhaps they were asking it to do too much with the jagged terrain.

"Hernandez, you read me?"

"Loud and clear, Cap."

"You see Liu?"

"I can see them, but I can't hear them," Hernandez hissed into the miniature microphone. "Nothing, Captain," he said finally.

"Can you get close enough to tell them to hold on until Powder's in position?"

"Gotcha, Cap."

Danny glanced at the firing mechanism of the gun, as if reorienting himself to the machine gun. Powder had already climbed nearly halfway up the rock. Slowly, Freah began to crawl to his right, coming around the face where he could have an angle at anyone trying to attack his man.

The communicator suddenly cracked with an ungodly noise. A submachine gun began firing from the other side of the hill and something exploded upward. Danny pitched up the barrel of his gun, and had already begun firing at the dark shadow above before he realized what was going on.

"Hold your fire! Hold your fire!" he said.

The crackle over the radio was laughter.

"Buzzards," Powder was saying. "There's a fucking nest of vultures on the ledge. Liu toasted three of them, but another got away."

"I thought he had a marksman badge," somebody said with a laugh as Danny's heartbeat returned to normal.

ZEN WAS IN HAWK ONE'S COCKPIT NOW, BARELY twenty feet over the tallest building in downtown Tripoli. He flung himself back toward the outskirts of the capital, feeding live video back to the JSTARS and from there to the SEALS, already en route from the Mediterranean. The route had been carefully chosen, with intricate zigs and zags to avoid defenses; whoever had laid it out had done a damn good job, because he didn't notice anything deadlier than a water pistol. Nudging his sticks left, Zen put himself on a direct line to the bunker, now less than three miles away.

As critical as the video was for the SEAL team following him in, a good hunk of Jeff's attention was pasted on the threat indicator in the bottom left visor screen. He was whizzing through green and yellow fingers, ducking an array of radars as he came in. The jammers weren't set to go on until the SEALs were almost overhead.

A large ring of concrete appeared on his left. A lollipop of a road led to it, lined with tanks and missile launchers.

"SA-6 radar active, attempting to lock," warned the computer. "Scanning."

Thirteen seconds to his turn point. He had to crisscross the top of the bunker, catching two air-exchange units with the camera. Then he'd jump to Hawk Two, concentrating on antiair guns at the west end of the complex.

The computer continued to count down the programmed course for him. He took the turn, pushing the throttle for the last ounce of thrust.

Everything was a gray blur, even the bunker facility. He clocked past, noted a set of missiles that hadn't appeared on the satellite.

"Computer, Hawk Two optical feed in visor," he said, pushing the computer disengage switch at the stick base as he did. "Computer, take Hawk One on programmed course."

The images instantly switched, and he saw the world again, as if he'd jumped back in time, not location. A large 57mm gun loomed straight ahead, turning. A row of antiaircraft weapons were arrayed at ten o'clock in the view screen, looking like sewer pipes in a supply yard.

"Team One is inbound. Thirty seconds," reported Cascade.

The guns started to move.

"Jamming now," said Raven's operator.

"They're firing," reported Jeff.

Two Navy Prowlers as well as Raven clicked on their fuzzbusters. The interference was so severe the UM/F control computer immediately complained, giving him a red light on the radar altimeter and then warning that it was having trouble maintaining the connection with Hawk One.

"Raven, I need us closer to the Flighthawks," said Jeff, switching back into Hawk One as Two completed the run of the antiair guns. He flew up the coast, the plane responding well to his controls despite the computer's admonitions that the signal was degrading.

Somewhere offshore in the JSTARS, the operation co-ordinators were studying Zen's feed to make sure they had all of the SAM sites properly targeted. They were like defensive coordinators sitting in the press box during a football game, checking to make sure the blitz they'd called would work.

It did. With a vengeance.

Jeff caught the shadows of laser-guided missiles closing in on the SAM sites as he began to turn Hawk One south. The Libyans hadn't had a chance to launch.

Secondaries.

Turbulence.

A lot of shit down there.

He was between the two planes, spreading out over the coast. Fuel good, heavy air, almost stormy. His controls felt a little sloppy. Maybe it was the computer reacting to the wide spectrum of ECMs.

He could handle it. Zen nudged the stick up. The signal bar on Hawk One flittered into the red area, got strong again.

"Jeff, they're asking for another pass on the bunker," said Jennifer. Her voice seemed to descend from the clouds.

Zen told the computer to bring Hawk One closer. Then he pulled Hawk Two back in the other direction, away from Raven under a heavy cloud of black smoke and exploding tracers. Helos were coming in from the northeast; he saw a pair of Sea Cobra attack helos letting loose with rockets on an official building a half mile from the bunker. Jeff hunkered down, pushing his head into the windscreen, backing off the throttle, slowing down for the longest possible look at the bunker.

The east side of the facility was defended only by an armored car. He tilted his wing and banked off, the assault helicopters right behind.

He circled, watching them land. Raven was almost overhead now, beginning to orbit back. Hawk One flew in its set position behind the left wing. Jeff pushed Two around, came in on the bunker once more as the SEALS blew the cover on the southwest air-exchange portal. They immediately began disappearing down the large vertical shaft.

A second Seahawk came in over the back entrance of the bunker. An armored car moved toward them.

Zen was nearly lined up for a shot with the UM/F's cannon. He prodded the throttle slide but before he could activate his cannon, one of the Sea Cobras obliterated the vehicle.

"They're in!" shouted someone over the command circuit.

"How's the trial going now?" said Breanna sarcastically.

"It's still going," said the weapons officer, surprised.

Zen saw the main entrance to the bunker implode as he began a fresh circuit. Three satellite dishes collapsed with the dust as the front half of the football-field-sized upper building collapsed.

Had he said the trial was still going?

He pushed Hawk Two into a rolling dive to reverse course and overfly the bunker again.

"Missiles have launched! Flak batteries are shooting unguided in grid A-1. Evasive maneuvers," said the weapons officer.

"Losing control connection for Hawk Two!" warned the Flighthawk computer.

"Nancy, we need to double back," said Zen as he struggled to put Hawk Two's camera on the bunker complex. He jerked his right hand instead of his left, cursed at the infinitesimal delay.

"We have SA-2's in the air," said Cheshire calmly.

"Jam them."

"We are. But we're not taking any unnecessary risks now that the team is down. Evasive maneuvers."

Zen felt himself being pushed sideways as the Mega-fortress beamed the SAM site's pulse-Doppler radar. He lost Hawk Two and had to throw One's throttle to the firewall to try to keep up with the EB-52. The Libyans had launched no less than twelve of the high-altitude surface-to-air missiles at them. While the Megafortress's ECMs had no trouble thwarting their radars, there were an awful lot of them in the air; just dodging the debris was a chore.

Sixty 57mm antiaircraft guns were filling the air below the missiles with lead and cordite. The flak rose in plumes, hot coals for Raven and the UM/Fs to dance across.

The computer brought Hawk Two into a wide arc south of Raven as Jeff flew Hawk One to the east, cutting back on an intercept as an SA-2 exploded overhead. Sweat poured from Jeff's neck and back as the small UM/F began to jitter up and down, buffeted by a second explosion he hadn't seen or anticipated. He gunned the throttle, but got no response; the plane suddenly began nosing down and he tasted metal in his mouth, felt his stomach go sour with a wave of dread. For a moment he thought he was going in—he saw the ground loom and shapes dance, and his head began to spin. Then the UM/F picked herself up and he had only blue sky in front of him; he was clear, accelerating and climbing. The Megafortress was a bare two miles ahead.

"SEAL teams have secured the perimeter," reported Cascade. "SEAL teams are inside, encountering only token resistance."

"The prisoners aren't in the bunker," said Zen. He was on the interphone; only the others aboard Raven could hear him. "Where was that encrypted video transmission?"

"About fifty miles, south by southeast," said the weapons officer.

"Jeff?"

"Bree, get us back there. That's where Smith and the others must be."

"No offense, Major, but I'm flying this plane," said Cheshire.

"I'm sorry, Nancy. The bunker is a bluff. The trial broadcast didn't stop when the satellites were hit."

"He's right," said the weapons officer.

"Why do you think it's coming from that site and not somewhere else in Tripoli?"

"It's just a guess. Intuition," said Jeff. The computer noted that Hawk Two was now "fully communicative," and he acknowledged, though leaving it under the computer's command in the trail position. "The Navy's covering Tripoli. Let's go."

"Jeff, you're talking about deviating from our flight plan based on a hunch," said Cheshire.

"I trust hunches," said Breanna. "And I trust Jeff."

Thanks, babe, he thought as Cheshire jerked the Megafortress onto the new course.

Over the Mediterranean
24 October, 1050 local

JED SAT BACK AT THE JSTARS CONSOLE WHILE MS. O'Day left her desk in the White House Situation Room to take another call. The attack on Tripoli, planned by Madcap Magician and carried out mostly by the Navy, was still proceeding. But already the Saudi and Syrian governments had taken to the back channels to assure Washington that they had no interest in the Greater Islamic League.

It helped that they trusted neither the Iranians nor the Libyans. It also helped that America was demonstrating how easy it was to obliterate nearly a billion dollars' worth of military equipment.

Now if they could only complete the rescue.

"Jed, are you still there?" asked Ms. O'Day, coming back on the line.

"Yes, ma'am," he said, sitting back up at the console. The major was waving at him—he was needed on the other lines, where he was helping keep the SWAT team and Raven in contact with each other.

"Do they have our men?"

"Not yet," he told her.

"When?"

"Maybe soon," he said. The major was waving violently. "Ms. O'Day, I'm sorry, I have to go," he said, cutting her off by switching the simple twist knob that controlled the circuit input on the panel in front of him.

Felt weird. He'd never cut off his boss before.

What if the President had been listening in?

"Cascade, this is Big Bear. Can you get Raven to give us a feed on the base area?"

"Uh, I'm not sure," he said. He looked around for the major, but he'd gone off to help someone else. "Hang on."

The screen before him was a live situation map. It showed Raven heading south, away from Tripoli.

Shit. Why the hell were they doing that? And where the hell were their prisoners?

Obviously not in the bunker, if Big Bear was looking for a feed.

"Bear, I'm going to have to get back to you," said Jed, twisting into the Megafortress's frequency.

Libya
24 October, 0955 local

EVEN WITH THE STEINER GLASSES, THEY WERE MUCH too far from the action to see anything, not even smoke on the horizon, though all of the Whiplash members fixed their eyes in the direction of the coast. The Osprey pilot had moved the rotorcraft to the foot of the hill and was monitoring the raid via the SATCOM circuit back to the JSTARS command plane. He'd alerted Danny when the raid started; laconic to a fault, he remained silent as the attack continued.

The desert before them gave little hint of the battle raging seventy miles away. The sand seemed permanent, uncaring; the only sign of mankind was a highway about twelve miles to the northeast, as barren and destitute a stretch as Danny could imagine.

"Captain Freah, Raven is hailing you," said the Osprey pilot over the com set.

"Patch me through." Freah stood and looked directly down over the side of the cliff, as if that would somehow help the pilot turn the switch and allow the connection.

"Raven proceed."

"Danny, this is Breanna Stockard. Are you on the line?"

"Affirmative," said Freah. He could feel his heart pounding now in every part of his body, worried that the Megafortress had been hit.

"Stand by for Major Stockard," Bree told him.

"Captain, we have an encrypted microwave signal being beamed to a satellite from a grid in B-2, we think about eight miles east of you. What do we have there big enough to house a transmitter?"

"Stand by."

Freah dropped to his knees, carefully pulling the maps and satellite images from his rucksack. There were only two candidates. One was a small military post, the other an abandoned railroad depot with some old warehouses and support buildings. The sites were separated by about a mile and a half. He gave the positions.

"What do you think of checking them out?" Zen asked.

"We're en route," said Danny, not even waiting for the explanation as he signaled his men to reboard the Osprey.

THE BROADCAST HAD ENDED A FEW MINUTES AGO, BEfore they were able to pinpoint it; both sites were close enough to have been the source. Zen worked Hawk Two ahead toward the the coordinates of the military base that Freah had supplied. It seemed logical to start there.

The threat screen was blank. Gray asphalt rose beyond the desert sand, bounded by trenches and a ramshackle fence. Two long, dull yellow buildings stood at the far right; a pair of ancient antiair guns were behind sandbags in the middle of the installation. Behind one of the buildings was an earth station, surrounded by a tall chain-link fence.

"Losing command link!" warned the computer.

"Jen, I thought you said we increased our control distance." Zen throttled back. The signal-indicator bar slowly began to climb. "I'm having trouble at seven miles now."

"I'm not sure what the problem is," she yelled, working over the control. "We should be fat."

"Yeah. Raven, can you bring our distance parameter on the UM/Fs to within five miles?"

"Affirmative," said Cheshire. "We're dropping to ten thousand feet, staying on your programmed flight path. Cascade is trying to hail us. What should I tell them?"

"The truth—we're on a wild-goose chase."

Jeff started Hawk Two on a slow orbit around the base perimeter. Hawk One, meanwhile, was approaching the abandoned railroad warehouses. He toggled the view, saw nothing, went back to Two.

This sure did look like a wild-goose chase. Dust blew across the military base. Place looked like it hadn't been occupied since World War Two. He scanned for a radar dish, saw nothing.

Hawk Two's indicated airspeed dropped past two hundred knots, still falling. Zen walked over the gun emplacements. Damn things looked like they were rusted. Good trick in the desert.

Probably left by the Germans. Rommel had been out here, right?

He told the computer to take Hawk Two back to trail, and flipped back into Hawk One just as it closed to within two miles of the old railroad depot. He slipped down the throttle. Raven was five miles away, closing fast.

The terminal building's roof was missing, but the warehouses looked intact as he approached. One of the smaller buildings was just a collection of debris. There were two fairly large ones, maybe a hundred feet long apiece, at the edge of the track area. Between them there was a smaller, gray building, low-slung in the desert. It seemed to have collapsed or been swallowed by the terrain.

But was that a microwave dish next to it?

Zen pushed the throttle to close in. As he did, the roof of the nearest warehouse began to disintegrate. The thing seemed to be alive.

The radar-warning indicator flashed red. In the next instant, the sky perforated with explosions. Zen had walked into a minefield. A bank of antiaircraft artillery weapons had been hidden beneath the carefully camouflaged fake roofs of the warehouses.

"Whiplash, Target Two is hot. Hotter than hell!" yelled Jeff, goosing the throttle.

*   *   *

THEY RODE TOWARD THE VOLCANO, WATCHING THE massed fury of two dozen antiaircraft guns erupting upward. Raven jammed the radars, but the gunners flailed anyway. Danny, hunched over the pilots on the Osprey flight deck, saw the small Flighthawk ducking and weaving in the sky ahead, spinning back and forth like a peregrine falcon eyeing a kill. Major Stockard was trying to keep the gunners' attention focused on the miniature plane, not on the rapidly approaching assault team.

"Ten seconds," said the Osprey pilot. "Target building is dead ahead. I see a stairway down. Shit! I'll get you as close as I can."

"Okay! Okay!" Danny shouted. He spun back to his men, trying to hold down the bile and adrenaline. "We got stairs down to a bunker, I'm guessing."

"Vehicles coming up out of a ramp near the warehouses!" yelled the copilot.

"Get us down! Get us down!" Danny insisted. He was wearing the com device, but he yelled anyway. The Osprey pitched and weaved, swirling in the air. A second volcano opened up just to their right, bullets hissing like steam. The rear door began opening even though the Osprey was still ten feet off the ground. Powder leaped out.

"TV time!" yelled Danny, jumping out with Liu.

"Take him out! Take him out! There's a machine gun on the steps! Shit! Duck! Duck!" Powder screamed.

GUNNY HEARD THE RUMBLE OF THE ANTIAIRCRAFT BATteries above. The entire complex shuddered.

"About fucking time," he said to the pilot on the metal chair next to him. "Hey, you got any more questions before we go?" he called to the disembodied voice that had been questioning them from unseen speakers.

In the next second, the complex went dark. One of the camera technicians screamed.

"Hit the deck!" shouted Gunny. He reached to pull Howland down, got nothing but air. He found the captain on the ground.

"What now?" said Howland.

"Find a Sommie and get his gun," said the Marine, crawling toward the door.

RAVEN TOOK OUT THE FIRST BATTERY WITH A PAIR OF JSOWs, even though they were nearly on top of it. Zen barely managed to get Hawk One away from the second bank of ZSUs as the roof of the warehouse opened and the flak dealers began peppering the air.

"*Wing damage, Hawk Two,*" warned the computer.

Zen could feel it. Hawk Two began to wobble, threatening to yaw out of control.

Time to eject.

Shit, he yelled at himself. I'm half a mile away.

The computer helped stabilize the plane, but the damage was severe, and went well beyond the wing. Zen opened the warning/status screen; he had multiple hits, pending systems failures in the control and engine sections. Power was dropping rapidly.

Destroy the Flighthawk?

Better to land if he could. Whiplash could take it with them, lashing it beneath the Osprey.

He could always hit the self-destruct switch later.

Jeff did a quick check on Hawk One, just to make sure the computer had it under control; then he jumped back into Hawk Two. She was jerking up and down, wrestling with the air instead of gliding through it. He fought the wings level and aimed toward a nice flat piece of sand a quarter mile ahead. As gently as he could, he put her down on her belly, skidding and then spinning to a stop.

"We have the location marked," Jennifer said.

"Yeah," said Jeff.

He put himself into Hawk One, pulling the plane over him as the new image kicked into the top of his screen.

"JSTARS is sending reinforcements," said Cheshire.

"You have to keep me close," he told her, pushing the Flighthawk lower and back toward the flak.

DANNY TURNED AS A GRENADE WHIZZED FROM LIU'S launcher. There was a low, dull explosion and everything started moving in slow motion. He ran toward the building, ignoring the canvas-backed truck that had come out from the other side. There was a stairwell down; he grabbed the red metal pipe blocking off the side and swung himself down into the hole.

Powder had beaten him there. He was standing in front of the doorway inside a small alcove. He waved his right hand at Freah to stay back, then gripped his SAW at the handle. The door swung out toward them.

A set of metal steps led downward. Freah, leaping ahead of Talcom, took two at a time. A metal door at the bottom gave way as soon as he butted it with his machine gun; he stooped and rolled in a concussion grenade.

If they'd had a chance to plan this, to work the whole thing out, they'd probably be going in with masks, smoking the bastards out.

But hell, if they'd had a chance to plan the damn thing out, they wouldn't be the ones doing the attack.

"I got ya, I got ya," said Powder, taking a covering position as Danny plunged into the dark hall.

Nothing. No fire. Nothing. He ran for all he was worth.

"Door!" he heard himself yell. Powder was on top of him, throwing him down and in the same instant punching the door with the machine gun, ducking, rolling.

Two men fell out behind the doorway.

Light up ahead.

"We're taking fire up here," said Liu over the com set.

"Hold your positions."

"We are. Delta's en route."

"Room's empty," yelled Powder. Danny started moving down the hall. The boron-carbide vest gave him a dangerous sense of invulnerability—a foolish sense, since he knew that while the vest could stop point-blank machine-gun fire, it covered less than fifty percent of his body.

They came to a T. Both hallways were dark. Smoke curled at his nostrils, made him sneeze.

"Which way we goin'?" asked Powder.

"You that way. I'm this way," Danny said, wiping his nose.

"And I'll meet ya in the mornin'," said Powder, pushing forward.

GUNNY GRABBED THE SOLDIER'S LEG, YANKING HIM TO the ground. He grabbed for a gun, cursing as he realized he'd found one of the unarmed camera people instead of a soldier.

"This way. They've all left," the pilot was shouting. "Stay low!"

"Damn Air Force. Bunch of know-it-alls," grumbled the sergeant as he scooted for the doorway.

"MISSILES!" JEFF YELLED AS HIS RWR LIT UP. A LIBYAN Roland mobile antiaircraft battery had just activated its radar from inside a disguised post at the south end of the complex.

"We're out of JSOWs!" warned the weapons officer.

"Evasive action," said Cheshire.

"No!" yelled Zen. "I can nail them! Keep me close. I'll get them with the Flighthawk's cannon."

"We're too vulnerable here, even with the ECMs."

"The Roland will take out the Delta Osprey if I don't nail it," said Zen.

Someone shouted something back, but he'd stopped listening. He was in the UM/F now, butt tied to its seat, pushing for the dish spiking the mother ship.

The tanklike launcher sat behind a low wall a mile ahead. Its two-armed turret twisted toward the Flighthawk, its parabolic head spinning as it got a lock.

"Weapon," he told the computer.

The cannon bar appeared at the top of the screen.

Yellow, yellow. Red.

Locked.

Too soon, Jeff told himself, remembering how optimistic the gun radar was. Wait until you can't possibly miss.

The Roland seemed to move downward. There was a puff of smoke.

It had fired a missile.

The bar suddenly went yellow. His targeting radar was being jammed, probably by Raven itself.

"Boresight," Jeff ordered. He'd fire manually. The site cleared to a manual cross with a square aiming cue.

He was too high. He nudged, now less than a quarter mile away, moving incredibly fast through the haze.

Zen squeezed, saw the line of bullets move out ever so slowly, impossibly slowly toward the tank, saw the first one get the dish, saw the second, the third begin to unzip the metal as he nudged his aim point lower, the metal hissing.

Nailed the son of a bitch.

BREANNA FELT THE MEGAFORTRESS SLIPPING FROM their grip as they were buffeted by a wave of flak. Two missiles were in the air behind them; there was so much going on it was impossible to keep everything sorted.

"Roland on our butt!" yelled the weapons officer. "I've handed off ECM to auto mode, but we're not shaking it. Watch the flak! We're too damn low!"

Cheshire cursed, cranking the Megafortress into a tight turn, once more trying to beam the missile's persistent guidance system. The fact that the German-built antiair weapon was a known commodity wasn't making it easy to evade. The ECMs were blaring, there was more tinsel in the air than on a dozen Christmas trees, and still the damn thing was coming for them.

"Hold on," barked Cheshire.

In the next second she slammed the Megafortress in a full-bore dive, plunging straight for the earth. Finally confused, the Roland continued on for ten yards—but ten yards only. Realizing it had missed, its onboard circuitry lit the warhead.

Raven was shaken, but unbowed. Cheshire rolled out at two thousand feet.

Right into a wall of flak.

Rap heard the pops next to her, the sound of an old-fashioned percolator kicking up a fresh pot of coffee. Something flashed in front of her.

For a second she blanked. Then she realized she was shaking her head, her hand on Raven's yoke. The plane followed her nudge to the right.

"Jesus, that was close," she told Cheshire.

The major didn't answer. Bree glanced to the right and saw the pilot slumped forward in her seat. A good portion of the cockpit and fuselage beyond her had been mangled by triple-A.

DANNY PUSHED HIS BACK AGAINST THE WALL AS HE edged further into the complex. The com unit had gone dead; the guns seemed to have stopped. The hallway was filled with a dull red light, perhaps from an emergency lighting system further on.

A shape loomed ahead. He leveled the MP-5 at it, saw something flash.

A bee whizzed by him in the hall. Something ripped the floor next to him.

He squeezed off a burst. The shadow fell backward.

When nothing else came from behind the shadow, Danny slipped further along the wall. The Libyan soldier had fallen face-first, his AK-47 beneath him. Freah kicked the man, making sure he was dead.

He heard something ten yards ahead. He slid down, holding his breath.

Two shadows appeared, hugging the far wall. He raised his gun in their direction.

"I sure as shit hope you're a fuckin' American," said a low grunt.

"Hands up and move forward, fast!" he ordered.

"Gunnery Sergeant James Ricardo Melfi," announced the first shape, lunging toward him. "And this is Captain Howland."

"Where's Smith?" asked Danny.

"We haven't seen him since Sudan," said Gunny. "What the hell took you girls so long?"

"We had to do our hair," said Danny.

ZEN SWUNG HAWK ONE AROUND THE EDGE OF THE complex, gunning for Raven's wing. He was at bingo fuel. It was a long way back to base; if they didn't set sail soon the Ospreys would be towing both UM/Fs home.

But at least they'd be able to. The Roland was off the air. And the stream of antiaircraft fire had finally run dry.

"I need to get home or refuel, Nancy," Jeff said, punching the intercom. "You know what? As soon as that flight of F-14 Tomcats gets here, let's set course for that emergency base in Greece. My fuel won't be so tight. I'll meet you at fifteen thousand, okay?"

"I don't know that we can make fifteen thousand," answered Breanna. "We're chewed up pretty bad, Jeff. Triple-A chewed through the fuselage while we were trying to get under the SAMs. Nancy got hit, and she's at least unconscious, if not worse. I'm still assessing damage up here."

"Are you okay, Bree?"

He felt his heart leaping out toward the front of the plane. He felt like he was a million miles from her, as if he were here and she were back at Dreamland.

"I'm intact," she said. "How about you?"

"As intact as I get," he managed. His hands were starting to shake; he gave control over to the computer, settling the Hawk into a shadow trail.

"Hey, Bree?"

"Yeah, Jeff?"

"I love you."

"Me too, baby. Me too."

Tripoli
24 October, 0955 local

AS THEY GOT OUT OF THE HELICOPTER, FLAMES erupted from the building behind them. Tripoli was apparently under attack; the Imam's Allah had apparently stopped smiling at him.

One of the guards turned quickly, ducking with his weapon. The other pushed Mack down toward a set of cement steps that led to a long dock. Pleasure craft were arrayed in a marina to the left.

To the right, an ancient Piaggio flying boat strained a mooring at the end of the wooden gangplank. Mack took a step toward it, then threw himself down as a pair of F/A-

18's screamed less than a hundred feet overhead, en route to a target further inland.

The Imam pulled him to his feet. His voice remained resolute, but for the first time since Somalia he made it obvious that he had a pistol in his loose-fitting sleeve.

"Into the airplane," said the Iranian.

"Who's flying?" asked Mack.

"You," the Iranian said, motioning toward the seaplane. The Piaggio's cockpit sat in front of a high wing flanked by two overhead engines. "There has been a change of plans."

"Why don't we just stay with the helicopter?" Mack asked. He guessed that it didn't have the range to go where they were going—they'd had to stop several times along the way to refuel.

"You ask too many questions, Major. Go."

"I don't know that I can fly it," Knife told him.

The Imam lifted his arm, placing the gun next to Mack's ear.

"I've never flown a seaplane before," said Mack, half hoping to see a Marine—maybe even Gunny—pop up from the water. "I can't remember the last time I flew anything with a propeller."

Mack was telling the truth, but as a pair of attack jets screamed overhead, he realized he couldn't stall much longer.

The Imam's guards were up by the road; they weren't coming aboard the plane. Climb in, take off, then find some way to dump his captor.

"I'm telling you the truth," said Mack, ducking as another jet screamed overhead. "I don't know if I can fly this thing right."

"I will pray that it all comes easily to you," said the Iranian, gesturing with his pistol.

"Well in that case, let's go for it," said Knife, starting down the dock.

Libya
24 October, 1020

RAVEN WAS MANGLED, BUT FLYABLE. THE RIGHT STA-
bilizer was missing a good stretch of skin. One of the
leading-edge flaps on the right wing had locked itself into
a two-degree pitch, but the Megafortress's fly-by-wire
controls were able to compensate for the problem so well
that Breanna hadn't realized it until Jeff brought the
Flighthawk up to examine the battle damage. Jennifer
Gleason, meanwhile, had come up and helped Major
Cheshire, cleaning her wounds and making her comfortable, or as comfortable as someone could be while staring
at a mangled cockpit wall. The wind roared at the jagged
gash in the hull, adding a squeal to the rumble of the Pratt
& Whitneys, but as long as they kept their altitude and
speed relatively low, Rap didn't think they'd have a problem. She set course for Greece, the Flighthawk pushing
ahead like an Indian scout checking the area for an approaching wagon train.

"Raven, this is Whiplash leader, understand you took
some serious hits," said Danny Freah, punching into their
line from the Osprey.

"Affirmative," said Breanna. "We took a lickin' but we
are still tickin'."

"Glad to hear it," replied Freah. "Your Flighthawk is
secure. A Navy CH-46 is inbound to transport it. I left
two teams of SEALS standing guard."

"You trust 'em?" joked Rap.

"Hey, I had to give them something important to do,"
answered Danny. "We would have brought it along ourselves, but we have to expedite our passengers. We're
diverting to Greece."

"We'll escort you," Breanna told him. She had his position on the God's-eye-view screen; the Osprey was run-

ning just to the southwest, booking at close to four hundred knots—about fifty miles an hour faster than the stricken Megafortress. "That's where we're headed."

"Figured as much," said Freah.

The black bat-tail of Hawk One danced in the left part of her windshield, about a half mile off—the small size of the plane made it difficult to judge its distance without resorting to the screens.

"Hawk One, this is Raven. You copy Captain Freah's transmission?"

"Hawk," he said, acknowledging.

"Got your six," she said.

Kind of funny to be following behind Jeff when he was sitting behind her, she thought.

The rush of adrenaline that had pumped through everyone's bloodstream was starting to give way. It was a dangerous time—they were still nearly a hundred miles deep over Libya. While there were no enemy SAM sites left operating this side of Tripoli, Breanna realized they were far from home.

"Has Smith been recovered yet?" Freah asked from the Osprey.

"Mack? He's not with you?" Breanna shot back.

"Negative. The site has been searched. He was separated from the other prisoners back when they landed near Tripoli. We've been trying to get through to JSTARS directly on this. Can you?"

"Jeff—"

"Yeah, I heard," her husband told her.

"Poor Mack. I have to relay this to Cascade." One of the warning lights on the master caution panel came on. She asked the computer for specifics; it failed to respond. Unsure whether it couldn't understand her or was malfunctioning, she tapped the keypad for the error code.

"We're having some electrical problems," Breanna told the crew tersely. "I'm going to switch through some circuits. And please stay on oxygen, obviously."

"I'll talk to Cascade," Jeff volunteered.

"Thanks, hon."

JEFF WAITED FOR JENNIFER TO SET UP THE TRANSMIS-
sion, which had to be routed through a backup circuit
because of the damage to Raven. It seemed to take forever.

"Go," she told him.

"Cascade, this is Hawk Leader."

"Hawk Leader?"

"With Raven."

"Damn, your voice sounds familiar," said Cascade.

"So does yours."

"Jeff?"

"Shit, Jed," said Stockard, recognizing his cousin
through the synthetic rendering. "What the hell are you
doing out here?"

"Long story, cousin. What's up?"

Jeff relayed the information about Smith.

"Well, two thirds is better than nothing," said Jed.

"We'll catch up at some point," Jeff told him. "Things
are getting busy here."

"You guys okay?"

"We have damage, but we're flying," Zen told him.
"Later."

"Later."

Jeff hunkered over his joystick, concentrating on the
view projected by the forward video camera aboard the
Flighthawk. There were a number of civilian airplanes in
the air, including several rented news helicopters and airplanes from Europe, sent to investigate. Flights from the
Nimitz and *JFK* were challenging each aircraft. At the
same time, Navy helos were doing the same with boats.

Zen found the coastline, turning ahead of the Megafortress. An F-14 approached from the west; he waited for the pilot's challenge. Instead, the two-place Navy fighter ducked off to the south.

"Hawk One to Tomcat bearing along 320, at grid AA-5," he told the airplane. "Have you visually."

"Hawk One, this is Shark Flight Leader. Not reading you on radar."

Zen gave him his heading. The Tomcat acknowledged, though his voice seemed so hesitant Jeff wasn't sure he really did see him.

"We're checking out some civilians," said Shark leader. "Do you require assistance?"

"Negative. Just checking positions."

Zen pushed the Hawk closer to the water. The Med glowed a greenish blue, the water a gentle ripple edged with sun-reflected light. Twenty or thirty boats lay ahead, apparently unaware of the rampage that had taken place a few miles further west. He checked back with Bree, who was already starting to look for the tanker. The Osprey was clearing the coast.

Zen punched through the Navy circuits, listening to the aircraft challenge flights in the vicinity. His attention was starting to flag; he had a long way to go and needed something to keep him awake.

One of the exchanges suddenly did the trick.

"Dreamland Playboy One, acknowledging," said a faint American voice. "We are following a filed flight plan."

The voice sounded a little hesitant, but the Tomcat acknowledged and cleared the craft to proceed.

Dreamland? Dreamland?

Playboy One?

Playboy One was Knife's old call sign, the one he'd used the day of Mack's accident.

Coincidence?

No way in the world.

"Shark Leader, request data on Dreamland Playboy One," Zen said, bolting upright.

"Hang on," said the Navy pilot. He gave him over to his pitter, or radar and weapons system operator, in the backseat of the plane.

"Italian flying boat," said the Navy captain. The backseater had lists of civilian flights to check against.

"Was his call sign filed as Dreamland Playboy One?"

"Unknown. We're not the FAA here. But it's definitely on our list. Civilian plane, registered to an Italian fishing and tourist company."

"Can you give me his last position?"

"No offense, Hawk Leader, but I'm a little busy."

"That's why I'm going to double-check him myself," answered Zen.

MACK STEADIED HIS HAND ON THE SPLIT THROTTLE, trying to even out the engines. The Piaggio wasn't particularly difficult to fly, though it did feel weird as hell. It wasn't so much because the controls and instruments dated from the late 1940's; they were classic stick and rudder jobs, dials and toggles. You went where you pointed.

But the props were mounted above and behind him, pushing instead of pulling. They sounded like a pair of lawn trimmers, and he just couldn't seem to get them at the same rpm. No matter how he played with the controls, the plane continued to pull slightly but definitely to the right, pushed by a stronger engine on the opposite side.

Worse, he felt like he was walking over the water. Or crawling. The Italian flying boat went incredibly slow, even though it had two engines.

Walking on the water. The Imam would like that.

The Iranian had been vague about where they were heading, but it was obviously Egypt. Mack guessed the

Iranians had made some sort of deal with the Egyptian Air Force to escort them over to the Red Sea if necessary.

Or Turkey. Could be Turkey. Plenty of fuel. But Turkey was pretty friendly with the U.S.

Egypt was too, though. Or at least it had been.

Mack had blown it when the Navy plane challenged him, not expecting that the Iranians or Libyans or whoever had set the plane up had actually filed a flight plan. The damn Tomcat pilot was off the air so fast Mack couldn't think of any way to tip him off.

Dreamland Playboy One. The old call sign had shot into his mind when the Imam poked him in the neck with his gun.

Those were the days, huh?

Would have been easier if the Tomcat had gotten down in his face. Then there might be a chance of getting out of this thing.

Now the best he could hope for was to take the Imam out with him. The question was, should he crash in the water or on land?

ZEN FOUND THE ITALIAN SEAPLANE HUGGING THE LIByan coast.

"Come on, Bree. Tighten it up," said Jeff as the meter began sinking downward.

"I'm doing my best, Jeff. We have a hole in the fuselage, remember? And about two thirds of an electrical system. Push it and you're going to be lighting candles back there."

"I don't have candles."

He eased the throttle back a notch, concentrating on making sure he was well inside the optimum control range. Then he clicked into the frequency the Navy plane had used to hail the Piaggio.

"Dreamland Playboy One, this is Hawk Leader. I am

an American fighter monitoring your flight. Acknowledge, please."

There was no answer.

"Dreamland Playboy One. Identify yourself and give your flight heading."

"Hawk Leader, Dreamland Playboy One acknowledges. We are following on our filed flight plan. Stand by for compass headings and position, as requested."

Son of a bitch. There was no mistaking that smooth, full-of-himself voice. Mack was flying the plane.

Jeff clicked the transmit button to dial into the JSTARS command frequency.

JED HAD JUST RECONNECTED WITH MS. O'DAY WHEN the major did his arm-waving routine again. Jed asked her to stay on the line this time, then clicked over to find his cousin.

"We have Smith," said Jeff.

"You're shitting me."

"Jed."

"Hang on," Jed told him, desperately trying to flag down the major so he could patch both lines together.

Turned out all it took was pushing a button near the switch.

"Hawk Leader, please repeat what you told me," Jed told his cousin when the connection was set.

"We have Smith in a plane heading east over the Mediterranean. We're not sure whether we can force him down or not, but we can try."

"Jed, I need to talk to you alone, please," said Ms. O'Day. "A single, secure line. Now."

He pushed the button quickly and got the knob back, holding on to the D.C. scrambled satellite transmission.

"The plane has to be stopped at all costs," O'Day told him. "No pilot. No trial in Iran."

"They're on it," he said.

"Jed, listen to what I said. No trial. And this does not come directly from me, do you understand? You're not running tape."

"Well, of course not."

"Hawk Leader probably is."

"Boss, are you telling me to terminate the pilot?" asked Jed, finally understanding what she had told him.

The National Security Advisor didn't answer.

"Ms. O'Day?"

"Jed, a trial now will prolong a crisis that you know must be ended quickly."

"I—"

"Why do you think you're there, Cascade?" she said.

Before he could say anything else, the line snapped clear.

DANNY FREAH AND THE REST OF THE WHIPLASH assault team practically whooped as they cleared the coast and headed out over the Mediterranean.

The ex-hostages didn't seem too disappointed either.

"Yo, hold it down," yelled the pilot. "We got a situation. I'm trying to hear what the hell Raven's doing."

Danny got up from the rack seat and made his way forward to the flight deck area. He leaned across the small bulkhead to speak to the pilot.

"We're still available for SAR," he told the lieutenant. It was a command, not a question.

"Raven and Hawk One are tracking a seaplane," said the pilot. "They think Major Smith is aboard."

"Shit," said Freah. "Get us there."

"Captain, hang on." The pilot pressed his hand against his earphones. "Task force is directing us to an assault ship. It's about ten minutes away, dead north."

"Where's the seaplane?"

"That way," said the pilot, pointing back toward the coast. "Captain, seriously."

"Seriously, get us there," insisted Danny.

"HEY, COUSIN," SAID CASCADE, SNAPPING ONTO THE line.

The scrambled line gave voices a synthetic, machine-like sound. Even so, Jeff heard a tremor in his cousin's voice.

"Hawk here, Cascade," he said.

"Jeff, I got bad news. That seaplane. It has to be stopped."

"We're working on it. Can you verify there are Egyptian fighters en route? Raven has them now maybe thirteen, fourteen minutes away on their present course."

"Yeah, we got that. They're not on our side. They are, but not in the way we need them to be."

"What the hell are you talking about?"

"We need the seaplane stopped. At all costs."

"All costs how?"

"All costs."

"Jed—you're telling me to waste Mack Smith?"

"I'm telling you. I'm telling you there are four F-14 Tomcats en route with orders to shoot it down. I gave them the orders myself."

"Shit. You gave orders?"

"Cuz, you have your orders."

"Fuck. Jed what the hell is going on?"

There was no answer. Cascade had broken the circuit.

MACK TRIED TO WILL HIS HEART TO SLOW DOWN, AFRAID the thumping would tip off his captor.

Zen's voice had sounded so foreign, so wild, it had

seemed like a hallucination, a last dream before dying. But it was definitely real.

Fate? Allah?

Holy shit. Talk about luck.

Maybe. Could go the other way too. The Imam still had his aura. And his pistol.

Mack worked the controls calmly, frowning in the general direction of the fuel gauge. He'd build a pretense to land. Get down in the water, wait for the Navy to arrive. Or whoever was coming behind Stockard.

"What is the problem?" demanded the Imam.

"The engine, the right engine seems a little flaky," Knife told him. "And I'm starting to run out of gas."

The Iranian slid his neck back against the seat. "Both engines are fine. You have plenty of fuel. Continue on your course."

"Good thing you're a pilot," said Mack. "You can take over if I have a heart attack."

"You will not die of a heart attack today. That I guarantee," said the Imam, moving the pistol out so there was no doubt that it was aimed at Mack's head.

"Didn't think so," said Smith. "I try to watch what I eat."

BY THE TIME THE OSPREY HAD THE ITALIAN SEAPLANE in view, they were barely ten minutes from Egyptian airspace.

"The Egyptians are scrambling planes," Breanna told Danny. "They may try and shoot you down."

"That's the least of our problems," said Zen, who was plugged into the same line.

"Easy for you to say," Danny shot back.

"We have to take them down before the Egyptians get there," said Zen. "And if we don't, four Tomcats from the *Nimitz* will. You're the only chance we have to get

Mack out alive. I'll make them ditch, you pick him up."

"It's a long shot, Major," Danny told him. "They go down in the water, maybe we fish him out, maybe we don't. Better to have them surrender and follow us into Greece."

"Not going to happen," said Jeff.

"You sure you don't want us to fly over them and jump on the plane?" said Freah. The pilot glanced at him as if he were being serious.

Danny wasn't entirely sure that he wasn't.

"If you think you can make it, sure," said Zen.

"No fucking way," said the Osprey pilot.

"I think I can take out their engines without completely destroying the plane," said Stockard. "You guys jump in once they're in the water."

"What do you think his guards are going to think of that?"

"Hopefully we catch them by surprise. Maybe we offer to let them go. I don't know. I do know that the plane has to be stopped, one way or another."

"One way or another."

"I can take out the engines. I guarantee it."

"How many soldiers does he have in there with him, Jeff?" asked Freah.

"Hold on and I'll find out."

Danny turned back to his men. "Liu, get the snipe gear."

"Yes, sir," said the sergeant. He jumped up and went to grab the kit.

"I don't know if I can hold us still enough for a sharpshooter," said the Osprey pilot.

Danny nodded. "Yeah, I don't think so either."

JEFF PUSHED THE THROTTLE TO MAX, WHIPPING THE Flighthawk downward in a screaming beeline at the Piaggio's bow. He pulled hard, cutting a near-ten-g turn almost on top of the seaplane's windshield.

The airplane stuttered downward. Mack's voice, obviously shaking, screamed a string of obscenities over the radio.

Jeff didn't answer. It was pretty stupid of Mack to transmit. In fact, he should have used the diversion to knock out his captors—or jump from the plane.

Right.

Did he want to die?

"Two people, both in the front," said Jennifer, reviewing the video at ultra-slow motion. "One on the right has got some clerical-type clothes."

"Hopefully Mack hasn't converted," said Jeff, relaying the information to Danny.

THE GUN WAS AGAINST HIS NECK.

"Honest to God, I don't know what the fuck's going on," repeated Mack. "They must have fired a missile at us. I just barely got the hell out of the way."

"If anything else attacks us, if you divert from the course I have set for you, you will die," said the Imam. "The border is ahead. When the Egyptian planes challenge you, fall in behind them."

ONE TARGET. WITH ANY OTHER WEAPON, IT'D BE IMpossible.

But gray-haired ol' Anna Klondike's magic gun?

Child's play, no? She'd said it could shoot through glass.

Too bad she wasn't here to take the shot herself.

Danny took the gun in his hand. Powder was the best shot, but he took forever to aim. On a quick see-'em, nail-'em, Liu was the man to go to.

Or Danny.

Had to be Danny. He couldn't let one of the other guys live with missing.

Because he was going to miss. They'd be moving, his target would be moving. They would be no closer than three hundred feet. He'd have an instant to aim and react.

Ha.

Danny pulled on the visor, clicked the edge to get it active. Then he edged toward the Osprey's rear door.

"All right, lower it," he said after strapping a belt around one of the toggle restraints.

"Let me take the shot, Captain," said Powder. "I can make it."

"Piece of cake with this gear," Danny told him.

"We're going to have maybe a half second when Major Stockard blows out the engines and we pass in front of them," said Powder. "No offense, Cap, but you know I'm a better shot."

The Osprey began bucking as the door was opened.

"Hold it steady!" Danny screamed. "This is going to be hard enough!"

"Fuck you. I'm trying," said the pilot over the com unit.

No way he was making the shot.

ZEN WAITED FOR THE OSPREY PILOT TO TELL HIM HE was ready. The Egyptian fighters were now less than thirty seconds away, as was their country's border. The Tomcats were about sixty seconds behind.

Sweat poured from every pore in his body, from his forehead to his back to his toes. His mouth felt like a smelter's forge.

"We're ready," said the Osprey pilot.

Did he want to kill Mack, get his revenge? He could, easily. Hell, he'd essentially been ordered to.

No one would know he'd done it on purpose. All he

had to do was stay on the trigger a hair second too long as the Flighthawk swooped in, or give just a hiccup's worth of rudder the wrong way.

Or miss altogether. Let the Tomcats take the blame for killing him.

Jeff didn't want to kill him. Just cripple him.

True revenge.

He couldn't. Too many things prevented him. Duty. His conscience. Bree, in an odd way.

"We're ready," repeated the Osprey pilot, and Zen nailed the Flighthawk down, zooming toward the Piaggio, nudging the right engine into the boresight.

An inch the wrong way.

He squeezed. A thin line of smoke appeared behind the propeller on the right engine. Before the line turned into a wedge he had leaned ever so slightly left, put three rounds into the second engine, depriving the Piaggio of power.

DANNY BENT HIS LEG AGAINST THE OSPREY'S MOMEN-tum as the rotorcraft shot forward. The seaplane seemed to stop in midair, tilting forward, its nose falling right beneath him.

He saw the bastard Iranian, right through the glass. The man had a gun, but Danny didn't see that, saw only the wide base of his neck above the canopy edge.

He squeezed the trigger.

THERE WAS A POP, THE SOUND A CHAMPAGNE CORK makes.

So this is what fate sounds like, Mack thought. This is what it feels like to die.

Then he realized he wasn't dead at all.

Mack pulled on the controls, trying to hold the seaplane in an unpowered guide into the water.

In the next instant he slammed forward, waves lapping and someone screaming in his ears. He heard himself say he was alive and he heard someone, maybe the Imam, maybe Jeff Stockard, maybe even his own conscience, tell him it was more than he deserved.

Dreamland
24 October, 0700 local

BY THE TIME COLONEL BASTIAN WAS ABLE TO GET TIME on the secure satellite line to Greece, he'd seen the CNN report on the raids twice. In the sonorous words of the overpaid commentator, the "Greater Islamic League is defunct and peace is once more assured."

Dog wasn't so sure. True, the Iranian mullahs had officially withdrawn their threat to attack shipping in the Red Sea and Persian Gulf. And since they no longer had Silkworm missiles or MiGs, perhaps their pledge to "work with the UN and OPEC" on "important matters of commerce" could be taken at face value.

And true, the Libyans had been so decimated by the attacks on their facilities that their exalted leader would have to dip into his dress allowance for at least a decade to restock supplies.

Only two U.S. servicemen had died in the entire operation: a Marine killed in combat, and another killed by his captors while a prisoner in Somalia. All other U.S. personnel were safe, including Mack Smith. The downed stealth fighter had been destroyed, preventing—at least for now—further spread of the technology.

Still, the conflict had proven exactly how volatile the post–Cold War world really was. This small-scale conflict had taken several aircraft carrier battle groups, a Marine

MEU, and units from Delta Force to resolve. Not to mention Dreamland.

Of course, some might argue that without Dreamland it might not have been resolved at all.

Some. Not him. Not directly anyway. He didn't have to—not with Magnus steering things above him.

"Colonel, that you?" snapped Danny Freah over the phone line.

Dog slid back in the chair at Dreamland's secure conference center, ordinarily used for reviewing projects and teleconferencing. With a few changes, it might work as a decent command bunker; it had a large projection screen at the front of the room that could be fed from the secure video, phone, and satellite lines.

At the moment, the screen was blank. It sometimes took a while for the video code to make its way down.

"Well done, Captain," said Bastian. "I hear congratulations are in order all around."

"We kicked butt," agreed Freah.

"Daddy?"

The video finally snapped on. Breanna stood front and center, her soft features and tired eyes staring upward at the camera. Danny was holding a phone receiver behind her. Jeff Stockard was near the back of the room, talking with an enlisted man. Jennifer Gleason and one of the Megafortress crew members were also looking on, sitting on steel folding chairs. Gleason had a sixty-four-ounce bottle of Pepsi in her hand.

But Dog saw only his daughter.

"Hi, baby," he said.

"Mission accomplished," she said.

"Good job, Captain," he said. He stood up, realizing that they were seeing him too. "Major Stockard, everyone, very good job. How's Major Cheshire?"

"She's okay," said Breanna. "She lost a lot of blood, but the doctors say she's in no danger. Mack is okay too."

She began to laugh. "Last we saw him he was arguing with the doctor about whether he was dehydrated or not."

"What's Raven's status?"

"It's going to take a few days to button up the cockpit properly," said his daughter. "Sergeant Parsons is on his way up from Ethiopia to assess the damage. We could get it home right away, but it seemed foolish to take the chance."

"No, I don't want you to take any unnecessary risks, not at this point," said Bastian.

He didn't really want her to take necessary ones either, he thought.

"I've had some good news about Dreamland—and Whiplash—in the last half hour," Bastian said quickly, hoping she wouldn't see the concern in his face. "We've got funding. We're definitely in the budget. And Whiplash is going to be up-rated to active squadron status."

"What exactly does that mean?" asked Freah.

"Whiplash is going to make use of Dreamland technology, working with some of the advanced systems," said Bastian. "In much the same way you did in Somalia and Libya. Only, we're going to plan for it from now on. There are a few details to work out," he added. "Well, a hell of a lot of details. But we have a green light, and serious support at the command level: And beyond."

"Congratulations," said Freah.

"You guys get all the credit," said Dog. "So listen, since you're all in Greece, and since it'll be a few days before your plane is ready to leave anyway, I suppose a few days' R&R would be in order. I hear there are some nice ruins to inspect."

"I've had my fill of ruins," said Freah. "I'm up for the beaches."

"Me too," said Bree.

"Personally, I like ruins," said Jeff, rolling forward.

"But the only sight I feel like seeing for a while is a nice thick mattress."

Breanna put her hand down to his shoulders. It was nice seeing people so committed to each other, Bastian thought. Good that they could survive all the adversity they'd seen.

And wouldn't Gleason look good in a bathing suit?

"My satellite time is almost over," said Dog. "If you need anything, you know where to get me."

"The hell with that," said Freah. "We'll just get hold of Sergeant Gibbs."

"Dreamland Command, signing off," said Dog.